ABOUT

PATRICIA GAFFNE[Y] America's *Golden Hea[...]* the *Romantic Times* Reviewer's Choic[...] torical Romance by a New Author. She is married and lives in Pennsylvania.

BETINA KRAHN is the award-winning author of eleven novels. She lives in Eagan, Minnesota, with her husband and two teenage sons.

EDITH LAYTON is one of the most widely read and acclaimed Regency and historical writers, and has won many awards for her novels. Her first Signet Super Regency, *Love in Disguise,* won her the 1987 *Romantic Times* Award for Best Regency Author, the 1987 *RWA Golden Leaf* Award for Best Historical Novel, and the 1988 Reviewers Choice Special Achievement Award for Best Hero. *The Fireflower,* Ms. Layton's first historical, won her a Romantic Times 1989 Reviewer's Choice Award. Her latest Super Regency is *A Love for All Seasons*.

MARY JO PUTNEY is a graduate of Syracuse University with degrees in eighteenth-century literature and in industrial design. In 1988 she received the *RWA Golden Leaf* Award for Best Historical Novel, and the *Romantic Times* Award for Best New Regency Author. In 1989 Ms. Putney won four awards for her Regency, *The Rake and the Reformer*. Her novel, *Dearly Beloved,* received the *RWA Golden Leaf* Award for Best Historical Novel in 1990. Her latest historical romance is *Silk and Secrets*.

PATRICIA RICE was born in Newburgh, New York, and attended the University of Kentucky. She now lives in Mayfield, Kentucky, with her husband and two children in a rambling Tudor house. Ms. Rice has a degree in accounting and her hobbies include history, travel and antique collecting. Her latest historical romance is *Devil's Lady*.

A VICTORIAN CHRISTMAS

Five Stories by

Edith Layton

Patricia Rice

Mary Jo Putney

Betina Krahn

Patricia Gaffney

A SIGNET BOOK

SIGNET
Published by the Penguin Group
Penguin Books USA Inc., 375 Hudson Street,
New York, New York 10014, U.S.A.
Penguin Books Ltd, 27 Wrights Lane,
London W8 5TZ, England
Penguin Books Australia Ltd, Ringwood,
Victoria, Australia
Penguin Books Canada Ltd, 10 Alcorn Avenue,
Toronto, Ontario, Canada M4V 3B2
Penguin Books (N.Z.) Ltd, 182–190 Wairau Road,
Auckland 10, New Zealand

Penguin Books Ltd, Registered Offices:
Harmondsworth, Middlesex, England

First published by Signet, an imprint of New American Library,
a division of Penguin Books USA Inc.

First Printing, November, 1992
10 9 8 7 6 5 4 3 2 1

Contents

The Bird of Paradise
by Edith Layton

ENOCH SCRUGGS WAS AN EXCELLENT BUSINESSMAN. HE was frugal, clever, and clear-sighted. The only flaw in his makeup, and it was one that he deeply regretted, was that he was deeply superstitious. Thus, on the day when his elder partner died, leaving him full share of their successful brokerage business, he could not help but feel a little thrill of terror accompanying his glee. Because his partner's name was Mr. Morley. And his best clerk's name was Pratchit. It was coincidence, and amusing, and had Mr. Scruggs not been an avid reader in his youth, and a confirmed old bachelor now, it might have been more so. As it was, Christmas was to perturb Mr. Scruggs from that day forth.

Miss Kate Thacker strode to work. That was one of the wonders of the age, she thought as she did. Because she was in the city of London, and she was a female, only just twenty years of age, and yet, here she was, walking along with crowds of men, on her way to a paying position in an office. It was true, she admitted, that she couldn't quite *stride;* not only would that be unladylike, but impossible, because of the narrow skirt of her walking dress. And she wasn't earning half so much as most of the men. But she was working, and earning enough to meet her needs, if not her dreams. It might have been her daydreaming that made her walk right into the gentleman in front of her.

"I'm terribly sorry," she gasped, as his hands came

out to steady her, and then drew back as she quickly drew herself up.

"My fault, entirely," he said, smiling, sweeping off his high top hat.

She smiled in return. She'd seen him before, on this very street—a fine, very tall, well-set-up young gentleman, with bright hazel eyes that had always noticed her, at least since she'd first noted him, a few weeks before. She thought he must work nearby to her own office because she so frequently saw him here at this hour. She recollected herself as his smile grew broader. And so her own smile disappeared almost as suddenly as it had appeared. Because she knew all too well that a young woman who worked was not wise to smile at strange men in the street, however fine they appeared to be. Not if she didn't wish to appear free. Free, and independent, were two entirely different things. She nodded, letting her hat's brim shadow her eyes, and went on, leaving him frowning in her wake. Or so, at least, she hoped he would be, because, of course, she couldn't look back to see.

It wasn't long until she started dreaming again, because her dream was too wonderful to abandon. In fact, she reached the office, said good morning to her fellow workers, sat at her desk, and was still at it, when her dream looked like it was finally about to become a reality.

"Miss Thacker? Mr. Scruggs wants to see you," Tim, the office boy, said and gave her a ferocious wink.

She tried to smile back, but was too nervous. She rose from her desk, smoothed down her skirt, licked her dry lips, and prepared to face her employer. She'd been waiting for this day for the full thirty-one preceding it. Because that was when she'd heard that she might receive a Christmas bonus. It was Tim's casual comment one cold November morning that had first alerted her to it.

"Christmas be coming, Miss Thacker," he said, rubbing his chapped hands together, and glancing to the fireplace where the coal was making its usual ineffectual contribution to the comfort of the season. "Time for celebrations, eh? 'Specially when we get our Christmas bonus from Old Scruggs, eh?''

"Christmas bonus? Oh!" Kate had exclaimed with sudden hope before her shoulders slumped, and she said with a forced smile, "How very nice for you, Tim. But not for me, I'm sure. I've only been with the firm for three months, after all.''

"Makes no never mind," Tim said, "Old Scruggs, 'e puts great store in Christmas, or so 'e says each year when 'e gives our bonus. 'Can't have you all thinking I'm a Scrooge,' 'e says, and cackles something awful when 'e does too. You'll see, not likely 'e'll leave you out of the fun," he added on a wink as he left her desk to deliver papers to another.

It had sent her spirits soaring. She could certainly use the extra now. She yearned to ask Mr. James, Mr. Hardcastle, or Mr. Pratchit more about it, but hesitated to be so familiar. The men were pleasant enough to her, but none of them had ever offered her more than correct greetings each morning and a proper good evening each night when she left the office, with perhaps a comment on the weather now and again to liven things up a bit. But it wasn't a lively office, nor was it meant to be. Mr. Scruggs wanted work, not socializing, done in it. As was his right. The scratch of pens across ledger paper, Tim's low, tuneless humming as he went about his work, and the clicking of her typewriter were the loudest things to be heard all day, unless Mr. Scruggs had something to say. It was only a small office, after all, and all the men in it were respectable married ones, and she was, as none of them ever forgot, the first, and only female to work there in all the long history of the firm.

But a Christmas bonus! she thought now, as she and Randolph had for the past weeks, planning the things they'd do with it. She hadn't gotten it yet, but it had already enlivened their lives. They'd discussed it almost every night.

"I think," she'd said just last night, "that first, we'll buy the present for Aunt Fenton, a house gift, something to show her how well we're doing for ourselves, when we come to visit her. Something nice, not a white mouse or a sticking plaster, you wicked thing," she added, slanting a glance to Randolph, remembering his past nonsensical suggestions. "Something suitable, but . . . sensibly priced. So that then we can get something wonderful for ourselves too!"

"Ho ho!" he crowed from where he was lying on the floor, reading his schoolbooks in front of the hearth.

He rolled from his elbows and stomach to his side and propped his head up in one hand as he looked at her, "Dear, sensible Katie. At last, you see the light," he said on a grin. "So! A handsome tea cozy for dear Auntie, and then a new sled for me, and that wonderful velvet hat you've been mooning over in the window of the shop in Piccadilly. No, no," he said, magnanimous as a banker after a turkey dinner, as she tried to speak, "don't say a word—you deserve it."

"Dear Randolph," she said in the spirit of things, "how kind, too kind, my dear, I'm sure. But that hat was sold yesterday. And I think we need a new coat and nightshirt for you, and new gloves for myself far more."

His grin slid into sadness. "I wanted you to have that hat, Kate," he said with oddly grown-up sorrow in his voice, before he added, with a mulish look she knew too well, "and bother the clothes. What can you be thinking of? A nightshirt, no less!"

"I am thinking of the fact that Aunt's maid will report to her on the state of our wardrobes, and that will speak louder than any of our words on the subject of our well-being. So if you want to stay with me, and not her, I suggest you think of nightshirts, not sleighs. . . . I'm sorry, my dear," she said with simple truth, as she saw the sudden fear he tried to conceal, "I'm doing all I can to see that never comes about. This bonus will be a god-send, but only if we use it right."

"I know," he said abruptly, and turned his face to the firelight.

She looked at the back of his head, seeing the gold hair, so like their father's, curling over his collar, and realized he'd need a haircut—not one of hers, done by the window in the morning light, with a dressmaker's scissors and a prayer on her lips. But one done by a barber this time, despite the cost of it. She saw his thin shoulders, already beginning to widen to the demands of his sudden rapid growth, and thought of the new shirts he'd soon need too. And then, gazing at his profile, she saw one tear coursing down it, before he lowered his head. She longed to go over and rock him as she'd done when he'd been the baby her mama had put in her arms to wonder at. Or to put her arms around him and hold him close, as she'd done when he was a toddler, and they'd watched their mama laid to her eternal rest. Or just to hug him, as she'd done when he'd been a boy, just the other day.

But he was all of twelve now, and she wouldn't want to jeopardize his tenuous new dignity. And she wouldn't lose him to Aunt Fenton. She'd take any loss if it would be to his benefit, but she knew her aunt. And so knew the two holy tracts she lived by: her bank account and book of etiquette. She'd offered Kate and Randolph a roof over their heads when their father died the year before. But not a thing more.

Etiquette and Finance had obviously waged war in Aunt's mind when Kate refused her offer. Because Aunt hesitated. She could have claimed the legal right to take them in whatever their wishes, since Kate was only twenty. But she hesitated. It gave Kate a moment to wonder why. It couldn't be due to Etiquette, so it had to be the money. Of course. It would be expensive. Two mouths to feed, after all. Because even if Randolph brought in a wage, as Kate then quickly pointed out, it was a fact that a boy always ate more than he could earn. And as Aunt pondered that, Kate mentioned that if they were free, they'd live in the heart of London, quietly, so no one in Enfield had to know, did they? So Propriety, being an expedient sort of god, bowed to Finance, who was an implacable deity, and Aunt let Kate go to London, and to work.

Kate was determined that her brother have what her Aunt would never give him—the education he deserved. She couldn't do it just yet. The fee to his boarding school was impossible to manage when father's estate turned out to be less than they needed, or Father had thought, scholars being wise but not necessarily clever. But at least she kept him going to school. Their house had been in a nice part of town, but it brought a nicer price. Their new rented flat was fine for their purposes, and their purpose, as Kate reminded Randolph whenever he urged her to some new extravagance, was to become solvent.

For now, he went to the local school and the only reason he didn't quit and take the job he kept threatening to seek was because of the hysterics she countered by threatening whenever he broached the subject. He grumbled, but accepted it, thinking himself at least useful for keeping her company. He was. But only until she could afford for him not to be. Because she was resolved that he go to the proper school. She was wise enough to know that in the world they lived in only the proper school would get him the proper profession. And so she determined that a lack in his early years not ensure a lack all his life long.

She'd spent a little of the little money they had, and had gone to Miss Akin's Academy for Young Women desirous of learning secretarial services and graduated with excellence: a fully accredited practitioner of the new typewriting machine. It had gotten her a position with Morley and Scruggs and allowed her to earn enough to keep Randolph and herself. For so long as she did, or at least so long as Aunt thought so, they were safe. Because although Aunt worshiped Finance and Etiquette, she did so at a private altar. Her public religion was Custom. If

Kate and Randolph looked as though they were needy, she would insist on taking them in.

And now they were going to Aunt Fenton for Christmas dinner, as was proper. But so were some of Aunt's friends and neighbors. What those worthies would see and gossip about might decide Kate and Randolph's fate.

"So, new gloves and a coat and a nightshirt—and if there's a bit left over—a sled," Kate said brightly.

"And a velvet hat," he said gruffly, not looking up from the fire, "because I don't think it will snow."

But it did; a glance out the window showed Kate that the hard white sky she'd walked beneath this morning had begun to shred down over London in fat white pieces. And so as she rose to answer Mr. Scruggs's summons, she was finally truly glad of the thought of new, warm gloves, and for more than Aunt's good opinion.

"Miss Thacker, well, well, well," Enoch Scruggs said when his only lady employee walked into his office, and, after a dip that was between a bow and a curtsy, waited for him to speak.

Pretty girl, Enoch thought approvingly, as he always did. Just the sight of her acted as a daily congratulations on his business acumen. Not many brokers had typewriters; none he knew had female ones. Moreover, she was enchantingly lovely. He often warmed his frugal heart by just gazing at her at work, thinking how he was getting double value—paying someone to prepare his documents in such a way as to impress his clients, as well as for providing a handsome furnishing for his drab office. And all for the same price.

He wasn't much of a fellow for the ladies, never had been. His monthly visit to Mrs. Eames overly decorated flat was a thing he'd done for thirty years, although now he regarded it solely as a sort of regimen done for his health, like taking a tonic in the spring. But just looking at Miss Thacker was a treat. That golden hair, those speaking amber eyes, that straight nose—and that impudent mouth! Her figure was ravishing, however decently she concealed it in proper working clothes. She'd be Mrs. Eames's prize employee if she'd chosen a different line of work. But still, she was prompt and efficient at the work she had chosen. He'd wondered if he weren't being too generous, including her in the Christmas bonus. But if the moral of the tale by Dickens he'd read in his youth hadn't been impetus enough, the sight of her now made him pleased with his decision.

"Well, well," he said again, delaying the moment. He wanted full value for his gesture. "Miss Thacker, you've been with us since . . . ah, only a few months."

Her lovely eyes grew troubled, and he saw her white teeth worry at her lower lip. "That's true, sir," she said softly.

"And here is Christmas almost upon us," he went on, delighted at how anxious she appeared. "As you well know, Miss Thacker," he added, shaking a gnarled forefinger at her playfully, "you asked for, and shall receive, an extra two days off in order to visit with your family, apart from the day itself. Which, in the spirit of the season, I have allowed. Without pay, of course," he added, so that season of glad tidings or not, she wouldn't get the wrong notion.

"So then, as to the Christmas bonus, the one that all the others are getting . . ." He paused and shrugged his bony shoulders helplessly.

"I understand, sir, I quite understand," she said, swallowing her bitter disappointment.

"Do you?" he asked merrily, enjoying himself very much. "Well, I take leave to doubt it."

She hesitated, looking deliciously puzzled.

"My dear, dear Miss Thacker," Enoch said gently, tears coming to his rheumy eyes as he thought of his generosity. "Now how could you think I'd leave you out at this glorious season of the year? No, no, child, never. Come see, here is your bonus—just the same as all the others are getting—except the men, having worked for me longer and having families to support, can expect theirs to be a little bigger, of course.''

He gestured to the table behind him, but she saw no envelope, bills, bank check, or pile of coins. All she saw was an enormous wicker basket of the sort used by laundresses. It was covered with a white cloth, which Mr. Scruggs whisked off, like a magician producing a rose, where there'd been only empty air.

"Happy Christmas, my dear," he said in a tear-glutted voice.

She stepped closer and stared. But all she saw was a large bluish white lump reposing in the basket, with a bit of parsley in its . . . beak?

"Yes!" Mr. Scruggs cried. "A beautiful Christmas turkey for you, with the best wishes for the season from Morley and Scruggs!"

As the pretty child tried to recover herself, reeling, no doubt, from her glad surprise, Enoch wiped his eyes with his handkerchief. It never failed to move him. How clever Scrooge had been even in his redemption. What a lovely Christmas present to give one's indigent employees. It was nourishing, necessary, but festive. And a bargain, if bought in bulk.

Kate couldn't bring herself to mumble more than a weak thanks, but that seemed to please him. She walked to the desk and tried to lift the basket, which weighed exactly as she feared a great lump of inert flesh might.

"Yes, a beauty, isn't it," he asked, "without feathers, too. Can't have our little lady typewriter's busy fingers bruised by plucking, can we?" he chortled. "Note the white color, the firm skin," he said, poking one finger into the bird, "a toothsome bird, a plum, a dandy; a veritable bird of paradise, isn't it?"

"Ah, yes," Kate managed to say since she was clearly expected to praise it, "and . . . and a lovely basket too."

"That," Mr. Scruggs said quickly, "is only for portage. That is to say, the poulterer expects it back after Christmas.''

"I'll bring it when I return," Kate promised, almost wishing she could leave it now. But she smiled, said, "Happy Christmas, sir," and left her employer at the door to his office, beaming as she struggled back to her desk with the basket.

Somehow, after work was done for the day, she managed to bump her basket down the stair without spilling the turkey out of it. She paused for breath at the foot of the stair, near the door. Tim was there, wrapping his scarf around his neck, before he ventured out into the snow. He stopped, picked up the corner of the white cloth that covered the basket, and eyed the turkey.

"Looks like a twenny pounder," he remarked. "Nice size. 'Course, ours is bigger. Ma thinks ours is a treat. Looks forward to it every year."

"Doubtless," Kate said, trying to control her laughter, or her tears—she wasn't sure which she was nearer to— "but she's probably got an oven," she added bitterly, thinking of the two rooms she and Randolph shared, and of how it would be possible only to cook her bird in her landlady's oven. And then she remembered she wouldn't even be home for Christmas. She saw Tim's expression as he saw hers, and fearful of his remarking on her ingratitude to Mr. Scruggs, added hastily, "But it was so kind of Mr. Scruggs; indeed, I don't deserve such a treat."

"Neither do we," Tim said in a merry whisper. "The old skinflint never squeezes out a penny he don't have to. Just like him to remember only the turkey when the story's got Scrooge giving out gold besides. Oh well, I know a trick or two. I can turn a turkey into gold. I just haul it on down to the poulterers every year, and he gives me good coin for it. It ain't much, but it's better'n naught, Ma says. Ah well, happy Christmas, Miss," he said, lifting his basket. And whistling a carol, he made his way down the snowy street.

Kate had never counted the blocks to her flat. But now she tried to. And had the time to. Because she had to pause every ten feet or so and put the basket down, and lean if she could, against a lamppost or a building, so as to draw in enough breath to continue hauling the turkey home. She didn't know what to do with it, but it was hers, she'd worked for it, it was all she had of her expected Christmas bonus, and she was more determined to get it home with every uncomfortable step she took. When she'd first gotten it, it had felt like Mr. Coleridge's albatross, she thought as she stopped and panted again, drawing in snowflakes with each breath because the snow was coming down so hard. Now it was like the Grail. She would take it home if it killed her. And it might, she thought, looking ruefully at her glove, because its threadbare surface had given up all semblance of unity after the rubbing it had got from the wicker basket handle. She sighed, held her hand to the street-light, and watched the snow settle in her naked palm, even though she still wore her glove.

"Excuse me, Madame? Ah, Miss?" a deep, pleasant voice said, interrupting her bitter ruminations.

She looked up to see the tall gentleman who smiled at her in the mornings standing in the growing dusk, snowflakes settling on the shoulders of his greatcoat. He must live somewhere near, she thought with dawning foolish pleasure, before she caught herself at it, and turned a blank, correct, and innocent face up to his.

"I noted the difficulty you had with your parcel," he said, looking down at her basket, "and wondered if you would like some help. I'd be glad to carry it for you, wherever you are bound. I'm in no hurry," he added when she didn't speak, "and it's a great burden for you, although nothing for me. Not that I'm bragging, but our respective sizes, you see . . ."

She couldn't help but see. He was a very large man

indeed. Well-dressed, as well-spoken as he was good-looking, with thick shaggy, sandy hair and craggy features. Not an Adonis, but nevertheless a great comforting giant of a fellow, and smiling at her so winningly. She blinked and straightened her spine. It was just as the cautionary tales had it. He was a complete stranger, if an engaging one. And everyone knew engaging strangers were the worst sort. She might have only lived on her own for a matter of months, but she had been accosted in the street many times, and off it as well. She didn't like to even recall some of the interviews she'd gone on before Mr. Scruggs had employed her.

Women had more opportunities in these modern times. This was the nineteenth century, and the world was hurtling on toward the millennium, but some things never changed. A woman alone in London was fair game. Charming as he was, she was alone. And too, it had been only a few years since Jack the Ripper had made headlines. This gentleman was far too normal in appearance, and they were far from Spitalfields, but she was far from home. And alone. She sighed.

"Thank you, but no, thank you," she said briskly, "I can manage."

She lifted her burden and marched on, the fact that she now had an audience giving her additional strength. Even so, she was surprised to find the burden growing lighter, and then nonexistent. He had simply plucked it out of her hand.

"Yes, outrageous of me, I agree," he said as he walked beside her, the basket swinging from his hand as effortlessly as though it were filled with strawberries, and he were just coming back from berrying on a May morning. "I know very well that a respectable young woman cannot strike up an acquaintance with any stray gentlemen she encounters. But I have my own set of scruples, you see. If my mama saw me letting a young woman half kill herself struggling with such a load while I strolled on by her—why I believe she'd half kill me for it herself. So

you'll have to put up with it. Unless you wish to call a
constable. We turn here, don't we?'' he asked as he
walked on, and she trotted beside him, anxious to keep
up with her turkey.

She paused and stared up at him. It seemed his face
grew a little ruddier in the gathering dusk.

"I, er, have noted the direction you sometimes take,
you see,'' he said uneasily, before he went on in a more
confident voice. "You don't have to take me to your door,
you know. Although there'd be no harm if you did. I am
a gentleman. But, yes, I know, so I'd say even if I
weren't. But even if I only can carry this to your general
destination, it would ease my mind. My name is Charles
Lyons, by the way. And you are . . . ? Ah, I see,'' he
said on a sigh, "you are cautious, aren't you? And
proper. So be it,'' he commented when she didn't reply,
"I can scarcely blame you, Madame X. Or is it Miss X?
That, at least, I should think you can say. Or is that you
think I'll set down this basket of gold bars—or are they
iron?—and abduct you if there's no husband awaiting
you? But there's folly, because for all I know you could
have a ferocious father and several large, menacing
brothers with filthy tempers.''

"My name is Katherine, Miss Katherine Thacker,''
she said, smiling, because she was almost home, and he
was being absurd and made her feel warm in all the snow.
"And no, it's only a turkey.''

"Good heavens!'' he said in astonishment. "What did
they do, fill it with shot in order to bring it down? You'll
definitely need help getting it into the oven, and if you
stuff it—why I hope your kitchen is in the cellar, because
the weight of this will surely bring down the floor.''

"This will be fine,'' she said firmly, seeing her house
just ahead. "I can take it now. I do have a brother awaiting me, and so I must go. Thank you, Mr. Lyons. And
a happy Christmas to you, sir,'' she said.

She took her basket from his hand, and somehow it
felt lighter to her now. He removed his hat, and they

stood gazing at each other until she saw the snowflakes had covered over his hair, making it look as though he was wearing a powdered wig. She flushed when she realized how long she'd been standing, staring. Then she curtsied, had a moment's difficulty straightening her back after she did, and then reluctantly, but dutifully, left him. She staggered on to her house with the basket. It wasn't until she'd opened the door and began to struggle up the stair that the full disappointment of the day descended over her again. Because although the gentleman had diverted her, it was nonetheless true that she was returning home with nothing to show for her Christmas bonus but a large, dead bird.

"We can't eat it, even if Mrs. Biggins lets us use her oven; we're leaving for Enfield tomorrow, and even if we cook it and eat it tonight, we'd never make a dent in it. And no use saying we ought to give it to charity, because we *are* charity, Katie, and don't forget it," Randolph argued, staring at the bird in the basket on their table with loathing.

"Well, we can't leave it here," Kate said sadly. "Oh dear, I should have used my head," she said sinking to a seat by the table. "I should have handed it to Tim and asked him to sell it for me when he sold his. I could have gotten the money when we returned. Better late than never. I think I could have trusted him, and if not, so what if he pocketed a few pence? We'd have had *something*."

"Tim was going to sell his?" Randolph asked.

"Yes, he said he does every year," Kate sighed.

"Well, then," Randolph said happily, "there's our answer."

"No, no," Kate said, shaking head in despair, "I don't know where he lives. And I can't find out because it's Saturday night. The office is closed until after Christmas, and we won't be back until then. Even if I do ask him then, what good is a turkey after Christmas, and who knows if it would still be salable then?''

''But you do know where I live,'' Randolph said. ''Silly geese oughtn't to try to deal with turkeys, my dear,'' he said, grinning at her puzzled expression. ''I'll sell it, of course. Yes, me. First thing in the morning. Tim's not much older than I, is he? If he can do it, so can I.''

''You don't know any poulterers,'' Kate began, but he cut her off saying, ''But I can read. And I distinctly remember they have signs with their names in big, gold letters over their shops. 'P-O-U-' '' He laughed at her and went on, ''And I have a wagon, and a great lump of a turkey, and so presto! We'll have our money, only a little later than we'd planned.''

She paused and thought, and then turned such a glowing face to him that he felt his heart swell with pride. ''Should we open a window and put it on the table nearby?'' she asked. ''So that it doesn't spoil?''

''I shouldn't think so,'' he said, circling the table like a shark, eyeing the turkey. ''What if a cat got in?''

''Oh yes, you're right,'' she said. ''We'll leave it here until morning then. What can I have been thinking of? Lord knows it's too cold for the living here at night. It ought to be just right for any sort of corpse.''

They giggled and made a great show of tucking the cloth over their turkey before they went to bed, wishing it a pleasant night until they were weak from laughter.

But each stayed awake for a while in the night, and not only because the cold pinched at their noses above the bedcovers, but because they were thinking about the bird in the basket and seeing hats and sleds, tea cozies, coats and gloves in its stead.

The morning dawned bright and cold, so Kate made Randolph wrap up well before she let him take a step outside. They inspected the turkey, found it unchanged, and tucked the cloth around it tightly. They took the bas-

ket down the stairs together, and then Randolph hurried
back up and got down the wagon he'd used so lately when
he'd been a boy with nothing on his mind but play. But
now he went to work. He promised again to note the
price of turkeys, so he could be sure of not being cheated
too badly. Then he saluted his sister and went down the
street, dragging his wagon through the snow behind him,
whistling like the happy boy he used to be. And Kate
went upstairs to pack and wait for his return.

She hummed as she packed their things, and then sat
by the window to wait for him. They lived to the back
and had only the sight of another wall. She counted the
bricks in it until she grew bored, and then tried reading.
But her book, so enthralling just the day before, dragged
like the time on her hands did now. So she rose and
paced, glancing out the window because at least the wall
showed the passage of the sun, until she saw that it was
growing later than she'd thought. He ought to have been
back by now.

She wondered how far afield he'd had to go in order to
get a fair price, and then found herself wondering if he'd
wandered too far, perhaps into a bad district where he'd
be set upon by other boys. She was amazed at how much
invention she was capable of, with one vision more ter-
rifying than the next occurring to her. So she sunk herself in self-reproach instead of fright, blaming herself for
not accompanying him, until she discovered guilt to be
as painful as fright. When she heard the knock on her
door, she leapt from her chair without thinking, ran to
the door, and flung it open. And froze in shock.

A constable stood there.

"Miss, ah, Thacker?" he asked.

"Yes?" she answered, her voice hollow and shaking.

"You have a brother by the name of Randolph A.
Thacker?"

"I do," she said, her eyes growing wide and wild.

"Then I'm afraid you'll have to come with me," he
said.

"Has he . . . is he . . . ?" she managed to stammer, as she felt her knees grow weak.

"He's been arrested, Miss."

"What?" she cried, enormously relieved and tremendously frightened, all at once.

"For theft. He was attempting to flog . . . er," he said, watching the girl and noting she was a lady, although her address hadn't led him to think it, "for, ah, attempting to sell stolen goods. One turkey, it was. A very nice one, at that," he added, fairly.

She hurried out into the rising day with the constable. The thought of Randolph in a cell! And with criminals . . . she couldn't speak she was so distraught. Until she heard what they told her at the police station.

"But what foolishness!" she blurted. "He's only a boy of twelve."

"There's them at twelve who'd murder their blind granny for tuppence," the officer in charge said wisely, and the constable who'd brought her nodded in unison with him.

"But it's *my* turkey," she cried, "I told him to sell it. We're going to Enf . . . ah, to my aunt's house," she said quickly, her eyes darting around the room, looking at the various miscreants and lawkeepers, not being able to tell the difference and not caring because if anyone breathed a word that might get back to Aunt, she was ruined.

"My employer, Mr. Scr . . . uhm," she began and hesitated again, because she was convinced she'd lose her position if Mr. Scruggs heard she'd even been in a police station.

"Ah," she said, seeing the officers looking at her with new interest and sad, knowing smiles, "that is to say, I received the turkey as a Christmas bonus, and not having any use for it, I instructed my brother to sell it for me. He did not steal it from anyone."

"That's as may be," the older officer said on a sigh,

"and I believe you, I do, Miss. But, see, 'tis the judge who has to do the final believing. And he don't sit 'til after the holiday. See, after the complaint's been sworn, and it has been—old Greer the poulterer was quick to do it, having had so many of his own fowl copped last year, you see, and not trusting a strange youth with such a fine bird in tow and for sale so convenient—things has got to go according to custom. And custom says he stays till the judge sits. 'Tis the law, Miss."

"Can nothing be done? Christmas is coming," she said and found, to her horror, that her composure had slipped as certainly as the tears that now coursed down her face. "I cannot bear to think of him in there over Christmas Eve, and Christmas morn. . . ."

"Well now," and "there, there," the officers said because she was such a winsome, lovely little miss, and it wrenched their hearts to see her weep, and it being so near to Christmas.

" 'Course he can be let out," the older officer said and smiled to see her smile come out, as much of a relief to see as the first rays of a constable's lantern when he thinks he's heard a noise in a dark alley.

"Yes. Well, of course, I thought you knew. Sorry," the other constable said with a sheepish grin. "I'm not used to dealing with a lady who has no experience with the law. But it's simple. All you have to do is to go bail for him."

"Go bail?" she asked tentatively, daring to hope.

"Aye, 'tis only a matter of . . . let's see," the older officer said, consulting a sheet of paper on his desk, "aye. Only fifty pounds."

She stared at him, doing rapid sums in her head. Then her lips trembled again—because she'd added it up and reasoned it out. And if she sold the turkey, the basket, her railway tickets, all the clothes in her closet, and herself, she reckoned she might have half that amount of money.

* * *

She couldn't go to Aunt, she dared not let her employer know, she was afraid of her landlady finding out, but that wasn't the worst of it. She could lose her position, reputation, and lodgings, and endure, but if she lost Randolph she could not bear it. But neither could she let him remain in prison. Christmas made it worse, but it was bad enough. She was so distracted, her eyes so filled with tears as she blindly made her way back to the refuge of her flat in order to think some more, that she wasn't surprised to find she'd walked into an obstacle.

"Sorry," she murmured and tried to go on her way. Only to find she couldn't.

"Miss Thacker!" the obstacle said with dismay, holding her back. "Whatever's wrong?"

"Oh, Mr. Lyons!" she said when she recognized the concern on his face through her blurred and smarting eyes.

She tried to say a thing to reassure him and realized there was no such thing. And then tried to tell him her woes and realized she couldn't. He was, after all, a stranger. So she decided to say something about how it was all nothing, and say it fast so she wouldn't weep. So of course, her next words were lost in sobs.

He reached for her, but stopped just as his gloved hands were about to grasp her shoulders. Then, thinking vile curses about custom and usage, and knowing them both too well to persist, he settled for finding his handkerchief and handing it to her, murmuring "there there's" in frustrated fashion as he watched her try to regain her composure.

He hadn't really expected to see her this morning. Even office workers had Sundays off. But now he knew where she lived and he'd hoped to get another glimpse of her before he left the city. It was foolishness, and he knew it. But whatever it was, it was, and there was no escaping it. He'd caught a glimpse of her by chance as she'd gone to work one morning, and then made sure he got another as she left that night. That was enough. But of course, he had to be sure she wasn't married, or otherwise unavailable. The next day a coin here and another there had told him that this glowing girl was an unwed lady typewriter for the firm of Morley and Scruggs, and exactly as proper as that august firm would wish its first female employee to be. But she was human.

She responded to smiles, and he'd been supplying her with more each day. He'd been about to risk more, but yesterday he'd been fortunate enough to find her risking injury as she'd dragged her prized turkey home. That was how he discovered her voice to be low and dulcet, her laughter music, her scent like the ghost of April, and her sense of propriety as firm as he'd been afraid it might be. He'd planned on tripping her to get another conversation going. But now fate had brought him this. And although he rejoiced for it, still, her tears were cutting little pieces off his heart.

"I'm so terribly sorry," she said, avoiding his eyes, dabbing at her own to try to still the flow of tears.

"You needn't be," he said. "Pray tell me what's amiss. It may be I can help. Or if it's a thing that's beyond human help," he added quickly, thinking of dying grannies and consumptive cats, "sharing a woe can ease it. And sharing with strangers," he said, with inspiration, "can often be easier than with someone one knows well. Please, Miss Thacker, tell me all."

"It is my brother," she said in a rush, before she could stop herself from sharing her misery with this broad-shouldered gentleman who looked as though he could move the world to suit himself if he wished to. "He's been arrested!"

Oh lord, he thought on a groan that almost became audible. Just his luck. She might be of unassailable virtue, but she came from a family of hedgebirds. Or was it that she had been stalking him even as he'd thought he was pursuing her these past weeks? Anything was possible, as he well knew. But he'd given his word. So he balanced on both feet, ruthlessly dismissed all sentiment from his usually acute mind, and prepared to hear her tale of woe. And wondered how much it would end up costing him.

"You see," she said, earnestly trying not to weep again, "my employer, Mr. Scruggs, gave me the turkey, the one you so kindly helped me carry, as a Christmas bonus. It wasn't what I was expecting, or could use, and I was so disappointed, but I would not leave it. Still, what I could do with a walloping great plucked bird like that I didn't know. But then I did."

She sniffed back her tears and went on with her story. And as she did, it came to him that she wasn't lying. It wasn't her amber eyes, awash with stifled tears, or her quivering voice, or even the look she gave him when she was done with the whole tangled tale. It was simply that it was too ridiculous a story to be an invented one. Those who played deep games, as he, of all people, well knew, told more straightforward stuff. The dying granny, or even the choleric cat, he would definitely have doubted. Not the luckless brother and the unwanted turkey. It was too bizarre to be anything but truth.

"Well then," he said when she fell still, "don't fret another moment. I'll just come with you to the lock-up and go bail for the boy, and the bird." He chuckled, but she did not respond in kind.

Her eyes widened; he could swear he saw her back stiffen, along with her lips.

"*We* shall not," she said, aghast. "I never told you so that you would think I expected you to . . . absorb my debts," she said, proud of how handily she'd phrased the awkward thing. "Thank you so very much anyway, sir and—"

And was doubtless about to snap his nose off with her good-bye and then storm down the street so she could go up to her flat and weep herself into a puddle, he thought. And so he interrupted her by exclaiming, "Of course not!" in equally horrified tones.

That got her attention, he thought with satisfaction, and went on, "I'd never wish to put you under such a

obligation. My dear Miss Thacker,'' he began to explain.
He paused. ''How awkward, under the circumstances.
May I call you, Katherine?'' he asked absently. Getting
a hurried nod of acquiescence, he allowed himself a little
thrill of triumph at how easily he'd accomplished that,
before he said, ''Katherine, I had quite another idea in
mind. One that wouldn't obligate you, or me. My cousin
is a lawyer. Never hold that against him,'' he added on
a smile, ''for he's a splendid fellow otherwise. A man of
great wisdom and absolute discretion. In fact, I've been
involved with some family legal matters for some weeks
now, which is how I come to be here. His offices are
nearby to yours, that's how we came to meet. I say we
call on him—promptly, because I know he'll soon be off
to spend Christmas with the family in the North. He'll
know just what to do,'' he added with such absolute surety that she let him take her arm and lead her on.

She didn't think of the impropriety or possible fool-
hardiness of going off with a perfect stranger, because he
was such a perfect stranger, until they reached the dark
inner hall to what he said were his cousin's lodgings.
It was true they were on a good street, and the building
was an elegant one, and the darkened entry where they
waited for the door to his cousin's flat to open was
dimmed even more by the expensive woods on the walls,
polished over the decades to achieve deep, glowing
shades. But dark was dark, and the strangeness of the
situation was borne in on her more with every second
they waited. Charles Lyons was gentle and kind, but he
was also obviously worldly, terribly attractive, and very
large and strong. And a stranger, really, when she got
right down to it. She was about to bolt when the door
opened.

The figure in the doorway was alarming, but not
frightening. A tall, thin young gentleman in a blindingly
colorful silk dressing gown stood there, regarding them
with interest.

"Ah, Somerset. Wonderful," Charles Lyons said with great relief, "you've not left yet."

And because Somerset found that a singular thing to hear from his cousin's lips, since he would hardly have left without him, as they'd made plans to leave the city together, he tilted his head to one side and regarded his large cousin with fascination.

"My manners!" Charles said. "Katherine, allow me to present to you Somerset Jones, Esquire: kinsman, friend, and lawyer of note. Somerset, this is Miss Thacker, a lady in distress."

"And no wonder," the tall young man replied, "since we're keeping her standing in the hall so long. Do come in," he said, throwing his door wide. When Kate hesitated, he added sorrowfully, "I'm afraid all evidences of the black mass have been removed, likewise the members of the orgy, so I can't offer you much entertainment. But if you'd care for a cup of tea? Miss Thacker," he said on a gentle smile when she didn't move, "I'm a wicked fellow, but mostly because I jest where I should not. Please do come in. If my jest made you doubt my morals, my cousin's size ought to make you feel more secure."

And oddly, it did. Kate ventured into the bachelor flat. She declined tea, but took the drop of sherry he offered, because she thought, as she perched in a chair in front of his hearth, it seemed they'd never get down to business if she didn't accept something to eat or drink first. Her host had very firm ideas of hospitality. He insisted on her seating herself comfortably and stoked up the fire as his cousin explained her difficulties. But still, he seemed to find nothing amiss with receiving a strange young woman while wearing his dressing gown. She knew there was everything improper about it for her, but propriety meant less with each additional moment Randolph remained in jail.

The room was lavishly furnished, with an eye to the exotic. It spoke of money and taste and a lack of care for anyone's taste but its owner's. Aunt would have worshiped at his hearth rug, Kate mused, as she eyed the room while Charles swiftly told her tale of woe.

"Well, then," Somerset Jones said when he'd done, "and who's sitting Tuesday? My dear Cubby," he added with fond exasperation as his cousin stared at him, "the judge who will hear the case on Tuesday morning is of utmost importance."

"I wasn't at the police station," Charles replied with annoyance.

"Oh," Kate gasped as though she'd been struck. When they turned to her, she said despairingly, "So he *will* have to remain in jail until then?"

"No, no, of course not," Somerset said, "I simply wanted to know who the judge will be so I know how much I'll have to jolly up when he eventually dismisses the case. You did get the name of the complainant?" he asked his cousin.

"Naturally—it is graven on Miss Thacker's heart. I'd thought to pay a call on him myself, and visit the police to see what can be done there too. They know me, as you well know," he said, with a rueful smile. "So if that's to be the extent of your assistance, Cousin, we need not trouble you further."

"Of course you must. I can do it all and clean up afterward in such a way as to delight the judge and assuage the constables. You may be acquainted with the constabulary, but I'm a favorite at the courts, you know."

"Yes. The back of you, perhaps," Charles said, grinning, "my dear gadfly."

"No time for compliments, time is of the essence," Somerset said as he shrugged off his dressing gown to reveal himself fully clad, except for his jacket. "For Christmas is coming, as Miss Thacker knows only too well, poor girl."

It was so simply done, and so quickly, that Kate could only wonder at the ease of it. And feel as foolish because of the very simplicity of it as she was wildly relieved. They made her wait outside the poulterer's shop as they went up the stair to his apartments above the store—and came down a few minutes later, grinning, as Somerset tucked a piece of paper away in his vest pocket.

"Christmas greetings from Mr. Greer," Charles explained. "He fully rescinds his complaint. It was so dim in the store, it turns out he couldn't possibly identify the boy he'd accused. He admits he has no fowl missing. He's terribly sorry for any inconvenience; it was all the holiday rush that made him lose his head as surely as all his merchandise was doing."

"*And* it only cost a guinea," Somerset said with satisfaction, patting his pocket. "I suppose because poulterers fatten before holidays even as their merchandise does. They do not come dear on the day before Christmas, in any case. A guinea is a bargain."

Kate swallowed hard. It was no bargain to her, except, she reminded herself, no price that freed Randolph was too outrageous. She stopped and opened her purse. She had exactly that, and two pence left over. It would have done for a snack on the train, coming and going, with enough left over for a gratuity for Aunt's maid, as well as a cab from the train station, and dinner for herself and Randolph the night they returned to London.

"Thank you so much," she said as she handed her coins to Somerset.

He drew back as though she'd offered him snakes. "A gentleman does not take money from a lady," he said in horror.

"A lady does not accept money from a strange gentleman," she insisted.

"I am not strange," he protested, and then paused, considering, "unusual, certainly. But not strange."

He refused to take the coins, putting his hands in his pockets so that she'd nothing to do with them but continue to hold them out to him, feeling a fool for doing so. But a determined one. Determination gave her inspiration.

"I consider that I have engaged you as a lawyer. I wish you to send me a bill for services rendered," she said proudly, wondering how many years she'd have to work in order to pay him in full, "and so certainly I should pay you out of pocket expenses in the pursuit of my cause."

"Extraordinary," he remarked to his cousin, who stood looking down at Kate with fond amusement. "You have the most wonderful luck, Cousin." Then he turned to Kate and said, speaking down his long nose with pride and disdain, and just enough humor to make it tolerable, "Very well. I will accept it. *After* I have done rendering my services. Then, you may be sure, I shall send you a full accounting."

"Very well," Kate agreed, putting back the coins in a businesslike manner, revising her estimate of his fee upward by double.

And those fees were nothing to the thought of the obligations she realized she'd incurred, and she was fretting about them as she entered the police station again, this time flanked by her two new protectors.

"Ah," the constable behind the desk said immediately, with a twisted smile, when he saw them, " 'tis Mr. Lyons. *And* Mr. Jones. Now to what do we owe this honor? Here I thought we'd done with you for the year, sirs."

"Scarcely," Somerset said in bored accents, "since there's a week left to it. You have in your possession one Mr. Randolph Thacker? Then, please," he said, producing the paper from his vest pocket, "produce him for us."

The constable hesitated, and Charles bent to speak with him in low, thrumming tones. Kate thought she saw Charles's hand go to his pocket, thought she saw him produce his wallet, but when she tried to see more, Somerset stepped in front of her. She craned her head, but he moved in the way again, and since it would have looked like they were dancing if she kept trying to see what he was blocking from her view, she gave it up. And despite his attempts at conversation, occupied herself with worrying about whether a suspected debt was a valid one. But then forgot about debts and obligations altogether.

Because she saw Randolph being led out of the recesses of the police station.

"He's all yours," the constable said.

The sight of her brother, grimy, blinking at the light, twisting his cap in his chapped hands as he looked at her, made her forget her audience and his dignity. She sank to her knees, swooped him up in her arms and hugged him hard, weeping as she did.

"Lor'," Randolph said in a thickened, wavering voice, patting her shoulder awkwardly, "don't cry, Katie. It wasn't so bad in my flowery dell. The old bucket and pail didn't get me down. I was Jack Jones, but once the lads discovered I was hearts of oak, we were china plates. Isn't that super?" he said gleefully, drawing back to see her face. "They taught me how to rabbit and pork!"

"I believe," Charles said, as Somerset grinned and Kate stared at him with great, grave eyes, "your brother was put in a cell with some cockney lads. It's rhyming slang. All he said was that it wasn't so bad in his cell, jail didn't get him down, he was alone but once his cellmates realized he was penniless, they became mates— and taught him how to speak."

As Kate turned to stare at her brother, Charles spoke to his cousin. "Just in time. A few more hours," he remarked in a soft, worried voice, "and the boy would have picked up far more."

But Kate heard him, and the sudden alarm that sprang to her eyes made him add, "Never fear. As it is, he only found it enlivening. Still, there's a chance you might find it even more so after he's been home an hour. Ah, I recommend he take a thorough bath before you set out for your aunt's house. Unless you want to bring her far more company than you'd reckoned on," he added gently.

"Oh! But our train tickets are for noon, that's only a half hour from now; we'll never make it if we stop at home for that," she protested, until she saw Randolph scratch his head in puzzlement, or . . .

"No. You must bathe," she said with determination, and a sinking heart, thinking of her tickets wasted and the holiday lost to them.

"But there's no problem," Charles said. "While he bathes, I can get a refund on your railway tickets for you. And then take you myself. You see, I'm going north. By myself," he added with a significant look to his cousin, who nodded in instant agreement, albeit with great amusement, "and would be glad of your company so far as . . . ?"

"Enfield," Randolph supplied, helpfully.

"Splendid," Charles said. "You see? No trouble at all, on my way, just a hop off the main road for me, actually. It wouldn't be in the spirit of Christmas if I didn't offer. And certainly there cannot be anything improper with young Randolph along to play propriety? After all, there'll be three of us."

"No, four," Somerset said after a brief whispered consultation with a constable.

Charles glared at his cousin in outrage. But that only seemed to please him enormously.

"Yes, four," Somerset said with great pleasure, as he accepted the basket the constable handed to him. "You forgot the turkey."

"Well, but I think you've rats in your turret, Katie," Randolph said as he combed his damp hair. "They're splendid chaps!"

"So it may appear," Kate said, "but the point is that Mr. Lyons is the only one who really knows Mr. Jones, and I scarcely know Mr. Lyons. Meeting someone on the street is hardly a proper introduction. Oh, dear," she added, sinking to a chair and biting her lip, "I wonder if it's worth it. I mean, to go careering across the kingdom with a perfect stranger, just so that we can get to Aunt Fenton, who will not be pleased with us in any case, no matter what we do . . ."

"And who will be less pleased if we don't show up at all," Randolph said. "Besides, I'll be there with you, so if you think Charles will turn into some sort of beast once we've left London, you've no need to fear at all," he said carelessly, as Kate frowned, trying to think of her dear brother in combat with someone like Charles Lyons—something like picturing David up against Goliath, sans his slingshot.

" 'Charles?' I know he told you to call him that, but it hardly seems right; we scarcely know him," Kate insisted, further upset by his familiar use of their savior's name.

"Please don't be such a prig, my dear," Randolph said, in those new accents that sometimes came out of his mouth these days, making him sound so much like a man that she blinked. "He's only a bit older than you are, after all. Yes. Seven and twenty. He told me so."

"That is seven years," she snapped, stung. "Seven is not 'a bit.' Nor is age a guarantee of innocence, for all we know Jack the Ripper is a stripling youth."

"Well, but he ain't Charles, I can tell you that! The lads at the bucket and pail say the inside word is that the Ripper's a flash gent, all right, but some say he's higher than that, high as a pig's eye and . . . ah," he said in response to his sister's glare, "that is to say, they say the Ripper's highly placed, maybe even a royal."

"I don't care to hear what *they* say. And certainly not in the way *they* say it. Please remember that. Nor do I believe Mr. Lyons is the Ripper. But how do we know what he is? He may be highly placed, or very lowly, indeed." She paused, thinking about what she'd seen and heard and tried not to understand, because she'd needed his help so much: that Charles was as well known to the police as Somerset was. And he wasn't a lawyer. Nor did she know what he was. But she didn't want to frighten Randolph, just put him on his guard. "After all, we know nothing about him," she finally said weakly.

"We know he's kind and helpful," Randolph flared, "and without him, I should still be in my flowery . . . ah, I'd still be in jail."

"Yes. True. And I'm grateful. But I'm not saying he's dangerous, love, only that we know so little that it's dangerous for us. But think. Why should he concern himself with us at all?" she asked. Randolph, looking at her in her new tightly fitted deep rose traveling dress, began to smile knowingly, but stopped when she added, "He say's he's going home—to what? Is he married? He's certainly old enough to be. Has he children? He looks the sort who likes children," she said in a soft, sad voice.

Randolph nodded, as chastened as if she'd scolded him.

"I'll be there, Kate," he assured her in that new voice of his, and she smiled at him, because it was comforting to feel he was growing to manhood, and she almost believed he could protect her from anything.

"But what are you doing with that?" he asked with loathing, looking at the great wicker basket that he'd learned to hate so well in so short a time.

"The turkey? It's for Aunt."

He stared at her in disbelief, and she said defensively, "What else are we to bring her for Christmas? It may not be elegant, but it is a thing of value. I don't make a great deal of money, but I did earn a Christmas bonus. It's not what we wanted, but it's not nothing. I *earned* it, Randolph," she said, half in defiance, half in entreaty. She stood before him, clutching the basket to her breast as though there were a child in there, and they were both about to be thrown into the storm.

"Well, of course," he said after a brief moment, "do you think they'd have clapped me in jail for something worthless? Why, in grandfather's day, I'd have gone to the scaffold for it! Of course, it's valuable," he said, so as to take that terrible look from her eyes. "Aunt ought to be proud to have it. Too good for her, in my humble opinion," he added, forcing himself to take the basket from her.

She was enormously proud of him. If the turkey wasn't what she'd wanted, still this—the way it showed her how grown up her brother was—was worth all the trouble and disappointment of it. Except, of course, that he wasn't grown up. He was only twelve, after all. And showed it only moments later.

"A motor! Just think, Katie, a motor!" he said breathlessly when he saw what was awaiting them at the curb when they came down the stair. "Is it truly yours? Or is your carriage just around the corner?" he asked Charles nervously.

"Mine, truly mine," Charles told him, although it was Kate he was watching as he did, "and not half so fitting as a coach and four, for going home to Christmas. But it's a matter of thrift. Horses eat their heads off in London, and motors do not."

"Pull the other one, if you please!" Randolph breathed with awe, forgetting his manners as he goggled at the auto and the uniformed fellow who was stowing their luggage in its boot. Because anyone knew there was nothing so expensive in the world as an auto: a fellow could buy seven horses for one of them, and no one but a very rich fellow would even think of it. Randolph had never so much as touched one, although he'd yearned to whenever he'd seen one in the streets of London.

"Should you like to sit up front with Mr. Hopkins?" Charles asked Randolph. And before Kate could bend an eye enough to let her brother know she'd rather not ride alone with their host, Randolph cried, "Would I?" and ran to join the chauffeur in the front seat.

"Ah, yes," Charles said, noticing the basket Randolph had left on the pavement, like an abandoned waif. "I remember this fellow well. How has he been? Recovered from his recent incarceration? Or has he lost . . .

anything in the experience?'' he asked, as he lifted a
corner of the white cloth covering the turkey and peered
in at it. ''He looks a bit pale,'' he said.

''He's quite intact,'' Kate said, a little stiffly, a little
on her guard now that she was about to get into the auto
with Charles, and not just because it would be her first
time in an automobile.

''Grown attached to the little fellow, have you?''
Charles asked with great sympathy in his deep voice,
taking the basket from her as she lifted it. ''Well, I can't
blame you. I can see anyone would. Such an ideal pet;
no trouble, no shedding or molting. No barking at the
door at night, no scratching the furniture, no sitting on
his perch and keeping you awake with raucous singing.
And if you get hungry, I'm certain you couldn't ask for
a better companion. What he lacks in animation, I'm sure
he makes up for in devotion. You won't find him straying!
Have you named him yet?'' he asked with great interest.

But Kate was trying to stop laughing and catch her
breath.

''Rover would be singularly appropriate, I think,'' he
mused, as he put the basket behind their seat and helped
Kate up into the automobile. ''For such a sluggish fellow, he's certainly managed to get around a bit, hasn't
he?''

''I don't believe in naming my dinners,'' she said as
starchily as she could, settling herself and starting to tie
her hat on with her scarf. But his fleeting look of disappointment and sudden polite expression made her feel
like her Aunt Fenton, so she added, ''How could anyone
sit down to consume a roast named . . . R-Ralph, for
example?'' before the absurd idea got the better of her,
and she started laughing again.

''Or a chicken named Charles, perish the thought,''
he said, looking very pleased, because she saw his lips
twitching.

''Or a fish named . . . Fred,'' she said, and they
laughed so much she neglected to moan in terror as she

thought she might do when the mighty engine of the auto started up, and the chauffeur hopped into the driver's seat again, proceeding to drive them down the street, and away toward the North, Enfield, and Christmas.

After a while Kate became used to the unsettling experience of traveling in a motor car. She even learned to disregard the terrible roar and chug it made as it went. When it did go, that was to say. Because it seemed to her that Mr. Hopkins spent as much time getting out to discover what caused the vehicle to cough and die, as he did sitting in it and steering. Getting used to the way they were stared at by all passersby, whether riding or standing still, was hardest of all for her. "Like riding in a howdah on an elephant down Drury Lane, yes," was all Charles said, imperturbably, when she remarked on it. She privately thought the journey would have been a deal faster and more comfortable in a simple hackney coach, but there was no denying there was a certain something to be able to ride in a coach with no horse in front of it. Like traveling in a howdah on an elephant down Drury Lane, she thought, yes.

She soon became accustomed enough to attempt conversation.

"I mean to give the turkey to Aunt Fenton as a house present," she told Charles. "I know it's not the usual thing to do. I'd planned to bring her a tea cozy, or somesuch. But, with all the commotion this morning, there was no time," she lied, unwilling to admit that money, not time, was the essence. "Still," she added bracingly, "I believe that if I tell her it's all the rage to give foodstuffs for house gifts in London, she'll accept it."

"All jest aside, it is a fine turkey," Charles said, looking at her oddly. "I can't imagine someone not accepting it with pleasure. Especially a hostess at Christmastime. Unless, of course, she's a vegetarian, like Mr. Bernard Shaw," he added with a grin.

"Oh no," she said, "it's never that. It's just that Aunt

is not a . . . a homey sort of person. If she thinks it's
not a proper gift, she won't be happy, not even if Tom
Turkey were the best in London. Or so it seems to me.
You see, we lived with her for five months after Father
died, and yet still aren't on easy enough terms with her
to really know. She's not motherly, precisely. Not that
Randolph and I require a mother, of course," she added
when she saw the sympathy that softened his keen hazel
eyes until she could no longer look into them—or away
from them.

"No, you've decided to be that for him. He won't stand
for it much longer, you know," he said. Before she could
deny it, he added, "Tom is it? How disappointing. I
thought you more original. Everyone's turkey's named
Tom. Every second dashing chap in Green Park calls his
turkey Tom these days you know. Why, a man only needs
cry 'Tom!' on Rotten Row, to have himself surrounded
by turkeys. Not to mention what happens if he does it at
a ball."

"How true," she said, wonderfully diverted, her eyes
dancing with glee. "Then Tim, I think. Tiny Tim," she
said, with sudden inspiration.

"Hmm. Yes. But in that case, we'd better divest him
of a drumstick immediately, don't you think?" he mused,
and she forgot herself enough to think of him as she
might any comical friend, and so cried, "Horrible man!"
and rapped his arm as a rebuke.

He caught her hand and held it, and said, "Yes," as
he gazed at her.

She wore gloves, and so did he, and they were alone,
but only by inches. But it had been so long since she'd
had anyone hold her hand. Randolph thought he was too
old for that, even crossing streets, and she'd not had a
beau since she'd been at home, carefree and eighteen.
That must be why she found herself shocked. Not the
fact that his hand was so large hers quite disappeared in
it, and the look he gave her was so warm she grew cold
enough to tremble.

"You're freezing, and no wonder, the bricks are all cold," he murmured. "Say, Hopkins"—he leaned forward to the driver—"let's stop at The Partridge just ahead, and have something warm to eat and drink. We've the time, and the horses need their rest."

The chauffeur nodded, and Kate was glad of the chance to recover herself.

"This is a horseless carriage," she pointed out when he sat back again, and she'd extracted her hand from his with regret and relief.

"So they'd have you think!" he said with animation. And proceeded to tell her about the teams of cleverly concealed miniature horses that were trapped on treadmills in the engine space, the ones that were really powering the auto. He told her about them until she was so weak with laughter she really needed his help to step down when they reached the inn.

They ordered far too much food, or so she thought, until she saw the short work Charles and Randolph made of it. When Charles excused himself for a moment, Randolph watched him go with as much admiration shining in his eyes as he had for the luncheon he'd just devoured. Which was to say, an enormous lot of it.

"He's top drawer, Katie," Randolph said, when he'd swallowed the last of the pastry he'd been chewing. "Not married, I'll have you know. And let's see—he does love children, and he's got heaps of money, and he plays tennis, and travels a bit, and rides to an inch, and would rather fish than hunt, and read than do either, and he gardens too. Imagine that. Hopkins thinks he's the best employer a man could have. So there's no sense being wary of him at all." He looked at her triumphantly.

"Hopkins is his dependent," she said softly, "and however grateful we are to Charles, we are nothing to him, and certainly not his dependents. Nor do we wish to be. We've already imposed on his good nature more than is proper, or wise."

"Lor', you sound just like Aunt Fenton," Randolph said in disgust.

She gazed at him steadily and told him what she had to tell herself. "But the world thinks very much as Aunt does. And Charles knows that too. We have no protector, please remember that. Charity is odious to me. But I take it if I must. To take more, however, is to ask for more than one deserves. And when one asks for more, there's always payment required. Aunt wants only our absolute obedience. I don't wish to find out what Charles might want."

Because, she thought as she saw Randolph pale, at last thinking along the lines she was—if I'm right, it might pain me to know what he wants. But what frightens me most is that if I'm right, I might not be as loathe to pay his price as I know I should be.

"Very glum indeed," Charles said when he returned to their table and found them silent, avoiding each other's eyes. "Is it because we're not at Enfield yet? Or so near to it?"

And since that was almost precisely what they'd both been thinking, they looked up at him with guilty surprise. And so gave him much to think about the rest of the way to Enfield.

"My dear," Aunt Fenton said, giving Kate her cool, powdery, wrinkled cheek to pretend to kiss. "My dear," she told Randolph as she allowed him to do the same. Kate was afraid she'd do the same to Charles, simply out of habit. But Aunt did worse. She stopped, drew herself up, and looked up at him with much feigned surprise. That was when Kate remembered there were introductions to be made before Aunt Fenton would deign to so much as ask who he was. Her aunt, Kate thought darkly, as she automatically introduced the pair, wouldn't cry "Stop!" to a midnight prowler creeping out from under the bed, if she hadn't been introduced to him first.

"How do you do," Aunt asked when Kate was done, but in such a way as to let him know she scarcely cared.

"Very well, thank you," Charles answered, "and you, ma'am?"

Aunt didn't reply, but looked to Kate, who realized there were explanations as well as introductions to be made before her aunt would say another word to the stranger on her doorstep.

"Mr. Lyons and I met in London," Kate said. When her aunt still said nothing, she added, a little desperately, "Ah, we met . . ."

"Through Randolph actually," Charles put in cheerfully.

"Yes!" Kate said at once, giving Charles a look of grateful entreaty, "just so. Mr. Lyons has a . . . a cousin who attends school with Randolph."

"I see," Aunt said, and then added, peering out her window at the amazing vehicle that had delivered her relatives, "you ride in an automobile, Mr. Lyons, and yet your cousin attends a day school in the City?"

"Poor relations," Charles promptly explained.

"Ah, yes. A common foolishness," Aunt told Charles, showing all her little yellow teeth in a terrible smile, "educating a lad above his station. As I tell our Katherine, and try to tell young Randolph: it little befits a boy to pass his days in ease at a desk when he could be out in the world earning his daily bread. And his sister's."

Randolph's fair face flushed, and he spoke up so quickly, he stammered, "Just . . . just as I tell Kate too, Aunt, depend on it. But I can't move her on the subject, nor can I vex her by disobedience. Next year will be different, I promise you. I'll be too old for the school then, and shall go to work and earn our daily bread, *and* cake. For they won't take me back then, Kate," he told his sister, his eyes glowing, "so there'll be more argument about it."

She bit her lip. She believed she might have enough for another term at his old school by then, if her mone-

tary debts to Somerset Jones didn't take too much from
her savings, if she kept her position at Morley and
Scruggs, and if there were no unexpected expenses. In
any case there was nothing she could argue now, nor
would she in front of Aunt, even if there were.

"And what do you do in London, Mr. Lyons?" Aunt
asked, as though they were not still wearing their capes
and coats and standing in the entry way. Kate could scent
fresh baked cookies, and knew that some neighbors and
all of Aunt's cronies were being entertained in the parlor
before a nicely burning fire. But she also knew that they
wouldn't be invited to join them until Aunt felt Charles
qualified for entry. Her cheeks burned for her aunt's high-
handedness. She was glad, once again, to remember Aunt
had only married into the family, but she could only stand
and shift from foot to foot and wish that Charles had an
urgent errand somewhere, much as she disliked seeing
him leave. But that might be better than having him see
how cheaply she was held here, in her only relative's
home.

"Do?" Charles asked as answer, as though he couldn't
believe his ears.

"I meant," Aunt asked with awful clarity, "how do
you earn your daily bread?"

"Oh, *do*," he said and his face, which had been looking rather grim, relaxed. "There is plain speaking! No
matter, no matter, I like it. I'm a bluff fellow myself."
Both Kate and Randolph stared at him in amazement,
because he'd become so much the hearty country squire
that they almost believed that was what he was. "Social
amenities might say: be gentle, be kind to the stranger,
especially on Christmas Eve. But your aunt," he said,
turning to Kate and Randolph so he didn't see Aunt Fenton beginning to swell with indignation at being accused
of a social lapse, "means to be sure you're not in the
company of a no-account charlatan. Quite right, ma'am,"
he said, facing his hostess, who was looking totally per-
plexed now, "good thinking, no matter if it embarrasses

the young ones, eh? But what do they know? Precisely. How do I earn my daily bread? I don't. In short, I don't, ma'am. Between what m'father left me, and m'uncle promises to, I don't turn a hand at anything that will bring more money. I'm not so greedy.''

He stood and grinned down at her.

''Do come in, Mr. Lyons,'' Aunt said, and Kate wanted to run for the door. She would have too, she thought bitterly, as she finally gave her coat to the maid, if she knew where to go. But it was Christmas Eve, and she didn't know when the next train to London was. That reminded her, belatedly, that in her confusion, she'd given Charles their tickets to and from Enfield. And that he hadn't given her back the return tickets, or the money for those he'd returned, either. So she was worried as well as shamed as they entered the fashionably overcluttered parlor, threaded their way through potted palms and ferns, found a clearing midst the statuary and knickknack tables, and faced Aunt's visitors.

Who were all, Kate discovered, just as charitable and kind as their friend, Mrs. Fenton, but twice as rude, because they didn't have to pretend to affection. But they were politely so, so she had to suffer them—and couldn't at all understand why Charles did. If she were he, she thought, she'd be in that motor and off down the highway before she was much older.

And he stood and wondered why Kate didn't take Randolph and her damned turkey and leave. He could bear the intrusive questions, the common stares, all the rude inquisition, because he'd a few terrible relatives of his own, and so had practice. And he'd been raised a gentleman. And he'd put up with almost anything, he discovered, so long as he was allowed to be in the same room with Kate when he was forced to put up with it.

He looked over the head of a singularly unpleasant fellow, whose breath was as bad as his taste in clothes, and gazed at Kate—bright, valiant, and beautiful. He was caught. Eyes and then loins, heart and then head—he was entirely hers now, though he knew he couldn't let her know it here and now. There was a legend in his family that the men in it knew their fate the moment they laid eyes upon her, and then never had eyes for any other female. He'd always laughed at it. Now he knew better. He sighed again.

"Just so!" the man he'd been ignoring said, and tapped at Charles's vest with one sharp finger to get his wavering attention. "*We* are supposed to be charitable at this blessed season, and so we are, so we are. But where is their charity, I ask you? Where? Do they help each other? No, no. No more than they help themselves, sir. They fill their bellies and put on the good used clothes we give them, and go out and drink and indulge themselves in all manner of vices—and come next Christmas, they're back with their hands out, just as woeful and needy again!"

"Indeed," Charles said in perfectly amiable tones, although he looked down at the fellow as though he were something he'd almost stepped in. "Just as if they couldn't turn those paltry rags and leftover bits of cheese into a fortune if they'd a mind to! Lazy shiftless louts if you ask me, and you did, didn't you?"

The tone of his voice made the fellow put on a smug smile, which faded as the sense of the words came clear. He was caught between satisfaction and dawning outrage, and so, momentarily speechless. Charles nodded and made his escape. By some intricate footwork, he managed to reach Kate's side.

"Oh, Charles," she said, seeing him join her, and glad to leave off getting advice from her aunt's friends for a moment. And yet sorry because she saw her aunt pointedly staring at the hands of her wall clock, "Have you come to say good-bye?" she asked fearfully.

He only left off gazing into her eyes when he heard her aunt speak. "Oh, do you have to leave us," she said, "what a pity. Still, it has begun to snow, and I imagine you have a way to go"—she tittered—"my, the holiday season has turned me into a lady poet, has it not?"

Her guests laughed, but Kate wasn't listening. She'd turned from Charles's burning stare to look out the window and saw the snow falling in huge, fat flakes. The day was growing darker, and yet the sky was filled with the curious luminous light that foretold a heavy snowfall. It was warm here in the parlor; there was a Christmas tree whose top scraped the ceiling, and its fresh green scent filled the room, competing with the wonderful odors of baking and spice and the applewood on the fire. It was a picture-book scene of a happy Christmas. And she would have left in a second to go out into the cold with Charles if she could, because she knew it was just as warm as a page in a picture book here for her. And not even so satisfying, because she knew this picture of content had no reality at all.

"Oh yes," Charles said, realizing he'd get no invitation to dinner, realizing he'd be wrong to accept one even if it had been forthcoming, because he was promised elsewhere, though his heart would stubbornly remain here. "So I suppose I must go," he said, shrugging. "It's been delightful, Mrs. Fenton. Thank you so much. Randolph," he said, extending a hand to the crestfallen boy who'd come creeping up out of the shadows to say good-bye, "it's been a pleasure traveling with you. All three of you," he added, to see the boy smile again.

"Oh," Kate said suddenly, remembering, her eyes widening, "how could I have forgotten? Randolph, before Charles leaves, do go out to the automobile and fetch Aunt's present in!"

"Oh, my dear," Aunt cried with patently false protest, as Randolph grinned and ran to the door, "a present! You oughtn't to have. The dear child, how considerate," she informed her guests, all of whom were watching avidly. "How good to see one's teachings haven't gone for naught."

Randolph came back, his hair and eyelashes covered with snow, but beaming, carrying the huge wicker basket before him. The guests all fell still as Aunt Fenton accepted it with little cries of pleasure, exclaiming over its weight. She had Randolph place it on a nearby table that the maid hastily cleared of its figurines, photographs, snuff boxes, shells, and various other objets d'art. Then Aunt hovered over the basket, as though too excited to lift the white cloth that covered its contents. She made it a moment of theater for her guests, and put a finger on her chin as she gazed down at it, kittenish as a girl, delighted at the attention and the size of whatever it was she'd just gotten. Then, too greedy to wait a moment longer, she ripped the cloth from it. And stared.

The bit of holly in the bird's beak was a little wrinkled at the edges, and its berries were puckering, but the bird itself was just as blue-white, plump, and cool as it had always been.

"Surely," Aunt Fenton said into the sudden silence that had fallen over the room, "you have gotten the wrong basket, Randolph."

"No, no," Kate protested, "it's exactly right. It's what everyone in London is giving this season."

The only sound was the sudden gulp the maid made as she tried to stifle a spontaneous giggle.

"Ah, foodstuffs, that is," Kate said a little frantically as she saw her aunt's lips tighten. "I thought a plum pudding rather mundane, and a fruitcake—well, everyone gives fruitcakes. Since no one actually seems to eat them, I thought, well, a turkey . . ."

As Aunt tried to think of a thing to say to save her face in front of her guests, and yet let Kate know what a wretched gift it was, especially to give in front of guests, who might now imagine her too poor to provide her own Christmas turkey, Randolph blurted, "It's over twenty pounds. The poulterer said so."

But his aunt said nothing. Kate looked desperate, and Charles was watching with no expression at all. The other guests all looked like hovering vultures, so Randolph went on, "He would have given me a quid for it. And the boys at the jail said it was worth far more. Ah. Ah," he said as he saw Kate's horror, "not that I stole it. It's Kate's, really it is. Mr. Scruggs gave it to her as a Christmas bonus. Her employer," he explained to the fascinated company. And then, realizing everything was now out, laid bare as Kate's turkey before them, he flushed red, and grew white, and then still.

"Your employer?" one of her aunt's friends asked with gleeful horror. "You are employed, Miss Thacker? In London?"

Kate looked at her aunt's furious face, and then at Randolph and feared for him. Then she straightened her shoulders. She might regret that the truth had been let out, but she would not bury it again.

"I do," she intoned solemnly. "At the firm of Morley and Scruggs. A respectable firm, a brokerage, and I hold a respectable position. I am a lady typewriter. Yes, in London."

"I never knew such a thing!" Aunt cried, turning to face the company. "As if I would countenance such! A gently bred female working among men! See what comes of letting the girl remain on her own? She goes to ruin in the fleshpots of London. I begged her to remain with me. Now I see why she would not," she said, putting her hand to her forehead. "The only good in it is that poor Mr. Thacker is not alive to see it. It is his family, you know," she hastily explained to her fascinated guests, "not mine. Not a drop of my blood."

Kate threw the cloth back over the turkey, as if embarrassed that she'd let them see it naked and vulnerable. She picked up the basket and took Randolph's hand.

"You did know, Aunt. I told you . . . ah," she said in disgust, though she was crying, not sneering. "There's no point to this. Good evening, Aunt, and a Happy Christmas to you," and so saying, she accepted her coat from the maid and marched out of the house, into the snow.

Charles stowed the turkey for her, sent Randolph to sit with Mr. Hopkins, and once he'd got a shaking

Kate into the vehicle again and heard no word of protest come from the house, he heaved a great sigh of relief.

"You've got the teams waiting at Bigelow's, I suppose?" he asked Hopkins. "Good," he said when his man smiled. "You were right, but don't gloat, it's not pretty. Take us there, before we're caught in a drift and have to leave this dratted machine to rust until spring. Hopkins respects the automobile," he told Kate as he sat back in his seat, "and does well with it, but his heart's not in it. Horses are his passion. He knew it would snow and suggested the carriage. But I wanted to impress you, and now he's got something to hold over my head for the next thirty years. Ah, don't cry, Katie, she's a wicked old thing, but everyone has a skeleton or two in the family closet. It's only that most of us have enough of the other kind to allow us to ignore those that are still rattling around. Ah, no, Katie," he said, taking her in his arms.

He couldn't feel much but a vague female shape wrapped in wool, shaking with sobs. But he knew he held her, and it was heaven for him to do so. And terrible too, because she was weeping, and trying so hard to stop. So he crooned to her, and rocked her, and she slowly stilled. By the time they got to the inn where Hopkins had stabled their teams, she was spent, and drained, and refused to meet his eyes.

"Thank you very much," she said stiffly, after he'd helped her down from the automobile. "I expect we can get a hackney cab to take us to the station now. Oh," she added, putting out her gloved hand, "I'd forgot, may I have our return tickets now?"

He stared down at her in the growing dusk. She looked like a little pilgrim, all snow-capped, and stern. He felt his heart wrenched, and steeled himself against it.

"No," he said simply. "No, you may not."

They argued for an hour, debated for another, and now that Randolph had fallen asleep in the seat opposite, they discussed the matter in tired, but determined whispers.

"I only came along because it was cold and growing colder, not to mention the snow, and I hadn't the energy to resist any longer. Not just then," she said, as she'd said so many times before, "but I will not come to your parents' house with you, and I want you to know that every mile farther north that you take us costs me more, because my railway tickets back to London will cost that much more too."

"You came because I'd have picked you up bodily and carried you into the coach, and you can't bear scenes," he said, sitting back and closing his eyes. "It's my grandparents' house; I told you there will be so many people there no one will notice you. Since you persist in your objections, I can only think you want to make a stir, and I must say I'm surprised at you being so vain."

She tried not to smile; she didn't want to leave but knew she could not stay as an object of his pity and charity. She couldn't remember when she'd been so confused. A Christmas alone with Randolph in London seemed pathetic now, but battening on Charles' kindness would be cheap. And what would his family think? He might say there was nothing wrong with a woman making her way in the world, only that she had to, but his family? She didn't dare risk more insult. But he looked so handsome with his eyes closed in the dimmed light of the carriage lamps, she'd never seen such long lashes on a man—well, she thought fairly, she'd never looked to see them on any other man. Then he said something that he hadn't said before—something that jolted her from thoughts of his eyelashes.

"Randolph deserves a good Christmas. That fiend of an aunt made him feel very meager indeed," Charles said very softly, so softly she had to lean closer to his big, solid, warm frame to hear. "We'll have a dozen boys his age at home; there'll be games and skating, food and frolic. Plenty of room and company, and the whole wide outdoors as his playground. He's not got that much childhood left. Give the boy this Christmas, Katie."

She sat very still, considering. Yes, she thought, with suddenly rising spirits, she could stay with that as her reason. And if his family thought her a pushy little upstart, so be it. She felt better than she had since her whole mad adventure began, since the moment she'd received her turkey. But then he spoke again, and now his eyes were open, and there was a look of pain in them.

"No," he said, frowning, "that's not worthy of me. You'd walk on hot coals for the boy. And though it's true what I said of him, I must be entirely honest. It's *this* boy I'm thinking of. I want you to stay with us over Christmas—and with me, forever after. Now don't gape like that, Katie," he complained. "I know it's early days yet. I know you don't know me, but you'll never get another chance to know a chap so well, and so quickly, as this opportunity offers. Still, I know you'll never know me better than you do now. Nor I, you. That's the way it is in my family. I know the etiquette books say a chap has to court a girl for a year, and then hint at his expectations for another, and then hold her hand for one more, before he declares that his intentions are honorable. But I hereby declare mine are. There's a savings of three years. Yours don't have to be," he added helpfully, "not immediately, that is. I don't approve such indecision, mind, but I daresay I can understand and wait a week more. Just stay for Christmas, Katie," he said soberly, "please?"

He laughed at her expression. "Goggling like a fishie, little Kate, close your mouth, do," he whispered fondly, "or rather, no, don't," he said with sudden inspiration, and murmured, "not just yet," as he lowered his head and placed his lips on hers. What he found there made him pull back after a long moment, start to speak, think better of it, and kiss her again, instead. This time when his lips left hers he said in an unsteady voice, "Please? I can't take much more of this convincing you. I'm a gentleman, you know."

She, all unknowing, licked her lips and nearly dashed

all his resolve as he watched. But she'd never felt any-thing more delicious, as spicy and hot as Christmas punch, and just as intoxicating—but she'd never yearned to totally immerse herself in a punchbowl, she thought with dizzy surprise. She gazed at him. Dazed and tired, happy as she'd never been and twice as fearful, she hes-itated. And then said, "Yes . . . but only because of Randolph, and because you have the tickets, and . . ." but before she could enumerate all the reasons, their coach had stopped, and they were at their destination.

She got a glimpse of an enormous manor house, glit-tering with light. She was shown into the house, and as she was divested of her coat, she was immediately sur-rounded by what seemed to be dozens of interested per-sons, who reported on what they were seeing to what seemed to be dozens of others coming to see who'd ar-rived. Charles's father was as huge as he was, and many of his brothers were the same size, but his mother, a few other brothers, and most of his sisters were built to a more delicate scale. His grandparents were enthusiastic in their greetings, as were their cousins, and there was much approval to be seen in the eyes of some of the octogenarians who sat in places of high honor in front of one of the biggest roaring fireplaces. Somerset Jones greeted her with ill-concealed hilarity before introducing her to his parents and grandparents and cousins, all over again.

Kate was shown to her room by a maid and helped to wash and change. She was glad she'd brought her fine coffee-colored silk dress, because it was the most festive thing she owned. She hardly had time to marvel over the size and comforts of her room before she was ushered down to dinner. There she discovered that Randolph had met two friends who'd been at his old school, and was busily catching up on old times with them. He sat across the long dining table from her. She was seated next to Charles and listened with fascination as he squirmed while Somerset explained how he'd gotten the nickname Cubby.

The table in the huge dining hall was long enough to seat a legion, and it seemed it did—a legion of well-dressed, laughing people of all ages. They were served so much food from so many dishes, there was scarcely room for it on their plates, so Charles urged Kate to finish it up so she could make room for more. Everywhere candles burned with pure and steady light; the fire that roared in the grate was reflected in all the prisms of the evergreen-swagged chandelier above them, and everyone, even the servants, seemed to be smiling.

Kate had a moment to herself when Charles became diverted by a discussion of another cousin's pet name. She sat back and watched the gay company, and thought perhaps that it was all some Christmas fantasy. She'd never known such welcome. When she gazed at Charles, she wondered if she'd run entirely mad. Because she simply could not envision going on with her life now without him. Then, during one of those momentary silences that comes over even the most boisterous company at times, she heard what Randolph was saying to his friends.

"Aye," he said, his clear excited boy's voice carrying to fill all the silences, "jail. Or as the lads there taught me to say, 'bucket and pail.' They said I had to stay over Christmas until Barnaby Rudge—that's the judge," he explained handsomely to his rapt audience, "sat on Tuesday, but my blister—ah, sister, and Charles and Somerset came, and got me out by proving that I hadn't stolen it; the turkey was ours by right. And they didn't have to fetch old Scruggs to prove it, either!"

Kate sat very still, and wondered how it was that she could feel all the blood leaving her head.

"Oh, I say!" one of the other boys said. "How splendid! What an adventure!"

"What a story!" another said jealously. "Nothing that fine ever happened to me."

Kate swallowed and put down her napkin. She wondered how far it was to the train station, to keep from wondering how she would be able to leave the room with her head still held high. Or see the doorway, her eyes were swimming so. But she began to push herself from the table, so she could rise without fuss, or oversetting any of the crystal.

"I'm sure," Charles's mother said gently, from the head of the table, "that Kate did not think it such a fine adventure, poor child."

"She'd have thought it even worse if they had to fetch old Scruggs to testify for her, let me tell you," Charles's grandfather crowed. "A hard-hearted old skinflint, as I remember him."

"Is he still such an old pinchpenny? He must be," Charles's father mused, "to give a girl a turkey for Christmas, when he's got money enough to gild her typewriter for her."

"Well, that's the way of some of these chaps," another cousin said, and as Kate sat, amazed into silence, she heard the company begin discussing the miserly ways of many of London's finest merchant families.

Charles looked at her with sympathetic understanding. He reached for her hand and held it in his as he remarked to Somerset, who was watching with interest, "I neglected to explain our family to Kate, I'm afraid."

"You should be. Afraid she'd throw you over, old boy? Let me try to smooth things out. Kate—I may call you that, mayn't I? After all, we're practically family. Oh, don't be so astonished. We've all got high expectations. Cubby's never brought a woman home—to our family home, that is," he said with a sly smile, as Charles coughed, and the rest of the company, who were hanging on their every word, laughed. "So we know it's serious with him. And if it is, it would be quite remarkable if he let you get away. He's tenacious. We all are.

"Now then, you see, the family's an extended one, founded when three fellows became friends in the infancy of the century we're about to leave behind us. All

were gentlemen, but some from less than gentle beginnings, and as there's been a good deal of intermarriage
between the families since—''

"In short," Charles broke in to say irritably, "which
is a thing my long-winded cousin never got the hang of—
since some of us had to scratch our way up, or love those
who did, we've a vested interest in those less fortunate,
and never give a fig about what your aunt would consider
proper. But we don't think proper is always right, nor is
right always proper—only respectable, which we do try
to be. Oh, we're wealthy enough, due to our elder's good
sense''—and here some of the oldest members of the
family drank their wine or fanned themselves, or looked
at the ceiling, or otherwise tried to appear oblivious to
the praise—"but we like to spread the wealth. I know
the grasshoppers—Hey! young Randolph, quick, what's
a grasshopper?" he interrupted himself to ask.

Randolph grinned and shouted back, "A copper, sir."

"Exactly," Charles told Kate. "I knew you were dis-
tressed that the police knew me, but were too polite to
inquire. Still, you should have done," he chided her. "I
might have been a rogue, you know."

"Might have been?" one wit called, while another
shouted, "Rogue would be the least of it, beware, Katie!"

"Yes, well," Charles said hurriedly, "I know them
because our family does what it can to alleviate the conditions which so vexed our great grandfathers, and so we
often have to deal with the magistrates in order to retrieve
young souls. I'm not an angel," he said to more general
merriment, "or at least no more so than any of us here,"
he added, glowering at them. "We all do what we can,
as well as our own work. I'm a broker myself, in the
family business. We're investors, you see. But as to the
other family business, Cousin Begood there''—and here
a cheerful middle-aged gentleman waved to her from
down the table—"and his clan oversee the orphan
schools. The Viscount Dylan's offspring are in charge of

the employment agencies, the Duke of Peterstow's family, particularly Somerset and his brothers, see to legal matters, and I and some of my brothers are coordinators, we oversee the lot of them.''

"Coordinator is a fine new word for lazy lump,'' Somerset remarked, and set them all aroar again.

"Well, then,'' Charles's father said, "speaking of fine things, we've heard a great deal about Scruggs's fine bird. What say we get a look at him now?''

"Rather peremptory, my dear,'' his wife reproved him. "It may be Kate has some other intention for the turkey.''

"Oh no,'' Kate protested, "please, will you take him as a house gift? He needs a home,'' she pleaded because she was so anxious to see the last of the bird. They all laughed at that, causing all promise of her bitter tears to fade, to be replaced by the more treacherous ones of joy.

"Yes, time to bed the fellow down, I think. He's done his work,'' Charles said, smiling at Kate so warmly Somerset commented on how old Cubby had certainly been treed at last.

A word to a young footman soon brought two more in, bearing the huge wicker basket between them. This time, when the cloth was whisked off, there was a cheer of delight as Scruggs's turkey met their gaze.

"A right handsome old bird!''

"Scruggs finally did something right!''

"Let's open him up—maybe he's stuffed with gold!''

"Aye, but cook him first!''

"Hear, hear!'' Charles's father said, rising, with his glass held high. "I propose a toast: to Scruggs, for being such a mean old skint—and so bringing Cubby his Kate!''

"Lord, don't ask the poor girl to drink to that,'' Somerset declared, "she hasn't even said yes yet!''

"She'd better!'' someone shouted, and was shushed when they saw the color rise in her cheeks.

"Will she, I wonder?'' Charles whispered. "I know it's an odious, overbearing sort of proposal,'' he told

Kate softly, under cover of the merriment at the table, "but since you said no in a closed carriage, albeit with your brother playing chaperon, I thought I'd try my hand at dinner. I always do well at table," he added hopefully, and she laughed until she was dizzy.

"A toast!" Charles's grandfather said, rising, with some help from a footman. "To young Charles and lovely Katie, and all the little cubs to come!"

"God help us every one," Somerset observed, but though he laughed, it could be seen that he raised his own glass high to that, and drained every drop in it after.

But as Kate had already whispered yes, no one paid any mind, because they'd all been eavesdropping and so were busily congratulating the newly engaged pair.

"You've done well, son, she's a lovely girl, bright and beautiful. With a mind of her own; I like that in a girl," Charles's father said, as he'd said from the moment Somerset had told them all about the young girl Charles was so interested in.

"It's of utmost importance in this family," Charles's mother commented, grinning at Kate.

"Well, how could I resist her," Charles asked, his arm tightly around his new fiancée, "with such a dowry as she brought. Now I have a lady typewriter of my very own. And I ask you—have you ever seen such a turkey?"

Christmas Angel

by Patricia Rice

"The Queen may decorate her palace as she pleases, but this is a place of worship, Marian, and I cannot allow it! It's pagan and ungodly."

"Even pagans worshiped a god, Bernard. And there is no where else to put it. I promised the children a tree, and a tree they shall have."

The young woman with her arms full of evergreens proceeded boldly up the church aisle toward the altar rail, the unfashionable gray serge of her gown swaying modestly over full petticoats. The anxious vicar in his dark coat followed close behind, nervously fingering his mustache.

"What if the family should come? They will think I have allowed their church to fall into sacrilegious rites. Just think of what they might say, Marian."

The shadowy figure at the rear of the church halted at this turn of the argument. With amusement, he waited for the outspoken lady's reply.

"Bernard, should Lord Sedgwick miraculously take up residence for the first time in twenty years, he would not be bothered to attend services. From all I've heard, he never attended when he was here. And even should God have sent some revelation that brought him into these hallowed interiors for the first time in his life, he would no doubt be carried in on his death bed and would not see nor care that we have brightened these dreary walls a trifle for the holidays."

The young vicar flinched at these cynical words, then

shoving an unruly lock of dark hair back from his face, he helped lay the arm load of evergreens on the first pew while the young woman in a plain coiffure too solemn for the season brought a ball of bright red ribbon from her pocket.

The figure in the background unashamedly took a seat in the last pew.

"It's not seemly, Marian," the vicar offered in one last protest. Perhaps the evergreen for the Christmas pageant, but not the tree. This is the Lord's house, not someone's parlor."

"Perhaps the Lord would like to have a parlor, too." The determined woman called Marian unclipped the scissors at her belt and began to snip equal lengths of ribbon. "The children have suffered so much this year, Bernard, you cannot deny them. First it was that dreadful influenza that took so many lives, then the cholera over in the factory town, and then the flood came and took everything along the river. Now the factory is closed down, and while I might be the first to say good riddance, it has left so many unemployed and hungry, we simply cannot deprive them of this one small treat. If you will not do it, I shall transfer my services to the Methodists."

"Marian, you would not!" Aghast at this traitorous threat even though he suspected she was not serious, the vicar absentmindedly held the evergreen against the altar rail while his antagonist tied a big bow around it. "Your family has been Anglican for centuries. They would turn over in their graves did you do such a thing," he reminded her for good measure.

"Moldering bones aren't going to care if I play here or over at the river. And the children won't either. I am sure I will find a choir just as eager as yours, and I have already spoken with that new Methodist minister. He is having an apple-bobbing and then they are going caroling. I have offered to help him find evergreens for that small box of a church of his, and he has eagerly accepted."

She threw too many defiant subjects at him at once, and Bernard shook his head to clear the way for argument. "You should not speak of the deceased so disrespectfully. And you have your mother and brothers and sisters to think of. They have always attended church here and will not be happy if you go elsewhere. And I suppose I dare not ask where this abundant supply of evergreen comes from. I can think of only one place. And besides," he added triumphantly, as an afterthought, "the Methodists do not have an organ."

Ignoring the reference to the instrument, Marian took up the argument where it was pertinent. "Well, I scarcely think the Sedgwicks will notice some missing greenery, after all. And the gatekeeper's children are in the pageant and he allows me all I like. Here, if you will loop this branch, I will tie it off and come back later to finish. It's almost time for the children to arrive, and I'm not certain Mama is at home to keep them in order." Marian straightened, brushed the pine needles off the gray serge of her heavy gown, and offered a smile of reassurance to the bemused vicar. "I believe God loves little children as much as I do, Bernard. He will not object."

With that little concession, she swirled around and hurried out the side door, leaving the vicar to stare helplessly at the mound of fresh-smelling pine. Fingering the lengths of bright red ribbon, he bent to pick up another branch for the chain when a slight cough at the rear of the church caught his attention.

Embarrassed, he hastily brushed his hand against his coat and stepped down the aisle toward the approaching figure in an elegantly cut short frock coat in the gray of half mourning, with top hat carried respectfully beneath his arm. The cut of the coat was slightly foreign to the London fashions with which he was familiar, but definitely of an expensive nature. Hopes rising, Bernard hurried forward to offer a proper greeting.

"How might I help you, sir?"

Despite the soberness of his formal attire, the gentleman's eyes appeared to be twinkling with some hidden laughter, and his slender face seemed almost incapable of containing the grin twitching at his long, firm mouth. His hands, however, were appropriately gloved and strong as he held one out to the vicar.

"Your lady friend is a mite strong-willed, I'd say. Your fiancée?"

Bernard's frown turned to confusion at this assumption. The stranger's accent was nothing like any he had ever heard, combining something of the polished tones of the aristocracy with an odd twang that reminded him somewhat of an American cousin who had once visited. But speculation was not part of his job.

"A good friend," Bernard asserted firmly, shaking the stranger's hand. "She lost her fiancé last year in a tragic accident at the factory."

"And has been bent on reforming the town ever since, no doubt," the stranger replied wryly. "Have you noticed how women seem ill content to stay at home anymore?"

Bernard offered a diffident shrug. "The world moves much too quickly, even in this small village. How might I help you?"

The stranger looked slightly embarrassed as he brushed invisible dust from his immaculate black hat. "Well, it seems I am temporarily discommoded. I had thought to take rooms at the inn, but there has been a serious coach accident; two vehicles collided at great speed, I believe. I gave up my room to some ladies who seemed in more need of it than I, thinking I might call on Sedgwick for hospitality. I knew the family wasn't in residence, but I had rather thought there would be someone in attendance. I was ill-informed it seems. Now I am temporarily without lodging. I thought, perhaps, you might know of someone hereabouts who might take boarders."

Bernard hesitated somewhere between doubt and delight. "You know the family?"

"You might say that. I'm sorry, I should have introduced myself." Holding out his hand, he offered, "I'm Alan Ellington."

Reassured by this use of the Sedgwick family name, Bernard shook his hand gratefully. "I'm honored to meet you, Mr. Ellington. We've not had a member of the family in residence in many years, since before my time, I fear. It's a pity you must come this year, when they have closed up the Hall. Bess and old George would have been delighted to put you up, were they still there. I am Bernard Dryden, at your service."

"Well, Mr. Dryden, it is my own fault for arriving unannounced. Would it be impossible to find somewhere else to stay until I can make other arrangements?"

Brought back from his fantasies of a member of the aristocracy moving back into the Hall, Bernard reluctantly considered the matter. He had no notion what relation the stranger was to the family or if he truly were who he said he was, but he seemed respectable and well-off. And if there were no room at the inn . . .

"It might be a trifle inconvenient for you," Bernard answered hesitantly. "We have no one putting up boarders per se, but the Chadwicks have an empty chamber now that their eldest son has married and moved away. And I venture to say that they could use the income, though don't tell them I said that. Shall I take you by to see?"

"I would be most appreciative." Replacing his hat on his head, Ellington followed the vicar outside into the gray chill of a December evening.

They had not far to walk from the church, and looking at the large house that the English called a cottage in their inestimable understated manner, Ellington ventured to think that it must once have been the residence of the local squire. Set back in a wilderness of trees and rampant rhododendrons, hemmed in on either side by meandering stone houses set against the street and awkward brick warehouses of more recent construction to the rear, the two-story Tudor style manor still retained much of its dignity. Mullioned panes sparkled warmly with the light of oil lamps behind them, and though the ravages of time marred the timbers and plaster, and moss and ivy covered much of the stone, the house appeared well-kept.

The impression was even stronger when a mob-capped maid hastened to answer the door, making a faulty curtsy in startlement at the sight of the visitors. A rush of warmth enveloped them as they entered the spacious front hall, and Ellington felt a sudden pang of hunger as the scent of spiced cakes and roasting chicken wafted around them. Childish voices sang in angelic tones from the room beyond while another maid managed to stretch up a ladder to hang a piece of holly while craning her neck around the doorway to observe the goings-on within. Somehow, the chaos of sight and scent and sound made him feel at home, and Ellington took off his hat with every intention of staying, whatever the cost.

While the maid scurried off to find the mistress of the house at Bernard's urging, Ellington allowed his gaze to stray around the gracious hall. Relatively barren compared to most of the houses with which he was familiar, it had a dignity all its own. An ancient sideboard along one wall held a basket of apples and a riot of greenery waiting to be hung. The faded carpet nearly blended into the gray flagstone floor, and Ellington imagined the owners of all those childish voices scampering over it without a care for muddy footprints, although he rather thought the design resembled a rare Persian he had once admired in his travels. An oak staircase circled upward along the wall to his right, its banisters gleaming with years of beeswax. A slight movement from the space beneath the stairway caused him to nonchalantly turn his head away, while still keeping an eye on the cubbyhole. Without surprise, he noted a cherub's golden curls peeping out, followed by a pair of brilliant blue eyes that looked slightly familiar, and then a chocolate-rimmed mouth. Grubby hands held the remains of a stolen treat from the kitchen, and Ellington grinned. He had the sudden feeling he knew whose house this was.

He wasn't in the least surprised when the angelic tones suddenly erupted into shrieks of joy, and a slender figure in drab gray appeared in the parlor doorway. While the infants in the room behind her apparently launched into a frenzy of biscuit munching, Ellington studied the young woman he had seen so briefly at the church.

Thick chestnut tresses were drawn back and held loosely in a heavy net adorned only with a velvet ribbon. Her simple day dress belled out over a modest petticoat and not the large crinoline he had come to expect on ladies. The brilliant blue eyes Ellington had noted in the child under the stairway stared back at him from a face with no particular claim to beauty, but creamy skin and sooty lashes and generous mouth combined with a striking attractiveness to hold his gaze. He didn't dare allow his gaze to wander farther, for she was already frowning at him, or at the vicar. Ellington wasn't quite certain.

"Mama's still over at the Donaldsons', Bernard. Mrs. Donaldson hasn't recovered enough to be allowed out of bed yet, and with all those young ones, there's so much to do. I daresay she's helping with supper and will be back after a while. Would you prefer to come back then?"

"You and your mother take too much upon yourselves, Marian. Visiting the sick is very well and good when there's no one at home to depend upon you, but did you know little John is sitting in his nightshirt underneath the stairs, no doubt eating himself sick on Christmas cake? And with Laura still recovering from the influenza, it seems you have enough to do here. Did you ever stop to think that charity might begin at home?"

Blue eyes snapped with anger. "That's a fine idea, Bernard, were there anyone else to do what we do. Since the noble Sedgwicks have seen fit to leave the village to struggle on its own, someone must look after the unfortunate. Perhaps you should marry someone ready to carry out the duties of vicar's wife, but since you seem in no hurry, who else would you recommend to see after the ill and elderly? Perhaps you can persuade the town parish to provide for those who have not?''

Momentarily abashed, Bernard still managed to hold his own. ''You know perfectly well that this is not a wealthy parish, Marian. Everyone gives as they can. Now let us not argue in front of Mr. Ellington. I fear he has already received a wrong impression.'' Anxiously, the vicar turned to indicate the tall stranger watching with amused eyes as he made the introductions. ''Marian Chadwick, this is Mr. Alan Ellington, come to stay a few days with us.''

Given permission to turn fully toward the stranger, Marian offered a hand in greeting while observing the suspicious laughter behind black-lashed gray eyes. His complexion was more swarthy than any proper Englishman's, but even she could recognize the quality of his starched linen and the silk cravat that was obviously not the made-up kind. Wearing only short side-whiskers without the mustache of fashion, he had a slightly exotic appearance for this small town. Looking away from the laughter in his eyes, Marian's gaze fell on the band of mourning on his coat sleeve, and her hand squeezed his lightly in sympathy before returning to her side.

''My pleasure, Mr. Ellington. You are some relation to the Sedgwick Ellingtons, I presume?''

She didn't waste time. After hearing her opinion of all things related to Sedgwick Hall and its owners, Alan thought it the better part of wisdom to hold his tongue. ''I understand there is some relation, yes. I have spent much of the last year traveling and thought it might be interesting to see the ancestral beginnings at Christmastime. I had not realized the Hall would be closed for the season.''

Marian made an inelegant noise. ''For the season? You might tell Bess and George that. They've kept that drafty monstrosity for the best of their lives, only to be told their services were no longer needed, just in time for a merry Christmas. Your ancestors might have a lot to answer for, Mr. Ellington, but it's the present Earl of Sedgwick who ought to be taken out and shot. Poor old Bess crippled up with arthritis like she is and no home of her own after all these years of looking after someone else's, and he sends her a letter saying she's no longer needed. I swear, if I ever meet that man—''

Bernard took her arm warningly. "Don't, Marian. It does no good to rail against what cannot be changed. I'm certain the earl had very good reason for what he did. Farm prices are not what they should be, you know that. It's possible the upkeep on the Hall has become unmanageable. And he cannot know about Bess and George. At least he left the gatekeeper on. They will be fine there until we can find somewhere else for them to go.''

Ellington was beginning to look uncomfortable beneath her wrath, and Marian took a breath and tried to remember he was a stranger and had no part in their troubles. "Pardon me, sir. I'm certain you had naught to do with any of this. Since Mama is not here, is there anything I can help you with?''

Bernard answered for his guest. "There's been a coaching accident and the inn is full. Mr. Ellington gallantly gave up his room to the injured but now has no where to stay the night. I thought of Robert's room. Would it be too much to impose on you if Mr. Ellington stayed here while he makes other arrangements?''

Having gauged the full measure of this lovely virago, Alan offered, "I will make a large charitable donation to any cause you espouse, Miss Chadwick, and pay well for my keep for the short time I must stay. I have no family on these shores and thought to find some homecoming at Sedgwick for the Christmas holidays, but I can see that is not to be. Would you extend your charitable indulgences to a wayfaring stranger?''

He was laughing at her, Marian knew, and she felt rather uncomfortable at being a figure of fun to this elegant stranger. She supposed she ought to be wearing a pretty pink gown and offering him tea and batting her eyelashes. She was quite certain that was what he expected from the females of his acquaintance. But as a country miss with little or no prospects, she did not have to cater to his expectations.

"I would not send you out in the cold homeless, Mr. Ellington, but I cannot offer what is not mine to give. We will need to wait for Mama. Perhaps you would care to come in for some tea while we wait? I'm afraid the children are becoming a little restless and I must return to them."

Turning without waiting for his answer, she hurried back into the parlor where the sound of rising voices indicated impending warfare. Bernard looked resigned as he met the stranger's questioning look.

"The choir is preparing for the Christmas pageant. Miss Chadwick is the church organist and choir director. There are so very few of the old families willing to help any longer, and I fear the youngsters nowadays are not all that they should be. We need an older woman capable of maintaining order, but Miss Chadwick tries her best, I'm sure." He added this last hurriedly at the questioning lift of Mr. Ellington's disapproving brow.

Wishing to investigate the youthful noises further and not averse to seeing the redoubtable Miss Chadwick in action, Alan followed her through the doorway without answering. Although the scene unfolding before him had the sound of Bedlam, he could readily discern a certain order to the madness. The warriors had already been separated under Miss Chadwick's firm direction. The one with vanilla icing smeared in his hair was already kneeling obediently beside a makeshift cradle and doll obviously representing the Christ child in the manger. The more recalcitrant combatant was still pouting as his face was being cleaned from what could be blood or an excess of red candy or both. The other children were returning to their various formations as a choir of angels and participants in the manger scene. It very much appeared as if three of the children were portraying donkeys or sheep, and Alan bit back a smile as they curled into appropriate animal-like attitudes. Unfortunately, one could not resist the equally animal-like urge to nip at another, and another tussle was about to ensue when he marched forward to grab their attention.

"I may have heard that animals talked the night the Christ child was born, but I'm quite certain that they did not fight or bite," Alan said thoughtfully, piercing one antagonist with a steely look while coming to stand closely by the other.

Just that one comment—or perhaps his presence—sent the chattering to new levels of excitement. The sheep and donkeys sat up and regarded him with silent awe, but talking animals was a subject for much speculation and strangers in their midst were an opportunity for attention. Each individual in the choir had an opinion on the matter, and the young shepherd with icing in his hair found a fascination with the shine of the newcomer's boots that required him to lean over and admire his mirrored image.

Marian threw up her hands in despair over this collapse of decorum, but whatever tirade she meant to unleash went unspoken by a second interruption from the doorway.

"My goodness! Is practice over already? Bernard, how good to see you. Did you come to see how the pageant progresses?" A swirl of bonnet and shawl and gloves swept into the room to come face-to-face with the aristocratic stranger who seemed to dominate the small parlor. She came to a halt before him and opened eyes as wide and blue as her daughter's as she gazed up into his face. "My goodness, if you aren't the image of Bartholomew. Has he come home, at last?"

Alan gracefully bent over her hand, issuing a small squeeze of warning. "Mrs. Chadwick, I assume, it is good to meet you. Mr. Dryden, here, has asked me to presume upon your hospitality for a while."

Elena Chadwick shot him a look of wry surprise when

he did not respond to her question, but she politely turned to the vicar. "Of course, we will be happy to put up your guest for as long as he needs. That is, if he does not mind the confusion. Oh dear—" She dropped the subject of their guest as she hurried to rescue an urchin whose curiosity had led him too close to the fire.

Resolutely, Marian gave up any attempt at regaining order. The older girls were whispering and staring through dreamy eyes at the exotic stranger, and the boys were on the brink of dissolving into wrestling matches to catch his attention. With brisk efficiency, she began gathering up their coats and shawls and dismissing them with a reminder of their rehearsal on the day after next. It would be a wonder if everyone knew their songs by the day of the pageant. She could only pray they would know their places.

Sending Mr. Ellington a look of curiosity as he retreated to a far corner with Bernard, Marian wondered who he really was and what he was doing here, but there wasn't time enough to find out. Perhaps in the morning, in the kitchen, she could winkle the information out of her mother. Her mother had lived here all of her life and knew everyone and everything. Marian was quite certain she could not know the stranger for he was not that very much older than she, and she would certainly remember anyone with so distinctive an appearance as Mr. Ellington. But it was very possible that her mother knew the stranger's family, particularly if he really were an Ellington.

Remembering her disparagement of the Ellington family and her cynical comments about their return, Marian turned pink about the ears but disguised it with her industriousness in bundling up one of the youngest children. Surely he couldn't be one of the Sedgwick Ellingtons, or he could have ordered the house opened rather than imposing on their small household. He was undoubtedly some distant cousin touring through the countryside looking for his wealthy and aristocratic relations so he might take home stories to brag about. Although he certainly didn't look as if he needed someone else's stories to tell.

"Who is he, Mama? You said he resembled Bartholomew. Who is Bartholomew? An old beau?" Folding raisins into the cake batter while her mother arranged toast and jam on a tray, Marian valiantly attempted to extract the information that had eluded her all of last evening. Mr. Ellington and her mother had got on very well, to the extent that Marian had to oversee sending her younger brothers and sisters to bed. By the time she was ready to join them in the parlor, Mr. Ellington had politely bowed out and retired to Robert's room, pleading the exhaustion of the journey.

"Old would be the correct term, I should think, were it so. Bartholomew was married and had a child while I was still a young school girl. Such an imagination you have, dear. Your father was my only beau. Now do not beat that batter too hard, you will make it tough."

With that, she whisked out of the room, not to be seen again before Marian turned the cake over to the kitchen maid and prepared to leave on her round of morning visits. Wrapping warmly in a practical mantle of navy wool over a pale blue alpaca gown that successfully hid a flannel petticoat and muslin drawers, she lifted the basket of little gifts to her arm and was prepared to go out when Mr. Ellington appeared on the stairway.

"Miss Chadwick, might I impose on you for a while this morning?"

Marian turned to watch him approach, thinking he was quite the most elegant man she had ever met for all that he was dark and rather slender compared to the husky young men that she knew. For the first time she noticed that he held one knee stiffly but not so much as to be immediately apparent. He still wore the black band of mourning, but his informal sack coat was of a dark blue, and she smiled at the realization that their choice of colors seemed to be identical.

"I am about to make my rounds of some of the elderly shut-ins, Mr. Ellington. They expect me at this time of the week and would be concerned were I late. Is it something I might do during the course of my visits, or can it wait until I return?"

"I only meant to ask you to show me something of your town. I would be happy to accompany you, if you would not mind." Despite the dreary practicality of her attire, she looked quite enchanting this morning, Alan decided. The thought caught him up abruptly, and he concentrated on pulling on his gloves.

"It is more of a village than a town, sir, but I would be happy to show you about if you will not be too bored listening to the chatter of people who have too few listeners."

"I stand corrected. In America, we seldom have villages. Every settlement claims to be a town. And I understand you have a factory. I should think that would qualify you for town status."

He took her basket and assisted her down the front stairs to the drive. The gray clouds of the prior day had blown away, replaced by weak sunshine and a crisp breeze.

"The factory is very small and is currently not in operation. Perhaps that is why Sedgwick Hall was closed. They must have invested considerable sums in the factory and all those warehouses along the river. And now they say trains will carry everything and the rivers and canals will go to waste."

Ellington glanced down at her with surprise, then up again to the walls of ugly brick behind the wooded property. "Those warehouses over there? Is that the river, then?"

Marian followed his glance. "Yes. We once owned the land down to the river, but mother was forced to sell it after father died. And the land on the other side has always belonged to Sedgwick. The factory is much farther down, though. There are new little houses cropped up all around it for the workers. I suppose that's the earl's doing, also. I don't suppose you know the earl, do you?''

But Ellington's mind had fastened on the factory, and he ignored the latter question. ''We have factory towns in America. I trust these are a little better maintained. Most of ours are little more than slums.''

Marian looked at him with curiosity. ''You are from America, then? Your accent is nothing like Bernard's cousin's.'' That certainly answered the question about his acquaintance with the earl. American cousins very seldom knew the families who stayed behind; the connection was much too distant.

''My parents' accents apparently stayed with me. Now I talk odd on two shores.''

His smile gave her unexpected palpitations, and Marian looked hastily away. He seemed genuinely interested in the century-old cottages leading into the village, and she tried to behave as a lady ought. Perhaps this was a wealthy American cousin who might be interested in staying here and helping where his aristocratic relations would not.

''You are still wearing mourning. Is it for one of your parents? Is that why you have returned here?''

''My parents are still alive and well in Arizona Territory. My wife died almost a year ago, and my grandfather just recently. I think that is why I am here now. I don't seem to have a home of my own any longer, and I thought perhaps I would see what there was of the ancestral lands. I had some business on the Continent and did some traveling, then thought to stop here for the holidays before returning to Arizona. I had a vague impression that these larger houses stayed open with a staff to oversee their upkeep even while their owners were away. That was a trifle foolish of me, I see now.''

A man who was willing to admit to foolishness was one in a million, and Marian stared at him more openly.

He did not seem to be aware of the unusualness of his statement. "Not so terribly foolish," she reassured him. "The Hall has had a small staff until just a few weeks ago. Your timing was unfortunate. Here is Mrs. Jessie's now. You might prefer to wander about while I go in and talk to her for a little while."

Ellington looked at the faded stone cottage with the murky panes and tiled roof and raised his hand to the knocker.

In the end, the American accompanied Marian to every cottage, seeming to enjoy the reminiscences of the residents as much as they. It was easy enough to steer the conversation to the old days when the "family" was in residence, and Marian learned as much as her guest before the morning was out.

"The earl must be quite elderly, then," Marian mused as they carried the empty basket back toward the house and their noon meal. "I wonder where he stays? Probably in some much more modern house in London instead of the drafty old Hall. I'd heard he was in India, but I hadn't realized he had taken part in the government during the French Revolution. That must put him in his seventies or more. I daresay he's returned from India long since."

"I understand the climate in India is much different from here. Sometimes it is difficult to re-acclimate after so many years, particularly if one is very old. He might not have had as much to do with the changes at the Hall as you think."

Marian's chin set determinedly. "It is his property and his responsibility. The village has always been dependent on the Hall. That is the only reason the village exists, and he should know that."

"Things are different in America. Towns crop up because everyone in the area needs them, not just because of one family. I had not realized how different things are here."

"How medieval?" she asked with a hint of sarcasm.

"There are modern towns in England, great smoking, filthy stretches of factories and tiny houses. You might enjoy visiting some before you leave."

Ellington regarded her solemnly. "Factories are the way of the future. Why are you so set against them?"

"They are inhumane!" she nearly shouted at him. "They employ young children and keep them bent over machines from sunrise to sunset instead of allowing them to grow up in sunshine and health. They are filthy, dark caverns where dangerous machines can yank off arms and mangle bodies. And after all that, they pay their employees barely enough to afford the rent on the pitiful housing they so thoughtfully provide. They are a scourge and a blight on the face of the earth!"

"I understand your fiancé died in an accident in one of them. Could that not color your opinion somewhat?"

Marian glared at him with tears of betrayal rimming her eyes, before turning and marching off toward the house at a pace that slowly left Alan and his stiff leg behind.

By the time he reached the house, she had already disappeared somewhere in the recesses, and he hung up his hat and removed his gloves under the undisguised interest of the tow-headed child he had observed under the stairway the day before. Remembering the appellation the vicar had given him on the prior day, Alan addressed him casually. "John, are you ready for Christmas yet?"

Bright blue eyes met his solemnly, and the cherub's head nodded slowly. Not having a great deal of experience with youngsters, his own sisters being only a few years younger than he, Alan wondered if all children were quite so silent as this one. He appeared to be four or five, well above the age of speech. Perhaps he was just shy.

"Does Father Christmas visit here? What do you think he will bring you?"

The boy smiled angelically, hugged himself and swayed back and forth, then scampered down the hall toward the kitchen stairs.

"He never talks to strangers. He was just learning to speak when father died, and after that, he hardly said anything at all. But he knows how, when he wants."

The girl coming down the stairs resembled her sister in the most superficial ways such as hair coloring, but she had little of Marian's sparkling vitality. The shadows under her eyes and the pale skin gave evidence of illness, and Alan surmised this was the one still recovering from influenza.

"I don't believe we have been introduced, Miss Chadwick. I am Alan Ellington." He made a graceful bow over the girl's hand which brought instant color to her cheeks.

She giggled slightly which made her look more her fifteen years than earlier. "I'm Laura. Marian is the only Miss Chadwick around here. She said I might come down for a little while. It's very dreary staying in a sickroom all day."

"I know that from experience," he said with conviction. "I had to spend weeks in bed once, and I didn't like it at all. What do you usually do at this hour of the day when you are not ill?"

"I go to school." She smiled prettily, revealing a tiny dimple at the corner of her mouth. "Marian gives music lessons there, so they let all of us attend for half the usual fee. It is much better than sitting around this dreary house."

"Should you not be learning to help your mother cook and clean and do the mending? Or do they teach that at school?"

She giggled again as he led her into the parlor and assisted her to sit on the horsehair sofa as if she were a real lady. "Oh, no, we learn lots of things, like where America is and who is the prime minister and how to sum great long columns of numbers. I don't like the numbers, but I like hearing about other places."

"Then who helps your mother with the cooking and cleaning and mending?"

"We all do, and what doesn't get done waits for another day." This voice came from the parlor door, and Alan recognized its firm, angry tones with ease.

Standing, he watched as Marian stalked in, bearing some of the maligned mending. She gave him a glare he felt certain was meant to put him in his place and settled on the window seat.

"We are not quite so backward in these parts as you must think, Mr. Ellington." She picked up a small shirt and began to thread her needle. "Minds are meant to be used, particularly if one is to survive in this modern world. Laura knows how to help in the kitchen and how to sew a straight stitch, but she can also read a newssheet and sum a ledger and discuss intelligently on the Corn Law. Women cannot always rely on men to support them."

"I shouldn't think either you or Miss Laura would need worry about such things," Alan replied pacifically. "You are both too lovely to go unmarried, and too intelligent to choose husbands who would not look after you."

Marian gave this flattering reply an angry glare. "And I suppose that you agree with Bernard and believe women's place is in the home, and that we need not concern ourselves with anything more serious than seeing that the pots shine and the children behave."

"Where I come from, that's about all they have time to do, Miss Chadwick. Admittedly some of the older women, once their children are grown, might help their husbands occasionally with the farming or in their stores, but they are of poorer families and do it of necessity. I shouldn't think you would have to worry about such things."

"Oh, heavens, no!" Marian mocked. "Why, all we have to do is choose what lovely frock to wear this evening and decide which beau we will cast our glance upon. Undoubtedly, whichever fortunate male we choose will fall at our feet and pledge us undying support for the rest of our lives, and then all we need do is choose frocks forever after. Our simple female minds need no more than that.''

''You have the tongue of an adder, Miss Chadwick,'' Alan replied fiercely, finally angered by her constant stream of sarcasm. ''I believe my wife was quite content with her life, and she felt no compelling need to espouse women's suffrage or engage in politics. Her only regret was that we had no children.''

Marian didn't appear properly chastised, but she withdrew her larger guns. ''I did not mean to stir painful memories, Mr. Ellington. I am certain your wife was as happy as you say. That does not mean that all of us would be content with the same life. I, for one, mean never to marry. Men seem incapable of recognizing a woman's mind, and I am incapable of closing mine.''

Alan wanted to remind her that she had been engaged to be married once, but the memory of her earlier reaction to the subject made him hesitate, and Mrs. Chadwick entered to announce dinner before he could find a suitable reply.

After the noon meal, with the remainder of the household engaged in their usual activities, Alan returned to the village on his own. He was beginning to realize that he was not going to get away from here as quickly as he had imagined. He had anticipated a brief visit to admire the old Hall and hear of his family's early lives as a means of healing old wounds, but instead, he had found a war going on. He wasn't certain that any of the inhabitants recognized it as a war, but from his more objective viewpoint, he could see the clash of cultures very clearly. In America, where everything was new, the war wasn't so very evident. But here, the clash of modern against ancient was visible in everything from the new brick warehouses against the old manor cottage to the factory against the backdrop of fields cultivated in the same strips as they had been for centuries. There was a certain excitement in the clash of different energies, and he wanted to view it a little closer.

Alan wouldn't admit that there was a certain excitement in his clashes with the very modern and very pretty Miss Chadwick, though. Isabel, his late wife, had been scarcely in her grave a year, and he had adored her for years before that. He had waited impatiently for her to reach a marriageable age, and she had been younger than Miss Chadwick when she died. He didn't wish to think of the tragedy nor to consider the contentious Miss Chadwick in any other light but that of hostess.

There were too many other things to occupy his mind here. With determination, Alan located a livery and hired a horse. He needed to see how much of Miss Chadwick's rebellious nature colored her words. The times couldn't be as desperate as she made them.

By the time Mr. Ellington returned that evening, his polished boots were mud-caked, his fawn-colored top coat was covered in dust and cobwebs, and he was frowning distractedly. The maid who let him in looked at him with surprise, but he paid no notice as he took the stairs to his room two at a time.

The children playing in the old nursery grew quiet and giggled as they peered out the doorway when he stamped by, but Marian hushed them as she entered shortly after. Even she threw a second look over her shoulder when their guest's door slammed. He had given her no more than a curt nod when she had passed him in the hallway.

His humor did not bode well for the supper table. With the children fed upstairs, Robert married and in his own home, and Laura still too weak to be allowed downstairs again, there were only the three of them at the table. Marian chose the innocuous subject of the Christmas pageant and her mother offered advice while their guest frowned into his soup.

"Did you know that there are children living over in the factory town who have no shoes?" he asked abruptly in the midst of the discussion of Joseph's costume.

Marian raised her eyebrows slightly but replied reasonably, "Many of them have lost parents during the influenza and cholera epidemics. Then the factory closed and now many families have no income. So far, most of them have been scraping by helping with the harvest and doing odd jobs. But now that winter's here, I suppose they will have to go to the workhouse. We're a poor parish, as you heard Bernard say yesterday. There is little more we can do."

"Workhouse?" Alan looked up, his gray eyes more steel than warm. "What is this workhouse?"

"Do you not have workhouses in America?" Elena Chadwick asked with surprise. "What do you do with your poor?"

"We don't have them in Arizona, that's for certain. There's more work to be done there than there are people to do it. Do workhouses give people work?"

"I'd advise you to see for yourself," Marian said quietly. "Bernard will take you. Tomorrow is his day to visit. Then you will see why parents prefer to let their children go without shoes than to go there."

Alan could tell by her tone that he wasn't going to like what he was going to see, but he had set himself a challenge and he meant to go through with it. He nodded and turned the subject to more pleasant ones.

"I heard you discussing a Christmas tree with Mr. Dryden yesterday. I will admit to having a fancy to see one myself. Has he finally consented to allow it in the church?"

"He has no choice," Marian replied calmly, sipping her soup. "The church is the only place large enough to allow all the children and their parents. And I mean to see that they have a tree." She smiled at a sudden thought. "Old Mrs. Jessie and some of the others are making ornaments to go on it. Mrs. Jessie has crocheted an enormous red star that will have to go on top somehow. I cannot imagine it hanging from any branch on any tree I have ever seen."

Alan set down his spoon. "Let me provide the tree. It

is the least I can do in return for everyone's hospitality. And I shall take care of Mr. Dryden's objections.''

That turned the conversation to a happier note that even lasted later, when Mrs. Chadwick was called out to attend a birthing and Marian was left to put the children to bed. However, before they could take the opportunity to lay aside their differences, another message came from an elderly neighbor asking for assistance in reading a letter that had arrived that day. Alan resignedly agreed to spend the evening alone while Marian went to read the letter and share the cake and tea the woman would have waiting.

With the children ostensibly in bed under the supervision of a maid, Alan was left with naught to do but put his feet up before the fire and read the newssheets. He really ought to take up pipe smoking like his father, he decided a while later, when the silence of the house began to impose on him. The smell of the newly hung evergreens and the warmth of the fire curled around him, and he felt contentedly at peace for a change. It had been a long time since he had felt that way, and he stared at his stiff leg with consideration.

The accident had crippled him in more ways than one. The day's riding told him that. The ancient hack horse had made more muscles ache than he knew he possessed. He would never be able to ride a more spirited mount again. But the physical damage wasn't the only damage done. The accident had taken Isabel and all hopes of a future with her. He had once envisioned building another house on his father's acres, expanding the ranch to breed horses as well as cattle, raising his children to follow in his footsteps. Now that all seemed some ephemeral dream with no relation to the man he was now.

His father was young and didn't really need his help. Alan's interest in breeding horses had ended with his inability to ride them well. He had become accustomed to the independent life and didn't feel at home in his father's house any longer. And he had not looked at another woman in so long, he felt uncomfortable in even thinking about it now. The pain of loneliness lingered in his eyes as he gazed up at the greenery adorning the mantel and discovered a small painted star done in a childish hand.

It was then that he heard the patter of small feet and looked down to find little John in his rumpled nightshirt standing beside the chair, his fist wiping sleepily at his eyes. Without thought to what he did, Alan held out his arms, and the lad eagerly scrambled up to his lap, curling contentedly against his chest.

He couldn't remember any bedtime stories and this wasn't a rocking chair that would soothe the child with its motion. He merely said, ''The bed is cold with no one in it, isn't it?''

The child nodded vigorously, closed his eyes, and cuddled in the warmth of Alan's arms before the fire, promptly went off to sleep.

Marian and her mother returned home together, whispering so as not to awake the household. Upon entering the parlor to turn off the lamps, they discovered the sleeping pair before the dying embers, and exchanged heartrending looks. Once upon a time, another man had sat so, holding the other children. Little John had still been a toddler when his father died. He could not possibly remember those nights. But the women did, and tears formed in their eyes as Elena bent to lift the sleeping child to take him to bed.

Ellington woke instantly, his gaze coming first to rest on Marian as she hovered nearby, hands clasped before her. His leg was stiff and would undoubtedly not move should he try to rise immediately, and he hid his embarrassment by running his hand through his hair and glancing toward the sleeping child being carried away.

''He must have got cold,'' he offered by way of explanation.

''I'll see he gets an extra blanket.'' Awkwardly, Marian watched her mother leave the room. She didn't want this feeling of warmth curling in her middle right now, dredged up by the sight of this man holding a child in his arms. His hair was as tousled as little John's, and his eyes equally sleepy, but she didn't think this feeling was at all sisterly. Stepping to the fire, she began to cover the embers. "Thank you for looking after him," she murmured.

Now that her back was turned, Alan gingerly lowered his leg to the floor and moved it about until he felt confident it would work. Then rising, he began the process of checking windows and doors and blowing out lamps. He remembered his own father doing that every night. It seemed a perfectly natural thing to do.

They went up the stairs together, Alan holding the candle and offering his arm, although he was much more likely to need assistance climbing than she. He grinned at the thought, and as if understanding the jest, she smiled back. For once, they managed to part without hostile words.

"They say he's going to open the factory up."

"I heard he's rich as Croesus and means to buy the old Hall."

"Bessie tells me the old earl is dead and the estate is selling everything. Is that true?"

"Tell us, does he mean to open the factory? Is it true the Hall is for sale?"

Marian heard all these rumors and questions as she shopped for vegetables for the noon meal. Walking home from the village, she allowed the voices to play and replay again in her head. Surely the man who slept in her brother's bedroom and held a sleepy child could not be the one who had started the gossip mill flowing. Men as rich as Croesus did not come to insignificant places like this. They sat in London and sent their men of business to do their work. Did one need to be rich to open up a factory? Her pace increased with her thoughts.

She took little notice of the sound of a horse coming up the road beside her until a familiar voice intruded.

"Are you marching off to war again?"

Startled, Marian looked up just as Mr. Ellington dismounted. She could almost feel his wince of pain as his stiff leg hit the ground. Torn between her need to express concern for his pain, her ire over the possibility of his opening the factory, and her confusion after last night's intimate scene, she said nothing but resumed walking as he fell into step beside her.

"Obviously, another foolish question," he said aloud to himself. "Christian soldiers must always march to war. There are so many ungodly enemies, after all. Perhaps the question I should have asked was which enemy did you mean to slay today?"

"You are being facetious, Mr. Ellington," she replied stiffly. "I do not enjoy being made a figure of fun. Should I ask what dragon you slayed today, would you have a reply?"

"No, because I seem to have stirred many but slain none. They are gossiping about me in the village, aren't they? That is one way in which both our countries are much alike."

His straightforwardness always caught her by surprise. Marian glanced up to see his wry expression and had to suppress a smile. He was too charming by far, even when he discarded his elegant city clothes for the more suitable tweeds of the country, and his boots were as muddied as his gloves.

"I daresay we could visit outer Mongolia or the depths of Africa and find human nature much the same. You are a stranger, and thus open to much speculation did you do no more than sit on a bench and whittle. Apparently you have found a great deal more to entertain you than whittling this morning."

"Indeed, I have, but nothing so good as whatever it is they are saying about me. Did you know the grounds at the Hall have the most delightful evergreen trees? We have nothing at all like them in Arizona."

Marian had to laugh at the incipient mischief his words

betrayed and had no doubt of the direction of his
thoughts. She, too, had considered the trees at the Hall
as ideal candidates for Christmas. "I suppose you offered
to buy one and that is the reason the town thinks you are
about to take up residence in the Hall?"

"Is that what they think?" He looked surprised, but
not in the least concerned. "Well, someone ought, I suppose, but at the moment it looks better suited for a hospital or an institution of some sort than a home. I
persuaded the gatekeeper to give me a tour. I don't believe the entire town where I grew up has as many rooms
as that place does. Why, there is one room there so large
that the entire village could attend the Christmas pageant
and there would still be room for more."

At the tone of his voice, Marian turned to stare at him,
aghast. "You wouldn't!"

They were walking up the drive and Alan stopped to
rest his arm against his horse's saddle while he met her
dazed expression. "Why not?" he asked gently. "No
one is using it. I shall write the solicitors for permission.
How could they possibly deny such a charitable cause at
the Christmas season?"

Marian breathed a sigh of relief. "Well, if you mean
to ask permission, that is different. I cannot imagine such
a thing happening, but perhaps with your connections it
might be so. Still, I'll not say anything to anyone.
Enough hopes have been dashed around here without
asking for more."

She resumed walking and so did he, but the hesitant
drawl in his reply caused her to swing around and face
him once again.

"Well-l-l, I have already sent a few people up to begin
cleaning out the gallery, but I haven't told them why,"
he finished hurriedly at her astonished expression.

Marian had the urge to cry, "You did what!" but it
seemed purposeless in the face of Alan's sheepish expression. Perhaps all Americans were so self-confident
that they thought they could turn centuries of behavior

around in a day. She didn't even want to begin to imagine how he had charmed Bess and George and the gatekeeper to allow him these liberties. She sighed and began to walk again.

"There are people who could use the money, I suppose. I trust you won't be too terribly disappointed when naught comes of your endeavor. I still cannot believe you just walked in there and ordered them to begin cleaning."

"People like to take commands, I have found. It makes life so much simpler if someone tells them what to do. And then, I have the name of Ellington. I suppose that makes all the difference."

"I suppose it does." She turned to watch as he tied the horse to the post. "But why on earth they should believe you is beyond my understanding. Do they think you a Christmas angel dropped from the sky to answer their prayers?"

"It's just a pageant, after all." Alan shrugged and offered his arm.

"You've not heard the rumors, then. They are pinning all their dreams on you. I trust you'll not go near the factory again. I cannot imagine what else has brought about the belief that you mean to open it."

He made no reply as he held the front door for her.

When he remained ominously silent as they removed coats and gloves, Marian watched him warily.

"You do not mean to open the factory, do you?" She tried to keep the accusation out of her voice, but incredulity entered instead.

"It's well-built and modern. There isn't any reason it can't turn a profit. But I've made no decisions. There are men more experienced at these things than I am."

"Like Will Harris. You've been talking to Will Harris, haven't you?" This time, the accusation was obvious. "He would say anything to see that hateful place opened again."

Alan answered slowly, his gaze never leaving her face.

''He admits that some of the machinery is ill-designed for safety. That mangle should never have been left unshielded. Improvements can be made. People do not have to die there.''

Marian went white at the mention of the machine that had taken her fiancé's life. Then, without another word, she gathered her skirts and swept from the hall to the kitchen, leaving Alan to fend for himself.

She scarcely spoke to him over dinner, and with the children home from school to eat, there was little opportunity to expound upon his discoveries. Unexpectedly frustrated by his inability to speak with her, Alan left soon after the meal to continue his explorations. No doubt the choir would be arriving to vent their mischief for the afternoon. There would be no place for him here now, or perhaps ever. He should never have mentioned the factory.

Feeling oddly cheated of a glimpse of heaven, Alan turned his mind to more practical things and tried to forget Marian's white face and the childish voices and the smell of hot cider and spice that for him embodied the Chadwick home. It wasn't his home, but a temporary lodging until he took himself out of here.

But the more he talked to people like the vicar, and the Methodist minister, and the former factory manager, and the people who had served at the Hall, the more engrossed Alan became in this rural world. The place had a feeling of permanence that the crude Arizona town of his origins did not. He felt he could make a difference here, while his father would not. For a man who has lost all goals in life, these things mattered, and Alan's excitement mounted rather than diminished as he returned to the house to begin his letter campaign.

He was immediately assaulted by childish caroling when he entered the foyer, and he had to hold back a laugh at the two maids sneaking a peek into the parlor. His stomach rumbled at the smell emanating from the kitchen, and he couldn't help but wonder what happened to all the goodies that were being made daily. No one family could possibly eat them all. When he found little John sitting on the bottom step watching him, Alan decided to find out.

Holding out his hand, he took the little boy's, and they made a show of tiptoeing down the hall to the kitchen in search of the treats that surely must be piling in great mounds in some pantry. The maids watched them with laughter but made no attempts to put a halt to their mischief.

Replete with spiced currant cake and hot cider, satisfied with a child's beaming smile, Alan retreated to the relative solitude of the study to put his thoughts about the factory down on paper. Floors buckled from the flood were easily replaced. Retaining walls could be built at a minimum of expense. Safety features could be added. Costs would rise, but it was worth the attempt if people could be kept from starving. Remembering his tour of the workhouse with Bernard, he shook his head and applied his pen industriously. Something had to be done.

But before he sanded the ink and folded the paper and mailed it off, Alan hesitated over the memory of a white face and angry words and a feeling of desolation as a slender figure marched away. He was being unnecessarily foolish, but he really needed to hear her arguments, seek her approval. It seemed the only hospitable thing to do.

Piping voices had faded into shouts of farewell not long before. Alan could hear the children of the house scampering up and down the stairs with restless energy as their mother attempted to round them up and herd them into the nursery for their supper. He was aware that there were two or three more he had not yet really met except over the noon meal, but Mrs. Chadwick courteously attempted to keep them from annoying their gentleman guest. That was what he was here, a guest. He really ought to think about moving out. It could be arranged, he knew, but he was not yet ready to make the break.

Laying the sheets of paper on the desk, Alan went in search of the one voice he had not heard in the confusion outside.

He found her straightening out the chaos of the parlor after the children's departure. Returning an antimacassar to a chair back and unrumpling a corner of the carpet as he traversed the room, Alan waited for Marian to take notice of him. When she did, it was only to ask him to return the candlesticks to the mantel.

"They are a rowdy lot, aren't they? I don't know how you keep them in line." He attempted a placatory note.

"According to Bernard, I do not. Did they disturb you? I am sorry." Her reply was clipped and perfunctory as she gathered a tray of punch cups and crumb-smeared plates.

"They did not disturb me in the slightest. It is I who should be apologizing for disturbing you. I am the intruder here."

She gave him a startled look but continued at her task. He always seemed so irritatingly sincere. Even the dark lock falling over one eyebrow had a certain sincerity to it. There was no need to even consider the expression of his lean features or the warmth of his eyes. She wouldn't think about him sleeping in the chair, holding little John. She didn't want to think about him at all.

"You are our guest. You do not intrude. Supper will be ready shortly. Or would you prefer it sent to the study? You seemed quite absorbed there."

"No, I need to hear more opinions before I can continue with my work there. I am a stranger to this place, after all. I need insight from those who live here."

Marian lifted the tray and regarded him from beneath raised brows. "Shall I invite Bernard and some of the gentlemen from the neighborhood? I am certain their opinions would be of far more value than that of a couple of women."

Alan gritted his teeth and attempted to hold his temper. She had to be the most irritating woman he had ever encountered. The women he knew seemed content to anticipate his needs and see him happy, but this one seemed determined to plant herself in his way and challenge him. He didn't understand why he valued her opinion, but he did.

"I know their opinions. It is yours I seek. Or have I done the unforgivable and dared to think differently than you?"

Properly chastised, Marian glared at him but nodded her agreement. "The London paper is on the table. Make yourself comfortable and we will call you when supper is ready."

Alan had the urge to offer to help, but he knew nothing of kitchens or women's work and wasn't certain where to begin. The Chadwick women seemed to have more than their fair share of tasks, but he could think of no simple way of relieving them. From things he had heard, he knew they were not as well off as they would seem, but they had much more than most in this place. Perhaps he needed to discuss with Bernard how much he should offer for his room. The cash might be welcome at this time of year. Which made him think of the impending holiday and gifts. He needed to consider that, too.

As it turned out, Alan received very little of use from the women when he discussed his tentative theories concerning the factory. Marian listened dispassionately as he expounded on the opportunities, then returned to her meal while her mother all but patted him on the head with her soft flatteries.

When he confronted Marian with a direct question, she merely answered, "It does not really matter what I think, does it? You will do as you wish."

Frustrated, Alan wanted to throttle her, but he awaited his opportunity instead. When Mrs. Chadwick disappeared upstairs later with the children, he cornered Marian in the dining room while she polished the silver tea set on the sideboard.

"I am tired of apologizing to you, Miss Chadwick. We seem to be at constant odds, although I cannot fathom why. Before, you chastised me for not thinking women had minds or opinions. Now, when I ask for your thoughts, you ignore me. What do I need to do to please you?"

"I cannot think why you need to please me." Marian rubbed briskly at the tea pot, trying not to look at him. It was difficult to do. He stood too close, and she could sense his masculine shoulders near to hers. He was nearly a head taller, she noticed. A perfect size. Embarrassed by that wayward thought, she rubbed harder.

With firm hands, Alan reached over and removed the pot from her grasp. He had meant to take her shoulders and steer her toward the parlor, but somehow, her startled gasp at his touch provoked other instincts. Beneath the crisp serge of her gown, her shoulders were soft and malleable, and her parted lips and wide eyes seduced his thoughts away from rationality. Without giving any thought to what he did, Alan leaned over and touched his mouth to hers.

Marian stiffened and backed away, only to discover the sideboard against her spine. She touched a hand to his chest to push him away, but the heat of him scorching her palm paralyzed any protest. His kiss wasn't demanding or hungry as she remembered other kisses. It was gentle, exploratory, and almost as eager as her own.

She couldn't help it. She'd not been held in longer than she cared to remember. The comfort and security of Mr. Ellington's arms as they closed around her tempted her, and the tenderness of his kiss drew her closer. When she found herself responding eagerly, she shivered and reluctantly pulled away.

Alan didn't stop her. He touched a wondering hand to the curve of her cheek and stared down into her eyes for a moment before stepping back to a proper distance. "I didn't mean for that to happen,'' he murmured, but there was no apology in his voice.

Marian closed her eyes and wished down her embarrassment. "We'll just have to see that it doesn't happen again," she whispered in response. "You wished to speak with me, I believe."

Her full skirts swaying, she led the way into the parlor, lighting another lamp and stirring the fire before taking a chair, not the sofa.

Alan followed her in but his thoughts were suddenly full of a slender, supple waist and firm breasts pressed against him, and he could scarcely remember what it was he had meant to discuss. She looked at him with curiosity, and he wondered what she would do if he pulled her back into his arms again. It had been a long time since he had held a woman in his arms. He had forgotten how good it felt.

He had to get his thoughts back where they belonged. He didn't know his future, didn't know whether he would be here one day or one week or one month. And he was quite certain Marian Chadwick was not a woman to dally with for whatever time he had here. They scarcely knew each other. There would be time to wait and see what the future might bring. But he was having great difficulty getting that message across to the rest of his body.

Plunging in, Alan finally said as he paced before the mantel, "I think I understand some of your objections to the factory. There is the safety factor that can be remedied with the proper engineering. You mentioned the children and the hours that they worked. Although it is against common practice and will undoubtedly be costly and cause a furor, I see no reason why children must be employed. I suppose if the family is needy, children might be employed for a few hours a day sweeping or doing other simple jobs. There will need to be some discussion as to the age hiring begins. Some of the girls down there are married at fourteen and fifteen. I would think of them as children, but they have families to support just as any other.''

Marian's eyes widened. ''You have thought this through very seriously. You really do mean to open the factory, don't you? Why? Aren't there factories enough in America?''

Alan shrugged and met her gaze briefly, before turning to stare at the fire with empty eyes. ''Why does one decide to do anything? Because it feels right, I suppose. The opportunity and the need is here. I believe I have the ability to make things right again. Isn't that reason enough?'' He could have listed several more pertinent reasons, but he wasn't ready to reveal that much of himself yet. He wasn't certain why. Perhaps he had just become accustomed to keeping to himself this past year.

Marian shivered and stared into the flames as he did. She remembered the sounds of the factory, the suffocating closeness in the heat of the summer when all the machinery groaned and creaked and backs bent over moving metal for hours without stop. She didn't really remember the mangle to differentiate it from the other horrible pieces of metal. Nor had she been allowed to see Robert's body when they carried him out. But she could imagine it, and tears welled up in her eyes.

''You mean well, I'm certain,'' she whispered, choking back her sob. ''But you cannot know what it is like. There is no light. The air fills with this terrible dust until everyone is coughing and sneezing. The noise is something that nightmares are made of. There must be some other way for people to make a living. That cannot be called a life.''

''It is not so pleasant a life as you have here, admittedly.'' Alan spoke slowly, seeking the right words. ''But starving in the streets is much worse. Farm prices are going down. There aren't enough jobs in the fields. And those families without fathers or husbands to support them have nothing. I haven't seen the books. I don't know yet if it can be done. But the factory seems to be their only hope. Would you deny them that one chance?''

"I think I should prefer starvation," Marian replied stiffly. "I told Robert that, but he thought he would make our fortune by working hard and long in that evil place. He was just out of Oxford and the earl's solicitors hired him to make the place profitable. He was of good family but not wealthy and he wanted to buy us a house. Instead, his savings went to pay for his funeral. He was but a year older than me." Marian turned her tear-stained face in Mr. Ellington's direction. "Are you sure there is no other way?"

Alan didn't answer her directly, but finally taking a seat, he clenched his fingers over the curved claw of the chair's arm. He focused on a point somewhere above her shoulder as he answered. "Isabel and I had been married only two years when I decided to take her traveling. She had never been beyond the small ranch and town where we grew up. I had traveled considerably by then and knew the dangers involved, but there are always dangers in living. I wanted her to see something of the country, decide if she wanted to spend her life on the ranch, or if she would prefer a more civilized world."

He released the chair to rub absently at his knee. "She wanted to ride a train. Your railroads here are more advanced than ours, especially the ones we have out west. But traveling in a train is faster than by coach, and I agreed. The engine spewed smoke and ash night and day and the cars rattled and shook incessantly. Isabel became nauseated from the smoke and noise and motion, and we agreed to abandon the train at the first large stop. The train derailed in a canyon before we made it."

He didn't say any more, and Marian understood that was all he would say. Just as she couldn't speak of how Robert had died, he would not indulge in the details of the train wreck that had taken his wife's life. They had both suffered tragedies, he was telling her. But they seemed to be employing different methods in coping with them.

"I'm sorry," she said quietly. "I suppose all trains can't be banned because of one accident. Life does go on; I understand you. I just can't see why it can't go on in a more civilized fashion. If the Sedgwicks aren't going to return to the Hall, they could at least sell it to someone who might return the estate to what it once was. That would take care of much of the problem without ever looking at the factory."

She rose and started for the stairway before he could pluck any more of her heartstrings. Despite his kiss, she was well aware she wasn't the sort of woman that a man like Alan Ellington addressed his attentions to. A man who was widely traveled and had wealth enough to open a factory was from a different circle than a rural miss like her. She couldn't allow herself to become involved in his private pain.

Alan stood up when she did, grasping the chair briefly to balance himself, not daring to strike out after her until his knee caught. He wanted to say something that would make her stop, keep her here a while longer, but he could not imagine what it would be. She was not being realistic, of course. She was living in hopes of a return to a world that no longer existed. But there was just enough truth in her words to grate against his conscience. So there wasn't anything he could say, and he watched her retreat to the safety of the upper story without offering one word to stop her.

"I cannot believe they are allowing him to open the Hall just for our Christmas pageant," Marian whispered as she and her mother carried the tins of Christmas delicacies out to the waiting carriage that Christmas Eve. "Do you think he is doing this without the earl's permission?"

"I doubt it," Elena Chadwick replied, smiling, as she carefully lodged the tins among the other packages burst-

ing from the carriage boot. "And I doubt that the earl
could do anything if he was. It is Christmas. No one
could be hard-hearted enough to deny little children a
pageant and a tree."

That was the conclusion she had drawn, and Marian
breathed a sigh of relief. If her mother thought it was all
right, then there could be no harm in it. She had just
been too afraid to fall victim to the excitement of finally
having the opportunity to see the Hall, only to have her
hopes dashed. This would be as much of a treat for her
as for the children. Just the idea of having the Hall opened
was excitement enough, but decorated with a tree and
filled with the people she loved—that was a memory she
could keep forever.

Finally accepting that the miserable year would end on
a happy note, Marian allowed herself to indulge fully in
the laughter and joy of the children around her. It was
almost a dizzying sensation to breathe deeply of the cold
air and laugh out loud as she slid on an icy patch and
went skating down the drive with her arms full of packages. Even Laura, bundled carefully against the cold, followed her example, until the ground was alive with
kicking, laughing young bodies as they fell into one another and onto the ground.

Eventually everyone was crowded into the old carriage, and Bernard clicked the horses into joining the
caravan of other wagons and carriages rumbling steadily
up the hill toward the Hall. The pageant wasn't scheduled
for another hour, but it seemed everyone had one excuse
or another for arriving early. The Hall that had once been
the life blood of the village had been closed for the better
part of two decades; everyone wanted the opportunity to
take a glimpse of the past, when everything seemed much
simpler.

The gatekeeper waved them through, and Bess and
George were there to greet them at the front steps and to
help with the packages as they unloaded the carriage.
The air inside was little better than that outside as they

entered the massive foyer towering three stories upward, but Marian's excitement carried her through the cold as she followed Bess up the grand staircase, past the gold-framed oils of Ellington ancestors, and down the long hallway dotted with marbled tables laden with ancient statues and guarded by gilded mirrors, into the long gallery sweeping the entire width of the building.

Marian heard Mr. Ellington before she saw him. Her gaze was too busy taking in the fairy-tale illusion of the gallery to concentrate on people yet. The fact that there was very little furniture beyond the fragile chairs lined along the wall did not detract from the gleaming stretch of waxed floor beckoning for dancers, nor from the wall of mirrors reflecting the wintry light from the windows on the opposite side. Between the mirrors and windows there were looped garlands of holly and evergreen, and candles glittered bountifully in the polished chandeliers over their heads. But the crowning glory was the tree at the far end of the room, and Marian could not resist floating toward it just as surely as the excited, chattering children.

"Is it what you wanted? I have never seen a Christmas tree before. I just did everything Bess and Mrs. Jessie and the others told me to do." Alan caught her elbow as he guided her toward the package-laden tree.

"It is glorious," Marian whispered with awe. "I have never seen anything like it. How did you get the candles to stay on? And Mrs. Jessie's star, it is perfect! You have made it perfection. I shall never get the children to stand still for the pageant now. Just look at them!"

Garbed in bits and pieces of their costumes, all from the youngest to the oldest were poking and exclaiming over the bits of gaudy tinsel and lace and fruits and carved and painted toys hanging on every branch. Little John was crawling among the packages at the back of the tree, searching for more hidden depths, apparently, while others were doing impromptu jigs of excitement.

But Alan was more interested in watching the woman on his arm. She vibrated with life and love; he could

almost feel the intensity through the places where her
fingers touched his arm. The vague sorrow and often
sharp bitterness that had haunted her face these past days
dissolved with the laughter filling her as she watched the
children. And it suddenly came to him that she was a
woman meant to have children of her own. He didn't
know where that thought had come from or what it meant,
but he allowed her happiness to spill over and fill him.

With the authority he wielded well, Alan shepherded
the troops onto the makeshift stage he'd hired village car-
penters to build for the occasion. The young Mary instantly began cooing over the porcelain doll lying in the
crude manger borrowed from a local barn, while Joseph
and the shepherds leapt into a hasty duel with the shepherd's crooks made of tree limbs, until Alan called a
halt to their antics.

By the time costumes were arranged and the choir in
place, the elegant Hall had filled with hundreds of warm
bodies shuffling and stretching to get a better glimpse of
the Christmas scene. Bernard and Mrs. Chadwick hastily
pulled out chairs for the elderly and the disabled, placing
them toward the front, while the children not part of the
pageant dodged in and out between their elders' legs,
looking for the best spot to observe the proceedings.

Marian gave Alan's hand a squeeze of gratitude as he
boosted the last angel into place on the newly built tiered
planks for the choir. With all the children settled and the
crowd waiting expectantly, she suffered a moment's agony as she realized she was bereft of the church organ,
but Alan caught her elbow and steered her toward a discreet niche beside the choir.

The piano was obviously an old one, but when she sat
down and tried a few chords, the quality belled out in
elegant tones to fill the gallery. She shivered with the
pleasure of playing such a beautiful instrument, then after one last glance to Mr. Ellington's anxious expression,
she smiled and began the first piece.

The children had learned their parts well. Watching

Marian carefully for the nod signaling the start of the first song, they swept into the notes with all the vigor and pleasure of their youth. If solemn hymns held a touch more jollity than was required, nobody objected, and the old carols became a sound of joy that brought tears to the eyes of everyone listening.

Standing to one side, not a part of the crowd so much as an observer, Alan felt the tug of sentiment and resisted valiantly. This wasn't his home, and the majority of these people were strangers. He was merely indulging himself by providing them with the Christmas he wouldn't have had otherwise.

But when he watched Little John curl up in his mother's lap and nod contentedly in time to the music, then noted Mrs. Jessie's beaming smile as she caught a glimpse of her star on top of the tree, he couldn't lie to himself any longer. He wanted to stay here. He wanted these people to want him to stay. As he glanced to the lovely woman singing along with the choir as her fingers danced along keys she knew by heart, he wanted her to be the one to tell him to stay.

Which was an entirely ridiculous notion. He knew better than anyone that he was entitled to stay here if he wished. He could make this his home. But in doing so, he was in all probability going to earn the contempt of Marian Chadwick.

This was Christmas Eve. He didn't have to contemplate such thoughts tonight. Tonight was for enjoying, and he fully meant to do so. Mourning was over when one was ready for it, and he felt ready. Smiling, Alan led the applause when the choir finished the first half of their selections, then took a place near the Chadwick children while Bernard and Marian coached the little tableau into the words of the Christmas story.

Alan tried not to think how well the vicar and his choir leader worked together. Helping eight-year-old Matthew to a better position on the window sill, Alan tried not to imagine Marian finally agreeing to be the vicar's wife simply because she wanted children, and she could help the parish by doing so. She was perfectly capable of reaching that decision, he knew too well, despite the obvious differences between her and Bernard. And he was a fool to think there could be any other outcome whether he stayed or not.

But did it matter so much? He could be happy here, he knew. He could make a difference in this place. The challenge would keep it exciting. Maybe one day, when he was ready for it, he might venture into the life of London society and meet someone there with whom he might share his life. The possibilities were endless. And meanwhile, he would have good friends like the Chadwicks to keep him in check. Alan heard Matthew's scorn at the flubbed lines of Joseph, and grinned inwardly. There would be no doubt that he would be subject to very definite opinions should he elect to remain.

As the babe was laid in the manger, the crowd broke into a spontaneous applause that would never have occurred had they been in the church. The children grinned with this attention, and Marian hastily struck the piano keys for the final songs before the young thespians could improve upon the story.

The hall rocked with a lively carol as childish voices were joined in the chorus by their audience. By the time refreshments were served, the room rang with laughter. The sorrows that had haunted the village throughout the year disappeared for at least this one day. Neighbors chatted with neighbors as pounds of puddings and cakes disappeared. Electrified with excitement, children chased each other up and down the gallery, and were only prevented from playing hide-and-seek throughout the Hall by the presence of Bess and George in the doorway. When it came time to distribute the small handmade gifts for the children, the eldest practically tumbled over each other to reach the front of the room first.

Usually Bernard did the honors, but this year he and Marian had decided to confer that award upon Alan.

When informed of this decision, he stared at them incredulously and almost refused, until Marian told him he could not.

"It's an honor you can't give back," she told him, laughter lighting her eyes. "It is terribly *de trop* to try to give back honors, you know. All you need do is remember the red ribbons go to the girls and the green ones to the boys. They'll take care of the rest."

Her laughter swayed him. She really did have the most incredibly blue eyes, Alan decided as he gallantly fetched the first gift from beneath the tree and handed it to the first tot standing nearby with mouth open in astonishment. It was quite unfair of Marian to have blue eyes. He had always thought blue the loveliest of colors. And he was glad that she had worn the blue gown today. Perhaps she, too, was ready to release the bans of mourning.

Children jumped excitedly all around him as Alan tried to hand out packages fast enough. Scrubbed faces, shining eyes, polished braids, and tight collars abounded. One impudent miss kissed his cheek, and a toddler crawled up in his lap when he sat down to reach the packages buried behind the tree. Bernard and Marian were there to steer off the more daring children who tried to get back in line for more, but most were so busy exclaiming with joy and laughter over their unwrapped presents that they didn't have time for mischief.

When the last of the packages was handed out and even the toddler in his lap had crawled off, Alan felt exhaustion seeping through him, but it was a good exhaustion, a happy one, one that he had missed for longer than he could remember. Closing his eyes briefly and stretching his knee prior to making the attempt to stand, he felt a warm body huddling at his back and knew instantly who he had missed.

Opening his eyes, he turned and pulled Little John from beneath the branches. The disappointment in the child's eyes nearly erased all the happiness he had just been feeling. Glancing quickly to see Marian and her mother engrossed in their endless tasks, Alan held a finger to his lips to indicate quiet, then staggering to his feet, caught the boy's grubby hand and led him through the crowd.

If anyone noticed, they made no indication as the two of them slipped past Bess and George in the doorway to make the descent of the long staircase. Alan lifted John to the banister, and holding him tight, let him slide to the bottom. It was something he had wanted to do himself, and the child's glee was worth every ache he would suffer later from the run.

But the banister wasn't his goal. He had meant to wait until later to distribute his gifts for the Chadwick family, but Little John would no doubt be in his bed by then, and Alan was highly uncertain as to Elena Chadwick's reaction to this gift in her house in any case. So it was much better now, with just the two of them, while everyone was too busy to notice they were missing.

The cold night air was crisp and brilliant as man and child hurried across the cobbled drive outside the stable. No horses whinnied their greetings when they entered the musty barn. They breathed in centuries of hay dust as John clung trustingly to Alan's hand while they traversed the long corridor to one of the center stalls. Once this place would have been warm with the heat of a dozen horses and all the grooms and stable lads who cared for them. That time was gone, but the barn seemed to be sitting there, waiting for them. Alan drew in a sharp breath at the thought, then threw open the door to the stall he had marked the night before.

He should have brought a lantern, but the chinks of moonlight from outside seemed to be sufficient for childish eyes. John gave a cry of ecstasy and fell to his knees, his hands hovering wishfully over the tiny brown puppies cuddled up beside their mother.

The mother dog sniffed carefully at Alan as he knelt beside her, and satisfied with his familiar scent, made no objection when he lifted one of the sleeping puppies into John's hands. The animal was just a stray the gatekeeper had allowed in, but she had an intelligent collie's face and looked as if she had once been a pampered pet. With all this empty barn to fill, Alan had seen no reason why the dog couldn't stay. And there were a half dozen squirming little reasons for him to bring John here.

"The puppies have to stay with their mama right now, because they're too little to eat by themselves. But when they get bigger, you can have one if you'd like. You'll have to ask your mama if it's all right, but I'm sure she'll let you visit them here."

"Can I keep them?" The child looked up to him with hungry eyes, eyes that knew better than to hope but couldn't resist hoping still.

"All of them?" Alan laughed. "They will be as big as you are before long. Where would you put all of them?"

"Here," he announced firmly. "They belong here. Where is their daddy?"

That was a tricky question, one he wasn't prepared to answer. How did one explain to a child of five that life was uncertain, that daddies didn't always stay where they were supposed to be, that eventually even mommies and sisters and brothers sometimes went away? And wives. And boyfriends. Life happened, and one went on.

Alan lifted another pup to his shoulder and felt the rasp of a tiny tongue against his neck. "I don't know where their daddy is. Maybe God sent us to be their daddies. Do you think so?"

That simple notion went down well. Little John nodded firmly and happily. "I'll take care of them. What do we feed them?"

The child could talk, then. As Alan explained they wouldn't need to feed them right away, John interrupted with a dozen different questions. As he took the child's hand and led him back toward the departing party, John chattered as excitedly as any of the others spilling from the Hall right now. It wasn't a miracle, but it was a warmth that Alan kept to himself even as he greeted the others and helped load weary children into wagons and carriages for the ride home.

When it came time to help the Chadwicks into their ancient barouche and it was quite apparent there wouldn't be room for him, Alan waved them off with hearty reassurances of the rented hack waiting for his return. Then he watched them drive off, heard the laughter and chatter spilling behind them as the carriage rolled away, and felt the towering loneliness of the empty Hall at his back. That was when he began to doubt if he could go through with this.

He wanted to stay, but the home he had in mind wasn't the grandiose building he turned toward now. The home he wanted was rolling away on cracked wheels and sagging springs.

"Alan, how lovely! You really shouldn't have." Elena Chadwick held up the soft folds of the brilliant cashmere shawl, her delight evident in the way her hands stroked the warm wool.

"I wanted to. You have given me a Christmas to remember wherever I go. I'll not likely ever forget your generosity to a stranger." Alan came to his feet as his hostess did.

"That is what I meant to do," she replied with satisfaction, kissing his cheek lightly. "Now I'll go see that the children are settled in bed. It's been a long day. Don't keep my daughter up too late."

Embarrassed at her mother's obvious ploy, Marian stared into the dying embers of the fire after she had gone. Cups for the wassail they had enjoyed after returning from midnight services needed to be returned to the kitchen, but they could wait until morning. Satiated with the happiness of the day's activities, she couldn't bring herself to call the day at an end. She wouldn't admit that the man crossing the room toward her could be part of the reason she wished to linger.

"You haven't opened your gift," Alan said softly as

he took the cushion beside her on the sofa. He had been aware all evening that she was sitting there instead of in her usual chair. He hadn't dared take advantage of the opportunity until now.

"I'm not sure I want to," Marian replied, in the same whispers as he. "I have had so much happiness this day, I feel as if I ought to postpone some of it for another time."

"I know the feeling." Alan took the gift from her fingers and set it aside. "The gift is too paltry for all that I have been given this day. I can remember many happy Christmases at home with my family, but I cannot remember one like this. I keep thinking . . ." He hesitated, uncertain whether he wished to reveal his deepest desires right now. But the day had stripped away his caution. He wanted someone else to share his happiness. "I keep thinking perhaps I ought to make my home here. I'm not certain I want to go back."

Surprised and not a little cheered at this prospect, Marian turned to meet Alan's gaze. The warmth and the question in his eyes made her shiver with apprehension, and she fought to remain practical. "Has the idea of the factory so caught your interest then?" she asked demurely.

"Now is not the time to play those maidenly games with me, Miss Chadwick," he chastised her lightly. "We know each other's opinions on the factory very well, and I have no desire to fight with you about it tonight. Nor is it the reason I wish to remain, as you very well know. I am asking your honest opinion. Do you think I will be accepted here if I stay? It's sometimes difficult for people to accept strangers."

"I think you belong here." Even as she said it, Marian wondered how she knew it to be true, but it was. Alan Ellington belonged here, and she wanted him to stay. "Stay, and let us argue over working conditions on the morrow."

The laughter was back in those incredible blue eyes,

and soot-smudged lashes beckoned him teasingly until he could do no other than lean over and press his lips to hers.

Marian gave a sigh of contentment as Alan's fingers brushed her cheek and turned her more pressingly into his embrace. Until now, she hadn't realized this was what she had been waiting for to make this day perfect. Her fingers went tentatively to his waistcoat as his arm closed around her, and she gave herself up to the deliciousness of his kiss.

He was very good at kissing, she decided moments later when his mouth moved to the edges of hers and her head stopped reeling briefly. She really shouldn't allow him such liberties, but if he meant to stay . . .

His lips returned more forcefully this time, and she had to gasp "Mr. Ellington!" and try to push away.

"Alan," he insisted, daring to touch the shimmering silk of her pinned tresses. "You must call me Alan, and then I will kiss you just one more time and let you go."

"Alan," she breathed with a smile as he brought their lips together once more. And it was more than one kiss later when he finally caught his breath and forced himself away.

"I am rushing things. I tend to do that a lot. You must make me slow down when I go too fast. It's just this day has been so lovely, I don't want it to end." Alan knew how he wanted it to end. He had been married. He knew what it was like to retire to bed with the one he loved; he knew how to extend this happiness. But she did not, and it was much too soon to ask it of her, too soon to even consider it. So reluctantly, he stroked her cheek instead.

"Will it be the same tomorrow?" Marian asked wistfully, leaning her head back into his protective palm, basking in the heat of his gaze. "Or will everything be back to normal? Do animals only talk on Christmas Eve?"

Alan laughed and lifted her hand to kiss it and put

some distance between them before they both regretted it. "I can't answer for the animals, but I hope tonight will last until the dawn. The world is seldom peaceful, but two reasonable people ought to be able to iron out their disagreements. Shall we find out in the morning?"

Marian squeezed his hand and reached for the gift he had set aside. "I shall take this with me and open it in the morning and pretend today has started all over again. That should make me much more reasonable."

Alan watched her retreat to the security of her feminine bedroom and found himself wishing for the right to follow her. He'd thought something in him had died with Isabel; he was only just discovering it had not. He wanted a warm and willing woman, and not the kind that he could buy. He was more than certain that Marian Chadwick could not be bought, perhaps not even with a wedding ring, particularly not when he was forced to admit the truth.

Not wanting to contemplate that subject, Alan banked the fire and checked the locks and windows before taking his candle up to his lonely bed.

It was obvious he couldn't stay here much longer. Sooner or later, he was going to have to leave the Chadwick house and make his own home. He wanted it to be later.

"You cannot mean it! You've bought the Hall?"

Christmas Day had been nearly as splendid as Christmas Eve. Alan admired the glitter of the sapphire brooch at Marian's throat, avoiding the incredulity in her eyes. She had only accepted the gift because she thought it a pretty piece of glass. He doubted that she had ever seen a valuable piece of jewelry. To him, it was merely a bauble, but he was quite certain she wouldn't look at it that way had she known the cost.

But Christmas Day was over, and though there were many more celebrations to come, reality was already beginning to set in. There was no point in delaying the inevitable any longer, not if he really meant to stay and plant his roots in this soil.

"My family owns the Hall, Marian," he explained patiently, but she still stared at him in disbelief.

"I'm glad one of the family has finally decided to return." Elena Chadwick smiled sensibly as she drew her yarn around the knitting needle. "I thought perhaps it might be one of your sisters. It was too much to hope that one of the wandering males of your family would come home."

Alan grinned at the aptness of this remark. "Grandfather evidently set a bad example. I've just returned from visiting one uncle in Italy and another who was about to explore Africa. I think there was a time when my father would have returned, but that was before he met my mother. She feared his consumption would worsen should he leave Arizona. And he's quite content to stay there now. And I must admit to a certain amount of wanderlust of my own, but that's only because I have never been here before. Now I know what I've been looking for."

His gaze drifted back to Marian, but she was still looking at him as if he had developed two noses and horns. "You said you wished to see the Hall opened," Alan reminded her. "Do I not deserve some show of appreciation?"

"Your family is the one who closed up the Hall and the factory? Your grandfather is the earl who built those warehouses and ignored the people who worked for him? How could you? How could you sit here and pretend you were what you were not?"

He had been afraid of that. Threading his hand through his hair, Alan tried to explain. "My grandfather left everything to his solicitors. The distance between here and India is too great for him to have made the everyday decisions. Perhaps he was wrong, but there is no one to say that his decisions would have been any better had he been here. I have seen other towns much worse off than yours, and the noble families in their districts still live and play there. They're not any better or worse than the wealthy families in my country who put business first. Surely you cannot blame me for a life I have never known?''

''I can blame you for pretending you aren't who you are. I should have known when you opened up the Hall! Shall we call you Lord Ellington now, or is there some other title that goes with it? I can't believe you . . . Oh, damn!'' Unable to scream at all the little lies that were causing all the little hurts right now without coming to blows or tears, Marian picked up her skirt and ran from the room.

Drained by the scene he had known had to come, Alan bowed stiffly before his hostess. ''I am sorry for that, ma'am. I didn't want people to get their hopes up, or to say the things they thought I wanted to hear just because of who I was. I thought perhaps you understood . . .''

''I understood, Alan, but my daughter is far too young to understand. She still has ideals and dreams, and perhaps you shattered them just a bit. When she sees the good you can do, she will come around after a while. You mean to remove to the Hall, then?''

''I thought it would be best. I will have to go up to London and work things out with the solicitors. They know I am here, and my father has written them with his permission to allow me full rein, but I haven't told them my decision to stay yet. You're the first to know.''

''I thank you for that. I'd always secretly hoped that Bartholomew would return and make things right again. I had forgotten about his little boy. You've grown into quite a handsome young man. Sometimes, it makes me feel old to see the children growing up, but you'll know the feeling soon enough. You are always welcome to stay here; I hope you know that.''

Alan smiled at the gracious lady who had made him feel at home even knowing who he was. He was nearly thirty and hadn't resided in this town since he was a toddler too young to remember, but she made him feel

as if he had belonged here all his life. "Perhaps I can
return the favor and have you stay with me sometime. I'll
call when I return, shall I?"

Alan felt the parting more strongly than when he had
left his parents. Then, he had known he could return at
any time. Now, he knew he might never spend another
Christmas as he had with the Chadwicks. As he carried
his bags down a staircase still wrapped in evergreen and
adorned with ribbons, he felt as if he were leaving home,
and he didn't want to go.

Another person had the same thought. Before Alan
could let himself out the door, a small figure in mussed
shirt and knee breeches came hurtling out from behind
the stairs, his dirty face streaked with tears.

"Don't go!" he wailed, clinging to Alan's leg. "Don't
go!"

Despite the protest of his knee, Alan crouched down
to hug the little boy. "I'll be back, I promise. Somebody's got to go up and keep an eye on the puppies until
they're big enough to run by themselves. When I get back
from the city, I'll take you up there to see how they've
grown."

"Don't want you to go," John repeated resentfully.
"Stay here."

How he wanted to. Throwing a last glance around the
now familiar foyer, Alan hugged the lad, then let him go.
Someday, he wanted children of his own, but none would
ever replace this grubby little one in his heart.

Telling himself it was all for the best, Alan Ellington,
Viscount Coke, carried his bags out to the waiting carriage.

"Where is Little John?" Marian stopped in the nursery to count heads. John seldom joined his older brothers
in their rough games, but she hadn't found him anywhere
else in the house. Alan had scarcely been gone a week,
but already she missed his ability to attract her youngest
brother like a magnet.

"Probably down in the closet sniffing boots again,"
Matthew declared disdainfully. "Want me to go get
him?"

"I just looked there. And he's not in the kitchen,
either. Where did you see him last?"

The lads looked from one to the other and shrugged
their shoulders. Worried but trying not to be, Marian
picked up her skirts and went searching for her sisters.
Perhaps one of them had grown bored and agreed to read
him a book.

Finding the girls involved in their own activities without any knowledge of their youngest brother, Marian went
nervously down the staircase to check under it one more
time. Her mother entered with a cold draft of winter
wind, and throwing off her scarf, lifted a questioning
brow.

"Lost John again? Did you check with Matilda? The
child's always hungry."

She had, but Marian joined her mother for a second
search of the kitchen. When no one claimed any sign of
the child since luncheon, Marian felt fear, but her mother
calmly went off to the upper story to look for herself.
John was a peculiar child given to hiding in strange
places. With that thought, Marian lit a candle and turned
to the cellar. He could very well have found the key and
locked himself in.

Supper was delayed while the entire family joined in
the search, scouring the old house from top to bottom,
unburying old boots and ancient canes in unused closets,
stirring up coal dust in the cellar and spider webs in the
attic, without any hint of a tow-head or a sleepy smile.

Quite certain that they would find the child sound
asleep in some unlikely cubbyhole, Elena Chadwick refused to be alarmed, but she agreed to allow Marian to
call on Bernard to do a hasty check of the neighbors. The
wind was achingly cold with a hint of snow in the air,
but John was quite capable of wandering into someone's
backyard in search of some elusive toy. He could easily

be sitting in a neighbor's kitchen munching biscuits and
drinking hot chocolate while they waited for his family
to claim him.

By nine o'clock that night, supper had been forgotten
while men wrapped in their warmest mufflers and hats
spread out to search the surrounding countryside for a
little boy no bigger than a large dog and with just as
much tendency to stray. Marian held back her tears for
her mother's sake, but she insisted on going with Bernard
when he took their carriage out to parts of town that had
not yet been searched. How far could small legs and an
empty belly carry him?

Farther than anyone expected, it was discovered when
dawn arrived and still no sign of the child was found.
Both women had given into tears by then, but they dried
them as they joined the others in searching up and down
the river bank with the first light of day. It was not the
way anyone wished to welcome the new year, but it was
the only other logical place to look.

When Alan rode up to the Chadwick home on his new
horse expecting to extend his good wishes for the New
Year, he discovered only a teary-eyed Laura and a house
full of children at home.

"They're all down by the river looking for Little
John." Her bottom lip quivered as she gazed up at the
elegant man who had made Christmas so exciting, as if
he might wave a magic wand and return the strayed child.

"The river?" Alan felt a shiver of apprehension as he
realized the abandoned horses and wagons along the drive
and roadway had naught to do with an excess of visitors.

The story came spilling out then, and Alan felt a cold-
ness creeping up inside of him. He had just begun to
accept that life must go on, but he couldn't accept the
passing of a child who had not yet begun to live. With a
brisk nod to the shaken girl in the doorway, he strode
through the back gardens toward the river where he could
see even now the bright red wool hats of some of the
searchers.

News of his name and title had already spread through the village like wildfire, and Alan disregarded the irritation he felt as men removed their hats when he appeared and women bobbed ancient curtsies. His gaze sought and swiftly found the women he had come looking for.

Elena Chadwick appeared a ghost of herself with haunted eyes lined with shadows as he approached. Marian wouldn't even look his way, refusing to acknowledge his presence by plunging into bushes, tearing at her clothes and hands as she thoroughly searched the surrounding shrubbery. Already victim to more emotions than he cared to decipher, Alan grabbed her arm and jerked her back to a safer level of the river bank.

"Have you searched the Hall?" he demanded of both women, conscious of those who listened around them.

"It's much too far," Marian protested. "They've searched half way there, but he couldn't possibly walk farther than that."

"I only just returned late last night. I gave Bess and George a holiday, so there's no one there, but I think I know where he might be. Grab a blanket and some food and we'll go look."

Ignoring Marian's remonstrations, Alan began pulling her up the hill. Several of the men offered to accompany them, and he nodded curtly, more in dismissal than agreement. He couldn't bear to see the hope rising to Elena Chadwick's eyes. If he were wrong, he would never forgive himself. But he could not be wrong. He wasn't going to let that mischievous little cherub get away so easily.

Marian gasped for breath as she tried to follow Alan's long strides. If his knee gave him pain, he showed no sign of it as he hurried through the garden toward his waiting horse. She wondered what on earth he meant to do with her if he intended to ride back to the Hall, but she learned the answer to that swiftly enough when she returned with the blankets and basket of food he had ordered her to fetch.

The new viscount had hitched his expensive horse to the old pony cart from the stable and was checking the strength of the traces as she hurried down the front steps. Without a word, Alan helped her into the cart and threw the blankets and basket behind the seat. In a motion, he had joined her and was whipping his horse down the drive before she barely had time to get settled.

Clinging to her hat and the side of the cart as they barreled down the road, Marian prayed fiercely that Alan was right, that somehow John had trundled his chubby legs the miles up the hill to the Hall, but she could not imagine how he had done so. The cart and horse seemed to take hours bumping over the rocks and ruts of the main road, then turning off onto the overgrown drive up to the Hall itself. It was a torturous stretch of road, and she heard Alan's curses under his breath as the horse gallantly pulled them out of ruts large enough to swallow a pony.

When they finally stopped in the cobbled stable yard, Alan leapt out, but instead of running toward the house, he went directly to the stable, forgetting her presence entirely in his haste. Marian jumped from the cart and ran after him, hope finally flooding her veins.

"You didn't come back!"

Marian heard the heart-breaking sob as she dashed into the darkness of the chilly stable, and she felt a sob of her own being wrenched from her throat. She couldn't hear Alan's low murmurs but judged their direction and found the stall just as he knelt to take Little John into his arms.

The child was sobbing wretchedly, and Alan looked up to her for guidance. On the floor near him lay a lovely collie and her squirming puppies, and Marian felt light-headed as she kneeled beside them and reached for her youngest brother. He clung determindedly to Alan's neck, however, and wiping a tear from her eye, she managed a smile.

"You came all the way up here to see the puppies, Johnny?"

The little boy nodded vigorously, rubbing his wet face against Alan's collared greatcoat. "They don't have a daddy," he explained between hiccups.

"And John and I were supposed to be the daddies for them, but I went away, and John thought I wasn't coming back." Alan looked up to her with pain in his eyes. "I packed my bags and left and he thought I would be gone forever."

"Just like father and Robert. Oh, dear, I never thought . . ." Marian brushed a piece of hay from John's hair. "Johnny, Alan isn't going away. He's going to live here, just in a different house than ours. You can see the puppies anytime you like, but you have to tell us. Mama's so worried, she's out looking for you."

"I want to stay here," he sniffled.

Alan shifted the boy so he could remove his handkerchief and wipe a grimy face. "I don't have a mama and sisters and brothers here, John. There's nobody to look after us and make us pies and cakes and mend our clothes. Let's go back down and tell your mama we're sorry for scaring her."

This time the child didn't protest, and Alan held him easily as he stood and waited for Marian to join him. The emotion she met in his eyes burned a pathway straight to her heart, and still blinking on her own tears, she hurried from the barn to the waiting cart. She hadn't thought how all alone Alan would be if he stayed here in this great barn of a house, thousands of miles from his family. He had chosen to stay here to help people he scarcely knew, but at what cost to him?

The trip back into town was a quiet one. Marian wrapped John in the blanket they had brought and fed him sandwiches from the basket, and he was nearly asleep by the time they returned. Beside her, she was conscious of the silent man expertly guiding the horse past the rough spots in the road. His hands were clad in expensive

leather gloves, and his heavy greatcoat would protect him
from all but the worst of winds, but inside the trappings
of wealth, he was as human as her little brother. It had
been simple when she thought of him only as a faceless
nobleman who deserved her insults and tirades. But he
wasn't even the man she had cursed. He was someone
else entirely, and she couldn't lift her eyes to meet his
gaze when he looked down on her.

The New Year's celebrations began when they drove
up the drive with their sleepy burden. Women came
streaming from neighboring houses, crying openly as
they hugged each other and the Chadwicks. Men pulled
off gloves and hats and shook hands with the new viscount and pounded each other on the back with an excess
of cheer. The house opened to allow the tramp of feet
into the warmth of open fireplaces and hot cider and the
puddings and cakes that had been waiting for the round
of New Year's visits.

Alan and Marian held back from it all. After the first
round of explanations, the story repeated itself throughout the room, and there was no further need for them to
tell it. But there was a need for them to be together, to
explore the emotions they had just encountered, and no
way in which it could be done in this room full of people.

Alan finally took a deep breath and pulled her from
the parlor, flinging the first cloak he found around her
and drawing her out into the cold sunshine of the dying
day. Marian followed eagerly, and he breathed a sigh of
relief as he led her through the winter-barren garden toward the river.

"I'm staying. The arrangements are under way. I'm
going to have men up to look over the factory and make
suggestions and others to undertake repairs. I'm going to
have to hire people for the Hall. The money's there; the
solicitors simply didn't want to spend it. Do you still hate
me?"

This all came out in one breathless sentence, but Marian understood every word of it. She came to a halt and

stared up at Alan's lean features, the thin, rather sensuous mouth twisted into a self-deprecating grimace, the dancing gray eyes warm and eager as they watched her. When a particularly strong gust of wind made her shiver, she immediately found herself wrapped in the immensity of his coat, caught against the heat of his chest, and she curled up there, oddly comfortable with the arrangement.

"I can't hate you," she whispered against his heartbeat.

"Is there any chance, if I behave particularly unlike a viscount, that you might come to more than not hate me?"

Marian giggled at this odd phrasing. "I already not hate you." More softly, she finished, "I think I already like you much too much."

Joy flowed through Alan's veins and the winter berries bursting through their wrappers could have been roses for all his senses knew. The warmth he felt now was a summer warmth as he bent to ply eager lips with his.

"By spring, perhaps you'll like me even more," Alan ventured as he brushed his mouth against the sweetness of hers.

"I'm afraid so," Marian answered, her hands creeping up his waistcoat to the vicinity of his neck.

"Would that be so terrible a crime?" he murmured, pulling her closer. "If I can play daddy to puppies, maybe I can graduate to little boys after a while?"

"You can't forget little girls," Marian whispered breathlessly as his hands began to do strange things to her through layers of clothing. "There is a great house full of us. You will want to run away in dismay before spring ever arrives."

"Not if the most troublesome one of them all keeps me in kisses. I don't want to be your daddy, Marian. By spring, do you think you might be willing to reconsider your decision not to marry?"

"I may have to," she answered honestly as his hand

touched a sensitive place. ''Especially if you mean to keep doing that. Alan, we are behaving wickedly—''

''Oh, no, we're behaving naturally. Do you have any idea how glad I am that there was no room at the inn?''

''I refuse to believe you're a Christmas angel,'' she murmured against the mouth warming hers.

''Then believe there were angels watching over us. I almost never knew you were in this world.''

''You may regret it later.'' Laughing, Marian looked up into warm, gray eyes.

''When Christmas falls in July.''

With that firm announcement, Alan wrapped her in his arms and proceeded to show her how unangelic he could be. As the snowflakes finally began to fall, a small creature in the shrubs stuck out his tongue to taste them. Then deciding there was nothing more for him out here, he removed the hat from his tow head and ran back toward the house for the last of the Christmas pudding. The nice stranger was going to stay.

Second Chance

by Patricia Gaffney

1

AT FIRST CODY THOUGHT IT WAS TWO HOUSES, MAYBE even three. Or not a house at all; maybe he had the address wrong and this was the public library. Or City Hall. But as he stood on the sidewalk across Thirty-first Street in the snow, he saw that all twenty-three windows of the four-story wall of glass and carved granite were lit up because there was a party going on behind them, and every window belonged to one house. In that case they all belonged to one man. Marion Gladhill.

Shivering, Cody turned up his collar and huddled deeper into his sheepskin coat. Kentucky winters were mild and kindly; he hadn't felt cold like this in three years. He'd walked across the bridge from Brooklyn and halfway up Broadway before the thick, soggy snow had penetrated his clothes, then his brain, and he'd finally had the sense to hail a hansom cab. He'd been too numb from the news to care about the weather, and the grim message of the young girl who lived next door to Hettie's old house on Clinton Street had rung in his ears all the way uptown: "Hettie O'Rourke? She's gone, moved away a month ago at least. Getting married to that fella's been courting her for half a year—Gladhill's his name. Marion Gladhill, owns the big department store on Fifth Avenue. Fella like that must be rich as God."

Carriages lined both sides of Thirty-first Street between Fifth and Madison. The fine, well-mannered horses

stamped and blew while their drivers huddled close by,
nipping brandy from flasks to keep warm. Hell of a way
to spend Christmas Eve, thought Cody. It reminded him
of the Colorado blizzard he'd gotten caught in back in
'79, riding herd on forty thousand head of Texas long-
horns. The memory dampened his sympathy for the shivering coachmen. At least they'd sleep inside tonight, and
tomorrow they'd wake up dry and warm, not half-starved,
near-frozen, and dog-tired.

A new carriage clattered to a halt in front of the house
with twenty-three windows, and an elegant-looking lady
and gentleman got out and hurried up the slippery marble
steps. A blast of genteel merriment rang out on the snowy
air when the front door opened, ceased when it closed.
In the next block, carolers were chanting the second verse
to "It Came Upon a Midnight Clear." That reminded
Cody of something else. Something he didn't care to remember, ever, but especially tonight. Wet snow worked
a path down the back of his neck, making him shudder.
He decided he could stand out here all night until he
froze to death, or he could screw up his so-called courage
and join the party. Squaring his shoulders, he threw his
cigarette in the gutter and stepped off the curb toward the
Gladhill mansion.

The massive front door, almost invisible behind the
biggest Christmas wreath Cody had ever seen, opened
before he could knock. Thank God nobody was checking
invitations. He handed somebody his coat and hat; the
butler or footman, or whatever he was, gave the coat a
skittish look and bore it away at arm's length, as if the
sheep might still be alive and fixing to butt him in the
chest. A second later somebody else glided up, this one
definitely a butler, duded to the cheeks in black and white
like an undertaker, and said in an English accent, "Most
of the guests are in the reception room; if you will follow
me, Mr. . . . ?"

"Darrow. That's okay, don't bother, I'll just follow the
noise." It looked to be the kind of party where people

got announced, and Cody didn't intend to spring himself on Hettie that way. Without waiting for permission, he strode off down a hall as big as the entire first floor of his mortgaged house in Lexington. The fancy plaster-work ceiling was twenty feet high, with about that many marble columns holding it up. Between the columns were statues of naked people with names like *Demosthenes* and *Zenobia* and *Fisher Boy* printed on bronze plaques underneath. It struck Cody as a peculiar thing to put in your hall, a bunch of nude sculptures—although *Water Nymph,* on second glance, had a certain something he thought he could learn to live with.

He paused in the entrance to the reception room, scan-ning the occupants warily. When he couldn't see Hettie, he let out a long, deep breath, half relief, half disappoint-ment. Relief because he needed a minute to reconnoiter, get his bearings—hell's bells, he was nervous. And dis-appointment because he was dying to see her. He hadn't really known how much until he'd found out she didn't live on Clinton Street anymore and he might not be able to find her. He ran his fingers through his damp hair and adjusted the chain of the gold watch he'd bought last week to show her how solvent he was. His tailor had assured him his dark blue suit was sedate and dignified, his but-terfly bow tie in the height of fashion. Now he wasn't so sure. Like the butler, most of the men at this jamboree were all in black. And unlike Cody, they all had on shoes. But hell, he felt barefoot without his boots; he wouldn't have parted with them even to impress Hettie.

"Champagne, sir?"

"Sure. Thanks." He lifted a glass from the onyx and silver tray a waiter held out to him. A moment later he saw an empty spot across the room against the wall, be-tween a window and a huge Christmas tree decorated with about two hundred dolls, and excused himself through a wall of murmuring guests until he reached it. He'd thought it would be a good vantage from which to see without being seen, but already a woman across the way was giving him the eye. He was used to that sort of thing at home, but it gave him a boost tonight to think a sophisticated New York lady would find him worth looking at. Boots and all. She sent him a smile and he returned it, but his eyes slid away easily and he didn't look back. He was looking for someone else.

"You're in my spot."

"Beg pardon?"

"I've been standing here all night, except for the two minutes it took me to go to the gents'."

Cody looked down at a tiny man with thin, silver hair combed to a point in the center of his forehead. "Oh, well, sure, I'll—"

"No, don't leave, just move over. There. Friend of the bride or friend of the groom?" the little man asked pleasantly, leaning back against the wall and tucking the crook of a cane over his forearm.

Cody stared at him in horror. "You mean to say they're already married?"

His pencil-thin eyebrows jerked up in surprise over mournful eyes the color of wet slate. "Not yet, they're not." He patted his chest vaguely, then reached over and pulled Cody's watch out of his waistcoat. "But they will be in"—he squinted down at the dial face—"about fourteen hours."

Cody took his watch back between numb fingers. It was worse than he'd thought.

"Hettie was against it, but Marion thought it would be a nice touch to get married on Christmas Day." His sad eyes narrowed on Cody in speculation; he pursed his lips. "Friend of the bride?" he guessed cannily.

"That's right." He tried to sound positive. "You?"

"Oh, both, I like to think. My name's Elmore, by the way."

"Cody Darrow." His palm swallowed his new friend's bony bird claw of a hand; he kept his grip gentle for fear of breaking it. "Where is Miss O'Rourke?" he asked, voice amazingly casual. "Haven't paid my respects yet."

"In the drawing room, I expect."

He indicated a distant door, and through it Cody saw a crowded room with another high, prairie-sized ceiling, this one with gods and goddesses and overweight babies gamboling across it in florid pastels; beneath it, between the people, were more gilt and plush, mirrors and glowing gaslight globes, white marble and burgundy velvet. His spirits sank a little lower. When a new waiter appeared, he swallowed what was left of his drink and lunged for another.

Elmore grinned at him. "Merry Christmas," he said, clinking glasses.

Cody echoed the sentiment gloomily. Which one of these swells was the groom? Probably that pork-bellied geezer in the boiled shirt, stuffing himself at the buffet table. "Is that Gladhill?" he asked, nodding toward the geezer.

"Who? That, no, that's Buffy Sloan. One of the Peabody Sloans," Elmore added helpfully.

Cody hummed as if that meant something to him.

"That's Marion over there, talking to his mother. The lovely Olympia." The lovely Olympia happened to look over at that moment. Elmore toasted her with his glass; she returned the salute with a faint nod and a tightening of the lips.

Cody sagged against the wall. "That's Marion? Tall, good-looking fellow with the beard?" The one built like the statue of Apollo he'd just walked past in the hall?

"That's Marion." Elmore studied Cody's stricken face curiously. His mournful gray eyes softened. "The beard hides a weak chin," he confided kindly.

Cody felt like a trapdoor in a barn had given way under his feet, and he was falling through it in a cloud of dust and straw. He stared morosely at Marion Gladhill and his mother, noticing they were both tall and handsome and imposing, like proud thoroughbreds in the winner's circle. If Marion had a weak chin, his curly blond beard hid it well. But his mouth had a sulky look, Cody decided, stubborn instead of strong, like a little boy's when he's contemplating the pros and cons of a tantrum. And he wore a monocle. How could anyone marry a man who wore a *monocle*?

"Does he really own a department store?"

"Oh yes, indeed. Gladhill's, you know, in Madison Square."

"Isn't he a little young? Where's his father?"

"Bradford passed on about two years ago. The fair Olympia took over for a time, but it's pretty much Marion's show now." The gnomelike features lifted. "Ah! Here's Hettie."

Cody took a firmer hold on his drink and turned his head, trying to ignore the explosion in his chest. He had a quick, chaotic impression of light green silk, Irish-white skin, copper-colored hair piled high. Then she turned her back to him, and his heartbeat had a chance to steady. He hadn't known exactly how he would feel when he saw her. Glad, of course, but maybe with a tiny bit of belligerence mixed in. Aimed at himself, because he'd treated her so bad, but a little of it touching her too, on account of proximity or something. A good defense for his guilty conscience. But all he felt now was a bright, powerful, chest-jarring delight. It was as if everything in him had suddenly gotten centered and put right, after years of crookedness and confusion.

Elmore was staring at him, and he realized he'd made some strangled sound in his throat. He grinned stupidly, then looked back again at Hettie. She was in profile now, and a flood of memories came to him all at once—how sweet her mouth was, how pretty her eyes, how much he loved that spray of freckles across the bridge of her nose. Even from here he thought he could hear her easy, good-humored laugh; the sound made his throat swell and something humiliatingly close to tears sting in the back of his eyes.

"Shall we go say hello?"

"What?"

Elmore disengaged Cody's tight fingers from around the stem of his glass. "Come on, Mr. Darrow. I'll introduce you to the groom."

"My dear, have you met the Castletons? Helene, Ogden, this is Henrietta O'Rourke, Marion's lovely bride-to-be."

Hettie shook hands and said how do you do to the Castletons, while Olympia looked on with that air of tragic cordiality Hettie was getting used to by now. As if she were bravely awaiting the inevitable moment when her future daughter-in-law finally committed a social blunder so egregious that the Gladhills' place in society was lost forever.

"O'Rourke," Mrs. Castleton repeated pleasantly. "Your father isn't by any chance Lawrence Jamison O'Rourke, is he? Something to do with railroads, isn't it, Ogden, or was it real estate?"

"No," said Hettie, "my father—"

"Henrietta's father passed on a year ago, quite tragically," Olympia put in with a bit too much funereal gravity. "A wonderful man. In the hotel trade, you know."

Hettie kept her face blandly blank, but it was an effort. The *hotel trade*? Her father had worked as a doorman, off and on, at the Winchester Arms on Lafayette Street. It was a good thing she'd never told Olympia about Petey's short-lived career as a hansom cab driver; otherwise she would surely be telling people that he'd been in the carriage trade.

Oh, if only Petey were here right now! He'd made her laugh and cry in about equal measure over the years; but in spite of his faults, her father had loved her with all of his big Irish heart, and tonight she could've used a friend.

She smiled at something Marion was saying, wishing she could touch him, or better, that he would touch her. A little affection from a girl's sweetheart wasn't too much to ask, was it? But any expression of fondness in public was anathema in the Gladhill household—as she'd learned the hard way: she'd held Marion's hand one morning in the parlor and suffered a stern rebuke for it afterward from his mother. It wasn't what she was used to, but it was something—one of many things—she was learning to live with.

She thought of telling him, just saying straight out, *I don't fit in with these people, Marion, and sometimes I'm scared*. What would he do? Laugh his hearty, upper-class laugh, which she could never quite believe in, and tell her not to be a goose. Oh God, yes, that's exactly what he would do; she knew it with total, demoralizing certainty. She stared down at the glass of flat champagne she'd been holding for an hour; her tense fingers felt as if they were welded around the stem permanently.

"Marion, there's Monty Beck, talking to the Lansers. Go and speak to him," Mother Gladhill ordered, the well-known tone of authority jolting Hettie out of her reverie. The Castletons had drifted away. She watched Marion's lips take on the petulant droop she knew equally well, and listened without surprise as he reacted with thoughtless, automatic defiance to his mother's command.

"You go. He's your friend, I can't stand him. The loan's secure, there's no need for me to go toadying up to him now."

"Don't be childish. Go and say Merry Christmas or whatever else comes to your infertile mind."

Marion's handsome face pinkened; Hettie tensed for another fight. In the four weeks since she'd moved in with the Gladhills she'd witnessed dozens, but the timely arrival of a new group of well-wishers prevented it. She smiled some more and said suitable things, while inside the gnawing thought nagged again that part of her appeal to Marion—she didn't want to consider how big a part— was that his mother detested her. She thrust the idea away, as she did habitually, and tried to pay attention to what these new people—the Worthingtons? the Washingtons?—were saying.

"Roger tells me you and Marion met *in the store*,"

exclaimed the wife, all eager interest, "and that you were actually employed there, Miss O'Rourke."

"Yes, I worked—"

"Isn't it too droll?" Olympia cut in, squeezing Hettie's elbow in the vise of two steely fingers. "Henrietta would do anything for a lark—so delightful. She took it into her head to sell lingerie in the ladies' ready-to-wear department." Her laugh was hearty and indulgent; the others joined in immediately. "Young people nowadays . . ." She trailed off, smiling her benign, condescending smile, and Mrs. Worthington, or Washington, launched into an affectionate anecdote about Missy, her own silly, irrepressible daughter. Hettie subtly disengaged her elbow and glanced at Marion. He raised his handsome brows, lips curling in a small smile, as if to say, "I know, darling, but what difference does it really make?"

None, maybe, but it rankled all the same. She'd had employment of one sort or another since the age of thirteen. If she'd depended on Petey, they'd both have starved to death within a year after her mother died, and at Gladhill's Department Store she'd worked her way up to lingerie department manager on the strength of ability and determination alone. To hear Olympia call it a lark out of sheer snobbery made her furious.

But she was marrying out of her class; she knew it as acutely as Olympia, and so she supposed she could forgive her future mother-in-law's compulsion to gloss over the more squalid details of her past. She'd conquered her initial indignation and accepted, a month ago, Mother Gladhill's invitation to move into the house on Thirty-first Street, even though she'd known full well that the motive wasn't hospitality; Olympia simply could not bear the thought of all those wedding invitations and newspaper articles announcing that her son's intended was from *Brooklyn*. But the thorn that still chafed was her insistence, with Marion's uninterested concurrence, that Hettie give up work altogether now that she was to marry into the family. Ladies didn't work. To work meant one

thing: one needed money. Nothing was more socially ab-
horrent in the Gladhill circle than a hint, a whisper, that
one wasn't rolling in wealth. Therefore Hettie would certainly never work again. End of issue.

A wave of fatigue washed over her suddenly. She had
to clench her jaws to smother a yawn and blink to keep
her eyes from glazing over. The conversation at the moment seemed to be about tea. Green tea versus black, the
English preference for blends, the demise of high tea at
Newport in favor of cocktails. It was too much. Hettie
lost the battle she'd been waging for hours and remembered another Christmas Eve party, three years ago. In
Brooklyn, not Manhattan. The male guests had worn
denim and plaid, not frock coats and striped trousers,
and the highlight of the evening had been an impromptu
lassoing contest in the parlor. She remembered hanging
onto the arm of her chair, laughing until tears streamed
down her face. How long had it been since she'd laughed
like that? Later, Cody's friend J.T. had brought out a
guitar and sung "Silent Night" in his gravelly voice, so
sweetly that she'd wept again. Cody had put his arm
around her shoulders, thinking she needed soothing;
when no one was looking he'd stolen a kiss. And then
he'd—

The knife-sharp clarity of the memory frightened her;
she gave it a violent mental shove and forced her mind
to return to the present. The here and now. Sometimes
the very solidity of the rooms in this great mansion of a
house could soothe her. She looked across at the wide
marble mantelpiece, heavy as a ship, and the gilt-framed
mirror above it soaring to the ceiling. Pictures graced
every wall, by painters whose works she'd only seen in
museums before now. The magnificent entrance hall's silent, icy-white parade of sculptures never failed to impress her with a sense of the weight of the ages, of
steadiness and endurance, security and dependability,
qualities not much in evidence in her own life up to now,
and consequently of great value. The Gladhill name was

solid if not exalted in old New York society; ''Mrs. Marion Gladhill'' printed in Florentine script on Hettie's new calling cards made her feel secure and protected. It was so patently a name that could never, ever belong to a woman whose rent was overdue, whose father regularly drank up the housekeeping money, whose three jobs left her exhausted even though they never quite managed to earn enough money to drive the creditors away once and for all. ''Mrs. Marion Gladhill'' was safe from such sordid concerns, and she always would be.

A gentle touch on her shoulder made her turn. Her set, pasted-on party smile softened in genuine welcome, and the vague heaviness on her spirits lifted. ''Uncle Elmore,'' she chided in a low voice, eyes twinkling, ''you've been trying to hide. Don't deny it, I saw you trying to blend into the Christmas tree a few min-mi . . .'' The man behind Uncle Elmore came into focus, and Hettie lost her train of thought. Then she lost her grip on her wine glass, and it shattered into wet fragments on the floor at her feet.

Stepping back, blind and deaf, she bumped hard into Marion's arm; he reached out by reflex and steadied her. ''Excuse me,'' she mumbled, also by reflex, and held on. Even though she couldn't take her eyes off Cody, her vision seemed to be operating in peculiar fits and starts, so that now she saw nothing but his dark-lashed blue eyes, now his arrogant nose, and now his straight, wide, devastating mouth. Uncle Elmore was speaking, introducing him to Marion and Olympia, she assumed, and then it was her turn to talk—she could tell by the cadence of Elmore's voice and the expectant look on Marion's face—but she had no idea what she was supposed to say because she hadn't heard anything anybody had said so far. Cody spoke instead, and the sound of his voice, low and smoky, polite and sexy, did something to her stomach muscles that hadn't happened in three years. To the day.

"Yes, Miss O'Rourke and I know each other, we were acquainted some time ago. How are you, Hettie?"

Acquainted. That was the word that snapped her out of her trance. *Acquainted.* "I'm fine," she uttered, lips barely moving. "I'm perfect. I have never been so well in my life." But one of the ubiquitous Gladhill servants was kneeling at her feet, vigorously scrubbing champagne out of the priceless Turkish carpet, and his bobbing industry had a destabilizing effect on her dignity. She watched as Cody gave Marion's hand a hearty shake and Olympia one of his ruthlessly charming grins. To her credit, Olympia returned it with only the courteously neutral facade she reserved for persons whose social status she hadn't quite nailed down. And Cody's social status was bound to present a puzzle, Hettie couldn't help noticing in spite of her agitation, because his face was distinguished and intelligent but his glossy black hair was much too long, and his clothes were fashionable and expensive but he wore them with the most outlandish pair of cowboy boots.

"Mighty fine house you've got here, ma'am," he was saying to Olympia.

She thanked him and then asked, "Are you from New York, Mr. Darrow?"

"No, ma'am, I come from down around Lexington." When she looked blank, he added, "That's in Kentucky."

To cover her surprise, Hettie looked straight ahead and didn't blink.

"How interesting. And how did you meet our Henrietta?"

She hoped no one else noticed his hesitation before he answered, "We met at an exposition."

"Oh," said Olympia, "an art gallery?"

He made an ambiguous sound, slanting Hettie a look, but she avoided it. A *rogue's* gallery was more like it, she huffed to herself. Exposition, indeed. They'd met at Buck Culver's Wild West Show and Congress of Rough

Riders of the World in Madison Square Garden, where Cody had distinguished himself by falling off his roping horse and almost breaking his neck.

She missed the next few exchanges, then heard Cody say, "I was in your store a few years back, Mr. Gladhill, the last time I was in New York."

"Is that so?" Marion didn't quite know what to make of him either; Hettie could tell by the way he sawed his monocle in tighter and squinted, trying to get a better look.

"Yep. I bought a present there for a lady friend of mine. You lowered your prices any since then?"

Everyone tittered, certain he was joking. Cody grinned back, hands in his pockets, rocking a little on his low-heeled boots, looking as much at ease in the Gladhills' drawing room as he did in a dusty rodeo ring. Hettie's anger and alarm burgeoned as he talked and laughed with her future in-laws, even bringing something close to animation into Olympia's pinched face with an amusing anecdote about his train trip up from Lexington. *What was he doing here?* He said something she didn't catch, and Marion's braying laugh grated in her ears like fingernails on a chalkboard. Intolerable! She wished she'd thrown her drink in his face instead of squandering it on the rug.

Elmore waved to someone across the way, and Olympia turned around to see who it was. "Monty Beck is leaving, Marion," she said quickly, reaching for her son's arm. "You *will* go and speak to him. And I'll go with you."

Her tone brooked no disagreement. Mother and son told Cody they were delighted to have met him, then Marion let Olympia lead him away. Hettie had time to be grateful he hadn't asked Cody to the wedding—they'd been getting along so damn swimmingly, it wouldn't have surprised her—before Uncle Elmore muttered something about another drink and excused himself. All of a sudden she and Cody were alone. The abruptness of the maneuver left her speechless.

Almost.

"Go away," she ground out in a whisper. When he leaned close, pretending he hadn't heard, she jerked back as if he'd pinched her. Still whispering, she said, *"Get out of here."* He actually cupped his ear and said, "Eh?" Seething now, she said in a suddenly too-loud voice, "What are you doing here?"

"Why, Hettie, I've come to see you. Not a minute too soon, either. You don't really mean to marry that jackass, do you?"

She glanced around in a subdued panic, terrified that someone had heard. No one seemed to have. "Will you leave?" She was back to hissing again. "Just go."

"Not until you talk to me."

"I have no intention of talking to you."

"You're looking mighty pretty tonight, Hettie. You're even prettier than the last time I saw you, and I'd've said that was downright impossible."

If only she had a weapon. A gun, a sword. A cannon. But she didn't, so she walked away, half-blind, almost running into Lula Wilkes, one of her least favorite new acquaintances. "Lula, how lovely to see you," she gushed, then remembered she'd greeted her already, about twenty minutes ago. "What a becoming dress, that color suits you perfectly."

"What do you call that color anyway?" asked Cody at her elbow, and she went stiff as a spear. "Pink? No, not pink. Gray?"

"Mauve," simpered Lula, big brown eyes widening as if she'd just opened an early Christmas present. "I don't believe we've met." She looked at Hettie expectantly.

Through gritted teeth, Hettie introduced them.

"What sort of work do you do, Mr. Darrow?" Lula purred, eyeing him up and down in blatant appreciation.

"I'm in the horse business, ma'am."

Hettie almost snorted. He was as good at euphemism as Olympia. She couldn't help it; smiling sweetly, she asked, "Oh, then you're still riding steers and lassoing calves?" Lula laughed as if at a great joke. Cody turned away from her and looked directly at Hettie, and the sudden intensity in his piercing blue eyes made her catch her breath.

"No, I'm not in that line of work anymore," he said levelly. "Nowadays I breed and train thoroughbred racehorses on my own stud farm in the Bluegrass."

"Why, I declare," Lula exclaimed, touching his sleeve to reclaim his attention. "Racehorses. My goodness, how interesting. What's the name of that race they have down there in the spring? The Kentucky something—"

"Derby."

"That's it, the Kentucky Derby." Her fingers on his wrist tightened when Cody turned from her again because Hettie had murmured, "Excuse me, won't you, there's someone I . . ." Captured, helpless, Cody watched her glide away like a ghost, while the girl in mauve chattered away like a grackle about the time her parents had taken her to England and they'd gone to Ascot and she'd gotten a glimpse of one of the queen's daughters although Mama said it was probably only a cousin, and the horses looked so handsome in their satin colors and the jockeys were the cutest little things you ever saw. . . .

By the time he finally extricated his arm and got away, Hettie had disappeared. He went back into the reception room, searching for her. She was gone. But Elmore was back in his spot beside the Christmas tree.

"Where is she?" Cody asked tersely.

"Who?"

"Hettie—Miss O'Rourke."

"Why, I have no idea."

Cody didn't believe him. His sad eyes were twinkling as if he knew all kinds of secrets. He had skinny arms and legs and a little pot belly. If he'd had on shoes with long, curled-up toes, thought Cody, he could've passed for one of Santa's elves. "You didn't tell me you were

Uncle Elmore,'' he accused, trying to remember if he'd made any insulting remarks to him about Marion.

''Well, I'm not *your* uncle,'' Elmore pointed out.

''Whose uncle are you?''

''Marion's.''

''So you're Mrs. Gladhill's—''

''Good God, no, I'm Bradford's brother. No blood kin to Olympia at all, I assure you.''

Cody felt almost as relieved as Elmore looked. But they were getting off the track. ''Listen, I've got to see Hettie, to talk to her. Tell me where she went.''

''What do you want to talk to her about?''

He might have told him—under the eccentricity there was something trustworthy about Uncle Elmore—but the past was Hettie's secret as much as it was Cody's, and he didn't have the right, or the heart, to give it away to a stranger without her consent. ''It's personal. Something between us.'' Elmore just blinked at him. ''Look, all I want to do is talk to her. I know it's a bad time''—now there was an understatement— ''but there's something I have to tell her.''

''What if she doesn't want to listen?''

For some reason the light, penetrating question settled his nerves. He told the truth. ''She won't, Mr. Gladhill, that's a dead cert. But I still have to try. I swear I won't do anything to hurt her; I give you my word.''

Uncle Elmore's shrewd gray eyes measured him for so long, Cody felt like loosening his collar and fidgeting. He refrained, and at length the little man came to a decision. He launched himself off the wall with his elbows, reminding Cody of a cricket, and headed for the door. Cody followed.

''She might be in the library,'' he said once they reached the marble entrance hall. He pointed with a long, bony finger. ''Down this corridor, the door at the end.''

Cody faced him gratefully. ''I'm much obliged to you. If you're ever in Kentucky and you need a friend, I'm your man.''

Elmore looked intrigued. ''I'll remember that.''

* * *

She couldn't stay here much longer; she was bound to be missed soon at her own wedding-eve party. Pacing before the closed French doors, Hettie caught a glimpse of her reflection in the long black panels and stopped in surprise. She hardly knew herself anymore. In her new Worth's gown, whose style, fabric, and color had all been chosen by Olympia without even a pretense of consultation, she looked tall and distinguished, almost aristocratic. Almost as though she belonged in this house and among these people. Did that mean the beautiful green gown was a disguise? Perhaps. But not for long, not if it killed her, because Hettie intended to submit to her mother-in-law's tutelage and learn to suppress all the things about herself that Olympia considered vulgar and common. Things such as her taste in clothes or the way she wore her hair, her informality, her habit of saying what she thought. That last would be the hardest to give up, she knew, but by God, she meant to try.

She turned from the windows and glanced around the library, which was decorated for the holidays with the muted restraint that was Olympia's specialty. Muted to the point of inaudibility, Hettie thought rashly, but then, she was used to Petey's exuberant insistence on displaying every ball, bell, ribbon, and ceramic Santa Claus he could lay his hands on at Christmastime. But this understated show of a few greens on the mantel and a little ivy over the French doors was much more tasteful, she told herself. Tasteful, yes, but then why did the sober spectacle vaguely depress her? No matter; the library was her favorite room in the house, predictably perhaps, because of all the years she'd worked in the Brooklyn Heights Lending Library. But that wasn't the only reason. She also liked it because it was a beautiful room, and because no one ever came here. *This will be my home,* she thought. *This house.* After tomorrow, there would never again be lonely, two-room apartments over noisy Brooklyn streets. No more working at two or three jobs to make ends meet. This would be home, and finally she would be safe.

She couldn't stay here, she reminded herself, starting to pace again. But if she went back now, would Cody still be there? How cowardly of her to hide from him like this. She knew it, but she couldn't help it. If she saw him again, she was afraid she would disgrace herself by bursting into tears. Or socking him in the eye. *Why had he come?* She'd thought many unkind things about Cody Darrow over the last three years, but she'd never thought he could be deliberately cruel. But then, why not? After all, this was the man who had called off his own wedding at the ceremony with a message sung by a ragged group of children to the tune of "It Came Upon a Midnight Clear."

The dreadful memory flooded her, hot and humiliating as ever. Damn him! Damn him for coming back now and spoiling her second wedding as thoroughly as he'd spoiled her first!

"Any Bronco LaSalle books in here, sweetheart?"

She whirled in shock.

Cody sauntered the rest of the way in, closed the door, glanced around, and whistled. "Guess not. I don't remember your books ever coming out bound in leather. Not that they didn't deserve it."

Hettie flushed to the roots of her hair. Her brief career as "Rick Chase," author of a half-dozen "redback" westerns detailing the exploits of Bronco LaSalle, cowboy extraordinaire, was a secret she hoarded in fear and dread, one she would die before admitting to anyone— especially anyone carousing sedately this very minute at the other end of the hall.

In a low, fierce voice she said, "Did you come here to torture me?"

"No, I—"

"Or did you get the date wrong? Our wedding was supposed to be on Christmas Day, 1883."

He shook his head sadly, coming closer. "You never used to have such a sharp tongue, Hettie girl."

She made a sound of revulsion and moved backward, then sideways, putting the heavy mahogany desk and chair between them. "I want you to go."

"Not until you hear me out. I've got things to say to you."

"You've had three years to say things to me. Not a word in all that time and now, *now*, you want me to listen to you." She was wringing her hands. "Well, I won't. I can't believe you've come here like this. It's too much, Cody, even for you."

"Well, I sure as hell didn't mean it to be like this."

"How did you mean it to be? Were you just in the neighborhood, so you decided to drop by and ruin my life for the second time?"

"No." Her bitterness dismayed him; he was acutely aware that he was the sole cause of it. "I came here to tell you that I'm sorry." She whipped around, turning her back on him. He couldn't blame her. *Sorry?* he thought, disgusted. He'd practiced what to say to her all the way up on the train, but now all his sincere phrases sounded lame because he was hearing them through her ears. "I know I hurt you," he went on doggedly. "I hurt myself too. But what happened didn't have a thing to do with you, Hettie; it was all me." She didn't move. "Look at me, will you?"

"No."

He stepped to his right until he could see the reflection of her pale, stricken face in the window. "That last night before the wedding, after I left your house." He rubbed the back of his neck, searching for the words. "I kept thinking about selling suits and hats and neckties in a store, like you wanted me to. Having to be inside all the time. Dressed up like a mannequin, smiling all day at a lot of city swells. Hettie, honey, I just couldn't do it. And then—then I couldn't face you, to tell you. I thought maybe not seeing me would make it easier for you." He cursed under his breath. "No, that's a lie. I thought it would make it easier for *me*. Stupid. Stupid. I found these kids, caroling for pennies on the street on Christmas morning. I, um . . ." He stopped because he couldn't say it. He just couldn't.

Hettie turned back. "Taught them some new words to an old song." Eyes closed, she recited the first verse to herself, as clear in her memory tonight as on that dreadful morning in St. Stephen's Church three years ago.

It came to me in a vision clear,
A horrible sight to behold,
Of shirts and inseams and trouser cuffs,
It made my blood run cold.

Cody sent her a pained grin; he was remembering the chorus:

I'll love you always, I'll love you true,
It grieves me to leave you alone.
I'd stay but I'd only break your heart,
Sweet Hettie, this cowboy's gone.

"You should've heard the one we made up first to 'Good King Wenceslas,' " he tried. But she didn't smile. Heartbroken, he watched her bottom lip start to tremble. "Aw, Hettie . . ." He moved around the desk, desperate to touch her, but she sidestepped him again.

"Thank you for explaining why you jilted me," she said, head high. "Better late than never, I suppose. But I'd already figured all of that out for myself, so you've told me nothing I didn't know."

He caught her hand as she swept past him to the door. "Wait, Hett."

The old nickname shocked her. She yanked her hand out of his. "Let me by."

He held his ground, blocking the way. "Just tell me this: are you in love with Gladhill?"

"Of course I am. Yes. Yes! Of course I'm in love with him."

He thought her persistence rang a false note. Hope swelled. "I don't believe you, you just want to be in love with him. Anyway," he aid, clinching it, "how could anybody marry a man named Marion?"

"It's better than Cuthbert!" she crowed.

He flinched and she looked away, guilty-faced. He saw her soften and pressed his advantage. "How's Petey?" he asked. "How come he isn't here tonight? I bet he can't stand *Marion* any better than I can. Hettie?" He watched her face go still, close up. "Honey, what's wrong?"

"My father died a year ago."

He dropped his arms to his sides. "Oh, no. I'm sorry. God, I'm really sorry. If I'd known . . ." He broke off, ashamed. Even if she'd wanted to tell him, she couldn't have, because he'd never let her know where he was. "How did it happen?"

"In his sleep. His heart just . . . stopped."

"That's a good way," he said gently.

"Yes."

"He was a good man. I'm sorry he's gone."

Her eyes flashed. "He stayed mad at you for a long time, Cody, longer than I did. But he got over it. And so did I. I never think about you now." She took no pleasure in watching the hurt darken his somber blue eyes, but she didn't regret the lie. "Now let me go, I can't talk to you anymore."

"Wait." He reached for her arm again as she tried to pass, and this time he hung on. "Listen to me. Hettie, I have to tell you something."

"No, I won't. Let go. Let go, or I'll call Marion and he'll throw you out." His amused expression incensed her. "I mean it, let me go this minute!"

"Not until you listen to what I've come all the way from Kentucky to tell you."

"I don't care if you've come all the way from Mars, I'm not—"

"Children, children, what's all this bickering? On Christmas Eve, too. Keep on this way and you won't get a single present."

Uncle Elmore stood in the doorway, cane in one hand, a toddy in the other. Cody dropped Hettie's arm in frustration. "Marion's looking for you, Hettie," said Elmore.

"I'm just coming." She forced herself to face Cody. "You didn't give me a chance to say it before, Mr. Darrow, so if for nothing else I'm grateful to you for the opportunity to say it now." She raised her chin and looked him straight in the eye. Her voice didn't falter. "Good-bye."

"Fine girl." Elmore stepped across the room to the fireplace, struck a taper against the stone hearth, and touched it to the kindling under the split oak logs in the grate. Straightening nimbly, he whacked at the logs with his cane until the fire blazed up, then looked back at Cody, who hadn't moved and was still glowering at the closed library door. "I say, fine girl."

He finally turned around. "Fine girl," he agreed in a monotone.

"Best thing to happen to the Gladhills in a long time."

Cody was silent.

"Known her long?"

"Three years ago, I knew her for all of a month." He came toward the fire, in need of its warmth. "We were engaged." Now, why had he told Elmore that?

Elmore filled two glasses from a liquor cabinet beside the fireplace and handed one to him. "To marriage."

Cody took a morose sip. His eyes watered and he held back a choked cough by swallowing repeatedly. "What is this?"

"Usquaebach. Scotch. Smooth as silk."

He sampled it again, cautiously. "Not bad," he decided, as the fire in his throat died down to an amiable blaze.

Elmore filled his own glass again and waved at the two leather armchairs in front of the fireplace. "Have a seat.

"Yes, indeed," he said after a few minutes of companionable silence, "Hettie's a fine girl. How is it she can't seem to stand the sight of you, Mr. Darrow?"

Maybe it was the Scotch, but for some reason the question seemed natural, didn't even take him by surprise. And for some reason, he realized, he didn't mind telling Elmore the answer. Some of it, anyway, even though the end of the story didn't do him any credit. If nothing else, Elmore deserved to hear it for not throwing him out in the snow. He was freezing inside already; if he had to leave now, he reckoned he'd die of the cold in this god-awful city.

"I'll tell you if you've got a few minutes."

He leaned back, stretching his long, lean legs closer to the fire. Elmore stretched out too, but his legs barely reached the floor, much less the hearth. "I used to be a cowboy," Cody began, setting the scene. "Texas and Oklahoma, Arizona, Wyoming, Colorado, I worked cattle all over the West from the time I was fifteen years old. In between—"

"What did you do before that?" Elmore interrupted.

"Before that? Ran away a lot. I just wasn't successful at it till I was fifteen. When I wasn't—"

"What were you running from?"

Maybe this was going to take longer than he thought. "Orphanages and foster homes. People who wanted a farmhand more than they wanted a son. Anyway"—he waved his hand; that wasn't the story he wanted to tell. "Herding cattle is seasonal work; if you don't get hired on for the winter at somebody's ranch after the fall roundup, you're out of a job for the next six months. So what I used to do was follow the Wild West shows." Elmore's eyes widened with interest. "Bronc stompers and carnival boys, they called us. Open-air delinquents is what we were," he admitted, recalling the fighting, drinking, whoring, and hell-raising. "It can be a pretty rough life. But at least you're working for yourself; none of us would've been caught dead at the blister end of somebody else's shovel." He still wouldn't. But he didn't expect Elmore to understand the pride a cowboy took in his work, or his belief that a man on a horse was a breed apart, or his passion for independence.

"I've never been to one of those Wild West shows. What are they like?"

Cody grinned. "They don't call 'em wild for nothing. Some are just circuses with a few horse acts thrown in between the snake charmers and sword swallowers and clowns. But the ones I liked were the real rodeos, with roping and tying contests and bronc-riding and steer-wrestling. Bulldogging, we call that."

Elmore rubbed his tiny hands together. "My goodness, that sounds like an exciting life."

"Yes and no. It gets old fast, and it's hard on a man's body. Once you start thinking about all the bones you might break, you're finished."

"Did you ever break any bones?"

He smirked. "I can't even count how many."

"So is that why you gave it up?"

"Nope." He settled lower on his spine until his boots were only inches from the flames. "Three years ago I was touring with Buck Culver's show. We were doing a week at Madison Square Garden. One night I was dogging a steer on this little sorrel gelding when I got in a storm. To make a long—"

"Got in a what?"

"A storm—when a rider gets in trouble, drops his pigging string or misses his calf or falls off his mount. This time, I bobbled a throw, my horse broke and cut left, I leaned too far out to compensate, and ended up in the dirt. The slack rope threw a half-hitch over my leg, and when the horse cut back right he dragged me for about a hundred feet before the loop finally unhitched and fell away. Four men had to carry me out of the ring."

"Good heavens!"

"I wasn't hurt bad, not after I woke up, just bruises and cuts. Sore as hell, but no real harm done. But anyway, that's how I met Hettie and her dad. Did you ever meet Petey?''

"Never had the pleasure. You mean to say Hettie and her father were in attendance at this cowboy exposition?''

"Yep. It was Petey's idea; he made her go. He was crazy about rodeos.''

This was an out-and-out lie. But Cody had no intention of telling Uncle Elmore that it was Hettie who had dragged Petey to the show, because she'd wanted to research her latest Bronco LaSalle book in person.

"Hettie's dad came back to the changing room afterward to see if I was still alive,'' he went on—and kept to himself as well that Petey had done that at Hettie's insistence. One of the sweetest memories he had was of the time, days later, when she'd admitted to him how scared she'd been when he'd fallen off his horse. She'd noticed him from the opening act, the obligatory cowboy and Indian fight, because, she'd said, he looked so much like the image she had in her mind of Bronco himself, her cowboy storybook hero. "Petey asked me and some of the boys to go have coffee with him and his daughter when the show was over. We said sure.''

Elmore looked skeptical. "Coffee?''

Cody laughed. "That's what we thought, too, until we got a look at the daughter. Then we'd've drunk muddy water just to sit next to her.''

"Ah.''

"We went to this café on Twenty-third Street called Brother's, that night and then every night after the show for a week.''

Was it still there? he wondered. He stared at the crackling logs and took another sip of his Usquaebach. Elmore was right; it was going down now as smooth as hot velvet. He thought of that first night at Brother's, with Buck and Junior, Monroe and Olan and Tater. And Petey and Hettie. The boys had been on their best behavior; nobody had smoked, spit, or uttered a single swear word. They'd all been half in love with her already. He could never remember how the subject of Bronco LaSalle had come up; more than likely Petey started it. The boys all said they loved the books, couldn't wait for each new one to come out, thought they told the story of a cowboy's life with great truth and fidelity. Cody, who liked the books too but wanted to impress Hettie and set himself apart from the herd, had launched into a long speech about how stupid they were, how childish and unrealistic; why, they bore about as much resemblance to a real cowboy's life as a flea did to a dog's.

He would never forget her face, pink, crushed, close to tears. She'd excused herself a minute later, leaving a pall of bewildered silence behind her.

"Why, you damn fool," Petey cursed him.

"What did I do?"

"She writes 'em, you moron! She's Rick Chase!"

It took Petey five minutes to convince them. When Hettie came back to the table, everybody but Cody toasted her, praised her, begged her for her autograph. Cody could hardly look at her; he'd wanted to crawl under a rock and expire. Later, she'd told him she could've killed Petey for revealing her secret and exposing her to Cody as the author of the very books he said he hated, because she'd wanted to impress him, too.

"That first night, when the party was over, I took the trolley down Broadway with Petey and Hettie as far as the Brooklyn Bridge. I said I'd never seen it before and wanted to look at it all lit up at night, but really I just wanted to be with her." Make peace with her, if he could, after hurting her feelings so badly. Tactful for once in his life, Petey had left them alone at the horsecar stop, going off a ways to smoke his pipe. At first she wouldn't believe him when Cody told her he loved the Bronco books and had only said he didn't because he'd wanted her to notice him. He told her cowboys loved to brag and swagger, and sometimes he was the worst of the lot, the purest damn fool God ever made. But what really got her

was when he'd confessed—after swearing that she was the
only human being on earth who knew it and making her
vow never to reveal the secret to a living soul—that his
given name was Cuthbert. After she stopped laughing,
she'd had to forgive him.

"By the time we said good night, she'd agreed to go
out with me after the show the next night. With Petey
along for a chaperon, of course."

Elmore poured more Scotch for both glasses. "I
thought you said you only knew her for a month."

"Right."

"And you were engaged to be married?"

"Right."

Elmore cackled. "Must've been quite a month."

Cody put his drink aside and smiled back. "I asked
her to marry me three days after we met, Mr. Gladhill.
She hemmed and hawed for about three more. On the
last night before I was supposed to leave with the rest of
the troupe for Buffalo, she said yes." He grinned. "Yes,
sir, you could say it was quite a month."

Elmore waited a decent interval before asking, "What
went wrong?"

Cody's smile faded and died. "Mind if I smoke?" Elmore said no, go ahead, and Cody pulled out his tobacco
and started to roll a cigarette. "Hettie's mother passed
away when she was thirteen," he said slowly, "and from
then on she was always working at some job or other.
Sometimes two." Three if you counted the Bronco
books. "Petey was a good man at heart; he'd've given
you the shirt off his back if you needed it, but he wasn't
what you'd call reliable. If they had a stable home, it was
because Hettie made it that way. So she . . ."

"Wanted a reliable husband," Elmore guessed when
Cody trailed off.

"Yeah. And she *deserved* it. And I wanted to give it
to her, be everything she needed." He hauled himself up
to his feet; the fire felt too hot all of a sudden. He went
behind his chair and leaned against it, arms folded across

the top. "I tried to talk her into coming with me after we got married. Go on the road with me, see the country. I wanted to show her the West." He could keep on being a cowboy and she could keep writing cowboy books, he'd figured. Perfect.

"But she didn't want to go?"

"No. Not that I blamed her; she needed stability, and I was asking her to leave everything she knew and start living the most unpredictable kind of life you can think of."

"Is that what made you part?"

"No. Not that exactly." He kept his gaze on the fire because the last part of this story was the hardest to tell. "I was crazy in love and I . . . didn't want to lose her. But I could see it happening unless one of us gave in, gave up what we wanted for the other. So I did it. I said I'd quit my old life and live in New York, get a real job. She said she could find work for me in the store, talk to somebody she knew in the men's department."

"At Gladhill's?"

"Yeah. Not forever, but for a start, a first job."

"That was quite a concession." Elmore nodded approvingly. "Anything for love."

Cody straightened and walked over to the French doors. Outside, he saw that the garden was filling with soft, silent snow. He kept his back turned. "Anything but that," he said flatly. "At the last minute"—*literally*, but he couldn't admit that to anyone, he was too ashamed— "I realized I couldn't do it after all. Couldn't be what she wanted. So I went away." He sagged against the window. He'd made a life for himself since then, had triumphs, even been middling happy. But the stupidity and wrongness of what he'd done had never left him, and right now he could feel the full, mean, miserable weight of it.

"But you came back tonight."

Cody turned back. "I always had swell timing."

Elmore crossed his legs and propped his chin on his

hand, elfin face alight with new curiosity. "Why did you come back?"

"Because I was stupid enough to think she might give me another chance. I've made good in Kentucky; I thought I could talk her into starting over. I didn't count on this." He shoved his hands in his pockets and shot a resentful glance around the dark, opulent room. He thought of how proud he'd been of his new suit and his gold watch. His hopes of sweeping her off her feet. Pathetic—he embarrassed himself. "I didn't count on finding her in a damn mansion, engaged to a damn tycoon," he muttered bitterly, then remembered he was speaking to the tycoon's uncle. "Sorry. No offense."

"None taken." Elmore was pulling thoughtfully on the little point his silver hair made in the middle of his forehead. "Well, that's a mournful story, Mr. Darrow. A very mournful story."

"Yes, sir."

"Because Hettie O'Rourke is a fine woman."

"Yes, sir. She is."

"And the Gladhills could certainly use some healthy new blood."

Cody grunted, depressed.

"Too bad Marion's such an idiot."

Cody blinked.

"Mr. Darrow?"

"Sir?"

"You strike me as a man in need of a little help."

2

HETTIE'S ARMS FELT HEAVY AS LEAD AS SHE REACHED UP to wind her hair into its long nighttime braid. Staring at herself in the dressing table mirror, she took steady, depressed stock of her wan coloring and forlorn expression, and she thought, *This is not how a bride is supposed to look the night before her wedding.* She heaved a sigh and let her hands drop in her lap, then leaned forward to torture herself with a good, long look. *This is your fault, Cody Darrow. Look at me, I can hardly hold my head up.* Dejection always had that effect on her, of making her limbs go limp and loose like a rag doll's. She doubted if she had the strength to get up, walk across the room, and fall into bed.

She'd always taken pride in being sensible, strong, and self-sufficient. She'd had to be or she wouldn't have survived, but right now all Hettie wanted was her mother. She watched a tear well up in her right eye; one in her left followed immediately. What was wrong with a little self-pity every great, long, infrequent once in a while? Whom would it hurt? All the same, she dashed at her cheeks and started straightening combs and creams and jars on her dressing table, brisk and efficient as ever. Because even if her mother were here, she would only tell her what she already knew: that she was a very silly girl to hold a three-year torch for a man she'd known for one month, and who'd proven unworthy of her in the end, anyway.

Knowing something and feeling it were not the same, though. Cody's reappearance had opened a hundred old wounds. She'd never forgotten him, and now she had to ask herself if she'd ever even stopped loving him. Whatever she felt for him, until now she'd kept it hidden away in her secret heart, a sweet, private memory with a sad ending. How unkind of him to turn up now, how cruel to hurt her like this all over again!

A soft knock sounded at the door—the maid come to turn down the bed, no doubt. Would she ever get used to servants, and the pointless-seeming tasks they were always doing for her? She went to the door and opened it.

She repressed her first impulse to scream and put everything into her second, which was to push the door closed in Cody's face. But he was stronger than she was, and he also had his foot in the door. A wordless, undignified struggle went on for endless seconds until he rasped, "Let me in, somebody's coming!"

"Good!" she cried. They could rescue her! Immediately the flaws in this plan became clear, and she let go of the door. Cody's momentum tumbled him inside, almost on top of her. He righted himself, spun around, and closed the door. When he turned back, the look of triumph in his eyes made her clench her fists and take a boxer's stance. "You were lying!" she marveled furiously. Before she could take a swing, another knock sounded, and they jumped like murderers caught in the act.

"Hettie? Sweetheart?" Marion's voice was low and insinuating.

She bit down hard on the knuckles of both hands. Cody glared at her, whispered an earthy curse, and squeezed himself behind the door. "Well, open the damn thing," he muttered darkly.

Aghast, irresolute, she looked back and forth between him and the closed door. Marion knocked a little louder and said, "Darling?" Her shaking hand went to the knob and turned it.

"Hello, sweetheart."

"Marion, what are you doing here?" Good lord, he was in a dressing gown of purple paisley and leather slippers without socks. Hair, she couldn't help noticing, grew out of the tops of his very white feet.

"I came to say good night." He pulled something spindly and green from the pocket of his gown and held it up. With a sinking feeling, she recognized it. Mistletoe.

"We already said good night."

His eyes narrowed in surprise at the sharpness of her tone. "I wanted to say it again." Smiling to charm her, he let his eyes drop to her bosom. "You look absolutely adorable."

She pulled the two halves of her robe together to hide her nightgown, which she suddenly remembered was sheer. ''Marion, you shouldn't be here! What if your mother caught us?''

The familiar petulant droop pulled at his lips. ''I don't care, I hope she does. What business is it of hers? Anyway, we'll be married in a few hours.'' He took a step over the threshold and reached for her. ''Man and wife.''

If she stepped back, he'd follow her in. So she didn't move, not even when he put his arms around her. ''You're sweet but you have to go,'' she blurted, panicked.

''Kiss me.''

''Oh, Marion—''

''Oh, darling.''

Something, a snarl or perhaps the grinding of teeth, sounded from two feet away behind the door. Terrified, she put her arms around Marion's neck and kissed him, thanking God when he made a satisfied humming sound in his throat: it drowned out that noise Cody was making.

She broke away with abrupt relief, as if from a task performed unwillingly but well. ''Good night.''

''Wait. One more.''

''No, Marion, go.'' It was disconcerting to see the same sulky but submissive look come over him that he wore when his mother gave him an order. ''Please,'' she added, in an effort to sound less like Olympia. The distracted thought struck that she wasn't ready yet to be anybody's mother.

''All right, darling, if I must.'' He seized her hand and pressed it to his lips. ''But I'm counting the hours until you're mine.''

Another tiny noise, like a groan.

''I'm counting them, too,'' she said in a rush. ''Now go, Marion, you really must. Good night.''

''Good night, my dear. Sweet—''

She closed the door in his face.

Cody had her by the arms almost before she could turn around, and he was kissing her before she even knew he meant to try. He pressed her back between the door and his hard body, his fingers tangling in her hair. After the first few seconds of near-violence, when all he cared about was erasing the feel of Gladhill's kiss from her mouth, Cody forgot about jealousy and frustration, and thought of nothing except how much he'd missed her. How much he loved to touch her. It all came back, everything, all at once. When she embraced him, it was as if no time at all had passed since the last time he'd held her. Just like this. "Hello," he whispered, and kissed her again. A welcome home kiss, deep and emotional and unconsidered.

For her, the idea of resisting came and went with astonishing quickness, and deserted her at exactly the same moment she felt his anger fade to tenderness. It wasn't that she lost her mind; she knew what she was doing. She disapproved of it heartily. She did it anyway. Her arms came around him naturally, automatically, as if falling back into an old habit. A lovely old habit. A hot fire that had gone out in her heart burned bright again, and she was nothing but glad.

The kiss ended in gentleness. He let her go when it was over, not trying to hold her. She drifted away slowly, not trying to escape. She wasn't hypocrite enough to call him a name. But as the seconds passed, what they'd just done began to seem less real and more unthinkable, like the guilty morning memory of an illicit dream.

"You shouldn't have done that." She said it without rancor; she hoped he didn't know that she said it without conviction.

"Maybe," he agreed, watching her. "I couldn't help it." It wasn't an excuse, he realized, it was the truth.

She backed up to the high bureau and leaned against it. Looking at him for the first time since he'd come here tonight, really seeing him, she noticed he no longer wore the rakish mustache that had so infatuated her three years ago. But that was no consolation; if anything, he was more dangerously attractive without it, because now he looked open and forthright. Trustworthy. A new, cynical part of her wondered if he'd shaved it off for that reason.

He was handsomer too, something she wouldn't have thought possible. Now there were no distractions from the strength and evenness of his features. The bones in his face were hard and prominent, the sky blue eyes crinkled at the corners from squinting into the sun and rain and snow. He raked his dark hair back with both hands, still watching her, trying to gauge her mood. Such strong hands, sensitive and stirring, and how well she remembered them. Holding them, studying them, playing with his fingers, because, at first, her scruples had dictated that their intimacy could go no further, that his body was off limits but his hands were acceptable sexual territory. So she'd focused all her girlish sensuality on them—at first.

"How did you get here?" she asked, needing to break the risky, widening silence. "How did you find my room?"

"I promised not to reveal my accomplice."

"Uncle Elmore," she guessed, without anger or even much surprise.

"He reminds me of Petey," Cody said softly.

She nodded, and suddenly she felt like weeping. It was important to dredge up the old bitterness and hurt, but somehow they wouldn't come now. Her shock at seeing him had deserted her, too. "I'm getting married tomorrow," she reminded him, or herself. "Nothing you can say or do will stop me."

He cocked one dark eyebrow at her, turned around, and locked the door. Then he sauntered over to the wide tester bed and lay down on it. "Too soft," he observed, bouncing a little. "Join me?"

Hettie folded her arms. "I can start screaming."

He rolled to his side and reached over to the bedside table, turning toward him a framed photograph of her and Marion. The formal pose, him seated, Hettie standing behind him with a dutiful hand on his shoulder, annoyed Cody intensely. "I hear he's hardly got any chin at all. You know what they say about men with little chins?''

"Listen, Cody," Hettie bristled, pointing at the door, "I want you—"

"How did you meet him?" he asked in a disarmingly reasonable voice, folding his arms behind his head and crossing his boots at the ankles.

He looked so permanent on her bed, so immovable; and she knew as well as he that the last thing she was going to do was start screaming. It looked as if they were going to have a chat. Deciding she might as well be comfortable during its extremely brief duration, she took a seat on the padded stool in front of her dressing table. Back straight, hands clasped, she tried for a formal air, which was not all it might have been, considering she was wearing her nightgown and robe.

"We met in the store, of course. You might remember that I was working there two days a week, to supplement my income from writing and my job at the library. Marion's father was still alive then, and Marion was working as a floorwalker, in training for the day when he would take over. He noticed me."

Cody's lip lifted. "I'll bet."

"He noticed that I was reliable and competent," she snapped. Which hadn't stopped him, she remembered but didn't say, from inviting her out to lunch, to dinner, tea, the theater, and anywhere else he could think of, for months on end. She'd refused all his invitations, partly because of the social chasm between them, but mostly because she hadn't trusted his intentions. "Eventually he offered me full-time work for more than I could make at the library. I accepted it. A few months later he promoted me to head of the department."

"The lingerie department."

"Yes."

"All because you were reliable and competent."

"Yes! We had a business relationship."

''Okay, okay,'' Cody said placatingly, ''I believe you.''

''I don't care whether you believe me or not!''

''So when did it turn romantic, this business relationship?''

''I'm not discussing this with you!''

''Why not?''

''Because it's none of your business. You of all people.'' But a second later she heard herself say, ''It was gradual. We fell in love slowly, not . . .'' She pinched her lips together.

''Not like us,'' Cody murmured. ''Not like a cyclone hitting a dusty cornfield. If you marry him—''

''*When* I marry him.''

''If you marry him, will you keep working there?''

''No.''

''No?''

''No, I'll be . . .'' What? She didn't quite know.

''A great lady,'' he finished for her. ''Much too fine to work in a department store. Well, I can't blame you.''

She went stiff. ''First of all, I couldn't care less whether or not you blame me. Second, Mother Gladhill insisted that I stop working when Marion and I became engaged. It wasn't my choice; I did it . . . out of respect for her feelings.''

''Mother Gladhill,'' Cody repeated, lips curling. ''Now, that's something Marion's got over me, I can't deny. A ready-made family to come into.''

She was silent, contemplating that mixed blessing.

''I think I can remember my mother,'' he said unexpectedly. ''I was about two and a half when she took off, so I might be wrong, but I've got a memory of a woman leaning over me, changing a diaper, I guess, frowning down, with a cigarette in the side of her mouth. Squinting one eye against the smoke.'' He smiled crookedly. ''That's a hell of a memory, isn't it?''

Hettie felt a dangerous softening. ''You never told me very much about your childhood.''

He stood up. "Nothing to tell." He reached for the photograph again, then put it down, restless. "Remember that time we had our picture made, Hett?"

She didn't answer.

"You had on a fur hat. I'd just taken you riding in Central Park. Remember? You'd never been on a horse before and you were scared; you thought that little mare was going to run away with you. What was her name?"

"Chloë," she said, in an unwilling murmur.

"Chloë. And mine was Thunder, a big roan stallion. You looked beautiful on that little mare, Hettie. I wanted to ride off with you into the sunset. Like . . ."

"Like Bronco LaSalle and his girl."

"Yeah." He smiled, and her heart clenched. "That was a low-down trick, what you wrote in that last Bronco book," he told her in a gruff, gentle voice. "How could you make him a *farmer*?"

She couldn't help smiling back. "You should've read the first draft. They refused to print it."

"What did you do, kill him off? Torture him to death?"

"No more than he deserved." He moved toward her, and her smile faltered. When he reached for her, she let him pull her to her feet, but she drew her hands out of his immediately.

"I knew it was me you were paying back in that book, honey. I knew, and I didn't blame you for a second. After I left, it took about a week to figure out I'd made the worst mistake of my life." His low voice deepened. "I'd die before I'd hurt you like that again."

"I'm not going to let you do this to me," she whispered. He laid his big palm on the side of her face and said her name. "I'm not, Cody, I'm not, I'm—" He leaned closer.

Behind her the door knob rattled twice. She jumped, muffling a shriek of pure panic.

"Henrietta? Why is this door locked?"

"Olympia!" she mouthed, wide-eyed. "Hide! Oh, dear lord. Will you hide?"

"You want me to hide? Where?"

"Under the bed!"

"Too short. My feet would stick out."

"Henrietta?" Mother Gladhill sounded impatient.

"The wardrobe!"

Cody looked askance at the huge upright trunk with mirrored doors in the corner. "Well, now, I don't—"

With a strangled cry she caught him by the arm and hustled him over to it. "Just a minute," she trilled in a light, ludicrously chipper voice. "Get in," she muttered, frantic. "Quick, quick!"

Grumbling under his breath, he pushed yards of cloth and frothy lace out of the way and climbed inside. "Hell's bells, I haven't had to do a fool thing like this in—"

"Shut up."

"Hurry and get rid of her, Hett, I've still got—"

She slammed the door on the rest.

"Henrietta?"

"Coming!"

She rushed across the room, paused for two seconds to press her hands against her hot cheeks and compose herself, then opened the door.

"Why was this locked? Doors are never locked in this house." Olympia, majestic in a voluminous yellow dressing gown of quilted satin, looked annoyed and suspicious.

"I can't imagine. I must've done it by accident, absentminded me. I'm all keyed up tonight, the party, bride's jitters . . ." Stop babbling, she commanded herself.

Olympia eyed her strangely. "You weren't trying to keep anyone out, were you?"

"Anyone," she knew, could only mean Marion. "No, certainly not." She almost giggled at the idea; hysteria seemed as close as the next breath. Olympia crossed the threshold and closed the door, and Hettie's heart sank. It wasn't going to be just a quick good night, then.

"I forgot to ask how the final alterations to your wedding gown went this afternoon. Did the seamstress lengthen the train all right? And tighten the bodice?"

"Yes, everything's—" Oh God! Her wedding dress was hanging in the wardrobe, and Olympia was moving toward it purposefully. "Everything is perfect," she blithered, "*perfect,* no need to—"

"And Trudy pressed it one last time?"

"Yes! Oh, Mother Gladhill, I'm so . . ." With her hand on the knob, Olympia turned to look at her. Hettie collapsed on the bed, holding her gaze, hands stretched out invitingly, imploringly.

"Yes, dear?"

"I'm so . . . so nervous. About everything."

Olympia smiled stiffly as a knowing look marred by condescension settled over her florid features. Her hand dropped away from the handle of the gaping wardrobe door. She crossed the room slowly, like a stately ship steaming into harbor. She avoided Hettie's hands, but unbent enough to sit beside her on the bed.

"It's entirely natural. You're about to undertake very serious duties and obligations that are, of course, completely unfamiliar to you. That is, one assumes they're unfamiliar to you. Are you aware of what's expected of a woman on her wedding night, Henrietta?"

Hettie gave up trying to peer over Olympia's shoulder to see if Cody was visible in the wardrobe now that the door was half open. She flushed a bright crimson and said quickly, "Oh heavens, there's no need to go into that now."

"No? Do I take that to mean you already know everything?"

"No! I mean, no, that is, *some* things I . . . but nothing really, I wouldn't say—"

"You are innocent, are you not?"

"Yes, of course." And so she was.

Olympia looked incompletely convinced. Nevertheless, she sat up even straighter and fixed her with a baleful look, stern and joyless, like a schoolmistress obliged to administer the ruler solely for the pupil's own good. An unsavory task, but someone had to do it, the look said.

"A man has certain needs and desires that are difficult for a woman to understand because she herself does not possess them. Indeed, she must take it on faith, a matter of hearsay, that such needs exist at all, so foreign, so alien must they seem to a true lady. Nonetheless, they do exist, and I suppose the endless perpetuation of the human species is proof enough of *that*." This was said with a sniff of disapproval, as if the perpetuation of the species came very close to being, in her opinion, too high a price to pay. "But perhaps I am getting ahead of myself a trifle. Let us begin with the basics: the physiological distinctions between male and female."

"Oh, no, really—"

"It's the logical place to begin; and even though you may think yourself already familiar with these anatomical differences because of pictures and statuary in galleries and museums, the subject is a bit more complex than you might imagine."

There was no stopping her. In an agony of embarrassment, Hettie listened to her describe first, in alarmingly clinical language, the ways in which men differed from women; and then, in brief, somewhat euphemistic detail, which was nevertheless distressingly lucid, exactly what occurred between married ladies and gentlemen in the bedroom. Hettie's cheeks burned; she cringed; she squirmed. Not because of the information, none of which was news—her mother had explained everything to her when she was eleven—but because of the awful knowledge that Cody was listening to it, too. Snickering, she had no doubt. Holding his sides. Turning purple with mirth. The image of him laughing in the closet caused the most unseemly giggle to bubble up in her throat, at precisely the moment Mother Gladhill was getting to the very heart of things.

Olympia, who had been leaning toward her with great earnestness, stiffened in reproach. "I doubt you'll find it quite so amusing when it happens to you," she said ominously. "The marriage act is meant to produce children and to please men, nothing more. I know of no act a lady can perform that is as singularly unpleasant, distasteful, and repellent. And yet it is our duty, one we accept in silence and without complaint."

She softened a little at Hettie's expression. "There, it won't be so terribly bad. If you have children early, you'll only have to put up with it for a short time. I was fortunate in that way; Mr. Gladhill left me alone after Marion's birth, which occurred, luckily, only two years after our marriage." She patted Hettie's wrist briskly. "And there are ways to make it less of an ordeal, you'll learn. Never disrobe, that is my first piece of advice. Don't agree to remove your nightgown, no matter what the inducement; the indignity is less when one is fully clothed. Endeavor not to move, because the pretense of sleep has a wonderfully inhibiting effect on a man's enthusiasm. In my experience, silence and complete rigidity of the limbs are more effective even than—"

Hettie jumped up, to avoid crying, or laughing, or both. "Oh, Mother Gladhill, thank you, you're very kind, and I shall heed your advice to the letter! But I'm so tired now, do you mind if we say good night?"

Olympia rose too, looking faintly disappointed. "Of course. You'll have to get up quite early in order to be at the church by ten. Your dress—"

"It's just right, it's perfect, I absolutely adore it," she gushed, with a light hand on the older woman's arm to steer her toward the door.

Olympia looked at her curiously. "You're behaving very strangely tonight, Henrietta."

She gave a broad, almost Gallic shrug, moving sideways at the same time to block the view of the wardrobe. "It's the excitement."

Hettie stifled a start of surprise when Olympia took her by both shoulders and turned her so that they faced each other, nose to nose. "Far more important than the physical joining we've just discussed, my dear, is the merger of two individuals into one *socially* functioning entity. Tomorrow, you will become a Gladhill. I hope that means something to you."

"Oh, it—"

"I hope the age and eminence of our family name excites in you the humility it deservedly ought, and that you're fully aware of the honor—I trust you will not think the word too lofty in this context—the honor that this marriage confers on you."

"I certainly—"

"And I hope you'll make careful, discerning use of an opportunity that's been handed to you." On a platter, Hettie could almost hear her thinking, unrelated to anything you've ever done to deserve it. The patronizing lecture went on for a few more minutes, Hettie weakly agreeing to it all. When it was over she felt depressed, on her own account, and embarrassed, on Cody's.

"Well, then," Olympia wound up at last. "I'll say good night. I'll send the maid to you to turn down the—"

"No, don't, it's not necessary, I'm going to bed instantly."

"Very well."

Hettie put out her hand, thinking they would kiss now, or at least touch; but Olympia only said good night again and turned away from her.

After the door closed, she put her ear to it for a second, then silently turned the key in the lock. She went to the bed and collapsed on it, weary all of a sudden, that lifelessness of the limbs that seemed to afflict her after conversations with her mother-in-law-to-be. She watched the wardrobe door widen and Cody step out, groaning exaggeratedly and rubbing the back of his supposedly stiff neck. Then he grinned. "Don't you say one word, Cody Darrow," she warned tightly. "Not one word."

"All right." He crossed to her in three lithe strides and sat beside her on the edge of the bed. "Not one word." She looked so woebegone, and so damn young in her bathrobe and bare feet, her pretty hair hanging in a braid over one shoulder; she reminded him of a little girl trying not to cry after a scolding. "Old goat," he growled, and was rewarded with a limp smile. "Fat old bug. Big fat ugly old turnip." He gave her braid a gentle yank, and the trembly smile blossomed. Then it was impossible not to slide his fingers between the slippery plaits and release them. Hettie's hair spread out across her breast like a shiny, copper-colored flag. "So beautiful," he murmured, letting it flow through his fingers. Now she didn't look like a little girl at all.

She reached for his wrist and gave a half-hearted pull, but instead of letting go he moved his hand to the back of her neck and began a soft, tension-relieving massage. He watched her eyelids close and fly open, then close again. She whispered, "Don't, Cody," but he could tell she didn't mean it. He felt a different kind of tension building in his own body, fast and hard, and he clamped down on a dozen different urges, a hundred different ways he wanted to touch her. Mother Gladhill's sex lecture had tickled him, but it had also gotten under his skin.

It had gotten under hers too, she realized with dismay, all that talk about needs and desires and intimate physical connections. Her muscles gave in to a different kind of lethargy, not at all like depression. She could feel Cody's warm breath on her cheek, but she didn't seem to have the strength to open her eyes, and certainly not enough to turn her face away. The brush of his lips over hers followed so naturally, she couldn't help but sigh, even though the sound was like surrender. If she didn't think, if she blocked out every sober, sensible, clearheaded reason why what they were doing was unthinkable, she wouldn't have to stop. Not yet. She could let him touch her like this for a little longer. One more second. One more. Now another.

The slow, sweet stages of her acquiescence acted like gentle fingers urging Cody to let go of the grip he had on his emotions. He let his hands drift across her shoulders and down her arms, pushing the silky sleeves of her robe up so he could feel her bare skin. Soft. Oh lord, she was soft. The warm pulse at the bend in her elbow beat fast and strong. Their mouths were just touching, it was hardly a kiss at all. He caressed her lips with the soft, tentative slide of his tongue. "Please, Cody," she might have said, but neither of them took it seriously. He whispered, "Shh," taking little sips of her lips, remembering the taste, savoring it. "Don't talk, Henrietta. In silence and without complaint." She made a sound in her throat that might have been a laugh. His arms tightened around her. Slowly, urgent but still gentle, he took her down, never stopping the kiss, until her head touched the thick satin coverlet.

Her green eyes darkened, but not with fear, and when he kissed her again Hettie didn't once consider using rigidity of the limbs to inhibit his enthusiasm. She wrapped her arms around his neck and kissed him back.

Heat rushed through her. She felt his fingers tugging at the sash at her waist. Stop now, she advised herself, sleeking her fingers through his hair. They'd never gone this far before, and now he was working at the tiny buttons down the front of her nightgown. His hands were so gentle, his eyes so intent; she didn't make him stop when he pulled the silk aside and uncovered her breasts.

"I knew it."

"What?" she quavered.

"I knew you'd be beautiful. Ah, Hettie." He touched her with all the tenderness in him, even though he was burning for her. She moved her head restlessly. "I don't want *him* touching you like this," he growled suddenly, pleasuring her with the slow rasping pass of his palm. "I don't want him looking at you. You're mine."

"No—"

"Yes." He flicked his tongue across one taut, pink nipple, and she gasped.

The sensation was so strong, it jolted her out of the dreamy haze of sensuality she'd been floating in. Before it could carry her down to a deeper, darker, more dangerous place, she said, "Stop now. I mean it, Cody, stop." He didn't stop, and she could feel herself falling, flailing. "Please," she begged in a desperate whisper, "this is wrong. Cody, for pity's sake, don't shame me."

He opened his mouth wide and covered her breast, making her cry out. This couldn't be wrong; he'd prove it to her. Her stomach muscles were tight and trembling under his hand. He slid his fingers down to the soft mound between her legs and cupped it, his mouth still at her breast. Her thighs clamped tight together, and her whole body went rigid. "Darling, darling," he muttered. He raised his head to soothe her, and saw a tear slide past one closed eyelid and spill down her cheek. He sucked in a deep, shuddering breath of air. "Don't do that. Aw, Hettie." He flushed hot with remorse, sick because he'd made her cry, after he'd sworn he'd never make her cry again. The penalty was harsh, but he did it; he pulled her nightgown down, covering her. His body felt like a cocked gun, but he made himself roll away from her and sit up. He put his elbows on his knees and his head in his hands, and told her he was sorry.

She got up more slowly, light-headed but sluggish, as if her body had an excess of blood. She turned her back to him while she drew the front of her nightgown together with hands that shook. The sight of one pink, wet nipple shocked her; she tied the ribbons of her robe tight with jerky movements, desperate to keep her mind a blank for just a little longer.

But a memory intruded, familiar, shopworn even, harrying her now with new freshness. A memory of the night before she and Cody were to marry—the last time she'd seen him. The celebratory dinner party in the Brooklyn apartment was over, the guests had all gone home. Petey had stumbled off to bed, and she and Cody were alone together, ostensibly saying good night at the door. But they might as well have been in bed, a vertical one, so tightly did he have her pressed against the door, his hard thighs between hers, kissing her with the starkest kind of intimacy while his hands touched her through her clothes everywhere. Everywhere. They had both been utterly lost; he could've done anything and she'd have allowed it, joyfully.

But Petey was no fool, even though he'd been as drunk that night as Hettie had ever seen him. "Say g'night t' that boy, darlin'," he'd hollered from his bedroom. "You'll see 'im in the mornin'."

But she hadn't seen him in the morning.

Afterward, when she thought of his abandonment, she'd always remembered that night and the liberties she'd let him take with her body.

"What is it? What are you thinking about?" he asked from the bed. Her stillness worried him.

She turned around slowly. "Was that what I did wrong?" she asked seriously.

"What do you mean, honey?"

"If I'd been more chaste, more respectable, would you have married me? Or did you find me not to your liking, that last night? Or too much like all the others you'd known? Nothing special?" He stood up fast. "No, don't," she said quickly, one arm out to hold him away. "Just answer. Just tell me."

"That last time between us, Hettie." He looked at the ceiling, praying for the words. "It tortured me for months, years. But it carried me through, too, because I never forgot it, never could have. The hardest thing I ever did in my life was to walk out on you the next day."

Her throat tightened; she could just barely ask, "Why did you?"

"Because I was afraid."

He'd said that before. "What were you afraid of?"

He wondered if she had any idea how hard it was for him to admit weakness to her. "Of losing myself. Everything I'd made of myself. *By* myself." He tried to laugh. "Which wasn't much, I know, but I still couldn't give it up. Freedom, I called it. I wasn't cut out to be the kind of man you wanted, and I didn't know how to tell you. I knew I'd disappoint you, I knew it. I didn't have the guts to face it."

They looked away from each other at the same moment, both hopelessly aware that it always came back to that.

"Why did you come here?" she asked at last. "If it wasn't to hurt me again, why did you come? Nothing's changed."

The dejection left his face and his eyes flashed with determination. "No, you're wrong, everything's changed. Sit down, I'll tell you."

"Cody, it's late, this is crazy—"

"Please. It won't take long." He gestured toward the bed.

She hesitated, then took a seat on the edge of the spindleback chair beside her dresser. Folding her arms in a deliberately defensive posture, she waited.

He took up a position between her and the bed, legs spread, hands in his pockets; but before he finished the first sentence, he'd started to pace. "After I left New York, I caught up with the show in Buffalo. Ever been to Buffalo in January? I was pretty wild; you don't want to know what all I got up to. Trying to forget about you. But I was never drunk for a show," he pointed out hastily, defensively; "it never did come to that. Anyway, one night, I drew the rankest steer in the go-round, a crossbred Brahman with nothing in his brain except evil. I made my horn catch all right, from this big stout gelding named Strychnine, but somehow my slack rope got blown under both his forelegs. So I'm trying to untangle the

fouled rope when all of a sudden horse and bull take off
in different directions. The rope tightened like a banjo
string and Strychnine goes crashing down sideways. Me
under him. I was unconscious for twenty-eight hours.''

Hettie's white-knuckled fingers ached. She'd gone to
every show during the week Cody had performed in New
York, unable to stay away, but petrified that something
would happen to him. ''At least I didn't have to see it,''
she whispered. ''Thank God for that.''

''Afterward, I couldn't ride. Doctor said I'd be crazy
to get on a horse for six months at least.''

''What did you do?''

''The show left me, naturally. There I was in Buffalo
by myself. Didn't know a soul. Broke, drinking too
much, not feeling too proud of Cody Darrow, all things
considered. And missing you like hell.''

''This won't do you any good at all,'' she said suddenly, realizing how he affected her. ''You can't sweet-
talk me into anything anymore, Cody.''

''You asked me what happened.'' He held out his arms.
''Don't you want to know?''

She gave him her stoniest look. ''Go on.''

''One night in a bar I got into a poker game. I started
with my last dollar, and four hours later I'd cleaned 'em
all out, every last one of 'em. I couldn't lose. One of the
ones I'd varnished told me about another game, one with
bigger players and higher stakes. He took me to it, and
it happened again. I couldn't lose. These fellows were
high rollers, Hett; one was a New York City assembly-
man, one owned a big chunk of some railroad. I took
nine thousand dollars off of 'em before dawn.''

''Nine thousand dollars!'' Then, prompted by her new
cynicism, she asked, ''How long did you hold on to it?''

He didn't take offense; it wasn't her fault she didn't
know he was a changed man. ''Honest to God, I've still
got most of it. Not the original nine thousand, but money
I've made with it since then.''

''How?'' she asked suspiciously. ''No, don't tell me.

I don't want to know." All of a sudden the circumstances struck her. She couldn't believe he was here in her bedroom and they were having this conversation, any conversation. She jumped up. "You have to get out of here, Cody, now, and you can't let anybody see you."

"Then I better wait until they're all good and asleep. Besides, you want to hear this."

"I really don't."

"You don't lie very well."

"I'm not lying. Anyway, I never had to until—"

"Until you met me." He came close to her, but didn't touch her. "You won't have to anymore. I'm different, Hettie. I had to grow up."

"I don't care, I don't want to listen anymore." She turned away and began to fiddle with perfume bottles on top of her dresser.

"Why not? Afraid to admit you've made a mistake with Marion? Too bad, you'll have to learn to live with it. And fix it."

She whirled around. "You arrogant . . . bounder!"

He smiled benevolently. "You can say 'bastard,' honey. Go ahead. I'm not a Gladhill, you can speak freely to me."

She wanted to hit him because he'd put his finger on the truth so easily. Even after three years and all that had happened between them, she still felt more at ease with him than she did in the company of Marion, or Olympia, or any of their set. The only Gladhill she could really relax with was Uncle Elmore.

Cody saw he'd scored a point and was shrewd enough not to press it. He backed away from her and went to lean against the footpost of the bed. "I won something else in that card game. Something worth a lot more than nine thousand dollars."

"What?" She looked skeptical, expecting some platitude now, like "I won self-respect," or "I got my peace of mind."

"I won a blue-black yearling colt with champion's blood in his veins. Guess what his name is."

Petey had played the horses; she was aware of the absurd mental connections gamblers made between horses' names and dead-cert winners. Her lips curled. "I give up."

"Second Chance."

She held his gaze and said evenly, "So?"

"Second Chance," he repeated, patiently. "As soon as he told me his name, I knew it was a sure thing."

"As soon as who told you his name? The horse?"

He sent her a look. "The owner. I had him down to his long johns by then; he'd have bet his mother's gravestone next if he'd thought of it. Pendleton was his name; his father's rich as Croesus, rich as Gladhill, made his money in meat packing. This saphead never worked a day in his life, and he owned this colt." He shook his head in disgust. "He'd never even seen it."

"I don't know what you're talking about."

"I'm talking about drawing to an inside straight on account of the most powerful hunch I've ever had in my life. This colt's name was *Second Chance*, Hettie, and he was going to turn my life around." He grinned, cocky, standing up straighter. "And he did. I drew a seven of clubs and won him fair and square that night, and the next day I caught a southbound train and rode it all the way to Kentucky to see my new horse. I've been there ever since."

He drew his wallet from his coat pocket and went to stand over her. "This is my stud farm, Hettie. Look at it." She took the worn photograph from his hand. "I bought it with the money I won, plus a loan I took out using Second Chance as collateral. Look at it, Hett." His voice took on a reverent tone, as if he'd just entered a cathedral. "Two hundred and seventy acres of rolling pasture on the south fork of the Licking River. The house isn't much yet—needs a woman's touch—but the paddocks and stables are spic an' span, and so pretty you could almost live in 'em with the horses. My stock is still small, I've got six broodmares, a race mare, four blooded colts, and half a dozen yearling thoroughbreds, but we're growing fast.''

He took another picture from his wallet. ''This is Second Chance. Look at that Roman nose.'' Now he sounded like a new father, offering photographs of his firstborn. ''The first year, he couldn't get out of his own way. The next, when he was three, he won everything. I put him to stud this fall; I set his fee at a thousand dollars a leap, and nobody bats an eye. He'll sire champions for me, Hettie. For us.''

''Cody, stop.''

He dropped to one knee and pushed the photographs she was trying to hand him back into her lap. ''There's a lane up to the house, and the oak trees meet over it and make this long, leafy tunnel. There's acres and acres of open woods, with little creeks running through, and the trees are ancient black cherries and ash, coffee trees and huge sycamores. In the spring the catalpas and the dogwoods bloom, and the redbuds. Around the house there's peonies and irises and mock-orange hedges—''

''It doesn't—''

''But the best, the prettiest sight of all is when you come riding up the lane and see the mares grazing in the pasture with the foals, and the stallions pacing along the white paddock fences next to 'em, proud and arrogant. The yearlings look like fawns. They'll break into a sprint for no reason, and run and run and run. Or they'll surround you, all eyes and long legs, friendly as puppies.''

He had her hands now, squeezing them with unconscious force. Hettie shook her head mutely.

''I'm not a gambler. You don't have to worry about that. I don't care about racing 'em myself; it's the breeding and training I like. You wouldn't think it, but training a thoroughbred racer isn't that different from breaking in a roping pony. Any horse will snap if you push him too hard or too fast; the trick is to teach him to want to win, and I'm good at that, because I'm a patient man and I know how a horse thinks.'' He looked down. ''The breeding part's new to me, I admit, and it's complicated as hell. But I'm studying all the time, trying to figure out genealogy. The list of names for one horse can go on forever, but you have to know all about the matings of sires and dams and grandsires and graddams. I've hired a fellow to help me when—''

''Cody, it's no use. Let me go.''

''You'll love Lexington, Hettie. It's like a little English village or something with these narrow streets and old, old houses. They call it the Athens of the West because the architecture's Greek. It's a college town, the University of Kentucky's there. You could get a job in the library if you wanted to.''

She yanked her hands out of his grasp.

''Or you could write books again, or you could do nothing at all. Money's not a problem, I've got—''

She finally put her fingers over his mouth to silence him. ''Stop. It's no use.'' Twisting away, she jumped up and went across the room to the door, hugging herself. When she turned back, he was picking up the pictures that had fallen on the floor, and getting slowly to his feet. How many times had she plotted revenge on him, imagining lurid scenes in which he humbled himself to her and she scorned him? Now that the real-life opportunity was here, she found she hadn't the stomach for it. In fact, she couldn't bear it.

''It's no use,'' she said again, as steadily as she could. ''I'm marrying Marion. I love him and I'm marrying him.'' She didn't think about what the words meant. She used them for a shield, a meditation, which, if she simply said it often enough, would become the truth by itself.

The clock on the bureau struck midnight. They stared across the width of the room at each other, listening to the twelve measured strokes. When the echo of the last one died, Cody came toward her, pulling something else from his pocket. A small leather booklet, she saw when he stopped in front of her. With a little stab in the heart, she saw that it was his checkbook.

"I'm flush, Hettie. This is my bank balance. Look. No, look—"

"Please, Cody." She started to cry.

He gave an oddly harsh, embarrassed laugh and looked down at his last exhibit, a folded piece of paper. "There's a minister in Lexington. Reverend Perry. He knows me. I got him to write this. For you. It says I'm of good character and moral standing in the community." She didn't speak and, without looking at her, he slid the unopened letter back into his checkbook, his checkbook back into his pocket. His hands at his sides flexed and relaxed. Another minute ticked past. "I was too ashamed of the way I treated you to write you, to tell you any of this before," he said in a hollow voice. "I wanted to be able to prove it to you, show you I'd changed. It wasn't me before, the job in the store, the city life. I wanted to be what you wanted—"

"I know all that." She could not stand this any longer. "I've had three years to sort out what went wrong with us."

"Not us, *me*."

"It was nobody's fault, Cody. We were both young, and I was so in love I couldn't see what was real. I shouldn't have tried to press you so hard, force you into a life that wasn't natural." She wiped her cheeks with the sleeve of her robe. "I wanted to marry a man who wouldn't be anything like Petey. I loved you, but you weren't that man, so I tried to make you up."

"But I am now," he insisted.

"No, you're not. You're not." The certainty broke her heart. "And anyway, it's too late, I've given my promise."

"But you don't love Gladhill!"

"Maybe it's true that I don't love him the way I loved you," she conceded out of weariness. "But he'll be solid,

I think, someone I can depend on. That's important to me. I'm not the girl you knew, Cody. I've changed, too.''

"I know something that hasn't changed," he said grimly and pulled her into his arms.

"This won't make any—'' His hot mouth silenced her. This time his kiss made her feel nothing but sorrow, because she knew it was the last. When he left her mouth and put his lips on her throat, she managed to say, "Let me go, Cody. I won't deny that there's . . . this between us still. But it doesn't mean anything.''

"You're wrong." Desperate, he kissed her again.

"Please stop. Please.'' She started to cry again.

"I know a way I could have you," he snarled. "All I'd have to do is open this door and start yelling." He reached down and turned the key, unlocking the door. "You know what the Gladhills would do if they knew I was here?''

"Yes. Yes.''

"They'd throw you out in the snow, and it wouldn't matter to them if we'd been playing pinochle in here.''

"I know it.''

"That's all I'd have to do. Just open this door." He had his hand on the knob. "Last chance. Leave him and come with me to Kentucky.''

"I can't.''

"I'd make you happy.''

She shook her head.

"I love you, Hettie.''

Tears were blinding her, clogging her throat. "Too late," she whispered. "If only you'd told me that day, to my face, that you couldn't do it, I'd have gone with you anywhere. But you never gave me the chance, Cody.''

Heat rushed through him, a fire in his veins. He opened the door, stepped outside. Only a low-burning gas lamp beside the staircase illuminated the long, silent hall. He looked from one end to the other, as if calculating how loud he'd have to yell to wake up the household. He sent her a last look, took a deep breath, and then smiled, with a sweetness that slivered the last intact pieces of her heart. "Be happy," he whispered. He lifted his hand to an imaginary hat, saluted her, and moved away down the hall, silent as a ghost.

"There. Like that. No, don't move, try not to move your head until the ceremony." Olympia gave the graceful folds of Guipure lace that veiled Hettie's face a last careful fluff, and stepped back. "You look nice."

Nice. Not much of a compliment, thought the bride, from the woman who would be her mother-in-law in about ten minutes. "Thanks," she said, with matching enthusiasm.

Olympia looked at her watch at the same moment a frazzled-looking Mrs. Mainwaring, the genteel professional lady the Gladhills had employed to see that everything about this wedding went smoothly, poked her head in the doorway. "Everyone's seated and the choir is starting. It's time to take your place in front, Mrs. Gladhill."

"I'm coming." She turned back to Hettie, eyed her up and down in a last critical examination, and nodded, satisfied.

"Wish me luck?" Hettie said faintly, when it looked as if Olympia intended to leave without a word, or even one of her bracing pats.

"Good luck. And remember: speak your vows straight out, but not too loudly, neither too demure nor too bold. Just as we practiced."

"I'll remember."

"Good. Well." She looked behind her at Sally, the maid. "Don't let her forget the bouquet."

"No, ma'am."

She crossed to the door, resplendent in midnight-blue crepe de chine. "I'll send Elmore now to get you."

"Thanks, I'll be—" The door clicked shut behind Olympia. "Ready," Hettie finished to her own reflection in the full-length looking glass on the back of the door. As the maid began tidying the room, Hettie stared across

at her own white, virginal image, and felt thankful that
her face was only a lacy blur. From this distance she
looked rather sweet, she thought. The blushing bride, all
eager anticipation. What luck that her pale cheeks and
red, swollen eyelids weren't in evidence. The lace even
softened the grim line of her mouth.

She turned away quickly, but new tears stung like acid
behind her sore eyes before she could defend herself
against them. Damn! Damn! She'd honestly thought the
battle was over, that she'd finally subdued her emotions
around dawn this morning, just before she'd fallen into
an exhausted sleep. Why must she be cursed with all the
old doubts now, *minutes* before she was supposed to say
"I do" to Marion in front of four hundred wedding
guests? All night long her heart had done battle with her
head, and she'd been sure common sense had finally won
out, once and for all. For God's sake, she was a sensible
woman! Surely life had taught her the painful lesson by
now that charming, exciting, lovable men couldn't be
trusted, and that unless she wanted to rely only on herself forever, she had better cast her lot with a man of
substance. A *dull* man of substance. A man who was the
opposite of her father.

The opposite of Cody.

The maid finished straightening the room and started
plucking at Hettie's dress, her train, poking at this, patting at that. "Don't, Sally, leave me be," Hettie snapped,
with completely uncharacteristic impatience. She sighed,
and could have cried again, disliking herself for the
maid's look of hurt surprise. "I'm sorry. It's just that I'm
so nervous."

Disobeying Olympia's order not to move, she started
pacing, reminding herself of Cody last night and giving
the long silk train an irritable twitch with each pivot.
Cody, Cody, get out of my mind. The trouble with him
was that he wasn't serious. He was the lone wild oat she
would ever sow. A youthful indiscretion, as the saying
went. A learning experience, useful now to look back on

and solidify her adult inclinations. She could even admit, in an admirably adult way, that it hurt to give him up, like any bad habit. But surely her heart couldn't be broken a second time. Surely she was immune to him. Like a devastating disease against which she'd been inoculated, Cody Darrow could only strike once.

"Ah, how beautiful. How truly beautiful you look, Hettie." She turned to see Uncle Elmore in the doorway, tiny, almost doll-like in his three-piece black cutaway. She went to him, and he took her hands in his spidery grip, smiling; but his sad eyes went even sadder. "So cold," he mourned, rubbing her stiff fingers.

"It's the excitement." On an impulse, she lifted her veil and kissed his cheek. He actually blushed. "I'm glad it's you who's giving me away," she said softly. "Thank you for being so kind to me all these weeks."

"My dear, it's the other way around." He frowned, peering at her closely. "What's this?" He touched her face, one frail thumb grazing her cheekbone. "You've been crying."

She dropped her veil back into place hurriedly. What could she say? "Yes, a little. Nerves. It's an emotional day, I'm keyed up. Well! Are we ready?" Sally brought her bouquet of white orchids, heavy as a suitcase and completely scentless; as she held them, she saw that her hands were trembling. "Look at me." She tried to laugh.

"Good luck, Miss O'Rourke."

"Thank you, Sally."

Elmore took her arm in a steady, surprisingly strong grasp and led her out of the room. They stood at the top of a flight of stairs leading to the narthex of the old church. Organ music floated upward, slow and stately; Hettie, who hadn't been consulted on the program, couldn't identify the piece. She took a deep breath, preparing to descend, when Elmore announced matter-of-factly, "You know, it's not too late to change your mind."

She stared, positive she'd misheard. "What?"

"Watch your step, this marble can be slippery," he

recommended, starting down the stairs with a slow, careful tread. "I say, it's not too late to reconsider."

She laughed weakly, realizing it was a joke. If he only knew how—

"I like that Darrow fellow, now. Decent man. Devoted to you."

She halted in midstair. "Uncle Elmore!"

Mrs. Mainwaring appeared in the vestibule below. "Lovely, just lovely," she said distractedly, then signaled to someone out of their view. A second later the music stopped. "Come on," she urged with a tense, professional smile, puzzled by their motionlessness.

Elmore got them going again; Hettie followed his lead, puppetlike. "You talked to him, didn't you?" she whispered urgently, searching his impish profile.

He smiled at Mrs. Mainwaring when they reached the bottom of the stairs. "Talked to whom, dear?"

"This way." The woman smiled back, gesturing, as if they didn't know which door led to the nave.

"Cody."

"Oh, Cody, yes, we had quite an interesting conversation. Two, in fact."

"Two? Then you saw him—"

"After you sent him on his way last night, yes. He was terribly distraught, you know, quite inconsolable." They'd reached the portal to the long center aisle that led to the altar. "Well, my dear, what's it to be? Last chance, and all that."

"Uncle Elmore, what's got into you?"

"It's Marion, then?"

"Well, yes!"

He heaved a melancholy sigh, flimsy shoulders rising and falling with resignation. Tucking Hettie's hand more firmly under his arm, he gave Mrs. Mainwaring a nod; she relayed some discreet signal farther along, and immediately the organist launched into "Lohengrin."

Heads turned; well-dressed strangers gaped and smiled; a few made low sounds of approval. Hettie kept her eyes forward, grateful again for the veil that hid her face. Marion looked small in the distance, miles away in the enormous cathedral, but even from here the sight of him discouraged her. *Nerves,* she scolded herself violently. *He probably feels exactly the same way.*

"Absolutely sure, are you?"

She turned her head to stare at Elmore. He was smiling to an acquaintance on the aisle. She must have misheard.

But he looked up at her then and prompted, "Eh?"

Eyes ahead again, barely moving her lips, she mumbled, "I don't believe I'm hearing this! He's charmed you, too, hasn't he? Got you eating out of his—"

"No, no. The thing is, you know, Marion's not good enough for you."

Hettie nearly stumbled. "Will you stop?" she hissed. "Someone's going to hear you." It didn't seem likely, though, because the organist was playing the Wedding March with much verve and gusto.

"Oh, he'll provide every material comfort, no question of that, but what about the rest? The other things a woman needs. A man, too, for that—"

"Marion loves me!"

"Marion's a selfish little boy. His mother won't let him grow up."

"He loves me. Damn it, it's Cody who's the boy."

"If you say so. But I wonder which one of those boys loves you more."

She flushed. The answer to that came easily, too easily. She distrusted it. "Love isn't everything." She closed her mouth, aghast. What an awful thing to say at her own wedding.

Uncle Elmore made soft clucking sounds, which only added to her shame. "That can't be Hettie O'Rourke speaking," he chided gently. "That's some angry little girl I'm not particularly fond of."

"That's not fair. You don't know everything. Uncle Elmore, I don't mean to offend you, but will you please shut up?"

They'd only reached the halfway point because of the excruciatingly slow pace he'd set; the organist had already played the Wedding March twice and was launching into it a third time. She could see Marion clearly now, waiting patiently for her at the altar rail. He looked tall and substantial in his formal wedding clothes, but his face, she couldn't help noticing, had that fatuous look it took on whenever he was feeling self-conscious. The sight of his monocle dangling from his silk lapel plunged her into despair.

"Must be tough growing up in orphanages," Elmore mentioned wistfully. "And then in homes where all the foster parents want is another strong back to help them with their chores."

Hettie ground her teeth. "If you don't—"

"Might make a man a little marriage- and family-shy, if he was sensitive to begin with. Of course, that wouldn't excuse anything mean he might do to someone he loved. But then again, someone who loved him would probably have a big enough heart to forgive him."

"I'm going to kill you," she said seriously. A horrible thought struck. She focused her gaze on the congregation for once and didn't just see them as indistinct blurs gliding past and smiling at her. "He's not *here,* is he?"

"No, no. Not that I know of. I suppose it's possible."

"Oh, dear God."

"We're almost there. I guess you're really going through with this." Ten feet away, Marion cleared his throat and shot his cuffs, preparing to take her hand. "He said to thank you, by the way."

"What?"

"Mr. Darrow said if you wouldn't have him, at least he could go back to a life that suits him. He said he owes that to you, and wanted me to be sure and thank you for it."

A huge lump rose in her throat. Not fair! she wanted to shout. I won't be bullied like this!

The last strains of Wagner died away. Uncle Elmore

let go of her arm and faced her. She expected one last piece of subversive advice now, even though Marion was standing right beside them. But he only gave her a quick kiss through her veil, lifted her right hand, and tenderly placed it in Marion's left. She thought his sad eyes twinkled before he turned his back on her and went to take his place on the aisle beside Olympia. Hettie had never felt so alone in her life.

Nonsense. She was with Marion, her intended, her betrothed, her beloved. Shoulder to shoulder with him before Reverend Toombs, who was smiling benignly on them and opening his prayer book. "Dear friends," he began, then stopped when an irritating rustling noise sounded from the direction of the chancel pews behind him, where the choir sat. He didn't turn at first; he waited, with a good-natured, professionally patient air, for the interruption to subside. Hettie, who couldn't see around him to locate the source of the disturbance, went still as a statue as a truly dreadful possibility occurred to her.

The rustling and scuffling noise didn't stop; on the contrary, it got louder and seemed to be coming closer. Disconcerted, Reverend Toombs finally cast a quick glance backward, and started in surprise. Hettie and Marion peered around him on opposite sides.

The rood screen was trembling; a small hand pushed it aside, revealing the choir and revealing as well, behind it and off to the right, a shorter, younger, less organized-looking choir. An auxiliary choir of sorts. Hettie said, "Sweet Mother of God," and let go of Marion's limp-fingered hand.

The new choir wore no robes and carried no hymnals. Huddling by the door to the north porch, they waited while their leader, the raggedly dressed urchin who had moved the rood screen, hurried back to their unkempt circle, ignoring the hissed commands of a shocked Reverend Toombs. "Mi, mi, mi, mi," the chorus piped at once but on different notes, searching for unanimity. The leader raised both of his grubby hands high in the air.

There was a breathless, soundless, endless moment of suspense. Then the youthful ensemble burst into song.

At first the off-key strains of "O Come, All Ye Faithful" were unrecognizable, and Hettie missed the words to the first verse entirely. But the sharp little soprano voices rose as the carolers' confidence grew, and the words to the second verse rang out with bell-like clarity.

"Oh come to Kentucky,
Hettie, I adore you,
Come, let's be man and wife, I swear I'll be truuue.
I'll make you happy, never make you cry again.
O Hettie, have a heaart,
O Hettie, have a heaart,
O Hettie, have a heaaaart, come home with meeeeeee."

Silence fell. The choir grinned and shuffled self-consciously, evidently expecting applause. There was none. The child nearest the door gave a shrug, then a jaunty little wave, and walked out. The others filed after him.

Marion closed his mouth, then opened it again to pronounce a word Reverend Toombs had never heard in his church before.

Behind them, the astonished voices of wedding guests whispered and buzzed; someone muffled a laugh but someone didn't. Hettie put a hand over her mouth, but whether to hold in a laugh or a sob she couldn't have said. Inside her a war raged, soul-wrenching and life-deciding, between fury and exultation.

"What the hell is the meaning of this?" Marion sputtered, yanking her around by both wrists until she had to look at him. She couldn't answer. She kept turning, even though his grip was painful, until she faced the long aisle. The first face she saw was Olympia's—red, fishlike, confounded. The second was Uncle Elmore's—hopeful, happy-sad, excited. He blew her a kiss, then winked and jerked his thumb over his shoulder.

Someone stood in the dim vestibule, fifty yards away. The great church portal stood open at his back, and snow swirled in circles behind his dark silhouette. Black on white; stillness on motion. But Hettie didn't need proximity or color or detail to know who it was. She took a deep, unsteady breath, pulled her veil aside, and turned back to her betrothed.

Cody's fingers clenched around the brim of his Stetson. Blind to the stares and deaf to the whispers of the hundreds of people craning their necks to look at him, all he saw was Hettie take Marion's hands in both of hers. Even from here her face looked sweet, and whatever she was saying looked urgent and earnest and heartfelt. The tension went out of him gradually, like a guitar string slowly loosening, and he lowered his head until he was staring at the snow-covered toes of his boots. He didn't regret anything. He'd do it all again, because there *had* been a chance, and he hadn't known and never would know a better way, except maybe by kidnapping her, to try to win her back.

He glanced back up and wished to God he hadn't, because now she was kissing Marion. He had to look away, and his heart felt like dry tinder somebody had just set a match to.

But something made him look up again, and when he did she was coming toward him. To punch him? he wondered, brain-addled. A low muttering began among the congregation, and by the time Hettie was halfway down the aisle it had become a roar. Cody stood still for one more uncertain second, and then her shining, smiling, tear-streaked face came into focus. He let out a raucous cowboy yell and threw his hat up to the vaulted ceiling.

She started running before the hat reached its vertex, and by the time a little girl in the seventh row caught it she was in his arms. Her impact almost knocked him over. But Cody hadn't been a prize-winning bronc-buster and bulldogger for nothing; he caught his balance easily and lifted her high in the air, her skirts flying, train billowing. When he set her down, she could hardly get her arms around the muscular breadth of him in his bulky sheepskin coat.

"Oh, Cody—"

"You won't regret this, Hettie."

"I love you, and I'm sorry I put us both through—"

"I swear I'll make you happy."

"I don't know how I thought I could ever have married anyone but—"

"I'll make you laugh a hundred times for every tear I made you cry."

"We wish you a merry Christmas, we wish you a merry Christmas, we wish you a merry Christmas and a happy New Year!"

They stopped hugging each other to look outside where Cody's rag-tag chorale had assembled on the sidewalk to sing a last carol. Hand-in-hand, they bounded down the steps. "Good job," Cody complimented the underage vocalists, dispensing coins and bills with wild extravagance.

Hettie saw a horse tethered to a telegraph pole a few feet away on the corner at Tenth Street. A roan stallion, he looked vaguely familiar. Then she remembered. "It's Thunder!" she cried, charmed. "It is, isn't it?"

"Yep." He kissed her hand impulsively, hurrying her along, delighted that she remembered. "Chloë foaled yesterday, she couldn't come. I gave the liveryman ten dollars to name the filly after you."

He put his hands around her waist and hoisted her up onto Thunder's back, seating her sideways on the western saddle. Then he leapt up behind her. The stallion sidestepped, nervous, but Cody calmed him expertly.

People were spilling out of the church door, gaping at them. Cody had no hat to lift. "Hang on," he cautioned, reached for the reins, and dug in his heels. Thunder reared perfectly, his forelegs pawing the air in a graceful salute.

"Which way to the train station, my heart?"

"That way." She pointed.

"Dang."

"What?"

"I was hoping we'd ride off west."

She turned her face, and he kissed her. Then he spurred the stallion to a canter and they rode away, a few degrees north of where, in about six hours, there would be a brilliant sunset.

Kidnapped for Christmas

by Betina Krahn

1

"THERE SHE IS. THAT'S THE ONE I WANT." SEBASTIAN Wolfe pointed across the snowy village square to a line of young schoolgirls dressed in matching navy blue cloaks and bonnets, marching along two-by-two. The pair of roughly clad men seated across from him in the elegant coach craned their necks to get a look through the frosted window glass.

"Which one, Guv?" the short, stout fellow with the florid face asked, squinting. "They all looks alike to me."

"Not the gulls, pea-brain." The taller, hook-nosed fellow, seated by the window, gave his companion a jab in the ribs with his elbow. " 'E means the slip o' muslin what's leadin' 'em."

"Oh." The ruddy, round fellow squeezed closer to the window and squinted again. "Ye mean that bit o' fluff in the gray . . . wi' the black feathers in 'er hat?"

"The very one." Sebastian Wolfe settled back against the soft, glove leather seat with a wry tilt to his broad, expressive mouth. He tried to imagine the horror that would bloom on Miss Victoria Howard's face if she were to hear herself being described as a "slip o' muslin" or a "bit o' fluff." But he was stopped because he had no idea what the intractable Miss Howard's face looked like. He had never set eyes upon her until two days ago, and then from a distance similar to that from which he viewed her now.

"So, ye want us to put the pinch on 'er," the round fellow summed it up with a glance at his partner, then turned back to Wolfe's searching gaze. Why the handsome and wealthy Sebastian Wolfe wished to kidnap a school mistress, when he had his choice of London's beautiful actresses and courtesans, and even a number of pedigreed ladies, was beyond both of them. But whatever the powerful and enigmatic Mr. Wolfe wanted, he got. Always.

"Well, ye picked the right blokes fer the job. Me and Horace can 'nap her clean as a whistle, we can. Just like we pinched old 'Lead-bottom,' that judge."

"Woke up an' found 'isself planted under a palm tree in Bermuda, 'e did, wi' no notion how 'e come there." The lean, horse-faced fellow beamed a toothy smile. "Me an' Edgar, we come back to London on the same ship, after . . . even bought th' old cod a snort in the bar. 'E never suspected a thing."

Wolfe's mouth curled up on one side at the memories they stirred; magistrate Edward "Lead-heart" Rathburn vowing to ruin him . . . former magistrate Edward "Lead-bottom" Rathburn arriving back from an unscheduled voyage to Bermuda to find that his wife and mistress had met under compromising public circumstances, the value of his investments was plummeting by the hour, and a number of his questionable legal decisions were being reviewed and correlated with suspicious upturns in his financial fortunes.

It didn't do to tangle with Sebastian Wolfe. And everyone in London's ruthlessly dignified, straitlaced, and cutthroat world of finance knew it.

"However, I suspect that pinching Miss Howard will require a bit more finesse." Wolfe's deep tones rolled softly as he watched the young woman in question ushering her charges into the local mercantile. When she was gone from sight, he lifted dark, twinkling eyes to the pair. "I doubt her bottom is made of lead."

But Miss Howard's heart, Wolfe thought, as Horace and Edgar sat back and chuckled, that was another matter altogether.

Victoria Howard oversaw the payment for goods in the little shop in the sleepy, snow-cloaked village of Bevis on the Wood. Then she escorted her young charges back out into the cold sunshine and led them down the cobbled lane toward the pillared gates of Grantley Academy for Select Young Women. She moved at a brisk pace; her shoulders square and her chin tilted at a confident but ladylike angle, which every young girl in the ranks behind her strove to imitate. Few, however, could ever hope to match the natural grace of Miss Howard's genteel, demurely bustled sway, or her shapely, statuesque form, or the exquisite classical proportions of her features.

Miss Victoria Howard was The Example, a product of Grantley Academy herself and the embodiment of all that the young girls at Grantley were taught to admire and admonished to work diligently to achieve. Possessed of coloring which was in vogue in elegant society—honey-blonde hair, peaches and cream complexion, and sky blue eyes—and accomplished in all the expected areas of languages, organizational skill, and the arts of conversation and entertainment; she was both the image and the substance of the well-bred and gently reared young Englishwoman.

But, for all her womanly gifts and glories, she suffered one deficit large enough and grave enough in the eyes of elite society to relegate her to presiding over the dormitory of an academy for young girls, instead of over the parlor of a wealthy peer's home. Miss Victoria Howard, granddaughter of a duke and daughter of a now deceased financier, was penniless.

"Come girls, quickly now. A vigorous step puts roses in your cheeks and twinkles in your eyes," she said, slowing a bit to let the head of the column pass and to give each girl a warm, encouraging smile. "Some of you still have gifts to finish, and all of you have packing to complete. The first carriages will arrive just after luncheon and you simply must not be late."

They picked up their pace along the snow-packed lane, heading toward the fir-and-ribbon draped doors of the sprawling graystone mansion known as Grantley Hall. The entry was decked for Christmas and in the lofty oak paneled entry hall, the scent of warm evergreen and beeswax tapers filled the air. In just a few hours, the girls would be packed off to their family homes to spend Christmas in the bosoms of their families, a tradition of upholding family ties at holidays, which Grantley insisted upon.

Upon the stroke of two, the first carriage arrived and for the balance of the afternoon, black lacquered coaches and polished chaise-and-fours lined the rounded drive outside. At dusk, Victoria stood on the front step with three other staff members, watching the last carriage rumble down the lane and out the gates of Grantley. As they re-entered the hall, Headmistress Meribah Chesterton halted Victoria with a hand on her arm.

"I've packing to finish, myself, Victoria," the gray, pinch-faced woman declared. "Are you quite sure you will not join me at my cousin the earl's home for the holiday? There are always so many *worthy* people to meet. And they can certainly find use for an accomplished young woman like yourself."

"Thank you, no, Miss Chesterton," Victoria said with a smile more gracious than her thoughts on that odious invitation. The idea of being a useful poor relation to her own wealthy family was distasteful; the idea of being useful to people she wasn't even related to was positively insufferable!

"You may recall, I did have an invitation from my cousin. But I am really quite content to stay on the grounds and look after things." She brightened at the thought of quiet halls, uninterrupted sleep, and two whole weeks without the strain of constantly exemplifying excellence in feminine deportment. "I shall take meals with Mr. and Mrs. Harrison"—the caretaker and his wife, the cook—"and attend Christmas Mass and have dinner with the rector and his good wife. The solitude will allow me to catch up on school correspondence and my own reading."

Headmistress Chesterton drew herself up with a smile that crinkled the papery planes of her thin face. "You are so marvelously dependable, Victoria. I knew I was right to insist the board appoint you Assistant Headmistress. Some of them thought because of your youth . . . But I convinced them of your rectitude and impeccable taste and standards. And you have proved so marvelously efficient. At the next meeting, I shall take pains to see that the board is apprised of it." She seized Victoria's hand and her voice lowered.

"In a year or two, when I step aside, I shall place your name before them with utmost confidence. And I trust that with my recommendation, they will see fit to place Grantley in your capable hands."

Victoria reddened and nodded with a reasonable facsimile of pleasure as Miss Chesterton hurried off to complete her packing. For some reason, the news that she would likely inherit the mantle of the Headmistress of Grantley had sent her spirits plummeting. She wandered back through the main hall toward the long gallery with its huge leaded windows overlooking the school's snow-draped tea garden. Feeling a sudden chill, she crossed her arms to pull her thick, Irish-knit shawl tighter around her shoulders and stood watching the phoebes and nuthatches foraging for seeds along the wintry paths.

It wasn't that she didn't like Grantley; indeed, the academy had been her second home. And it wasn't the sometimes disagreeable tasks Miss Chesterton assigned her as Assistant Headmistress; she had come to understand there was a price to pay for advancement. And it

certainly wasn't that she disliked the work; she loved the
girls and enjoyed helping them grow and prepare for their
lives as ladies of quality.

It was just that she had always expected that she would
have little girls of her own someday. And old dreams
died exceedingly hard.

She had tried being perfectly ruthless with herself, lec-
turing herself in the sternest and most bruising terms to
accept her lot and be grateful she had found a place of
value after her father's death five years ago. To an
eighteen-year-old girl on the brink of her first marriageable season in London, the double blow of losing her
only remaining parent and learning that her inheritance
must go to pay a mountain of debt, had been staggering.
Miss Chesterton's offer of a teaching post at Grantley
truly had been a godsend.

She had made quite a success of her teaching, and just
a year ago she had been elevated to the rank of Assistant
Headmistress of the prestigious girls' school. Now, at
twenty-three, she had established herself in a respectable
career and made a life for herself. But it was not the life
she had once planned. And that forfeited dream, a home
and loving family, still had the power to catch her heart
unawares and fill it with painful longings.

"Enough, Victoria Howard," she declared, turning
back toward the hall to lend a hand with closing the dormitory and seeing Headmistress Chesterton and the
teachers off on their respective journeys. "Be grateful for
your blessings, and for this rare bit of solitude."

A dark winter's night and a deepening silence settled
over the great hall of Grantley Academy. Victoria took a
bite of supper in the kitchen with the Harrisons, then
retreated to her sparsely furnished quarters on the second
floor, lighted a single lamp, and added lumps of coal to
the grate to warm the chilled room.

Seizing her buttonhook, she deposited herself in a worn
wing chair by the fire, unfastened her stiff, high-topped

Betina Krahn

shoes, and sighed in relief. With reckless abandon, she also unpinned her cameo brooch and pried open the buttons of her starched standing collar, savoring the feeling of freedom that came over her. Then she picked up the book of poetry lying on the parlor table and settled back into the chair, and into unaccustomed solitude.

The profound quiet slowly began to intrude on her awareness, then to work on her usually steady nerves. The polished marble halls outside her door began to echo with girlish whispers, the wind buffeted the frosty windows, setting them rattling, and the settling noises of the venerable old building were magnified to creaks and thumps in the stillness. Again and again, she found herself pausing in the midst of a line of verse, her shoulders tightening, her ears humming as she listened tautly for the repeat of a sound in the quiet.

Then an unmistakable noise came from the hallway, and she jerked straight in her chair and stared at the door in surprise. Setting her book aside, she rose and crept from the reassuring circle of lamplight, toward the shadowy outline of the door. As she listened, it came still again: a footstep, of that there was no doubt. She turned the door handle. The passage outside was dark and chilled, relieved only by the slice of light from her own doorway and the faint moon glow coming from the far end of the passage.

"Mr. Harrison?" she called, peering into the gloom, then inching out to search the hallway for the caretaker. "Are you there?"

There was no sound and no sign of him. Taking a quivery breath, she went to check the double doors at the far end of the hall, which led to the dormitory. All was dark and silent there. She retraced her steps then strode to the far end of the passage, to peer over the balustrade of the gallery that rimmed the cavernous main hall. Moonlight streaming through the long, leaded windows gave a silver luster to the checkered marble floor below and cast odd shadows over and around the massive old furnishings.

"You're hearing things, Victoria Howard," she declared as she retreated back down the hall and scrutinized the looming black shapes of doorways. "Don't be such a twitchit." She hurried into the glowing warmth of the lamplight, relieved to be back in her familiar quarters, and turned to close and latch the door securely.

Out of the shadows on either side of the door, they sprang at her. She gave a strangled cry of surprise and struggled as they seized her arms and waist in an iron grip. Men—there were men in her room! Hot, ruddy faces, burning eyes, pawing hands. She wrestled and shoved and fought with everything in her.

A hand with a cloth in it clamped over her nose and mouth, muffling her call for help, and as she dragged a panicky breath, her head filled with a pungent, sickly sweet odor that seeped strangely through her senses, causing her sight to dim and her ears to buzz. Her limbs grew alarmingly heavy and a second, panicky breath took her deeper under the spell of that strange vapor. Suddenly her knees were rubbery and she was sinking into a pair of restraining arms and into engulfing blackness.

Moments later, Edgar "Quickfingers" Quiggley stood before Victoria's wardrobe scowling at the meager choice that confronted him. "Ain't got room to take much," he mumbled, turning to his partner and holding up two hats. "Whaddya think, Horace? The gray with the black feathers or the dark blue with the white?"

Horace "The Ferret" Ferguson glanced up from tying a meticulous knot on the unconscious Victoria's hands and winced at her limited millinery. "Th' dark blue wi' white, no question." He regarded Victoria with a critical eye. "A bleedin' shame. Wi' 'er colorin', she oughter be wearin' that new 'Darlin' Primrose Pink' or 'Perky Periwinkle Blue.' " He craned his neck to peer past Edgar to the open valise on the floor beside him. "See if she's got anythin' to match. Laidies put stock in matchin' up.''

"Lor', she's heavier'n she looks," Horace grumbled when the pair of hired kidnappers had pinned the hat on Victoria's head, wrapped a blanket over her head, and hoisted her onto their shoulders. They carefully doused the lamp in her room.

"Right well plumped out," Edgar puffed, feeling his way through the gloom toward the darkened rear stairs of the dormitory. "Got a right purty face, too. Who'da thought?" he mused. "A schoolmarm, o' all things.''

"The Guv, 'e's got an eye fer the femmes, all right," Horace observed solemnly. As they inched along, Edgar stumbled in the dimness and nearly dropped his end of Victoria. "Edgar!" Horace shouted in a whisper. "Lookout where yer goin'! An' watch out where yer puttin' yer 'ands—this 'ere's a laidy.''

Victoria roused through the dark swirling mists in her head, to the sound of hooves and the sway of a coach or wagon around her. She moaned softly and tried to wipe away whatever was clinging to her face, but couldn't; her hands were trapped behind her, and she was lying on her side in a most uncomfortable position. Full use of her senses gradually returned, dragging with them a pounding headache and a slow-growing terror as she remembered how she came to be in such a miserable condition.

Noises, men springing at her . . .

Just then, the motions stopped, a door opened, and she was being hoisted and borne out into the chilled air. The blanket fell from her face and she glimpsed a wool-clad back below her, wet paving stones, then a door sill. Suddenly she was inside a building with polished oak floors that smelled of recent waxing. After several twists and turns, she was lowered into a sitting position and the blanket covering her was peeled back.

Taking a deep, shuddering breath, she looked up—

straight into a pair of dark, luminous eyes set in an angular male face. She recoiled and cried out, and not one but two hands clamped over her mouth to keep the sound from escaping.

"Miss Victoria Howard, I presume," came a resonant male rumble from behind those eyes. The sound of her name somehow both slowed her struggles and focused her fears. Whoever had abducted her had apparently intended her to be their victim! "Please, don't be alarmed, Miss Howard. I assure you, you are perfectly safe."

Safe. The word rumbled about in her head as those stunning eyes and that deep, penetrating voice retreated. She followed helplessly with her gaze, squinting against a torrent of bright sunlight streaming through several long, leaded windows. The man who greeted her by name was tall, dark-haired, and dressed in reassuringly fashionable clothing. Though why her kidnapper's gentlemanly taste in clothing should comfort her, she couldn't say.

She glanced frantically around her, taking in a large, walnut-paneled room lined with bookshelves that were crammed with expensive leather-bound volumes, oriental porcelain vases, bits of nautical-looking brass, and the odd stuffed owl. She was seated on a chair situated before a massive walnut desk and was being silenced by two men whose hands smelled strongly of . . . horehound drops and peppermint sticks?

"I hope you will excuse the forcefulness of my invitation, Miss Howard. But I doubt you would have accepted any other kind from me. I am Sebastian Wolfe." He made a small bow from the waist then gestured to the chamber around him. "And this is my London home."

Sebastian Wolfe. It took a moment to right itself in her mind: this was Sebastian Wolfe—financier, man of the world, the shadowy "exchequer" of London's less-than-reputable wealth. What could he possibly want with her? Then a cold drenching wave of recall sent a shiver of dread through her. Sebastian Wolfe, man of dubiously acquired power and questionable reputation, was also a *father*.

He pushed off from the desk and ambled toward her, his mouth curling into a smile which captured her gaze and would not release it. Victoria felt as if someone had set fire to her skin as he lowered his face to hers, crowding her senses and searching her face with those deep, thickly lashed eyes that seemed to perceive everything about her in a glance, including her jolt of anxiety at learning the identity of her captor.

"No doubt you are wondering what you're doing here, in my house, in my study," he continued in even, amicable tones. "It's quite simple, Miss Howard. You are here to spend the holidays with my little daughter, Margaret. Perhaps you recall her. You recently refused her admission to Grantley Academy."

The glint in his gaze probed for a response, but she felt her face flaming and forced herself to sit perfectly still. His daughter. She groaned internally. *Margaret Wolfe*. She did indeed remember. Miss Chesterton had assigned her to compose and pen the rejection letter; writing rejection letters was one of the more unpleasant duties that had fallen her way since her elevation to the post of Assistant Headmistress. And she recalled succinctly the headmistress's words on the occasion of this particular rejection: "Having dealings with a man of Mr. Wolfe's questionable character and connections could only bring trouble." Well, apparently *not* having dealings with such a man could bring trouble as well!

Sebastian Wolfe stared in surprise at the Assistant Headmistress's widening eyes—soft, velvety blue—and her ruined coif and the crumpled hat that dangled artlessly from the back of her head. Miss Howard was much younger than he'd expected and a great deal fresher; she had none of the air of fusty, withered femininity he had expected. And she was blond—rampantly blond. His eyes defied him to drift over her straining blouse and neatly cinched waist. She was nicely rounded. Indecently curvy, in fact, for an assistant headmistress. He felt an odd thickening sensation in his middle and shifted his weight on his feet. Against his better judgment, he nodded to Horace and Edgar to release her.

"How dare you abduct me from my post, sir," she declared, bristling away from them the instant her hands were free. "I demand you release me at once."

"I dare, Miss Howard, because I know the nature and the limits of power, both my kind of power and yours," he said matter-of-factly. "And, I dare because I adore my little daughter and will go to whatever lengths necessary to assure her future."

"To assure her future?" she choked out.

"Indeed. You see, you have made a mistake in judging my daughter unsuitable for your academy, Miss Howard. She is a bright, inquisitive, and delightful child who deserves the very best, including the celebrated advantages of Grantley Academy. I am certain that after a fortnight with her—studying her, coming to know her—you will see the error of your judgment and be more than willing to reverse your decision."

"You cannot be serious," she declared, sitting straighter, clamping a tight hand on her display of her disbelief. He expected her to credit that he had kidnapped her so she could meet and re-evaluate his daughter as an applicant to Grantley? The man was mad as a hatter!

"I assure you, Miss Howard, I am utterly serious." There was indeed a knell of conviction in his voice, which only served to nudge Victoria's anxiety higher.

"You cannot keep me here against my will." Her voice rose as she scrambled to think. "I'll be missed! The headmistress will contact the authorities and—"

"The headmistress and the teachers have all left the school grounds for the holidays," he countered, leaning closer with a smile that seemed to contain more amusement than malice. "You see, I was most careful in the timing of this invitation, Miss Howard."

"The caretaker and cook will find me gone and notify—"

"No one," he finished for her. "For they have found a letter in your hand this morning, stating that you have been unexpectedly called away to your dear cousin's house to tend an ailing aunt." She watched the satisfaction spreading through his expression and scrambled to think of another flaw in his wretched plan.

"They will find my things, my clothes, and know I would never go off without them," she declared.

"Oh, but your things came, too," Wolfe said, gesturing to the men on either side of her. "Mr. Quiggley and Mr. Ferguson were good enough to pack for you, weren't you, gentlemen?" She looked up to find two men in gaudily checkered wool coats tipping their bowler hats to her.

"Bro't what we could, Miz," the stout, fleshy-faced fellow informed her with an eager nod, pressing his headgear to his chest. "An' made sure everythin' matches."

"It was me an' Edgar what tucked th' letter under th' caretaker's door . . . slick as a whistle," the sallow, spindly fellow on her other side announced with professional pride.

Victoria stared between Sebastian Wolfe and his henchmen with mounting anxiety. They were madmen, the lot of them, albeit, remarkably efficient madmen. They seemed to have thought of everything in planning her abduction. A cool trickle of fear slid down her spine, drawing warmth and color from her hands and face. She was outnumbered, outmaneuvered, and in unfamiliar surroundings. The only chance she had, she realized, was to bide her time and watch for the means and the opportunity to escape.

"Well," she said with what she hoped would pass for reluctant surrender, "it would appear you have thought of everything, Mr. Wolfe. Except the possibility that I will find your daughter as ill-bred and unappealing as yourself."

The wry humor that had softened his face faded somewhat, allowing harder angles to emerge. "I deem that a rather remote possibility, Miss Howard. My little Margaret is . . . quite irresistible." His gaze flowed over her face, bodice, and waist, with insulting thoroughness, and the impressions he collected spun a strand of silk through his voice. "And I do not imagine that you are the sort of woman to resist the irresistible."

Under his intense scrutiny she sat immobile, unable to summon a proper, ladylike burst of outrage. Never in her comparatively sheltered life, had a man looked at her so directly, so intimately. She was instantly aware that her blouse was rumpled and partly unbuttoned, her hair hung in humiliating tangles, and her hat dangled haplessly from the back of her head. *Irresistible.* There were unsettling layers of meaning in his luminous eyes and provocative words—things she didn't quite understand—things she wasn't sure she wanted to know about. It was a long moment before she realized she was staring at him and jerked back, blushing.

"The apple does not fall far from the tree, Mr. Wolfe," she said irritably, scrambling for an appropriately disdainful response. "And it does not take much fortitude to resist a bad apple."

Wolfe's eyebrows flicked up as he studied both her reddened face and her remark. His wide, sensual mouth curled up on one end. "Allow me to show you to your quarters, Miss Howard." He extended a gentlemanly hand to her. "I think it might be a good idea if you rest and refresh yourself before you meet . . . the *bad apple* of my eye."

Spurning his hand, she shoved to her feet and found herself standing in only one shoe. She snatched her skirts aside and stared at her stockinged toes in horror. "My shoe, where is my other shoe?" She followed Wolfe's quizzical gaze as he turned to the two miscreants who had abducted her.

"It must 'ave come off . . . somewheres . . ." The plump one reddened and shrugged.

Her movement reminded her of her dangling hat, and she reached up to pull it off and inspect its crumpled felt crown and ruined feathers. She turned a scathing glare on Sebastian Wolfe. "My best shoes, now my best hat. You'll pay for this, sir!"

"No doubt I will, Miss Howard." His wide shoulders twitched oddly, and he seemed to be biting his lower lip as he seized her elbow to escort her to the door. "And I feel certain I can rely on you to keep an accounting for me."

2

SHE WAS PROPELLED ALONG A WIDE, WELL-LIGHTED hallway carpeted with thick-tufted runners that felt somehow indecent beneath her one naked foot. Her mind raced as she lurched along on one shoe, clutching her bedraggled hat and feeling her bustle sinking alarmingly down her derriere. She had to find a way out of here!

The passage ended in a stately entry hall, dominated by a massive, curved mahogany staircase. The soft rug gave way to cold, polished marble and the gaslight gave way to bright sun which streamed in golden shafts through long windows located along the gallery above. The hall was decorated with pilasters and intricate ceiling frescoes, a massive crystal chandelier, and large, ornately carved furnishings. But Victoria had eyes only for the huge brass-bound doors and the possibility of reaching the street outside.

As they reached the staircase, she jerked to a halt and bent to remove her other shoe. His hold on her arm slackened just enough, and she whirled and bashed him in the stomach with her shoe, then bolted straight for the front doors. He grunted and bent slightly, more surprised than hurt. After a stunned second, he raced after her. ''Ohhh, no!''

Her stockinged feet slid on the marble and she skidded into the massive doors and fumbled for the brass handles. But just as the door swung open and she glimpsed freedom, he plowed into the heavy portal with his shoulder, slamming it shut. She recoiled frantically, but he snagged her arm and reeled her to him. He managed to get a hand on her wrist, then an arm around her ribs, and hauled her hard against him, pinning her back to his front.

''You'll regret this!'' she cried, flailing and pushing at the arms clamped around her waist.

''I doubt it, Miss Howard,'' he panted, hoisting her off her feet and carrying her toward the stairs. ''As you will learn, I am a very determined man. I always get what I want.''

He wrestled her, kicking and squirming, up the great stairs, around a short gallery, and started down a broad hallway. The sight of bedchamber doors and the shocking feel of his arms clamped forcefully around her, roused new fears of a fate worse than mere captivity. But, outmuscled and out of breath, she was reduced to hoarse groans and frantic flailing.

''Papa!''

A clear, girlish voice penetrated their struggles and Sebastian Wolfe froze at the sound. His abrupt halt caused Victoria to slow, then stop midkick, as well. He wrested the two of them around to find a young girl in a starched ruffled pinafore and curls, standing at the end of the hallway, watching them.

''Can I play, too?'' she called eagerly, running toward them with a uniformed maid trotting nervously at her heels.

''Not . . . just now, Meggie,'' Wolfe caught his breath to reply. He straightened and his arms around Victoria tightened, as if cautioning her to remain silent.

''I'm so s-sorry, Mr. Wolfe,'' the nursery maid stammered, reaching for her charge. But Meggie tussled out of her grip and hurried closer, staring at Victoria's reddened face and wildly tousled hair. Her eyes widened.

"Is she the lady you said was coming to visit us?"

"She is." He sounded oddly hoarse. "This is Miss Howard, Meggie. Miss Howard"—his ragged voice was laden with undercurrents of warning Victoria understood without knowing just how—"may I present my daughter, Margaret." His arm cinched still tighter around Victoria's ribs and she stiffened, scarcely able to breathe and completely at a loss for how to respond to an introduction to her kidnapper's offspring. "Your manners, Meggie," he prompted the child.

"Oh!" Meggie giggled and made a perfectly charming curtsy. "How good to meet you, Miss Howard."

Margaret Wolfe was without a doubt the prettiest child Victoria had ever seen. She had huge hazel eyes set in a pixieish heart of a face, and a thick fall of auburn ringlets held by a pink satin bow on the crown of her head. There was no mistaking that straight little nose, that full, saucy mouth, and those thickly lashed eyes; she was a perfect miniature of her worldly, unscrupulous father.

"I'm glad you're here," she declared, beaming a smile that would have melted holes in armor plate. "Papa says we'll have lots of have fun together."

"Your father told you I was coming?" Victoria said breathlessly, scarcely realizing she had spoken her thoughts aloud. What sort of man informed his six-year-old daughter that he intended to kidnap a schoolmistress?

"Oh, yes!" Margaret nodded and held up four neat little fingers. "And that when you came that would mean there were only four days left until . . ." The significance of Victoria's presence suddenly dawned in her face. "Then there are only four days left until Christmas! And we can make the sweet treats and candies, and hang the greens around the door! And Papa will put up a big tree in the parlor, and we shall have presents and surprises when Father Christmas comes!" She bobbled up and down, then lunged toward them with open arms.

"Meggie, no!" Wolfe barked out, dragging Victoria back a step and halting Meggie in her tracks. He cleared his throat. "Manners, please. Miss Howard has had a . . . tiring journey. And I was just taking her to her room." The little girl looked a bit crestfallen, then frowned as her gaze dropped to the way Victoria was teetering on her toes.

"Why? Can't she walk?"

Wolfe's arms loosened around Victoria's waist to allow her to slide down his front, fully onto her feet. "Of course, she can walk. I was just . . ." Victoria glared over her shoulder at him as he explained his behavior to his little daughter. "She was limping a bit earlier," he said, conjuring an artful half-truth, "and I was just helping her along to her room."

"Oh."

"Go along with Odelle, back to the schoolroom, and we'll see you at dinner"—he nodded to the maid to retrieve her—"after Miss Howard has had a chance to rest and freshen up."

Meggie shoved her hands into the big pockets of her pinafore with a sigh, but she allowed the maid to take her by the shoulders and didn't have to be reminded of her manners this time. Dropping another perfect curtsy to Victoria, she produced a wistful smile. "I'm glad you and Christmas are both finally here, Miss Howard."

Victoria watched in complete turmoil as the little girl and her nursery maid disappeared around the corner of the gallery. Sebastian Wolfe had told his daughter that she was coming to be their guest for Christmas, and had actually encouraged the child to look forward to it! Then perhaps he truly had kidnapped her in order to change her mind about admitting his daughter to Grantley! She didn't know whether to feel relieved or outraged.

But her reaction to his scheme was only part of her mounting confusion, for at that moment she was experiencing a reaction to the man himself. His hard arms encircled her waist and his long, lean body had nudged her beleaguered bustle aside to mold tightly against her from her shoulders to her knees. She felt surrounded and engulfed by him . . . and the feeling wasn't at all unpleasant.

He was broad-shouldered, angular, and stood a full head taller than she. The warmth of his big frame was slowly seeping through the rumpled layers of her clothing, and faint but unmistakable wisps of sandalwood, tobacco, and soap curled on eddies of body heat through her head and lungs. A warm tide of sensual confusion washed her from head to toe, leaving her skin tingling and exquisitely sensitive wherever their bodies touched.

He seemed in no hurry to release her. His hold on her waist relaxed gradually, and she managed to turn within the circle of his arms and brace the heels of her palms against his fashionable shot-silk vest. But she was somehow unable to summon the force needed to push away. He flooded her vision; his wide, generous mouth with its full, velvety lips . . . his dark, absorbing eyes with their feathery lashes . . . smooth skin stretched over prominent cheekbones . . . aristocratic nose . . .

"You've nothing to fear, Miss Howard." Her eyes were drawn helplessly back to his fascinating mouth. "I have taken every precaution to see that you are not . . . compromised," he said in a hushed, intimate voice that somehow thickened her blood in her veins. "Your impeccable reputation is every bit as important to me as it is to you." Her gaze slid upward into his and as she watched, crinkles formed at the edges of his eyes. He was smiling. "After all, it is your good name that will give weight to your recommendation of Meggie to Grantley."

It took a moment to connect properly in her mind: reputation, Grantley, recommendation. Her heart gave an odd downward lurch in her chest. She thrust back forcefully against his arms, surprising him and briefly breaking his hold on her. He quickly recaptured her arm.

"You wretched bully," she declared, burning with a

uniquely feminine fury that he would take pains to preserve her virtuous name, only to serve his own selfish ends. "You kidnap me to force me to recommend your daughter—"

"Kidnap. Force. Such ugly words," he said, wagging his head as he reeled her toward him. He caught her other arm and pulled her close, searching her reddened face and rigid shoulders. "I cannot force you to recommend anyone, and we both know it. It is my intention to let Meggie herself convince you. And failing that, to try to persuade you."

"What makes you think you could possibly persuade me, after treating me in such an abominable manner? Why, I wouldn't—"

"You make me think that, Miss Howard," he countered smoothly. "You are highly regarded at Grantley. You are considered an excellent teacher and a promising administrator. A woman of your discernment will certainly recognize Meggie's worth." His voice lowered as his gaze slid over her with undisguised appreciation. "And a woman of your insight and compassion would not in conscience hold a father's conduct against a young, innocent child."

Victoria all but strangled on the hot responses clamoring on the back of her tongue. The man was totally without principles! He quailed at nothing, from brute force to bald flattery! He would not only trade on her virtuous reputation, he fully intended to take advantage of her morality, her character, and her professional ethics as well! She was speechless with outrage as he pulled her down the hall and into a large, formally furnished bedchamber bathed in gauzy, lace-filtered sunlight.

"These will be your rooms during your stay, Miss Howard. I think you will find them comfortable." He gestured to a door on the far side of a huge tester bed. "There is a bathing chamber through that door. I'll send someone up to light the grate and have Claudette come and unpack for you and draw you a bath. Dinner will be served at six-thirty. Not strictly fashionable, I know,'' he said wryly, ''but Meggie gets too hungry to wait until eight.''

''I can tell you now, it won't succeed,'' she declared, trying to pull her wrist from his grip and trying to not look directly at him. She lost both battles.

''But of course it will. You will find my daughter perfectly wonderful, Miss Howard. And you will be as eager to introduce her to life at Grantley as I am to have her attend school there.'' He produced another of those roguish and beguiling smiles that caused her pulse to jump, and the rise of his eyebrows and the way he glanced at her hand said he had felt her involuntary reaction.

''It won't work''—she tugged on her arm, scrambling for a verbal weapon and without realizing it, seized a remarkably potent one—''because it isn't your daughter that Grantley finds objectionable.''

It was true. The objections raised against Margaret Wolfe's admission to Grantley had concerned her father's questionable character and business dealings. Sebastian Wolfe, who had risen from seemingly nowhere with enviably deep pockets, had a canny—some said ''predatory''—sense for spotting failing business concerns and buying or lending heavily to gain interest in their stocks. In London's financial district, The City, few had escaped dealing with Sebastian Wolfe, and it was said that few of the shady, even criminal, elements in London's rough East Side avoided his broad financial web either. Around his name hung an aura of indulgence, spiced by vague whispers of ''actresses'' and ''liaisons.'' Sebastian Wolfe was simply not the sort of man Grantley's Board of Governors considered a fit association for a highly regarded girl's school.

''I am well aware of that, Miss Howard.'' Something in his dark eyes seemed to close, and he released her wrist and dropped his hands to his sides. Turning toward the door, he paused and looked back at her. ''I shall have to trust your discretion, not mentioning the forceful nature of your 'invitation' to Meggie. As you undoubtedly guessed, she knows nothing of your abduction. And I would hate to worry her.''

The tall, paneled door closed and there was a metallic scrape in the lock before she could react. A vivid picture of Meggie Wolfe flashed into her mind, those bright eyes, that bubbly laugh. She couldn't imagine the child's reaction to learning that her father behaved like a common criminal, abducting ladies to force them to comply with his wishes while demanding they behave with boundless compassion. She sat down with an unladylike plop on the brocade-covered bench at the foot of the tester bed.

As bad as Sebastian Wolfe's reputation was, she thought, Sebastian Wolfe himself was proving to be even worse! Her eyes narrowed as she rubbed the reddened wrist he had just released. And until her opinion of him changed, he hadn't a prayer of getting her to recommend his daughter, no matter how irresistible she proved to be!

Out in the gaslit hallway, Sebastian stared at the door he had just locked, but saw only Victoria Howard's tousled blond form. His arms, chest, and belly were alive with the tactile memory of her soft curves wriggling against them, and the heat generated by those lingering sensations poured straight into his blood and began to pool in his passion-starved loins.

Miss Victoria Howard, Grantley's grand example of efficiency, propriety, and accomplishment, had proved to be a curvy, blond bit of temptation wrapped in prim, schoolmistress trappings. Those long, sooty lashes and pout-prone lips, that delectably defiant body and responsive pulse—she was appallingly desirable!

The investigation he had initiated of her had provided details of her high family connections, her admirable record as a teacher, and her unassailable respectability. From such he had concluded she was just what he needed to implement his scheme: a woman of impeccable character, breeding, and reputation, who seemed to genuinely like children and might be persuaded to overlook his checkered reputation on his daughter's behalf. He closed his eyes, trapping the vision of her inside his head, and felt his loins tighten.

The last thing he had expected was to find himself roused and ranting after the schoolmistress he had abducted and decreed must spend the next fortnight under his roof! He groaned and jerked his eyes open, then strode hurriedly to the staircase and the safety of his study. Why the hell couldn't she have been a proper prune, like every other schoolmistress he'd seen?

When he reached his book-lined sanctuary, he found Edgar Quiggley and Horace Ferguson waiting patiently, hats in hand, for him to return and pay them for their services. He sank down in the high-backed leather chair behind his desk and settled a dark, turbulent look on the pair of them. They, of all men, knew what such a look on Sebastian Wolfe's face portended.

"Be somethin' wrong, Mister Wolfe?" Horace stiffened, shooting a glance of alarm at his partner.

"We didn' mean to loose 'er shoe ner squash 'er feathers, Mr. Wolfe," Edgar declared, nervously shifting feet and fingering the brim of his bowler. "Honest."

Sebastian leaned back in his chair, templed and tapped his long, elegant fingers, and scrutinized them. "Quiggley, Ferguson." He finally broke the silence and the tension. "How would you like to do another little job for me?"

Relief was visible in the sag of their shoulders and in the glances they exchanged. "We'd be purely honored t' help ye out, Gov," Horace declared.

"Miss Howard is something less than thrilled with the idea of being my guest for the holidays. I think it would be wise to have you stay and see that she doesn't try to leave before her visit is through."

Horace drew his long chin back and gave Sebastian a wily grin. "Say no more, Guv. Ye got jus' the blokes fer the job."

As they left, minutes later, Sebastian congratulated

himself on finding the perfect solution to both his problems. With "Quickfingers" and "the Ferret" guarding Victoria Howard, he wouldn't have to worry about her disappearing out a side door and wouldn't have any opportunity to act on the unholy temptation she presented.

Upstairs, the matronly serving woman was going about the unpacking and freshening of Victoria's garments, and when the maid disappeared into the bathing chamber, she saw her chance and darted for the door. But, throwing it open, she found herself nose to nose with the miscreants who had abducted her. They stood blocking the door, their hats in their hands, one looking like a Norfolk dumpling and the other like a rasher of bacon.

"Mornin', Miz." The short, stout one nodded and flushed.

"The Guv, he asked us to see ye don' get lost," the tall, thin one explained with an apologetic bob of the head. "Edgar an' me, we'll just be right out 'ere, if'n ye need anythin'."

"Sorry about yer . . . yer tail-feathers, Miz," the short one said, wincing as he gestured to her drooping bustle. "We didn' mean to drop ye. It's jus' ye were a mite heavy."

Victoria followed their rueful stares to her sagging bustle, turned beet red, and slammed the door. Jerking up her skirt, she tore through her limp petticoats until she came to her bustle frame. The metal bands were crumpled such that several of the rivets had popped. She hoisted the rest of her skirts, jerked the ties of the ruined contraption, and let it fall at her feet.

"My shoes, my hat, now my bustle," she hissed through clenched teeth. From the corner of her eye she caught sight of her ruined hair, stockinged feet, and bedraggled clothes in the cheval mirror. "You'll pay, Sebastian Wolfe."

* * *

Victoria arrived at the door of the dining room, under the close escort of her host's apologetic henchmen. She wore her best—her dark blue worsted skirt, her tucked-front blouse with the leg-o'-mutton sleeves, and her fitted jacket with the satin piping trim and the brooch watch pinned neatly to the shoulder—and felt ready to cross wits with Sebastian Wolfe again.

She took two steps into the huge dining room and stopped stock-still. Two delicate French cutwork chandeliers showered dazzling light over rich, claret-red brocades, gilded moldings, and dark, highly polished mahogany. The long dining table would have easily seated twenty and was situated on a huge red Persian carpet of purely regal proportions. The silver-laden sideboards were attended by four black-clad servants, and the table was laid with glittering china and crystal.

Dinner in Sebastian Wolfe's house was apparently an occasion of state. She was instantly aware of the unnatural droop of her bustle and of the chill of the floor against her shoeless feet. She wasn't here by choice, she reminded herself sternly. She had no reason to feel intimidated.

Wolfe stood in front of a massive marble hearth crowned by a large gilded mirror, looking tall, dark, and elegant in slim, piped trousers, an impeccably fitted black cutaway, and a pristine white vest and silk tie. Every aspect of his appearance, from the richness of his evening clothes to the casual authority of his posture, radiated supreme confidence. He was unlike any man she had ever met. It was all she could do to maintain a semblance of poise as she approached under his intense and highly personal scrutiny.

Sebastian watched her surveying his dining room, then himself, with her cool blue eyes and regal air. She had been born to privilege and authority, and even in her absurd circumstance carried a natural sense of them with her. She was an interesting woman, Victoria Howard. Cool and curvy, pink-cheeked yet proper, rigid one moment, responsive the next. He watched her hackles rising as she approached. Then she planted herself an arm's distance away, reached into her pocket, and without saying a word presented him a folded sheet of paper.

"Good evening to you, too, Miss Howard," he said, appraising the purposeful glint in her eye and trying not to let his gaze linger too long on the stubborn set of her delectable lower lip. "What is this?" He accepted the note from her and opened it, scanning the now familiar feminine script. "One pair of shoes, Taylor and Company, six pounds, nine and seven." His mouth twitched at the corner. Good Lord. She was dunning him for damages received!

"I'll have six pounds, nine and seven pence, sir," she demanded regally. "Or the equivalent in a pair of shoes." She jerked the tail of her jacket down and raised her nose a notch. "Unless it is a part of your plan to keep me shoeless as well as imprisoned for the next fortnight."

"One lady's hat," he read on, "finest silk-lined felt with white egret feathers, four pounds, nine and tuppence. One lady's foundation . . ." His eyebrows rose. "Your foundation has been damaged, too?" Taking full advantage of the opportunity she had handed him, he craned his neck from side to side to slide his gaze over her bosom, waist, and skirts with taunting thoroughness. "Just which part of your foundation isn't functioning up to snuff, Miss Howard? I must say, you look perfectly well put together, to me."

She flamed and took a step back. It was an outrage, having to discuss the calamitous state of her very most personal accoutrements with him. But she desperately needed shoes and was determined to make him replace them, along with her other ruined belongings. "My skirt frame," she choked out. "My bustle was severely damaged. And if I recall properly, you did invite me to keep an accounting of my losses."

He bit his lip. "Goodness." He paused, swallowed, then said with strained solemnity, "We certainly cannot have you going about with a damaged foundation." He glanced back at the paper. "Three pounds, seven and sixpence. Well, at least I shan't have to float a loan—"

"Papa! Miss Howard!" Meggie came racing into the dining room, but slowed at the sight of her father's chastising frown, and proceeded at a more mannerly pace to the fireplace. She gave Victoria a perfunctory curtsy and threw her arms around her father for a big hug. "I can't wait. Cook has made her special Tipsy Raspberry Trifle for dessert." Her eyes twinkled and she lowered her voice to a hush. "She says it could even sweeten up a sourpuss schoolmarm."

"Your cook said that, did she?" Victoria's eyes narrowed ever so slightly as Meggie nodded, grinning, clearly oblivious to the insult she'd just relayed.

"Cook is rather opinionated," Sebastian said, watching Victoria's reaction with a half smile. "She also tends to overestimate the power of her raspberry trifle. I personally think it may take a bit more to sweeten up a sour schoolmarm."

"Indeed," Victoria replied, feeling her face heat under his annoyingly personal regard. "Something more in the way of a good pair of *shoes*, perhaps."

Sebastian laughed quietly and took both Meggie and Victoria by the elbow, steering them to the table and seating Meggie in the chair to the left of the head of the table, then Victoria in the chair on the right. When he was seated and had motioned to the butler to begin serving, he found Victoria examining both the table service and Meggie with a questioning eye.

"Margaret is allowed at table with you?" she said, copying his mannerism of one raised eyebrow. Her question and her air of reserve declared her determination to resist his charm, his hospitality, and his daughter.

"She is," he said in clipped tones. "We take dinner together every evening, Miss Howard, in just this fashion." Irritation flared in him as her lush, perfect mouth tightened further with disapproval. "If I had a dozen children, they would all take their dinners with me at this table on this china. And they would all display impeccable manners.''

From any other man such a statement would have seemed an ill-bred boast. But Sebastian Wolfe was a man who knew what he wanted and let nothing stand in the way of getting it. If he wanted perfectly mannered children, Victoria couldn't help thinking, then he would likely find a way to produce such rare and exceptional creatures. Her gaze slid into his and couldn't stop the flush of her cheeks as he battered his way past her visual defenses to challenge her aloofness and the exalted standards of propriety by which she judged them.

Be fair, Miss Howard, his look said. See Meggie as a person.

She ripped her gaze from his and dropped it to the fine porcelain spread before her, still seeing the glint of his compelling eyes in her mind. When she raised her head, she spotted Meggie unfolding her napkin and placing it on her lap, then taking a drink from her water goblet, all with ladylike aplomb. His wordless challenge began to take root inside her.

By the end of the soup and the serving of the salad course, Victoria had to admit she was surprised by six-year-old Margaret's ladylike behavior. She could not help but contrast it to the deportment of the younger girls who arrived at Grantley each year. Some, even those from the finest of houses, behaved like little hooligans—snatching, squabbling, and squealing until the staff and the older girls took them in hand.

Then Meggie looked up from her fruited ice, between courses, and caught Victoria staring at her, and she smiled. It was a wary smile, one that sought approval as much as expressed it, and Victoria found herself utterly caught in those huge, taffy-colored eyes, which were so much like Sebastian Wolfe's.

There was an irresistible openness in that little face, an eagerness for all of living and learning and doing. As Meggie's smile warmed, her acceptance of Victoria and her desire to please tugged at something in Victoria's heart. Margaret Wolfe was an innocent. She had probably never known trouble or disappointment or rejection; she was the very picture of a child well loved and secure in her world. Victoria felt a sudden tightness in her chest. She had known that feeling of warmth and complete security, too, once. She had been a Meggie Wolfe herself, not so many years ago.

She returned Meggie a small but genuine smile, knowing even as she did, that it was probably a mistake. A smile here, a gesture there, and the barriers of sense and sensibility would soon come crumbling down.

Sebastian saw that smile. In the silence, every nerve in his body had focused on Victoria Howard, seeking some sign that he hadn't been wrong, that she could eventually warm to Meggie. And there it was: a small upward curve of her lips, followed by a telltale softening of her eyes and a slight relaxation of her perfectly straight shoulders. A huge burden seemed to slide from the middle of his chest. It didn't appear that Victoria Howard's heart was made of lead at all.

"Did you know, Meggie," he said in a buoyant tone, "that Miss Howard is a teacher, at a school?"

"She is?" Meggie glanced at him, then back at Victoria with piqued interest. "I'm going to go to a school, Papa said. He says it will be ever so much fun."

"He does, does he?" Victoria cast him an accusing look and he answered with a confident smile. Meggie nodded, then her shoulders rounded and she grew thoughtful.

"What do they do at a school?" she asked, studying Victoria.

"Well, they learn things," Victoria informed her. "The girls have lessons in drawing and music, in writing and languages. Sometimes they learn sports like badminton or how to ride horses. And they learn ladylike ways to walk and talk and behave and how to use proper etiquette."

"You mean manners?" Meggie perked up. When Victoria nodded she beamed at having gotten it right. "Papa says manners are ver-r-ry important."

"He says that, does he?" Victoria resisted the temptation to glare at Sebastian.

"Oh!" Meggie wriggled on her seat and drew her knees up under her to lean forward with her face aglow. "Who eats at a king's table but *never* uses a napkin?"

"I beg your pardon?" Victoria drew back, scowling at Meggie, then at Sebastian.

"I believe it is a riddle, Miss Howard." He seemed amused by her confusion. "Meggie and I often trade riddles at dinner."

"It keeps our wits sharp!" Meggie added, and she and her father nodded adamantly to each other. "Do you know what it is?" She turned an expectant look on Victoria and when Victoria frowned, thinking, she prompted: "Who eats at a king's table but never uses a napkin?"

"Certainly someone with very bad manners," Victoria pronounced.

"A fly!" Meggie crowed. "I have another one. When can you expect, to be quite correct," she recited in a singsong voice, "although you would wish, to serve milk in a dish?"

"Milk in a dish . . ." Victoria frowned, feeling herself being drawn into the game and telling herself it was probably a bad idea. She shook her head.

"When you feed a kitten!" Meggie declared, thrilled to have stumped their grown-up lady guest.

"Well then, I have one for you," Victoria countered, with a determined look. "Riddle me, riddle me, what is that? Over your head and under your hat?"

"That's easy," Meggie said, her eyes twinkling. "*My hair.* Papa told me that one a long time ago."

"Very well. No more easy ones, then," Victoria declared, leaning forward. "England, Ireland, Scotland, and Wales. What has no head but oodles of tails?"

Meggie squinted and muttered the last part of the line

to herself. She finally shrugged and looked to her father, who rolled his gaze toward the ceiling and scoured the glittering chandeliers as if he hid riddle answers in them.

"A book of stories," he guessed correctly, then turned a mischievous smile on Victoria. "I warn you, Miss Howard, we know a great many riddles. Riddle me this: What cannot be seen, but can only be heard; cannot speak unless it is spoken to?" After a moment, when Victoria had to shake her head, he turned to Meggie. "You answer, Pippin."

"An echo!" she cried. "Now, riddle me: You carry it everywhere, but it has no weight." She giggled when Victoria guessed wrong. "Your name!" she declared.

On they went, through fish and fowl and meat courses, riddling and answering, and with each exchange Victoria felt her anxiety melting into incredulity. Here she sat, victim of a kidnapping, dining in the most elegant surrounding she had been in for years, and trading riddles with a six-year-old child. After a while, Cook herself trundled in the Tipsy Raspberry Trifle on a serving cart and oversaw its portioning and distribution. It was absolute heaven, a delicate combination of sherry-laced cake, creamy pudding, thick swirls of raspberry preserves and mounds of whipped cream. At the first bite, her toes curled and she remembered her bare feet.

"I have one for you. I just remembered it," Victoria said, between bites of frothy cream. "Full at work and empty at rest, both of them are souls hard pressed. What are they?"

Sebastian and Meggie traded frowns, and he rubbed his chin thoughtfully. Victoria couldn't decide if he truly didn't know or was just holding back the answer. "Give up?" They both nodded, and she pinned Sebastian with a meaning-filled look and said, *"A pair of shoes."*

Sebastian leaned back in his chair and laughed softly at her pointed reminder of his debt to her. "Then answer this one, if you please, Miss Howard. What is round as an apple and flat as a chip, has two eyes, but can't see a bit?'' He glanced at his daughter's eager face. ''Don't tell her, Meggie.''

''Mmmm.'' She halted a fork full of trifle halfway to her mouth. ''A button?''

''A lucky guess,'' he said to Meggie and she giggled. Then a light seemed to dawn in her pixie face.

''I have one, a new one. Riddle me this: What is wild as a thunder clap, grabs you like a beaver trap . . .'' She puckered up her mouth trying to remember, then brightened. ''Given or taken with a squeeze, melts the bones right in your knees?''

Sebastian gave a short, surprised laugh. Squeezes, melting bones, and knees, he knew instantly what *he* would make of such a combination and that instinctive response sent an unexpected swirl of heat through him. ''That is a new one,'' he said thickly, stealing a furtive glance at Victoria's eminently squeezable curves and recalling too well the feel of them pressed tight against him. When she turned to meet his gaze, he reddened and shifted his attention to Meggie.

''Give up?'' she asked. When they both nodded, she announced: ''A kiss!''

Seized by some wretched impulse, Victoria looked straight at Sebastian. And that same unholy instinct must have seized him, for he looked straight at her. Their gazes locked. Heat bloomed in her cheeks. Crimson began creeping up his neck into his ears.

As if controlled by some other power, her gaze slid to his lips. And his slid to hers.

A kiss.

Meggie's movement brought them hurtling back to reality. Victoria jerked back, averted her eyes and stiffened; Sebastian snapped forward and fixed Meggie with a stern look.

''Where did you hear such a thing, Margaret? I want you to tell me this minute.''

''I-is it bad?'' Meggie looked between the two scarlet-faced adults with anxious eyes.

"It is not naughty. But such talk is not for your young ears." He glanced at Victoria's stiff face and rigid posture and ground his teeth together, praying that she wouldn't hold the riddle or his instinctively lusty reaction to it against Meggie. Whatever was he thinking, letting his personal responses get mixed up in so important a process? He knew better than that. "Tell me, Margaret."

She looked up at her father with a trembling chin. "Stephen the coachman said it to Odelle, and she laughed."

Repeating servant talk. He groaned privately. Here was certain fodder for Miss Howard's disapproval. And from her expression, she intended to make use of it. Of all the wretched luck, and just when he thought they might be making progress.

"In future, Meggie," he said, reaching across the immaculate linen to giving her hand a squeeze, "it's probably best not to repeat what servants say . . . in company." Meggie nodded, somewhat relieved. "Now, if we're all finished, I'll have Pearson serve our coffee in the drawing room."

Victoria hadn't thought anything could feel quite so humiliating as being forced to go without shoes. But she had just learned she was wrong. Being caught staring at a man's mouth like it was raspberry trifle, having her senses clamor hungrily after a pair of lips and feeling her body go all warm and twiddly inside as she imagined how they would feel, *that* was true humiliation. Especially when the mouth in question belonged to the unconscionable scoundrel who had abducted her and made no bones about taking advantage of her higher instincts to suit his purpose. If he ever discovered she had a few lower instincts, she thought with a shiver, he would undoubtedly try to exploit them, as well!

3

As they entered the drawing room, she stiffly removed her elbow from his influence and steered herself to the glowing fireplace. Like the other rooms of the house, the drawing room was the essence of baroque design—brocades, thick Persian rugs, carved furnishings decorated with gilt overlay, and intricate plaster moldings on ceiling and walls. Everything bore the stamp of Sebastian Wolfe's expensive taste, except for a small wooden rocker situated near the hearth, and a rather plain and somewhat battered piano standing nearby.

The chair was explained the moment Meggie settled herself in it, and part of the piano's purpose was revealed a short while later, when Wolfe asked Meggie to play a song for them. The chair and piano were Meggie's effect on Sebastian Wolfe's luxurious room, perhaps evidence of her effect on the man himself. As Meggie climbed up onto the piano stool and settled herself, Victoria couldn't help looking at him and recognizing the warmth and pride in his face. Whatever else he was, the thought surprised her, Sebastian Wolfe seemed to be a concerned father.

Meggie played a little Bach piece with careful, girlish precision, then was asked to play another. Victoria's fingers began to move on her lap, imitating, then anticipating the fingerings. A warm, unexpected wave of remembrance flowed over her and for a fleeting moment she was six-almost-seven again and her feet were dangling from a piano stool. It was a memory so keen, so sweet, that it left her with a tightness in her chest as the music died and it subsided. She came to her senses when Wolfe applauded quietly and went to give Meggie a hand down from the stool. They paused before Victoria as they passed the hearth.

"Meggie has lessons from a music master once a week," he said, searching Victoria's reaction. She ignored him to focus on the little girl's hopeful face and smiled.

"You play well, Margaret. I remember practicing those same pieces, years ago."

"You play, Miss Howard?" Wolfe asked, appraising her from a slightly different angle.

"I do, though not with any regularity," she admitted. "With all my duties, I have little time."

"Perhaps you would play for us now," he suggested. And before she could demur or protest her lack of preparation, he was reaching for her hand and ushering her to the piano. In short order, she found herself seated and facing a rank of ivory keys, with two pairs of eyes watching her expectantly. Annoyance boiled up in her at the way he had turned the tables, so that he now sat in judgment on her. He was a sly one, Sebastian Wolfe.

She limbered her fingers and began to play, surprised by the steadiness of her hands and the surety of her reach. The music began to tumble out, then to flow. When she ended her third selection, Wolfe and Meggie applauded, and she sat back, a little surprised by her own skill. It had been a long time since she played for enjoyment or for an audience.

"Lovely, Miss Howard," Wolfe said softly. "Truly." Then he turned to Meggie on the sofa beside him and said, "You see what practice can do, Meggie. Be diligent and perhaps one day you will play as well as Miss Howard."

Meggie hopped off the sofa and hurried to Victoria's side, leaning against her knees. "Do they have pianos at a school?"

"Yes, there are pianos at most schools for young girls." Victoria managed a polite smile.

"At your school?" she asked earnestly.

"Yes." Victoria stiffened and flicked a glance at Sebastian's interest, guessing where this answer might lead and suddenly furious with him for putting her in such a position. The man was an absolute cad. "There are pianos at my school."

Meggie whirled to face her father with a big smile. "I

want to go to Miss Howard's school, Papa. They have pianos!''

Victoria shoved abruptly to her feet, shooting him a scathing look above Meggie's head. Wolfe thrust to his feet and made a comment about waiting to see. He pulled the bell and when Meggie protested, he shushed her and put a finger against her lips with a frown.

''Go with Odelle, Meggie. You'll need a good bit of rest for tomorrow. In the morning you can show Miss Howard your schoolroom and your books, and help Cook and hang the greens and ribbons.''

Greens and ribbons and the prospect of Christmas worked a charm on Meggie. She went from willful to beaming in a blink. ''Good night, Papa.'' She threw her arms around his neck when he bent down, and gave him a noisy kiss on the cheek. When the nursery maid appeared at the door, she delayed just a moment longer to run to Victoria at the hearth and give her an impulsive hug. When she was gone, it was a minute before Victoria could compose herself and face Wolfe.

''That was nothing short of reprehensible. Using the child's innocence and affections to try to influence me,'' she ground out. He paused, studying the genuine coil of anger in her.

''And have they influenced you, Miss Howard?''

She lifted her chin and crossed her arms over her chest, refusing to answer. But her silence said all he needed to hear. He broke into a broad smile.

''I warned you that I intended to let her change your mind.'' He strolled closer. ''She is rather irresistible, isn't she? All wonder and curiosity, all earnestness and girlish passion for living, so fresh and genuine.'' His voice and gaze both softened. ''Do you know, I fell madly in love with her the first moment I set eyes on her.''

Those shocking words set something within her vibrating. She had never in her life heard a man speak of falling in love, of being in love. That heartfelt declaration and the quiver it generated inside her, jarred open a door in her heart and bared an emptiness she had never known existed in her. She had never even longed to hear such words; they were totally outside her experience. And she might have gone on in perfect, blissful ignorance if she hadn't stood in Sebastian Wolfe's drawing room and heard him speak things that she somehow knew came straight from his heart.

Falling madly in love. How dare he bring her here and make her hear such things? And think about such things, and want such things. . . .

"Meggie doesn't know about your plans for her, does she?" she charged, fighting both him and the feelings he conjured in her with the only weapon at her command. "She has no idea what a school is, or that you want to pack her up and send her off to one."

He sobered abruptly and turned away. Finding himself at the hearth, he seized a poker and gave the log on the fire a few prods before answering. "She has a vague idea. I thought it unwise to be too specific until I was certain she was accepted and could talk to her about the school itself. Meggie is a pliant, agreeable child. She will probably think whatever I—*we*—encourage her to think about school, Miss Howard."

"We?" She stiffened, her first impulse anger at his assumption that she would sooner or later surrender and agree to sponsor Meggie's admission. Then a startling thought intruded: the "we" might be him and someone else! Him and Mrs. Wolfe. She suddenly felt foolish and deeply embarrassed by her personal and conflicting impulses toward him. She didn't stop to think that she had seen no evidence of a wife and mother in the house. In the heat of the moment, all she could think was that there had to be a Mrs. Wolfe, since there was a Meggie.

"And what does Mrs. Wolfe have to say about your methods of securing Meggie a place at Grantley. Surely she cannot agree with such underhanded—" His usually genial face hardened before her eyes, and she halted, sensing she had crossed some forbidden boundary.

"There is no Mrs. Wolfe," he said firmly. His hands clenched at his sides and he shoved them behind his back, clamping them fiercely together. He considered lying, by omission or commission, leading her to think Meggie's mother was dead or had been long-since divorced. But there was something in Victoria Howard's eyes that demanded the truth. And for some reason he wanted her to know the truth, about Meggie, about him. He only wished this revelation had come later, after she had come to know them better. He took a deep breath and declared: "There never has been."

"Never? But Meggie . . ." She caught herself. She was thinking in schoolgirl terms again. It was a baleful axiom of feminine life: not all mothers were wives.

"You may as well know the truth, Miss Howard." He braced, obviously expecting the worst. "Meggie was born outside of legal vows."

It was the single most damning bit of information an administrator at an exclusive academy like Grantley could hear about a prospective pupil. Born out of wedlock. Illegitimate. And yet, Victoria found herself curiously unsurprised and strangely unaffronted by that news. The winsomeness and innocence of Meggie herself somehow eclipsed that damaging disclosure.

"And Megg—Margaret's mother?" she asked, her voice carefully neutral.

"She is gone, Miss Howard," he said, watching well-guarded emotions flicker through her expression. "Indisputably and irretrievably gone. She was an actress." He gave a short, self-deprecating laugh. "A very convincing one. She refused my offer of marriage in no uncertain terms, laid newborn Meggie in my arms and walked out." He turned back to the hearth and leaned one arm upon it, gazing down into the wheezing coals behind the screen. "And my life hasn't been the same since."

For a long moment she stood looking at his tall, arrogant form, refitting all the pieces she had to the puzzle of him into this new background. He was Meggie's only parent. He'd loved her from the moment she was placed in his arms and had raised her these last six years himself, teaching her riddles, teaching her manners.

When he turned to her again, his features were taut and his expression dark. He squared his formidable shoulders and raised his chin to an arrogant angle. Before her eyes, he had just gone from father to ''fortress'' once again, the unassailable maker and breaker of financial fortunes, the overlord of a financial empire that reached into every corner of London society.

''Now you know Meggie's deepest, darkest secret, Miss Howard,'' he said, with a finality that demanded a response. The one he got was not the one he might have expected.

''Yes, I do, Mr. Wolfe.''

She let her gaze linger on him for one minute more, then turned and walked out the door. Horace and Edgar scrambled up from their posts outside the drawing room door and hurried along with her to the stairs.

''Weren't that Tipsy Trifle somethin', Miz?'' Edgar asked, puffing up the steps beside her. ''Ain't never had nothin' like that before.''

''Purely a work o' art,'' Horace intoned. ''An' yer piano-playin', Miz, 'at were pure inspie-ration.''

It was a measure of her confusion that she actually thanked her kidnappers for their compliment, and when they reached her door, murmured a distracted, ''Good night, gentlemen.''

''Nice laidy, 'at Miz Howard,'' Edgar said, doffing his hat and sliding down the wall by the door, after they locked her in.

''A bloomin' peach, is what,'' Horace declared, taking up a seat on the floor on the other side of the door. ''It be a pure honor t' be guardin' 'er.''

* * *

After breakfast the next morning, Sebastian Wolfe appeared at Victoria's door to escort her to Meggie's schoolroom. The first half of Meggie's day was always spent with a tutor, he explained, leading her and the ever-watchful Horace and Edgar around the gallery and down a short, wide hallway to a pair of grand double doors. Flinging the doors wide, he led them into a massive, high-ceilinged room hung with breathtaking crystal chandeliers that glittered in the sunlight of a dozen long, leaded windows. Floor to ceiling mirrors in ornate, gilded frames lined two walls, and patterned silk brocades adorned the rest of the chamber.

"B-but this looks like a ballroom," Victoria said, staring at the grandeur above her.

"*Was* a ballroom. It's a schoolroom now." Sebastian urged her forward.

When her gaze floated down, it settled on an incongruous collection of tables and chairs, storage chests, and shelves—schoolroom furnishings. On one end of the huge room was a maze of bookshelves lined with volumes of every size and description, and with boxes of maps, drawings, and charts. A piano occupied space near the windows and the third corner was filled with desks and toy chests and cabinets stuffed with all manner of globes and mechanical toys, and the occasional animal cage. A large, thick rug bearing stuffed ottomans and strewn with huge brocade pillows filled the remaining corner.

"You're here!" Meggie jumped up from her desk and came running to greet them. Sebastian scooped her up into his arms and turned to Victoria.

"Miss Howard would like to see what your schoolroom is like, Meggie. Why don't you show it to her and read her a story or two?" He turned to the nursery maid and dismissed her with a nod. "And when you've read for Miss Howard and practiced your ciphers, Cook needs your help making the Christmas treats."

Meggie was more than happy to comply. As soon as he set her feet on the floor again, she reached for Victoria's hand and led her straight to the middle of the remarkable little library. "Lots and lots of books. Some of them I can't read yet, but Papa says I will someday. Look, these are my favorites." She dropped to her knees by a low shelf and pulled out book after book to hand to Victoria. Then she led Victoria past the piano to the corner filled with shelves and chests and low tables.

"Look, here's my bunnies. This one is Willie and that one's Beatrice. Want to hold one?" Before Victoria could decline, she found herself balancing several books in one hand and a small, floppy-eared bunny in the other. She handed the books to Horace and Edgar, who trailed close behind, peering over her shoulder and around her skirts.

The marvels of Meggie's unusual schoolroom seemed endless—books, models, toys, easels, and globes. Victoria was soon so absorbed in Meggie's world that she didn't notice when Sebastian backed to the edge of the group, then shoved his hands in his pockets and strolled to the doors. He lingered in the archway a moment longer, studying the light in his daughter's eyes as Victoria complimented her drawings, and watching Victoria's slender hands stroking the rabbit, then gently ruffling Meggie's auburn curls. With a bittersweet smile, he turned away.

Meggie showed Victoria her stuffed animals and mechanical toys, demonstrated how she made castle towers with blocks, and then got out paper and charcoal to show how her father had taught her to draw people and houses and animals. Horace and Edgar hovered nearby, watching raptly, and were soon seated on the floor by one of the low tables, trying their hands at charcoal and pencil, and arguing about which of them drew the better rabbit.

They read stories; first Meggie, then Victoria, while Horace and Edgar sprawled on the rug nearby, listening avidly and popping up at every turn of a page to demand what happened next. Meggie was a surprisingly accomplished reader for a child of six years old. It was only when they started to do ciphers that she displayed skills in keeping with her age. Victoria showed her a rhyming game that would help her remember her "adds and take aways," and soon they were on their knees on the cushions, doing that and other rhyming games until they were both laughing.

Victoria watched Meggie's girlish efforts to please her and the pleasure Meggie took in what they did together, and felt the spot of warmth in the pit of her stomach growing. It would be so easy to let down her guard, to absorb Meggie's innocent, unguarded affection, and then to return it. It would be so very easy to love her. For one stunningly vulnerable moment, Victoria glimpsed what it would have been like to have a little daughter of her own—the feeling of belonging, the poignant pleasure of discovery, the joy of giving and of watching the gift become part of a child's heart. And though it caused a painful swelling around her heart, she held on to those feelings for as long as she could, savoring them, storing them away.

The butler, Pearson, discovered them on the rug, trading riddles, rhymes, and learning rhythm games. Under the old fellow's quizzical stare, Victoria jumped to her feet, jerked her shoeless toes beneath her skirts, and tugged her jacket down firmly. She tidied Meggie's hair and smock, and together they followed the houseman downstairs to a light meal.

"Ye know, Horace," Edgar said as he and Horace trundled along behind, "if I'da knowed school was like that, I mighta gone meself."

With her morning's work done and anticipating an afternoon of Christmas fun, Meggie could scarcely sit still long enough to eat. As soon as the plates were cleared away, she slid from her chair and led Victoria back to the kitchen, where Cook and her helper were hard at work mixing huge batches of sweet dough. Plump, matronly Cook greeted Meggie with a hug, then draped a voluminous apron around her and set her to work straight away.

It was a big, friendly, brick kitchen lighted by windows set high on the walls and toasty warm from the heat of the ovens. Shelves, stoves, and ovens lined the walls, and a pair of long work tables ran down the center of the room. Meggie was given a stool to stand on and assigned to pinch and roll balls of sweet biscuit dough to make into thumb cakes.

"Thumb cakes?" Victoria said as Meggie dove into the mountain of dough in the great mixing bowl with both hands.

"Yea, Miz," Cook answered. "They're her favorite. Show her, Missy Meg."

Meggie scooped up a small spoonful of dough and began to roll it between her palms. "See, Miss Howard, you make a little ball, then you put it on the pan and push—"

"Your thumb down in the middle of it to make a big dent," Victoria finished for her as she demonstrated. "Then you drop a spoon of preserves in the dent and bake them." She smiled at Meggie's surprise and explained, "I made thumb cakes at Christmas when I was a girl, too." She glanced around the big chamber and her voice softened. "And in a kitchen much like this one."

Memories wafted into her consciousness, evoked by smells of fresh-milled flour and working yeast, cinnamon and cardamom, warm butter and raspberry preserves and orange peel. There had been such excitement in her girlhood home at Christmas—the decorations, the company, waiting for Father Christmas, the glorious Christmas dinner and plentiful sweet treats. It all seemed so long ago, another lifetime. A sweet stab of longing pierced her, a yearning to experience all the joy and mystery and excitement again, just once more.

Cook laid down her rolling pin and dusted her hands on the apron covering her ample middle, watching Victoria's faraway expression and reading the trace of longing

in it. She went to the linen shelf and carried a fresh apron
to Victoria, offering it up with a broad smile.

"Nobody stands idle in my kitchen, Miz Howard.
There's plenty o' work for all."

Victoria caught the twinkle in the woman's eyes and
after an awkward moment, accepted the apron with a wry
nod. She removed her good jacket, donned the bibbed
apron, and rolled up her pristine sleeves to dig into the
mounds of sweet dough with Meggie.

The kitchen bustled with activity as yet another batch
of pastry was started and Cook began work on her leg-
endary mince pies. When Cook looked up to find Horace
and Edgar clogging the doorway, she ordered them inside and soon had them shedding their coats and carrying
bags to fill flour bins and fetching down jars and bowls
from tall pantry shelves. Soon ranks of puff pastry in
patty pans and rows of thumb cakes with centers of lemon
yellow, raspberry red, plum purple, and apricot gold,
began to form, ready for the ovens.

Into that sumptuous swirl of rich aromas and festive
spirits, stepped Sebastian Wolfe. He had just returned
from a number of errands and his cheeks were still cold,
reddened from the carriage ride. He paused inside the
kitchen door and his eyes went immediately to Meggie
and Victoria. Both wore huge aprons; both had moist,
rosy cheeks and fingers caked with dough. He hesitated
a moment longer, absorbing the sight of them together,
hoping that time and close proximity had begun to melt
Miss Victoria Howard's determination against them.

"So, you've put them to work, have you?" he finally
said to Cook, loudly enough for the whole kitchen to hear
as he entered. Cook shot him a wide smile and plopped
her floury hands on her ample hips.

"That I have. And if you stay, Master Wolfe, you'll
find yourself employed as well."

"Forced to labor in my own kitchen?" he declared in
mock outrage.

"Use your elbows or use your heels, it makes no difference to me,'' Cook insisted, holding out an apron to him with a determined look.

To Victoria's surprise he accepted the apron from his saucy cook and began to unbutton his gentlemanly, charcoal gray coat. She watched, spellbound, as he peeled his outer garment off and hung it on the pegs next to hers, then proceeded to tie the apron around his neck and waist. There he stood in his bare shirt and vest, removing his gold cuff-buttons and rolling up his pristine sleeves to reveal bare arms, corded male arms, covered with hair. Her gaze slid down them to fasten on his hands—big, generous, long-fingered hands, so male, so very different from hers. He washed his hands and came to stand beside Meggie, drying them on his apron.

''She's a tyrant, that woman!'' he whispered, jerking his head toward Cook. ''Don't know why I put up with it.'' He made an outlandishly disapproving face and Meggie giggled.

''Here, Papa.'' She plopped a scoop of dough in his hands. ''We're making thumb cakes. Do you remember how?''

''Let me see . . .'' He pursed one end of his mouth, seeming puzzled. He rolled it into a ball then seemed at a loss for what to do with it, then promptly stuck it on the end of his upraised thumb. ''There, a thumb cake,'' he declared proudly.

''Papa!'' Meggie scowled, snatching the dough away and giving him an emphatic demonstration of just how it was done, all the while relishing the reversal of their usual roles.

Victoria stood watching them with a ball of dough getting warmer and stickier by the minute in her hands. He was suddenly approachable, accessible, human. It was as if he had shed his powerful, worldly persona along with his elegant coat and gold cuff-buttons. His angular face was slightly reddened, and a lock of his dark hair hung over his forehead. He was a stunningly handsome man. When he suddenly looked up at her and smiled, she felt all warm and tingly inside and her mind went back to the previous day in the upper hall. In a blink she recalled the feel of him pressed against her, his arms holding her, his breath bathing her face.

"It looks like Miss Howard could use a lesson or two," he was saying as she came abruptly back to her senses. He was staring at her hands.

She flushed and look down to find she had clenched her fingers and the sticky dough was oozing out. "Oh!"

"Is Cook working you too hard, Miss Howard?" he asked, watching her scrape the ruined dough off her hand with a spoon, then scoop and shape another ball. She looked up with her blue eyes wide with embarrassment, and he could see luminous traces of other, more interesting feelings in the depths of her gaze.

"No, I don't mind helping . . ."

She seemed oddly flustered and her lashes lowered protectively. He let his gaze roam over her. She had removed her brooch and loosened the buttons at the collar of her blouse, baring a small, tantalizing slice of creamy throat. Several wisps of her hair had escaped her upswept coif, and he had a sudden, overwhelming urge to seize her and pry open all the rest of her buttons, then to pull down the rest of her glorious golden hair around her soft, naked shoulders. Lord, she was an unholy temptation! A perfect blend of propriety and sensuality, of warmth and intensity cloaked in frosty reserve. She was a woman to be proud of in public, and to savor in private. Every nerve in his body suddenly vibrated with awareness of her.

"Meggie, I have a new riddle for you," he said. "Who is it that has a neck but no head, two arms, but no hands?"

He tried diverting his lusty thoughts by entertaining Meggie, and for a while the riddles and rhymes and guessing games distracted him. Then he felt that peculiar tension settling in him, tightening his sinews again, and realized his only hope was to raise her defenses, let *her* propriety put distance between them.

"You're very good at this, Miss Howard." He nodded to the tray of perfect dough balls in front of her. "Can it be that you've done kitchen work before?"

"She made thumb cakes, too, when she was a girl," Meggie informed him.

"Ahhh." He smiled. "And did you do anything else when you were a girl, Miss Howard?" She paused with her hands in the bowl to assess the impertinent tone of his question.

"The usual things girls do." She rose determinedly above his baiting. "At Christmas I helped hang the greens and ribbons and make up the poor baskets. And I planned the games for my younger cousins who came to visit. Then I helped our cook make her special sweet treats, just like Meggie."

"And what were your favorite treats, Miss Howard?" he asked, in a tone that made it seem a peculiarly adult and multilayered sort of question. She gave a determinedly obvious answer.

"I believe my favorite was thumb cakes. But after today, I'm not sure I'll ever want to see another bit of this dough again." She held up her gooey hands to Meggie and winced.

"You haven't been snitching have you, Miss Howard?" He met her eyes a bit more directly than he had planned. It was like being immersed abruptly in liquid heat, in the simmering blue pools of her eyes. His strategy dissolved in a swirl of rising need.

"No, I haven't, thank you. Snitching wouldn't be"— she caught Meggie watching her and phrased her answer instructively—"ladylike."

"And you're always a lady, aren't you, Miss Howard?" he said.

"I would hope so, Mr. Wolfe," she said, trying to ignore the taunting, or was that tempting, undercurrent in his tone.

The noise in the kitchen seemed to have dropped and when she looked around, she found Cook had dragged Horace and Edgar off to some new task, and she vaguely recalled hearing the kitchen and scullery maids being sent out to help with something in the servants' hall. Just the three of them were left in the kitchen. She looked with dismay at the mound of dough yet to roll and wished there was some way to gracefully escape the kitchen, and Sebastian Wolfe's unsettling comments.

Her predicament worsened when Odelle appeared with word that Mr. Evanston, the music master, had arrived for Meggie's lesson. Meggie protested and shrank from the nursery maid's hands, until her father reminded her that she had planned a surprise for Miss Howard and that they would see her later, at dinner. Odelle succeeded in pulling her away from the table and wiping her hands sufficiently for them to make it to the nursery for a thorough washing.

Suddenly there were only two people left in the kitchen.

"Perhaps we should leave this for the kitchen maids to finish," Victoria said distractedly, eyeing the sizable mound of dough still in the bowl.

"Abandoning the task before the finish, Miss Howard?" he said, with a challenging half smile. "I wouldn't have taken you for a wilter." He scooped another dollop of dough and rolled it doggedly, as if challenging her to do the same.

"What on earth does she intend to do with all these sweets, anyway?" she muttered, relenting and reaching into the bowl, the same moment he did. Their hands met in the sticky dough and she recoiled, but not quickly enough. He snagged her wrist and held it.

The silence thickened around them and between them. She felt him tugging at her downcast gaze the way he did at her hand. Against her better judgment, she raised her head to look at him.

His eyes, she thought helplessly, weren't quite as dark

as she remembered. They were a rich, creamy brown that reminded her of the cup of warm chocolate she had been served in bed that morning. Her eyes slowly widened as she realized she had just equated him with such sensual ladylike pleasures—chocolate, enjoyed in bed.

"I-I really must go and wash my hands. They'll be a disaster," she rattled out, tugging discreetly on her hand. "Really, Mister Wolfe—"

"Sebastian," he said in soft, compelling tones.

She swallowed hard, trying not to let her wayward impulses run away with her. But it was a losing battle, with him standing there in his bare shirt-sleeves, holding her hand in a bowl of sweet, sticky dough. Trills of panicky excitement were racing up her arm and through her shoulders. Her skin grew hot and sensitive where he touched it, and where she suddenly longed to have him touch it.

"Do you know what *my* favorite sweet treat is, Miss Howard?" he murmured, sliding around the corner of the table toward her. She could only shake her head; her throat was constricted, frozen by an alarming combination of anxiety and excitement. He edged closer, pouring the chocolaty persuasion of his gaze and his words over her hungry senses.

"Ladyfingers."

And he lifted her hand to his parting lips.

She watched, dumbstruck, as he ran his tongue up her palm and all the way to the end of her fingertip, licking the sticky dough from her hand. The sinuous rasp of his tongue on her skin penetrated all the way to her sinews, laving the bare endings of nerves that were newly exposed inside her. Then he grazed a second path across her itching palm, all the way to a second tingling fingertip.

He was licking her! Her seldom challenged sense of propriety convulsed with shock. It was positively indecent, an outrageous liberty! But her seldom roused womanly passions were demanding their rightful share of her experience. More, they wanted more!

Waves of new sensation washed through her—warm, undulant, softly pleasurable—drawing strength from her muscles and replacing it with a sweet, pliant ache of longing. He blazed a sinuous trail from the heel of her palm to the tip of each finger, then slid his tongue along the sensitive little valleys between her fingers, one after another, caressing, consuming her along with the dough. She shivered and drew a sharp breath. Those small, delicate strokes were telegraphed through her body and magnified by her mounting desire, until it began to feel as if he touched and licked all of her, everywhere, bit by sensitive bit.

Low, purring sounds came from deep in his throat as he worked his way to her fingertips again and nibbled them gently, one by one. The sound vibrated through her, setting her body's peaks and hollows quivering. Then he raised his head to look at her with fathomless eyes that invited her to lose herself in them. Promise, possibility, pleasure; there were uncharted worlds in his enigmatic gaze. She scarcely realized he was nudging her head up and bending.

"Victoria," he murmured. "You taste wonderful."

She stood breathlessly, waiting for, wanting, whatever he intended.

He lifted her chin on one finger, tilting her mouth toward his. Just one kiss, he tried to placate his better sense, just one. And he lowered his head to the lips that had haunted him from the moment he saw them. Soft, so wonderfully soft, was his first thought. And so unbearably sweet, was his second. She tasted of sugar and vanilla and almond, flavors that blended magically with the natural taste of her and made her into a tantalizing sensual confection. Perfect. Irresistible.

Her lips trembled slightly beneath his and her eyes fluttered closed. Her head shifted and her lips parted slightly to fit his, accepting and then seeking the feel of his mouth on hers. This was a kiss, she managed to think. It felt so unexpectedly soft and sensuous. That stunning

contact—warm, languorous velvet against lush oral silk—
sent ripples of pleasure spreading beneath her skin in all
directions. It was perfectly entrancing! It seemed a completely natural progression when his arms wrapped
around her waist and drew her against his body.

The bones in her knees seemed to be weakening
strangely, and she suddenly felt surrounded by his presence, caught up in a powerful flood of sensation. His
crisply starched shirt-sleeves beneath her fingers, his
sandalwood scent, the sugary taste of his hard-soft lips,
she experienced every detail of him in a stunning new
way. The pressure of his mouth on hers deepened, and
his tongue began to trace the edges of her lips, caressing
her, coaxing and tutoring her response. With each luxurious stroke of his tongue, her lips parted more, until she
yielded the satiny inner borders of her mouth and the tip
of his tongue slid sinuously over hers.

A noise intruded, seeming a thousand miles away at
first. Whether it was the shock of that deepening kiss or
the sound, she could not know. But suddenly a male voice
and a female gasp broke in upon them like a thunderbolt,
and they broke apart. Stumbling back a step, Victoria
turned dazed, darkened eyes on Horace and Edgar and
Cook, who stood six feet away with their hands filled
with bags and baskets of foodstuffs from the larder. They
were staring at her with drooping mouths, and it only
took an instant for their shock to become hers.

What in heaven's name was she doing, letting Sebastian Wolfe kiss her, kissing him back? She blushed crimson and backed into the table as she fumbled with the
ties of her apron. She jerked it over her head and wiped
her trembling hands with it, then strode out.

Sebastian turned on Horace and Edgar. ''Where were
you? You are supposed to be guarding her—'' He halted.
He could scarcely rant and rail at them that he had employed them to protect Victoria Howard from him!
''Don't just stand there gaping, you've a job to do! You're
not to let her out of your sight, from this moment on!''

When he flung a finger at the door, they scrambled for their coats and gave his glowering countenance wide berth as they scurried out. Ripping off the apron he was wearing, he washed his hands and strode off through the corridors to his study. There he flung open a frost-rimmed window and dragged in several icy breaths, waiting for the turmoil in his blood to subside.

Caught stealing kisses in the kitchen like some over-heated footman after a scullery maid! He groaned aloud. Victoria Howard wasn't the sort of woman to forget a little thing like being grabbed and licked and then kissed to within an inch of her virtue. He groaned and shut his eyes. *Licked!* He licked her fingers! Dear God. Whatever had possessed him? After this, he would be lucky to get Meggie past the gates at Grantley, much less inside the door!

Victoria Howard already thought him little better than a criminal, with a profligate past. He knew full well that it was his shadowy reputation and unusual business associations that had prevented Grantley from accepting Meggie in the first place, and here he was, adding fuel to all their disapproving and prejudiced notions about him with his licentious behavior toward their Assistant Headmistress!

Well, no more. He pounded a fist determinedly against the leather arm of his chair. Never again. He wouldn't risk Meggie's future for a bit of stolen pleasure, no matter how tempting Victoria Howard looked with her collar unpinned, her hair mussed, and her fingers all sticky and sweet.

Upstairs, at that moment, Victoria was sitting in a bewildered knot on the bench at the foot of her bed, fingering her tender, swollen lips and thinking that she would never, not if she lived to be a hundred, forget the feel of Sebastian Wolfe's mouth against hers. It was her first kiss. It would likely be her last. And it had been filled with tenderness and wonder and discovery, just as she imagined a "first, last, and only" kiss should be.

Not even her deep humiliation at being caught in the arms of her kidnapper could eclipse the rare splendor of that moment.

And not even the marrow-deep thrill of such a pleasure could make her repeat it, she thought plummeting back to reality. Sebastian Wolfe was a cunning, calculating opportunist, who intended to use her nobler impulses and affections to serve his purpose. He'd been quite open about that. He intended her to fall in love with his daughter and had said he intended to be persuasive. Apparently his persuasions included kisses and nibbles and warm, silky words. Wonderful, she tasted wonderful, he said.

She had no one to blame but herself for the hollow ache in her chest and the dismal, bottomless feeling in her stomach, she chided herself. More than once now she had allowed her personal feelings to interfere with what she knew was prudent for a lady of high moral standards and for an official of Grantley Academy. That had to cease, here and now. She wasn't here to relive Christmas memories, or to pretend she had a daughter, or to get into a twitter over a stolen kiss like some mooney-eyed debutante. She was a prisoner here, held against her will for nefarious purposes, and it was high time she remembered that and quit *enjoying it*!

4

LATE THAT AFTERNOON, MEGGIE APPEARED AT VICTO-ria's door with Odelle in tow. The greenery had just arrived, and her father had suggested that Miss Howard might like to help with decorating. Victoria looked at Meggie's taffy-colored eyes and hopeful expression and couldn't bring herself to refuse them. It wasn't Meggie Wolfe's fault her father was a cunning and manipulative scoundrel. Heaven knew the child would be punished enough, in the days to come, for her father's errant ways.

She let Meggie take her hand, and soon they were on

their knees in the vaulted marble entry hall, sorting through the prickly ropes of pine and fir and glossy green branches of holly. Odelle, Pearson the butler, and the doorman and the downstairs maids joined in, and soon Horace and Edgar, who had adopted a wary stance by the exits in case their charge might take it into her head to bolt again, were drawn into helping. Soon they were draping ropes of fragrant greenery and wide red ribbons around the mantels and door frames, on the elegant chandeliers, and around the newel posts and banisters of the great stairs.

The decorating was interrupted for dinner, which was served for just Victoria and Meggie in the small parlor. Mister Wolfe, Pearson informed them apologetically, was taking dinner at his club that evening and would not return until quite late. At first Victoria was both surprised and relieved to be spared facing Sebastian Wolfe that evening, after what had occurred between them. But as they returned to their decorating, she could not help but feel a bit disappointed that he had not deigned to face her.

Meggie was adamant about staying awake to see her father's reaction to their decorations. But as the hour grew late and Odelle insisted she go to bed, Victoria offered to come along and hear her prayers. They led Victoria upstairs to a bedroom filled with delicate, girlish furnishings, frothy blue voile and chintz, and murals of fanciful trees and flowers and animals frolicking in a woodland glade. As Odelle helped Meggie remove her clothes and don her nightdress, Victoria strolled around the exquisite little chamber touching and admiring the fabrics and polished woods and textured murals.

Sebastian Wolfe spared no trouble and no expense where his daughter was concerned. Despite his personal flaws, he had done a creditable job of giving a young child an enviably secure and balanced life. But admirable as that might be, she reminded herself sternly, it did not make him ethical or respectable, or the kind of man Grantley Academy was accustomed to dealing with.

Meggie knelt on the rug by her bed and said prayers and blessings on virtually everyone in the household, including: "Miss Howard, and let her find her lost shoes soon." Victoria felt her insides melting and draining toward her knees and knew it was already too late. Sebastian Wolfe's wretched plan was working; she was coming to truly care for Meggie and to want what was best for her, too. When Meggie climbed between the thick comforters and held out her arms, Victoria stood a moment feeling an alarming prickling in the corners of her eyes, then gave in to that overpowering, womanly urge, and gave her a hug.

It wasn't until the next day, Christmas Eve, that Victoria saw Sebastian Wolfe again. She had spent the morning in the schoolroom, meeting Meggie's tutor, listening to her recite, and helping her finish a small book of drawings for her father's Christmas gift. As Meggie worked she chattered away about her father and the things he had taken her to see: the Exotic Animal Park, Covent Gardens, Buckingham Palace, the ocean—and the things they did together: fishing, riding horses, swimming at the beach. Victoria found herself trying to imagine Sebastian baiting a hook or splashing around in the waves at the seashore and had found it strangely easy to do. She had only to recall how he had looked in rolled up shirtsleeves, with his hair slightly ruffled. And she spent the rest of the morning bolstering her righteous indignation and steeling herself for her next confrontation with him.

When they came downstairs for luncheon, he was standing in the entry hall looking over the decorations. His gaze transferred to the pair of them, then settled inescapably on Victoria's plain gray skirt and unadorned white shirt with the small, mannish, striped tie. He suffered a disastrously vivid recall of the taste of her and the feel of her delectably bound curves against him and realized that his purposeful absence last night and again this morning had been in vain. He had meant to remove himself from the situation and let time and distance diminish her temptation. But as usual, when it came to Victoria Howard, he had been wrong.

"Beautiful greenery, Miss Howard," he said, nodding toward the wrapped garland and ribbons on the railing. "You have a most artistic flair."

"I would have a word with you, before we lunch, Mr. Wolfe," she declared, stopping one step from the bottom of the stairs, so that she could meet him eye to eye. He studied the purposeful set of her jaw and sent Meggie ahead to the dining room.

"My shoes, Mr. Wolfe," she said with ladylike indignation. "I shall not go about without proper shoes for another single day, sir."

"You shall not, shall you?" he said, glancing at her stockinged toes before he could stop himself. "A pity. I was growing rather fond of the sight of your—"

"Mr. Wolfe!" She flushed hotly. "I insist you recompense me for the loss of my shoes and convey me to the nearest shoemaker to obtain—"

"Six pounds, nine and seven pence worth of shoe leather," he quoted. "You are aware, are you not, Miss Howard, that this is Christmas Eve Day. Many of the shops close midday. Only the poulterers and grocers and open markets will be doing business this afternoon." He glanced at her feet, then smiled. "I'm afraid you shall have to make do until the day after Christmas." His dark eyes twinkled. "Or, if you like, I could lend you a pair of my own slippers."

She gave an unladylike growl of frustration and stomped down from the step, jerking her elbow to avoid his helpful hand as she strode for the dining room.

He was in trouble, he thought, watching her angry stride and finding it dangerously appealing. It was harder and harder to take his eyes from her; he experienced phantom pleasures in sundry private locations when just looking at her, and, most alarming of all, he couldn't resist teasing her. He had always teased the women that truly meant something to him: his mother and Meggie. And now Victoria Howard. He had an overpowering urge to exasperate her, to make her laugh and blush and take pleasure in his company.

Yes, he was most definitely in trouble. And if he had a groat's worth of sense, he would turn on his heel this minute and walk straight out the door, or else lock Victoria in her room and ship her straight back to Grantley, come sunrise.

But instead, he sighed and tugged down his vest, and headed for the dining room.

Through the light meal of salad and cold pies and cheeses, Victoria refused to look at him or respond to his comments and answered his most leading questions with polite monosyllables. Meggie sensed the strain between them and grew anxious, unable to decipher the cause of it. In typical childish fashion, she began to worry that she might be to blame for their tension and to fear that it foreshadowed a disruption of their Christmas Eve celebration.

"Are you angry, Papa?" she asked in a small voice, her shoulders rounding.

"What? Of course not," he declared, searching her worried face.

"Is Miss Howard?"

"I don't know, Pippin." He gave Victoria a multi-layered look. "Are you angry about something, Miss Howard?"

"No. I suppose I'm just a bit cross-grained this afternoon. I miss my shoes," she said directly to Meggie, knowing she had just answered Sebastian's unspoken questions as well. She was sorely annoyed with him, but her wretched sense of fairness wouldn't allow her to hold it against his daughter, or to let it ruin Meggie's Christmas.

"Then will you still put up the tree in the drawing room?" Meggie brightened and turned to her father. "You and Miss Howard?" She turned to Victoria with hope so vivid and disarming that it was impossible to refuse. "Pearson let me peek at the tree in the alley," she said, with widened eyes. "It's big as a house! Papa always has trouble with the candles, so you'll have to make sure they're straight."

"Of course we'll put up the tree," he said with a determined smile. "Won't we, Miss Howard?"

Within the hour, Victoria stood by the closed sliding doors of the drawing room, her arms clamped around her middle, watching Sebastian, Horace, and Edgar wrestling a large, balky fir tree upright in the corner. They strained and grunted and grumbled about the scratchy bark and sticky sap as they pushed it upright and seated it in a great metal tub in the corner. They filled the tub with rocks, to hold the trunk in place and stood back to get a look.

"What do you think, Miss Howard?" Sebastian said, crossing his arms over his chest and tilting his head back and forth to evaluate it.

It was a marvelous tree, perfectly shaped, a deep, fresh green, and wonderfully aromatic, she thought. "It's crooked," she said, quietly.

He glanced at her tight stance and softening eyes. "So it is. Add a few more rocks on the right side," he ordered Edgar.

Pearson and the doorman arrived with boxes upon boxes of ornaments fetched from the attic and bundles of small wax tapers. When Sebastian thrust a dusty box into her hands, Victoria couldn't helping peeking in it, then unwrapping the ornaments packed inside. With each painted drum, velvet-clad doll, and gilded star she uncovered, her rigid posture softened. Christmas, she realized, was melting every bit of rectitude and good judgment she possessed. She looked up and found Sebastian giving her a searching sidelong glance. And Sebastian Wolfe intended to take full advantage of it.

"The tin taper holders go on first," he announced. "We must start at the very top, so the lightest person has to go up the ladder.'' The three men looked warily at one another, then turned in unison to Victoria, who shrank back, shaking her head.

"Ohhh, no.''

But she did climb the ladder, and in her stocking feet. She pinned the small tin candle holders on the ends of nearly all the higher branches. Then she began inserting the little wax tapers, leaning further and further off center to reach the branches. When the ladder started to tip, Sebastian abandoned his hold on it to grab for her. The tree shook wildly, and the ladder fell against the wall with a loud clack. She flailed and fell, squarely on Sebastian.

He staggered, but managed to keep his feet and break her fall so that she slid down him and landed more or less on her feet. There was a frozen moment of shock, and Horace and Edgar frantically rushed to see if she was injured.

"I'm all right, really,'' she said weakly, her legs turning rubbery with after-fright. Sebastian's arms tightened around her waist, to hold her up, and he sent Horace and Edgar running for Pearson and some smelling salts.

But, almost as quickly as it came, that peculiar wave of weakness fled, and Victoria found herself caught hard in the circle of Sebastian's arms once again. She could scarcely breathe as the fright of the fall blended with the pleasurable shock of being pressed so forcefully and intimately against him.

"I'm fine, really,'' she said in a breathless whisper. "You can release me.''

"Victoria, are you sure you're all right?'' He didn't want to release her, but when she pushed at his arms and arched away from him he had to let her go. She turned shakily and backed away, and stepped squarely on one of the tin taper holders that had scattered over the floor when the ladder fell.

"Owww!'' She crumpled and lurched, grabbing at her injured foot. A moment later she was in Sebastian's arms again and being carried to the settee. "Ohhhh, I stepped on something."

"Let me see." He knelt and gently inspected her hurt foot, finding nothing worse than a scratch and a ripped stocking. He heaved a sigh of relief. "You're not cut." He glanced up at her with a bit of a grin. "Unfortunately the same cannot be said of your socks."

Her throbbing foot, her fall, her fright; it all receded from her consciousness. All she could see was Sebastian. All she could feel was the tantalizing warmth of his hands on her stockinged foot, caressing and massaging, making the hurt disappear. It really was the most improper thing in the world, having him touch her bare foot like this. But she couldn't bring herself to move.

"One pound, three pence . . . for two pairs," she said distractedly, meeting his scrumptious chocolate eyes. The rumble of his laugh sent trickles of warmth up her leg.

"You cannot be too hurt if you're already dunning me for damages," he said, his voice thickening as he held her foot. "By now my debt must stand at more than fifteen pounds."

"Sixteen, eight and tuppence," she whispered, drawing a shivery breath as his long fingers began to move over her toes, her arch, and up her ankle. "I've ruined two perfectly good pairs of stockings." She had to fight for every word she uttered. "And I've had to ask your butler to send out my blouse to your laundress." When he looked puzzled, she confessed: "There was dough all over the back of it." The memory of how the dough had gotten there stirred a spark in his eyes.

"First shoes, hats, and bustle frames, now lady socks and laundry. You're an expensive woman to kidnap, Victoria Howard."

His hand slid up her calf exploring its sleek, sensual curve as his eyes explored her reaction. Her cheeks were reddening, her lashes lowering, and she wet her lips, both top and bottom. She shivered but made no move to pull away, not even when his fingers reached her knee and began to trace the rim of her garter. He roused, long-ing to run his hands higher, up her thighs, over her hips, over her narrow, corseted waist and full breasts. As his thoughts drifted up her body, he straightened and leaned toward her.

"Here it be, Guv!" Horace lumbered to a halt inside the doors, panting, and holding out a small brown vial. Edgar bumped into him from behind and the pair of them stopped dead, staring at the sight of Victoria's upturned petticoats and her stocking-clad knee captive in Sebas-tian's hands. "Ohhh. Well. Ye won' be needin' this, then," he choked out, jerking the bottle back.

Sebastian ripped his hands from Victoria's knee and sprang up, muttering an explanation. But Horace's and Edgar's accusing stares said they didn't believe a word of it. First they caught him kissing her, now they found him fondling her unmentionable lady parts. Their employer, the outraged looks they exchanged said clearly, was not behaving like a gentleman.

The next hour was a true test of Victoria's character and fortitude. She had to rise nobly above her utter hu-miliation to help complete the decorations as if nothing untoward had occurred, for to try to escape would have been to admit something had been amiss. But in her heart she knew something had happened between them. And if her two guards hadn't arrived when they did, who knew what might have occurred?

Horace and Edgar would scarcely look at her as they escorted her to her room later. She couldn't escape the feeling that she'd disappointed them somehow. And it was only when she was soaking in a warm bath, some time later, that she realized how inside-out everything in her life had become in the last four days and began to laugh. She was actually worried about offending or dis-appointing the two London street toughs who had kid-napped her!

* * *

That evening, after dinner, Sebastian led Victoria and Meggie to the closed doors of the drawing room. Meggie tried to peek through the crack between the doors and pleaded for her father to let them go in. But Sebastian waited patiently for the entire staff to assemble before throwing back the massive doors.

It was nothing short of magnificent. The lights were dimmed, but the room was bathed in the dazzling golden light of more than a hundred wax tapers. The tree was breathtaking, laden with ornaments, gifts, and paper garlands, and at its feet lay piles of gaily wrapped packages. Applause and ooohs and ahhhs broke out as they flooded into the great chamber. Sebastian raised his hands for quiet, then wished them all a Merry Christmas and thanked them for their faithful service in the year past. Victoria searched the faces of the household staff as they listened, finding only respect and attentiveness in their attitude toward him.

Then he called for Meggie to come and play for them. Pearson helped her onto the piano stool, and she settled herself like a seasoned performer and began to play. The second time through "Good King Wenceslaus," Sebastian invited all to sing, and to Victoria's surprise, they did. Soon the whole room, the whole house, filled with the sound of the rich old carol. "God rest you merry, Gentlemen" followed, sung in good order, and the German carol "Silent Night" came next. There was scarcely a dry eye in the room when the last notes died away. Sebastian scooped Meggie up from the piano stool and hugged her, amidst applause. Then, together, father and daughter handed out gifts to everyone on the staff.

The servants paid their respects, then migrated toward the mulled wine and food laid out in the dining room, leaving the family to itself. At last Meggie got to open the several packages with her name on them. She squealed and hugged a new doll and twirled around with a new dress. Then she gave her father the present she had made, hugged him, and climbed up on the settee between

Horace and Edgar to figure out how to work her new windup mechanical bear.

Victoria watched with a sweet ache in her chest: this was Christmas as she remembered it. She drank in the magnificent tree and heard the carols still ringing in her heart, and so missed Sebastian's words as he approached and held out a large box to her.

"I . . ." She blinked and stared at it. "I couldn't possibly—"

"Oh, it's not from me," he said with a twinkle in his eyes. "That wouldn't be proper. It's from Meggie."

She accepted the box, sat down, and undid the string with trembling hands. A moment later she was looking at a pair of elegant high-button shoes through a haze of moisture. Meggie came to stand by her knees and peered into the box. "Oh, look, new shoes!" On impulse, Victoria put her arms around Meggie and gave her a hug. But she was keenly aware that Meggie stood as proxy for the real giver of that gift. She looked up at him with a tremulous smile, then excused herself to put them on.

Pearson served them wassail and mince pies in the drawing room, and while Horace and Edgar were busy stuffing themselves and chatting up the coachmen and grooms, Sebastian found a moment to speak with Victoria alone.

"What did you think of Meggie's playing?"

"It was wonderful," she answered truthfully. Only then did she realize that Meggie's accompaniment of the carols was yet another attempt to convince her of Meggie's suitability for Grantley. She sobered. "Meggie is an exceptional child. I can see why you are so eager to have nothing but the best for her." He waited, expectantly, but she didn't trust herself to say more. Her profession and ethical judgements were getting all mixed up with her personal feelings and both were being swept up in a flood of poignant Christmas memories and longings. Of all the times of the year he might have kidnapped her he had to pick Christmas.

When the candles of the tree had to be extinguished, Meggie was ordered to bed. She asked Sebastian and Victoria to both come and hear her prayers and tuck her in bed. With the warmth of the Christmas spirit in her heart and the heat of the wassail in her veins, Victoria couldn't refuse. She took one of Meggie's hands and Sebastian took the other. Together they mounted the stairs and helped Meggie set her dress and shoes aside and crawl into her nightgown. They listened to her prayers, including "thank you for my new dress and Miss Howard's shoes" and "make Father Christmas hurry," then they both hugged her goodnight and withdrew.

"It's getting late," she said as they strolled back along the gallery. Every womanly instinct she possessed had just been roused by putting Meggie to bed. A veritable tide of the tender feelings had overwhelmed her as she and Sebastian stood side by side in Meggie's room, watching her, listening with affection and pride almost as if they were her mother and father. And she was painfully aware that only Sebastian had a right to such feelings.

She was on borrowed time here, a temporary intrusion into their lives. She would be gone in a few days and their lives would grow over and around the space she had occupied briefly and they would go on without her. But she had a terrible feeling that her life would never be the same. For she had indeed fallen in love with little Meggie Wolfe, just as Sebastian Wolfe had planned.

She paused at the top of the stairs. "I think I'll retire now, if you don't mind." She couldn't quite meet his gaze and her voice sounded small in her own ears. As she turned down the hall toward her room, he turned with her. She ventured a glance at him in the dimly lighted passage and her heart skipped a beat. "You don't have to escort me," she said. "I promise I won't try to escape tonight." The damage, to her reputation and to her heart, had already been done.

"I thought perhaps I'd retire, too," he said, gesturing

to the double doors across the hall from her room.
"Those are my rooms."

Victoria stiffened and paused with her hand on the handle. "Goodnight, Mr. Wolfe." The new tension in her voice was not difficult to read. He took a step back and made a small, restrained bow.

"Good night, Victoria."

5

SHE OPENED THE DOOR TO HER ROOM AND PAUSED JUST inside to turn up the gas light. As the light bloomed in the chamber, she looked around and gasped. On the floor beside the bed were rows and rows of *shoes*. Silk slippers, slender velvet pumps, fancifully colored high-buttons, warm fur-lined carriage boots, there must have been three dozen pairs! Her jaw dropped and her eyes widened as they shifted to the bench at the end of the bed, then the bed itself, which were both covered with hats—sun bonnets, pillboxes, high-crowned derbies, flower pots, and a jaunty straw boater. There were at least as many hats as there were pairs of shoes!

And by the head of the bed, on the floor, stood an elegant wire crinoline and an adjustable bustle frame.

Victoria's heart seemed to swell in her breast, crowding her breathing and sending blood rushing to her head. It was so much, so beautiful. A small movement by the door caught her eye and she looked up to find Sebastian standing on the threshold, watching her. The quiet pleasure in his dark-eyed smile knocked her emotions end over end. Her knees weakened and her heart began to skip every third beat.

"Those were from Meggie," he said in a husky rumble, gesturing to the shoes she had received earlier. Then he swept the sumptuous display with a casual hand. "These are from me."

Victoria shook her head, unable to speak. This was a

bribe, her reason whispered—a conspicuous and blatant persuasion. But her heart wasn't listening, and her entire body seemed to be melting into one big puddle of longing.

'Most improper of me, I know. But then, I've never claimed to be a proper gentleman.'' He took a step forward, then stopped himself and shoved his hands into his trouser pockets.

"I cannot accept them," she said in a forced whisper. "Perhaps you can get your money back."

A laugh boiled up out of his depths, thick and vibrant and stunningly sensual. "I won't take them back, Victoria. Think what it would do to my vaunted reputation as a fast-living scoundrel if I was seen dragging expensive lady-gifts back to shopkeepers for refunds. You'll just have to keep them." His smile was both teasing and tender. "Consider it recompense for damages received. Or consider it a Christmas gift, from an admirer." His hands slid from his pockets into fists at his sides. "For I do admire you, Victoria."

The ache those words produced in her chest was a very sweet pain indeed. Perhaps it was the magic of the special night, or perhaps it was the influence of the hour and the wassail; something had lowered the barriers between them. He admired her. And he wanted her. She felt his desire reaching for her as his hands would not.

"Or perhaps you could repay me for them," he said, his eyes darkening, luminous with need. "We could work out a trade. There is one thing I would have from you, Victoria."

Her breath caught in her throat. Here was the price.

"I would count myself well recompensed," he continued softly, "if you would call me by my given name."

"Your given name?" she whispered, feeling her defenses sliding. He was wearing the most heart-stoppingly earnest expression she had ever seen. That he wanted such a thing from her, something so small and gentlemanly and tender, revealed a great deal about the man inside him. The last protective barriers around her heart came tumbling down. In that moment she would have gladly given him whatever else he had asked of her, too. For, in that moment she had just given him her heart.

"Sebastian," she said quietly, watching and somehow understanding the small spark it struck in his eyes. "It's a wonderful name. Sebastian . . . Sebastian."

The intimacy of his name on her lips released his reined desires and he closed his eyes, trapping the pleasure of the sound and all it could mean, inside him. When he opened them again, they were hotter, brighter.

"I'm trying very hard not to move from this spot, Victoria," he said raggedly. She could see his breath coming faster, his shoulders swelling, and his fists tightening at his sides. Some instinctive, womanly part of her responded to those sensual signals. Her lips grew sensitive and her skin ached beneath her garments, yearning for the touch of his hand. But still, he did not move, and as she searched his tautly reined form, she finally understood. He was offering her a choice.

She took one step, then another, and saw them register in a tremor through his frame. He held out his arms and she walked straight into them. For a moment neither breathed as each drank in the heady reality of the other's closeness and warmth. Warm wool and starched cotton, a wisp of sandalwood and a hint of rosewater—their scents blended as their warmth merged. She lifted her face to him and he captured her lips with a groan that rolled up from the very bottom of his soul.

Clear, crystalline spirals of pleasure wound through her body, like ice laid against bare nerves, indistinguishable from flame. His lips moved over hers in lush, sinuous patterns, drawing passion and heat from her depths to quell the chills and shivers trembling her.

Pressed hard against him, she could feel the contours of his body against hers and ran her hands down the center of his back, learning his shape, discovering for the first time what a man truly was like. Ribs and spine and sinew and muscle, how could he be so like her and yet so different? She felt his tongue tracing her lips and parted them slowly, yielding, opening to him by small, luscious increments. And when his questing hands found the softness of her breast above her corset, her knees buckled.

With a husky, sympathetic laugh, he scooped her up in his arms and started for the bed. And he found it filled with hats. He groaned and made for the bench instead, pushing the costly millinery off onto the floor and sinking onto it with her on his lap.

"I want to touch you, Victoria," he murmured into her hair, gauging her response by the instinctive and languorous way her body arched into his.

"Then, touch me, Sebastian," she whispered, wrapping her arms around his neck and ruffling her fingers through his thick hair. He crushed her to him and kissed her breathless. His fingers worked the buttons of her jacket, then released the brooch at her throat, and encountered more buttons. Then his mouth lowered down her throat, between her parting collar, and onto the soft, fragrant skin of her chest. His hands slid over her, nudging buttons open, exploring the yielding curves of her breasts. When they dipped inside the stiff boning of her corset and found the budded tip of her breast, she quivered and pressed against his hand.

Their caresses grew bolder and kisses grew hotter. She felt his body swell and harden beneath her, not fully understanding what it was, but knowing it had to do with the pleasures she was experiencing and with the peculiar, throbbing heat collecting in her womanly parts. And when his hand dipped under her skirts and moved hotly over her thighs, she felt her desire focusing on those bold, possessing motions of his hands, and understood that he could somehow assuage that hollow ache in her loins.

Downstairs in the dining room, Horace turned to Edgar and found himself staring into a yawn of heroic proportions. It was clearly time for them to escort Miss

Howard back to her room. He rousted his partner and they lumbered along to the drawing room, finding it empty. Then they shuffled to the parlor and found it draped with woozy, wine-warmed forms, none of which was the least bit blond or pretty.

"Where did she go?" Edgar asked scratching his head and sobering as a thought struck. "Ye don' think she might of took off?" The words galvanized them, and they stumbled over their own feet as they rushed for the stairs.

"The Guv, 'e'll 'ave our guts fer garters if she's got away," Horace groaned.

Down the hall, they spotted a dim glow coming from Victoria's room and they lurched to a halt and heaved sighs of relief.

"Miz 'Oward?" Horace called softly as they approached and peered in the door opening. "Ye left yer door ajar." When there was no response they glanced at each other with fresh concern. They elbowed each other insistently until Edgar finally gave the door a halfhearted shove. It was enough to set the well-oiled hinges swinging, and a moment later they stood in the doorway, frozen by the sight that greeted them.

Miss Howard was lying half on the foot bench, half on the bed in a veritable sea of lady-hats with their employer pressed tightly against her and kissing her like he meant to do some business. Edgar choked on his own juices and Horace began to sputter. And the pair on the bench stilled, parted slightly, then turned to peer around the bedpost at them.

"*Dear God.*" Sebastian ripped himself from Victoria's warm, receptive body, rolled to the edge of the bench, and pushed to his feet to shield her from their gawking. "What in heaven's name are you—!" He broke off before he finished it. They were here because he'd ordered them to be here! And after a moment upright and away from Victoria's lush, intoxicating kisses, he honestly didn't know whether to bash them or thank them for their wretched interruption. His entire body was on fire, and that fact ignited his conscience as well.

"Mr. Wolfe!" Horace exclaimed, expressing the kidnappers' mutual horror.

"Be so good as to wait just outside the door, gentlemen!" Sebastian snarled, jamming his fist on his hips and trying to look as formidable as possible.

"Beggin' yer pardon, sir," Edgar growled, looking rather like a watchdog with its hackles up. "But we shull not. Not wi' you in Miz Howard's room."

Good Lord. Chided by his own hired henchmen for his ungentlemanly behavior toward the woman he'd hired them to abduct, it had to be the absolute low point of his manly life! Sebastian dragged his hands back through his hair and tried to get a grip on the situation.

"I would like a word with Miss Howard alone, before I leave," he declared irritably.

They glowered and exchanged doubt-filled looks, then grudgingly backed out the door. But he could feel their gazes piercing his shoulder blades as he turned back to Victoria. She sat on the edge of the bed, her skirts raised and rumpled around her shapely legs, her blouse gaping open above her grip on it, and her lips delectably swollen from their long and passionate kisses. But it was her eyes that rocked him to his very core. They were luminous and filled with equal parts of retreating passion and shame.

"Please believe me, I never meant this to happen," he said hoarsely. "I'm sorry, Victoria." When she closed her eyes and turned her head, he felt as if he'd been punched in the gut. There was nothing left to do but make an exit. He pulled himself together and strode out the door, closing it firmly behind him.

"I'm sorry, too," Victoria said in a tiny voice to the empty room, not knowing whether she meant she was sorry it began or that it had ended.

Horace and Edgar trailed Sebastian downstairs to his study and planted themselves before his desk with their arms crossed and their faces filled with shock at what they considered a foul and ungentlemanly betrayal of their trust in him.

"Miz 'Oward's a right bloomin' peach of a miz," Horace declared. "She deserves better'n a quick bit o' slap-an'-tickle on th' sly."

Sebastian ground his teeth and shot a glare at them from the corner of his eye. Of all the cutthroats, foils, and thugs he had to choose from in London's teeming criminal element, he had to pick the only two with a middle-class sense of propriety!

"Ye ought to make it right, Mr. Wolfe," Edgar pronounced authoritatively. "Ye ought to marry 'er."

Sebastian's eyes closed as those well-intentioned words flayed his already battered pride. Marry her? There was probably no humiliation deep enough or degrading enough to force her to such a thing with him, especially after his despicable behavior toward her.

When his eyes opened again, it was to a clear view of the awful irony of the situation he himself had created. He had kidnapped Victoria Howard, intending her to fall in love with his little Meggie, and he'd ended up falling in love with Victoria Howard himself. And now by letting his personal desires and feelings get mixed up in his scheme, he had probably just ruined whatever chance he had of getting Victoria Howard to look past him and his unsuitable reputation, to see and accept Meggie for just herself.

And the worst part of it was, given the same opportunity, he would probably do it all over again, just the same way. A few stolen moments in Victoria's arms, his heart was telling him, were better than nothing at all. He dragged his hands down his face. It seemed he had to choose: his daughter's welfare or his desire for Victoria. What on earth was he going to do?

Christmas Day dawned bright and crisp. Despite their night's celebration, the house staff rose well before the sun was up and scurried to prepare for a grand Christmas dinner. Sebastian emerged from his rooms, freshly shaved and groomed to perfection, but looking like he'd spent a wretched night. He prevented Meggie from hurrying straight to Victoria's room to show her the gifts Father Christmas had brought her by saying that Miss Howard didn't seem to be feeling well after last night and needed sleep. Then, after breakfast, he had Odelle get Meggie ready for Christmas Morning church service, as planned. Originally, he had intended this outing to show Victoria that he had provided for a moral influence in Meggie's life. Now it was just a way to remove himself from the situation for a while, to clear his thinking.

But as they donned their coats to go, Victoria appeared at the top of the stairs in her best blue worsted, her high-button shoes, and a saucy little pillbox hat awash in white feathers. Sebastian was caught speechless as she descended the stairs and paused, drawing on her gloves.

"I do hope the bishop won't be long-winded this morning," she said, then glanced at him. "We are going to the cathedral, aren't we?"

She honestly intended to go with them? Out in public? He felt an odd tug in his chest as he watched Victoria smile at Meggie and tuck some of her curls properly under her bonnet. It was a moment before he recovered his tongue and answered.

"We are indeed."

Sebastian glanced over at her as they knelt during the prayers at Westminster and thought what a remarkable woman she was. No hysterics, no maidenly outrage, and no accusations. She looked up at him, across Meggie's bowed head, and for a long, breathtaking moment their eyes met. And what he read in them made some of the burden he was carrying slide from his shoulders. She didn't hate him, and she didn't blame him, at least, not totally. He shifted his gaze back to his folded hands, feeling fortunate beyond words. Perhaps there was still a chance for Meggie. And if there was, he had to make sure his desires didn't endanger Meggie's future again, no matter how painful it was for him as a man.

Victoria stared at him for just a moment longer, seeing the regret in his eyes, wishing it had something to do with her, but knowing it had more to do with his plan for Meggie. She gave his handsome profile one last visual touch, then turned back to the service.

Her behavior of last night had handed him the perfect weapon to be used against her: a breach of her own exalted standards of propriety. If he was half as devious and unprincipled as she had believed, he would have called her into his office first thing and demanded a recommendation as the price of his silence. But he hadn't. He had packed her up with his little daughter and escorted her to Christmas Matins, of all places, and sat beside her in front of God and everybody, as if she were a part of his family. When she looked down, she had difficulty seeing the print in the missal she was holding.

Christmas dinner was sumptuous and peaceful, served in the grand dining room for the three of them and two additional guests, Horace and Edgar, whom Meggie was beginning to call by the sobriquet Uncle. The evening passed in peaceful and surprisingly amiable pursuits, though Victoria was painfully aware that Horace and Edgar scrutinized every exchange between her and Sebastian. When Meggie was sent to bed, Sebastian asked Victoria to have a word with him and led her to the fireplace in the drawing room.

"I want you to know, I will be staying at my club for the rest of your visit."

"You will?" Victoria felt her heart flutter in protest. "But, what about Meggie?"

"I'll come for dinner each evening, as always, and after she is in bed, I'll go." He stared down at the toes of his immaculate boots. "I don't know how to make up for my behavior toward you, Miss Howard. I can only hope you won't hold my conduct against Meggie." There was none of the familiar edge of arrogance in his tone and none of the outlandish impertinence she had come to expect from him. This was the same tone he had used in speaking of falling in love with Meggie. This came straight from the heart.

"You don't have to leave on my account, Mr. Wolfe. I accept your apology. Let us leave it at that," she said, hoping she sounded more convinced than she felt. When he looked up from beneath thick rims of lashes, her knees went weak. Chocolate eyes, she thought, hot and sweet. Longing trickled like a warm spring rain through her.

"No, I think it would be best, if I spent my evenings elsewhere," he insisted, searching her for a clue to what she was feeling. "I would not want you to fear a repeat . . ."

She drew herself up at bit straighter and clasped her hands a bit tighter. He was genuinely concerned for her, and she suddenly knew in her marrow that it was not just a self-serving fear of damaging her reputation and devaluing her recommendation of Meggie. He truly didn't want to hurt her. He had spoken honestly when he said he didn't want to coerce her, even in the matter of Meggie's application to Grantley.

Sebastian Wolfe was not the sort of man who coerced. Last night he had offered her a choice. If she hadn't gone to him, she realized, he would have turned away and made himself walk back out her door. And she suddenly had a deep and unshakable feeling that he would always offer her a choice. That was the sort of man he was.

"I'm not afraid. I trust you, Mr. Wolfe," she said quietly, meaning every word of it.

In the silence that followed a wondering smile began dawning over his taut face, softening it. And her heart paused, as if to collect that precious expression, before going on.

"You don't know how pleased I am to hear that, Miss Howard." He leaned instinctively toward her, then caught himself and stiffened back. "However, I'm not sure I trust me, where you are concerned." A wave of need swelled unexpectedly in him, freeing a reckless bit of candor. "I seem to have the most awkward craving for . . . ladyfingers."

Seeing her blush, he bit his lip and turned on his heel, making straight for the front doors. Victoria's didn't bother to suppress her soft-eyed smile. *Ladyfingers,* she thought. Well, at least he still thought of her as a lady.

Horace and Edgar pushed up from their chairs by the door as she passed, and they followed her upstairs. When her door had closed and they heard the key scrape in the lock, from the inside, they looked at each other, frowning.

"Did 'e see that? That look about th' pair of 'em while they wus parlayin'?" Horace said.

Edgar nodded. "Who woulda guessed? Th' Guv an' our Miz Howard. Horace," he asked quite earnestly, "ye think they know they're in love?"

The day after Christmas was always as much fun as the day itself, only for a different group of people. It was Boxing Day. And in Victoria's girlhood home, Boxing Day had been the time of year the servants received something extra from their employer, and the needy in the parish and on the estate were provided with food, clothing, and small household items which the family had "boxed up."

Victoria rose a good bit earlier than usual, intending to take breakfast with Meggie and to see if she would be allowed to take Meggie to the park for an outing that day. But the schoolroom and Meggie's bed were empty, and Victoria hurried downstairs to Meggie's favorite haunt, the kitchen. It, too, was quite deserted. She peeked into the servant's hall, intending to ask where Meggie, and everyone else, was, but it was empty as well.

She spotted Horace and Edgar coming around the gallery above the entry hall. "There ye be!" Edgar exclaimed, as they came puffing down the stairs.

"Yes, here *I* am," she said tartly. "But where is everyone else? Meggie is nowhere to be found, the kitchen is deserted and even the servant hall is empty.''

''Oh. Well, Miz . . .'' Horace lowered his head and shot a sidelong look at Edgar. ''They didn' e'spect ye up so early. We wus t' bring ye a spot o' tea when ye waked up.''

They were hiding something, Victoria sensed. ''Just where are Meggie and Mr. Wolfe, and all the others?'' When they winced at her sharp tone, she adopted her sternest schoolmistress demeanor and demanded: ''I insist you tell me. *Now.*''

''They went . . . t' the Guv's offices,'' Edgar said, looking a bit chagrined. ''They tho't to be back afore ye stirred too much.''

''To Mr. Wolfe's office? Whatever for?''

''Fer Boxin' Day,'' Horace answered. ''What else?''

Through judicious use of reason, indignation, and the threat she would have to be tied up to prevent her from going, she managed to convince her pair of kidnappers-cum-chaperons to escort her to Sebastian's offices. They hired a cab and soon were riding through the narrow and dirty streets of the near East End.

Whatever Victoria had expected, it wasn't that the offices of one of London's wealthy financiers were located in a series of huge brick warehouses wedged between a number of railway tracks and a sea of dingy, multistoried tenements. Outside the street door of the looming building stood a short line of ragged folk, huddled against the wind. And when Horace and Edgar opened a path for her through the people clogging the doorway, she saw that the line wrapped around through a massive warehouse, toward a set of offices.

Making her way through the crowd behind Horace and Edgar, she spotted the focus of their waiting: tables laden with food and kegs of ale and huge urns of steaming coffee and tea. The people in the queue were laughing and talking, greeting each other as they moved slowly along toward that festive meal, which was being served by Sebastian's butler, cook, and household staff. At the end of that line of now familiar faces was Meggie, dressed in her schoolroom pinafore, standing on a chair, handing out her thumb cakes to everyone who came through the serving line.

Victoria's attention fastened on her rosy cheeks and sparkling eyes, then slid to the thumb cakes in her hands. So that was where those wretched mounds of dough went! The cakes were being made to give away here.

Edgar nudged her arm and pointed toward the steps leading to the offices in the back. "There's the Guv'nor." At the foot of the steps stood Sebastian, talking with some of his guests and directing them to the clusters of people assembled along the far side of the empty warehouse. As she squinted and looked closer, a woman turned away from one group and Victoria glimpsed a big wooden box in their midst. In the woman's arms were two pairs of work shoes and what appeared to be either blankets or folded lengths of fabric.

Boxing Day. She suddenly found it difficult to get her breath. This was Sebastian's Boxing Day. She looked around her. At least two hundred people here and more outside waiting to get in. And he was giving them food and clothing and his own personal attention.

"The Guv, 'e remembers the little' folk," Horace said, studying the tumult in her face and unsure what to make of it.

"Does it twicte a year," Edgar put in. "An' if a body's got a need some other time . . ."

Victoria didn't have to hear any more. As Edgar rambled on about medicines and shoes and "make-work" that "tided a bloke over," she stared across the way at Sebastian, watching his changing expressions as he spoke to the people, his nods of encouragement, his quick, handsome smiles. He gave to them of his resources, his time, and his concern. She suddenly thought of three dozen pairs of lady-shoes and more than two dozen fancy hats. It truly hadn't been a ploy to gain her good will; it had been the boisterous impulse of a giving and generous heart.

She looked around the crowd then back at him and, as if touched by her gaze, he looked up. Surprise, pleasure, and concern all registered in his face and he glanced across the way to Meggie, then back at her. Instantly he was making his way through the crowd toward her.

"What are you doing here, Miss Howard?" he said, planting himself strategically between her and the sight of his daughter abandoning her post to investigate a game of jacks played by several ragged children. She peered around him to watch Meggie scrambling up onto some crates with the others. Then she glanced at Cook and the rest of his staff, behind the food table, before returning to him.

"It is Boxing Day, Mr. Wolfe," she said, removing her gloves and unpinning her hat. Then she paused with her ladyish accessories in her hand and gave him a look filtered through the fringe of her lashes. "I'm afraid I've nothing to give but my time and good will."

"The most precious gifts of all, Miss Howard," he replied. That muted, feminine glance went straight to his blood. For a moment it was all he could do to keep from dragging her into his arms.

"Put me to work, then," she said, sensing his desire and feeling reassured by it. "Anything but handing out thumb cakes. I believe I've had quite enough of those." And he laughed.

Shortly, she had removed her jacket and was serving tea and coffee, helping people find places to sit, and organizing the children to gather up the tin plates for washing. A number of Sebastian's office staff, who were also helping, introduced themselves; apparently everyone associated with Sebastian had a role in his unique Boxing Day celebration. And every time she looked up from her work, Sebastian was looking at her with that warm, teasing twinkle in his eye.

Three hours passed before she knew it. In the carriage,

on the way back to Sebastian's house, Meggie fell asleep, and Victoria gently lowered her across her lap and stroked her hair. For just that moment, there was no other place on earth she would rather have been, than seated across from Sebastian, with Meggie's head on her lap. She looked up to find Sebastian watching her, and she averted her gaze to stare out the frost-rimmed window.

But in her mind's eye she could still see him and realized she was seeing the whole of him for the first time. He was a clever, if somewhat unconventional, man who valued learning, honesty, and compassion. And there wasn't a more devoted and loving father anywhere. He was patient and generous to a fault, and she had just seen, firsthand, his sense of social obligation at work. Sebastian Wolfe was a man who could be counted on and could be trusted, whether with another man's money or with a woman's virtue.

He was the sort of man the Board of Grantley Academy should feel proud and honored to include in their list of patrons. And she intended to tell them that, as soon as possible.

Just before dinner that evening, Victoria found Sebastian helping Meggie build a huge tower of blocks in the schoolroom. She paused by the door, watching. They fit so well together—she glanced about the huge room—here, in this marvelous place. The love and pride that glinted in his eyes as he teased and taught her was so obvious. How could he even think of parting with her?

Later that night, when Sebastian came downstairs from hearing Meggie's prayers, Victoria led him to the hearth in the drawing room, under Horace's and Edgar's eyes, and put that very question to him.

"I've watched you with Meggie, the way you give her the encouragement she needs, the way you correct her. And there is one thing that puzzles me."

He frowned slightly. "And what is that, Miss Howard?"

''How you could bear to part with her.'' She paused, seeing she had struck a nerve. ''She is such a part of your life.'' His features smoothed and he stood straighter.

''For the last six years, she has been my life. Everything I did, everything I wanted, everything I was, it all changed the day her mother laid her in my arms and walked out. And I know it will all change again the day Meggie walks out.'' He paused and swallowed hard. ''I am prepared to accept that.''

''I still don't understand why it is so important to send her to school, at such a young age. Here she has tutors and lessons and a whole houseful of people who adore her. What could she possibly receive at Grantley that you cannot give her here?''

As she spoke fully five different emotions passed through his face, each leaving a trace of itself behind. And in the center of that dark swirl of emotion was a knot of pain so stark that she wondered how she could have missed it until now.

''Respectability,'' he said bluntly. ''At Grantley, Meggie will become *respectable*.''

She stared at him, shocked by his quiet vehemence. Then she was revisited by what he said on that first night, and it suddenly became clear. ''Because Meggie was born out of wedlock, you are afraid she won't have a decent future.''

''I know she won't have a future, Miss Howard,'' he said grimly.

''How can you know that for sure? She's still a child. And such a wonderful child—''

''I know, Miss Howard, because I am a bastard myself.'' His eyes burned as he searched her reaction keenly, looking for the tell-tale signs, the closing off, the withdrawal that occurred in respectable women's eyes when they learned of his parentage. He saw her surprise and saw her struggling with his revelation, and knew that both his heart and his hopes for Meggie hung in the balance.

"I know exactly what Meggie faces in the respectable world," he continued. "The Earl of Chatham was my father, and even with the best of educations and bearing noble blood, I was barred from many associations in the social and financial worlds. When I determined to make my own way, many resented my presence in the broker-ages of the City. They disdained my methods and my ethics, but what they truly objected to was my birth. Up-start Sebastian Wolfe, who didn't have the decency to stay on the wrong side of the blanket." He straightened and caught his emotions back under control. A pained smile curled half of his mouth. "And many who do not know of the circumstance of my birth, are still influenced by the cloud that it has produced over me. Your Board of Governors, for example."

She stood, rooted to the floor, stunned. She hadn't imagined. How could she? Illegitimate. Both he and Meggie. The pieces of the entire puzzle finally fell into place—his questionable reputation, the vagueness of the gossip about him, his burning determination to see that Meggie found a place in the hallowed and respectable halls of Grantley. The traces of pain in his expression caused an unbearable tightness in her chest. She suddenly saw him as a little boy, like Meggie, sunny, bright, innocent. Then she saw the man he had become and sensed the hurt that had tempered and hardened his determination to succeed, and his desperation to see that his daughter didn't suffer the same way.

"I have made my fortune my way. And I have no re-grets about that," he told her. "But my money will never be enough to give Meggie what she needs to have a re-spectable life, to make a good marriage, and to hold her head up in society. She needs a place to make the right associations, and friendships." He drew and expelled a deep breath, knowing the time for her answer had come. "She needs a sponsor."

Victoria swallowed hard and looked up at him through

prisms of moisture. It was all she could give to the man she loved, a future for the child they loved together.

"She has one, Sebastian."

A moment of shocked silence passed as he probed her gaze and found only warmth and acceptance there. "She does? Oh, Victoria—" He broke into a huge, boyish grin and picked her up and twirled her around and around. "How can I ever thank you?"

When he put her down, he seized her wrist and pulled her out the door and up the stairs, with Horace and Edgar hot on their heels. "We have to tell Meggie!"

"Meggie, I have wonderful news!" Sebastian awakened his daughter from a sound sleep and scooped her up into his arms. "You're going to go to school, young lady. What do you think of that?"

"What school? Where?" Meggie mumbled, rubbing her eyes. Then she saw Victoria and brightened. "Miss Howard's school?"

"The very one!" he said, turning a beaming, boyish smile on Victoria, too. "When Miss Howard goes back to her school next week, you can go with her."

"Next week?" Victoria scowled at him. "But I haven't even spoken with Miss Chesterton," she said, her emphasis reminding him there were still things to be settled. "Perhaps we should wait—"

"Wait not, waste not, Miss Howard," he said, with a raised and wagging finger. "I am sure Miss Chesterton would not want to delay a sizable donation to the school fund. And I know she will adore Meggie"—he leveled a meaning-filled look on Victoria—"especially when she sees her standing there in her best schoolgirl cloak, ready and eager to be a Grantley girl."

The man really was an outrage, she thought. How long had he been planning this little surprise? She heaved an exasperated sigh, then let herself be coaxed into a smile. Probably from the very beginning, she realized.

* * *

Over the next several days, Meggie was too busy and too excited to understand what it meant to leave the only home she had ever known. Sebastian seemed determined to make her last days at home as joyful as possible, and so packed Meggie and Victoria up each day for an outing—to the park, the shops, or the exhibits at the natural history museum. Then each evening they had dinner together and spent the balance of the evening playing games, listening to the awful stories Uncle Edgar made up, watching Uncle Horace try to juggle things, and learning the steps to a simple dance to Victoria's accompaniment on the piano.

They were golden hours, Victoria realized, watching the way Sebastian packed every scrap of his love into everything he did with Meggie. And when those precious hours faded, and it was time for Meggie's prayers, Victoria saw how Sebastian hugged her a bit tighter and a bit longer than usual, before settling her in her bed and tucking the covers under her chin. And it was all that much harder for her to say good night to him on the gallery, afterward, and to watch him descend the stairs and stride out into the frigid night.

The afternoon before they were to leave, the household was in a tizzy—assembling, pressing, and packing Meggie's things. As Victoria tried to insert some sanity into the process, she looked up to find Sebastian standing at the nursery door, watching her with a heart-stopping smile. He beckoned to her, and she joined him in the hall for a walk around the gallery.

"If Napoleon had had you at Waterloo, we would all be speaking French now," he teased.

"I'm sorry, I don't mean to interfere, but they're packing far too much. Half of those things will just have to be put in storage." When he chuckled, she felt her cheeks heating. "Well, when you see the dormitory, you'll understand."

He paused and took her hands, first one, then the other. It was the first time he had really touched her since that night in her room. She looked up and found his face troubled.

"I won't see the dormitory, Victoria. I'm not going to accompany you to Grantley."

"What?"

"I've given it a great deal of thought, and I feel it is best if I do not appear at Grantley with Meggie." Victoria's surprise turned to uneasiness as he continued. "And it will be easier for her if she parts from me here, in a familiar place. It will be as if she is just going to the park."

There was an undercurrent in his tone, words not spoken and intentions not shared. She sensed that his plan to send them to Grantley alone had broader implications.

"I'll be quite involved in my work for a while," he said thickly, fixing his gaze on her hair, then her mouth, avoiding her eyes. "I won't have much time to visit or to have her come home for holidays. And she'll have friends and she'll be so busy . . ."

She heard what he said, but this time, she also heard what he did not say. He was sending Meggie off to Grantley, intending to see little of her afterward.

"You cannot just pack her off to school . . . abandon her!" *Abandon us!* she thought. In all her innermost thoughts, she realized, she had believed that Meggie's presence at Grantley meant she would see him, too, from time to time, at parent days, at recitals . . .

"I'm not abandoning her—"

"Dearest heaven." She tried to jerk her hands away. "Think of her, all alone—"

"She won't be alone," Sebastian ground out, refusing to let her go. Then abruptly he transferred his grip on her hands to her shoulders and plunged into her gaze. "She'll have you."

Her breath caught in her throat as she stared through those stark windows on his soul, to the deep, unguarded places of his heart. In them she saw his anguish at losing

Meggie, his pain at forfeiting what might have been between them and a huge, immovable core of resolve.

"You love her, too, Victoria. I've watched you with
her."

"But I'm not her father," she whispered hoarsely.
"Why? Why would you do this?"

"You said it yourself, I was the reason Meggie was
rejected at Grantley. And as long as the taint of my
birth and my fortune hangs over her, she'll never be
accepted in respectable circles." Respectable. The
word suddenly sounded like the hiss of something foul
and corrupting.

"Can respectability be that important to you? That you
would break Meggie's heart, throw away her love?" she
demanded furiously. She couldn't believe that the same
man who had loved his daughter so lavishly and who had
made love to her so tenderly, could cut them both off
from him so ruthlessly, and for the sake of something as
empty as being respectable.

"You've never been without it, Victoria. You're the
granddaughter of a duke, the daughter of a lord. You've
always had an impeccable name, and a reputation se-
cured by generations of nobility—"

"Yes!" she declared, feeling tears welling in her
throat. "I have respectability. I have tons, mountains of
it!" She paused to swallow back her angry tears. *And
nothing else,* her heart cried out. *No family, no future,
no home of her own and no love.* And she hadn't even
realized how little she had until she was kidnapped for
Christmas.

"You're the richest man I know, Sebastian Wolfe. You
have all the things that make life worth living right here
and you're throwing it all away."

She turned and fled down the hall toward her room.
But he caught her halfway there and held her by the
shoulders. "Victoria . . ." After a long moment he released her shoulders to cup her face between his hands.

His thumbs stroked her cheeks and his luminous gaze trailed over her features. "I never meant to . . ."

The strain of the last several days finally cracked his self-imposed restraint. Just once more, he thought. He wanted to feel her lips against his and hold her softness in his arms one last time. And before his gentlemanly code or his sense of fairness could get the better of him, he lowered his lips to hers and sank into the receptive warmth of her mouth. His arms coiled around her, pulling her close, giving every part of himself to that kiss.

She met his lips and leaned into his embrace, drawing the strength she so desperately needed from his powerful frame. Her hands slid up his back, and she molded herself against him as fully as she could, seeking the imprint of his body on hers, something to carry with her in her heart. The pure physical pleasure of being joined to him flooded through her, driving out the pain and loss of the coming change. For a few splendid moments there was only him, only now.

Their brief pleasure encountered its own natural boundary and began to retreat. It could go no further. The intensity of his kiss eased, growing sweet and poignant as reality intruded. He drew back to look at her, caught between loss and longing.

"Victoria, I . . ." Again, he could not bring himself to say it. He pulled away, striding for the stairs, then for the front door. He was halfway down the block before he could finally form the words that would have broken both their hearts: "I never meant to fall in love with you."

The next morning the entire staff assembled in the entry hall to see their Miss Meggie off to school. They were under strict orders to make it a joyful occasion; no tears would be allowed. Accordingly, the staff excused themselves immediately after she hugged them, to prevent her seeing the moisture in their eyes. Sebastian was determinedly cheerful, though his usual teasing and banter were lacking something. Meggie didn't seem to notice at

first. But then she saw the looks he and Victoria exchanged and grew a bit concerned. When she asked Victoria what was wrong, it was all Victoria could do to say
that she was just a little sad to see the holidays go. Meggie touched her arm and looked up at her in all serious-
ness.

"Well, Papa always says next year will be here before
you know it."

Victoria's throat froze around an unuttered sob. *Papa
always says.* Would she feel this same rush of anguish
every time she heard Meggie say that? Sebastian bent and
scooped Meggie up for one last exuberant hug, then lifted
her into the carriage and tucked her under a lap robe by
a foot warmer. He turned and extended a hand to help
Victoria up the step.

She laid her hand in his and seized her skirts, then
hesitated and looked at him. His face was stiff with control, but his eyes glistened hauntingly.

"It was wonderful having you here, Miss Howard,"
he said thickly. Then he couldn't keep from squeezing
her hand and adding in a soft rush, "Take care of her for
me."

Victoria nodded and mounted the step.

Horace and Edgar, who were at last relieved of their
kidnapper-jailer-chaperon duties, had been engaged by
Sebastian to ride along with the carriage for the day-long
trip to Grantley. They mounted hired horses and waved
and grinned at Meggie through the windows. But as the
carriage lurched into motion and they fell in behind, their
smiles became sighs and they shook their heads.

Halfway down the street, Victoria couldn't help looking back and Meggie flew to the window across from her.
Sebastian was standing on the steps, alone, with his hands
in his pockets and his broad shoulders strangely rounded.
Victoria watched him until they turned the corner, then
she settled back in the seat and drew Meggie against her
side. The questions came.

"How far away is it?" "Why can't Papa come, too?"

and "Will we be back for dinner?" Victoria was barely able to detach from her own turbulent feelings enough to answer in a comforting way.

It was a long while before Meggie finally fell asleep with her head on Victoria's lap. In the lulling sway of the carriage, Victoria kept seeing Sebastian's face and reliving his last desperate kiss. How she wished she could hate him for doing this to her. He had stolen her from her safe, secure, limited world, awakened her emotions, and given her a taste of all the things she had long ago resigned to the world of her dreams. A love both passionate and tender, a gracious home, a beautiful child of her own; for a brief, splendid time she experienced it all. Now it was all gone, and in its place were only painfully sweet might-have-beens.

Meggie stirred and nuzzled her lap, and Victoria looked down and stroked a stray curl back from her face. Halfway through that motion, she stopped, realizing she was wrong. Sebastian had given her one lasting thing, something of great value, something she had longed for with all her heart. He had given her a daughter.

Sebastian hadn't bothered to go back into the house, not even to get his hat and gloves. He had walked to the end of the square, hailed a cab, and headed straight for the bar at his club.

Watching Victoria and Meggie ride away from him was the hardest thing he'd ever done. He had thought he was prepared for the emptiness that would follow, that he might even welcome its numbing effect. But instead of numbness he'd experienced physical pain. He hadn't felt hollow; he'd been on the verge of an explosion. He wanted to run after them, rip the door open, and drag them both down into his arms. He wanted to carry them back inside and bar the doors against the rest of the cursed respectable world, and never let them go. But he hadn't, and they were gone, and he was sitting in his club, unable to even swallow a shot of Scotch.

It had been managed and overseen down to the last

detail, carried out to perfection. His scheme had worked. He'd gotten exactly what he wanted. No, he'd gotten more. And it was that more that had him in complete turmoil. He stared at the amber liquid in the glass in his hand and shoved it back onto the bar. Then he strode out into the frigid afternoon, with no particular destination in mind. It didn't matter where he went, for it would never be the one place he wanted to be, with them.

The carriage stopped at a coaching inn, just before noon. They opened the food hamper Cook had sent along, but Meggie wouldn't eat and Victoria managed only a bite or two. When the driver said it was time to get started, Meggie looked around with frightened eyes.

"I want to go home," she said, tears welling. Then, as if the sound of her own words escalated her anxiety, she began to cry. "I want to see my papa," she gasped between sobs. "Please, let me go home, take me home. I don't want to go to an old school; I want to go home!"

Victoria had gone through this dozens of times with new girls at Grantley. But this time her own emotions were too fragile and too near the surface. Tears came to her eyes, too, and she pulled Meggie into her arms, overcoming her frantic resistance to hold her tightly. But the usual words of comfort just wouldn't come. Meggie wouldn't be going home for a holiday soon; she wouldn't see her papa on next visiting day, and there wouldn't be a summer in the country to look forward to. She sat down on the carriage step and cradled Meggie on her lap.

"I want my papa," Meggie sobbed into Victoria's shoulder.

"I know, Pippin," Victoria said, stroking her hair, and adding softly, "I want him, too."

Horace and Edgar stood by, watching Victoria's and Meggie's tears. Their eyes grew watery and their chins quivered. Horace pulled out a handkerchief and blew his nose; Edgar swiped his with the back of his hand.

"Can we do anythin' to help, Miz?" Edgar bent toward them, and Horace peered over his shoulder.

Victoria looked up into their grave, sympathetic faces and gave her tears a gloved swipe. The whole stupid, painful mess wadded itself into a combustible knot in her middle, and when she lifted Meggie's tearful face from her shoulder and cradled it in her hand, the misery in it provided the spark to set her ablaze with righteous indignation. Sebastian Wolfe didn't have good sense. And since he didn't, somebody else would have to take charge and sort out what was best for Meggie, and for him. She looked at Meggie's features, so like Sebastian's and knew that every time she saw Meggie cry for her father, she'd be seeing Sebastian's sadness for his daughter as well. And she simply couldn't stand it. She loved both of them too much to let that happen.

"Yes," she said emphatically, looking up at Horace and Edgar, "there is something you can do to help." She sniffed and looked back at Meggie with a teary smile. "You can take this little Pippin back to her father, right now, this minute!" Their jaws drooped.

"I don't have to go to school?" Meggie pulled back and drew a shuddery breath.

"No, you don't," Victoria declared. "You're going home to your papa, where you belong." She gave Meggie a tight hug. "I think you're a little young for my school, even if your father doesn't. In a few years you can come and stay with me if you want, and take piano lessons and learn to speak French. But right now you belong with your papa and Cook and Pearson and Odelle." She paused to try to swallow the lump in her throat. "Promise me you will study very hard and mind your manners." When Meggie nodded, she smiled as convincingly as she could, kissed Meggie's forehead, and whispered softly: "Give your papa a hug for me."

Then she gave Meggie a boost up into the carriage and

turned on Horace and Edgar with the most heart-breaking expression they had ever seen . . . part anger and part anguish . . . filled with hurt.

"You tell Sebastian Wolfe that he's worse than a fool to think respectability is more important than love," she said, her voice clogged with tears. "It's time somebody taught him better, and I suppose it will have to be me. So I'm sending Meggie back to him, and I don't want to even hear of him trying to send her to a school again before she is twelve years old. Tell him that if he still wants it, I'll be pleased to sponsor her to Grantley then. And tell him . . . a loving heart is too precious a thing to break." Tears streamed down her cheeks and she felt as if her heart was indeed breaking. It was a long, harrowing moment before she could get hold of herself enough to ask in a small, choked voice, "Please, be so good as to get down my valise. I can wait inside the inn for the next mail coach to Bevis on the Wood."

"But why can't she come home with us?" Meggie asked anxiously, pressing her nose against the glass, looking back at Victoria's figure, standing on the covered steps of the inn. Horace and Edgar glanced balefully at each other.

"Well, she cain't . . . 'cause she ain't part o' the fam'ly, I guess," Horace said.

Meggie looked as if she would cry again. "Well, why can't she be part of our fam'ly, with Papa and me?"

" 'Cause yer papa is too pigheaded to see what's plain as the nose on his face!" Horace answered with a glower. Edgar gave Horace a cluck of disapproval and took it over.

"He means yer papa didn' ask Miz Howard t' marry up wi' him."

"Oh." Meggie wiped her reddened eyes, then thought for a minute, and brightened. "Well, when we get home, I'll ask him to ask her; then she won't have to go to school either!"

Horace and Edgar looked at her, then at each other,

and a crafty light dawned in their faces. "Ye got a right good idea, there, Miz Meggie," Edgar said.

Sebastian paced his large, walnut-paneled business office like a haunted man. His clerks, lawyers, and assistants stayed discreetly out of his way and shook their heads in private at his unusual behavior. Late in the afternoon, two coarsely clad street-toughs came bursting into the office, with Meggie Wolfe in tow and went barreling straight into his inner sanctum.

"Meggie!" Sebastian looked like a man seeing salvation for the first time. He rushed to scoop her up in his arms, then he kissed and hugged her tightly, holding her as if he'd never let her go again. In that moment he felt as if he'd been given a second life. She finally peeled her arms from around his neck and pushed back. "What are you doing here? You're supposed to be with . . ." He couldn't quite bring himself to say her name.

"Miss Howard sent me home!" Meggie said.

"It were a big mistake, Guv, sendin' Miz Howard off like that," Edgar said, between puffing breaths. "Cried the whole way to Campden Station, she did. 'Er eyes swelled up like soaked prunes. It wus jus' plain pitiful."

"Pitiful," Horace affirmed, shaking his head.

"And Miz Meggie here, she wus bawlin' somethin' fierce. Callin' fer her papa," Edgar continued, looking to Meggie for confirmation. Meggie stuck her lower lip out and nodded. "Miz Howard had 'er hands right full."

"Right full," Horace echoed again, nodding gravely. "An' her in no condition t' cope, what wi' her eyes all swelled up like that."

Sebastian looked as though he'd been horse-kicked. He had been seeing horrible, wrenching visions of Victoria and Meggie before his eyes all afternoon. And now that he had Meggie back in his arms all he could think about was the other empty half of his heart, Victoria.

"Miss Howard said you were silly to like good names better than love," Meggie said, trying her best to look sad as she tried to remember all the words Horace and Edgar had asked her to say. "And she said I can't come to her school till I'm twelve."

"She said that, did she?" Sebastian felt a sliver of longing slice through him. Meggie nodded.

"And she said"—she glanced at Edgar, who nodded, urging her on—"'a loving heart . . . is too precious a thing to break.'"

Sebastian knew exactly the way Victoria's eyes must have looked as she said it, soft, filled with hurt, and rimmed with tears she was too much of a lady to let fall. "And did she say anything else?"

Meggie nodded. "She said for me to give you a hug for her."

As Meggie's arms closed around his neck, he closed his eyes and felt Victoria's arms around him, too. And that gesture of warmth and continued caring said everything his heart longed to hear. She had refused to help him ruin his life and Meggie's for the sake of respectability and social standing. She had sent Meggie back to him, with a message of love. She loved them too much to let his plan succeed. She *loved* him.

"Why can't you just marry her so she doesn't have to go to school either, Papa?"

"Yeah, Papa," Edgar said glaring, "why can't ye jus' marry Miz Howard?"

"Yeah, Papa, jus' marry our Miz Howard an' make us all 'appy," Horace growled.

When he and Meggie hurried out, through his outer office, Horace and Edgar traded smiles of delight. "We done it, Horace. He's goin' to get 'er," Edgar crowed, rocking up and down on his toes. When a door slammed in the distance, they started and scrambled to follow.

Victoria walked up the long drive carrying her own valise from the coach station. Her shoulders were damp and weighted from the cold drizzle that had just begun. She paused before the great doors of Grantley, dreading entering and knowing too well why she felt that way. The lights in the entry hall seemed cold and glaring as she stepped inside. From the direction of the dormitory, she heard girls' voices, footsteps, and door closings echoing along the polished halls. The place smelled of vinegar and fresh wax, musty books and starched linen.

Miss Chesterton greeted her and extended effusive condolences upon the illness of her aged aunt. The girls rushed down to see her, the minute one of them announced she was back. But all through the evening Victoria felt like a visitor inside her own skin, detached from it all, as if she didn't quite belong here anymore.

She tried desperately not to think of Sebastian. But in the way of stubborn hearts, the more she tried not to think of him, the more vividly he appeared in her mind and in phantom sensations through her skin. How long would it be, she thought while lying in her chilled, darkened room that night, before she would stop missing him, stop wanting him?

The next morning she made her rounds of the dormitory early, then spent some time at her desk in her room, dealing with school correspondence. When she heard the midday bell, she left her room, heading for the main stairs and found them littered with girls who had stopped to stare curiously at what was happening by the front doors. A voice drifted up from the entry hall, a male voice, breathtakingly familiar.

"It is imperative, madam, that I see Miss Howard at once." She rushed to the gallery railing and craned her neck to see past the knots of girls stopped on the steps. A tall figure in a charcoal greatcoat was hovering over Miss Chesterton. Dark hair, top hat in hand, features that she had seen last night, all night, in her troubled dreams. Behind him were two endearingly mismatched fellows in gaudy, checkered wool coats and oversized bowlers.

"Who are you, sir?" the old lady demanded, drawing herself up regally. "And what business could you possibly have with my assistant?"

"I am here on a personal matter, madam." Sebastian's voice rose, matching the imperiousness of hers, tit for tat. The old headmistress lifted her chin and folded her hands.

"Miss Howard has no personal matters, sir. She is a proper schoolmistress. Now unless you can produce a letter from a suitable relative, I suggest—"

"Sebastian?" Victoria called out, threading through the girls to stand at the top of the great stairs. He heard his name and looked around, then up the stairs. And when he saw her, it was as if the sun dawned in his face.

"Victoria!" he called, taking several steps across the hall, halting near the foot of the stairs. A ripple of excitement raced through the girls as they turned to watch between the handsome stranger and their Miss Howard.

"I warn you, sir, take not another step. If I must, I shall send for the constable!" Miss Chesterton declared, bustling after him like a roused mother hen.

"What are you doing here?" Victoria managed to say, despite a constriction in her throat. Her heart quickened at the sight of his dark hair, his wide shoulders, and lurched at what she read in his glowing eyes. "I sent Meg-Margaret home—"

"I'm not here about Meggie, I'm here about you," he said, pouring all his hopes into a bold, reckless smile that made her bite her lower lip and tuck her arms around her waist.

"Really, Mr. Wolfe." She blushed at the unshuttered desire visible in his face and heard Miss Chesterton sputtering: "Wolfe? Seb-bastian Wolfe?"

"I've brought you three riddles, Miss Howard. And

I'll make you a wager. If you get all three right, I'll grant your wish. If you don't, you'll have to grant mine.'' He set his foot on the bottom step and the girls nearby giggled and shrank back, staring between him and Victoria. ''What do you say, Miss Howard?'' He laughed at her confusion and plunged straight ahead.

''Riddle me this, then: What is a little bit shocking, a little bit sweet, when you're nearby, my favorite treat?'' He mounted one step, then another, slowly, watching her shifting emotions in her eyes. ''Do you remember, Miss Howard?''

Remember? How could she ever forget? The scoundrel! Her fingers were suddenly tingling, alive with the recollection of his tongue stroking them. How dare he invade her school, invade her privacy, invade her very memories like this? And how dare she be so joyful that he was doing it?

''Ladyfingers,'' she said, unable to stop herself from answering. She refused to think about why he was here or what trouble he might be making for her; she only wanted to follow wherever his outrageous behavior led. And not even the sight of Miss Chesterton's horror or the girls' tittering curiosity could deter her.

''Very good, Miss Howard.'' He grinned and mounted three more steps. ''Riddle me this: What is wild as a thunder clap, grabs you like a beaver trap, given or taken with a squeeze, melts the bones right in your knees?''

Meggie's riddle! A massive wave of longing crashed over her and, as happened the first time she heard it, her gaze went straight to his mouth. He was wrecking her career; she'd be finished at Grantley. But she just had to answer.

''A kiss.''

Miss Chesterton gasped and began clearing the entry hall.

''That's two correct, Miss Howard. My, you are a sharp one. But then, I always knew that about you.'' On he came, step by step, his voice growing more velvety and his eyes growing warmer and more irresistible. Four steps below the top he stopped, looking at her, telling her without words all that she meant to him. "One more, Miss Howard, and one of us will have our heart's desire."

Her heart's desire was standing on the steps before her, she thought, looking at her as if she were his heart's desire. The impact of that thought set her whole body trembling. He had come for her; he wanted her enough to brave Miss Chesterton and the board and the slings and arrows of indignant propriety. Each step he took up those stairs shouted that love meant more to him, she meant more to him than social respectability. He'd learned the lesson she'd intended by Meggie's return. And he was acting on it.

"What is stronger than steel, and more precious than gold, the sweeter it is, the older it grows?"

She couldn't think, her heart was hammering, her knees were weak. He was so close and the pull of his desire for her was so tangible. She couldn't seem to catch the words and string them together; she couldn't make any sense of them at all. Strong, precious, sweet. It was a message for her and she couldn't decipher it.

A huge, mischievous grin spread over his handsome face. "Give up?"

She hesitated, then nodded, looking utterly bewildered. He took another step, then another, and she was vaguely aware of Miss Chesterton on the steps below, frantically seizing girls and sending them down the stairs and out of earshot.

"A marriage vow," he said, stepping onto the gallery beside her. And he pulled her arms from around her waist and took her hands in his. "I win."

"As always," she said, her heart thudding wildly. She was suddenly lost in the dark, chocolaty swirl of his gaze. Her whole body migrated toward him of its own accord, pliant, yearning.

"Now grant me my wish, Victoria"—he lifted her hands and kissed them—"and take marriage vows with me."

"That's your wish?" she whispered, thinking that it couldn't be happening. Dreams weren't supposed to come true.

"That's my wish, Victoria Howard," he said, "and I pray it is your wish, too." Then he drew her captive hands against his heart. "For I do love you. And you said yourself: a loving heart is too precious a thing to break."

She couldn't speak; her stomach felt empty and her eyes felt full. He loved her! He'd said it! Without thought for propriety or consequence, she freed her hands and slid them up around his neck, pulling him down.

"Yes, yes, *yes*! I'll marry you!" she declared joyfully. "I'll marry you and go to live with you and . . . love you." There was only one way to fully express the joy erupting in her. "Oh, Sebastian"—she pulled his head closer—"make the bones melt in my knees again."

He wrapped his arms around her and gave her exactly what she wanted, a deliciously tender and loving kiss that did indeed turn her knees watery. She pressed herself tight against him, beyond propriety, beyond reason, reveling gloriously in a newborn sense of freedom, a newborn commitment to love. Neither of them heard the girls' embarrassed titters or Miss Chesterton's cry of indignation or saw the old headmistress charging up the steps toward them.

"Victoria! This is an outrage; think of the girls!"

But it didn't matter. Horace and Edgar both saw her and intercepted her, spreading themselves on the step below Victoria and Sebastian like a wool-clad wall. "Ohhh, no you don't." Horace said, glaring at her and jerking a righteous thumb at the pair of lovers behind him. "Them two's earned a bit of a smooch, an' they ain't doin' nobody no 'arm.''

"Well, I never!" she blurted out, snatching up her skirts and bustling back down the steps to try to herd the rest of the gawking girls from the hall, like an overwrought collie.

Edgar grinned, watching the old lady flee. "I bet she's right, Horace. I bet she *never*."

"I'm ruined," Victoria said against his mouth, when their lush, sensual kiss ended. She could scarcely focus her eyes.

"No, you're not, you're betrothed," he said raggedly, grinning. "And don't think you can back out of it, Miss Howard. I have witnesses. We've a verbal contract, sealed with something a bit more binding than just a handshake." When she laughed, he nuzzled her ear, then the side of her neck, murmuring. "And as soon as it can be arranged, I want to close the deal and seal it with something a bit more binding, and pleasurable still."

Victoria looked up to find two of her pupils, about thirteen years of age, staring wide-eyed at them from the far hallway. "Sebastian, I think we'd better stop." She pushed back in his arms. "Think what kind of example this sets for the girls."

"Ummm," he said, refusing to let her go completely. "A wonderful example. You're the best knee-melter in the realm, Miss Howard. And just think, in years to come, they'll be able to say they saw a dream come true, right before their very eyes."

It was just more than two months later that the wedding notice for Miss Victoria Howard and Mr. Sebastian Wolfe was published in the *Times*. Noteworthy in the story of the wedding was the fact that the bride was given in marriage by her cousin, the sixth Duke of Carlisle, and that the wedding guests included a number of dignitaries from the Home Office, the Exchequer, several leading banks, and the Board of Trade. Mention of the members of the wedding party included Mr. E. Quiggley and Mr. H. Ferguson, listed as "security specialists for Mr. Wolfe's varied financial enterprises," and serving as the sole attendant for the radiantly beautiful bride was Mr. Wolfe's daughter, little Miss Margaret Wolfe.

To Binnie, who has more Beauties and Beasties than anyone I know.

The Black Beast of Belleterre

by Mary Jo Putney

HE WAS UGLY, VERY UGLY. HE HADN'T KNOWN THAT
when he was young and had a mother who loved him in
spite of his face. When people had looked at him oddly,
he had assumed it was because he was the son of a lord.
Since there were a few children who were willing to be
friends with him, he thought no more about it.

It was only later, when his mother had died and accident had augmented his natural ugliness, that James
Markland realized how different he was. People stared,
or if they were polite, quickly looked away. His own
father would not look directly at him on the rare occasions when they met. The sixth Baron Falconer had been
a very handsome man; James didn't blame him for despising a son who was so clearly unworthy of the ancient,
noble name that they both bore.

Nonetheless, James *was* the heir, so Lord Falconer had
handled the distasteful matter with consummate, aristocratic grace: he'd installed the boy at a small, remote
estate, seen that competent tutors were hired, and thought
no more about him.

The chief tutor, Mr. Grice, was a harsh and pious man,
generous both with beatings and with lectures on the in-
escapable evil of human nature. On his more jovial days,
Mr. Grice would tell his student how fortunate the boy
was to be beastly in a way that all the world could see;
most men carried their ugliness in their souls, where they
could too easily forget their basic wickedness. James

should feel grateful that he had been granted such a signal opportunity to be humble.

James had not been grateful, but he had been resigned. His life could have been worse; the servants were paid enough to tolerate the boy they served, and one of the grooms was even friendly. So James had a friend, a library, and a horse. He was content, most of the time.

When the sixth lord died—in a gentlemanly fashion, while playing whist—James had become the seventh Baron Falconer. In the twenty-one years of his life, he had spent a total of perhaps ten nights under the same roof as his late father. He had felt very little at his father's death—not grief, not triumph, not guilt. Perhaps there had been regret, but only a little. It was hard to regret not being better acquainted with a man who had chosen to be a stranger to his only son.

As soon as his father died, James had taken two trusted servants and flown into a wider world, like the soaring bird of the family crest. Egypt, Africa, India, Australia; he had seen them all during his years of travel. He had discovered that the life of an eccentric English lord suited him, and he also developed habits that enabled him to keep the world at a safe distance. Seeing the monks in a monastery in Cyprus had given him the idea of wearing a heavily cowled robe that would conceal him from casual curiosity. Ever after, he wore a similar robe or hood when he had to go among strangers.

Because he was young and unable to repress his shameful lusts, he had also taken advantage of his wealth and distance from home to educate himself about the sins of the flesh. For the right price, it was easy to engage deft, experienced women who would not only lie with him, but would even pretend that they didn't care how he looked. One or two, the best actresses of the lot, had been almost convincing when they claimed to enjoy his company, and his touch. He did not resent their lies; the world was a hard place, and if lying might earn a girl more money, one couldn't expect her to tell the truth.

Nonetheless, his pleasure was tainted by the bitter awareness that only his wealth made him acceptable.

He returned to England at the age of twenty-six, stronger for having seen the world beyond the borders of his homeland; strong enough to accept the limits of his life. He would never have a wife, for no gently bred girl would marry him if she had a choice, and hence he would never have a child.

Nor would he have a mistress, no matter how much his body yearned for the brief, joyous forgetting that only a woman could provide. Though he was philosophical by nature and had very early decided that he would not allow self-pity, there were limits to philosophy. The only reasons why a woman would submit to his embraces were for money or from pity. Neither reason was endurable; though he could bear his ugliness and isolation, he could not have borne the knowledge that he was pathetic.

Rather than dwell in bitterness, he was grateful for the wealth that buffered him from the world. Unlike ugly men who were poor, Falconer was in a position to create his own world, and he did.

What made his life worth living was the fact that when he returned to England, he had fallen in love. Not with a person, of course, but with a place. Belleterre, in the lush southeastern county of Kent, was the principal Markland family estate. As a boy James had never gone there, for his father had not wished to see him. Instead, James had been raised at a small family property in the industrial Midlands. He had not minded, for it was the only home he had ever known and not without its own austere charm.

Yet when he returned from his tour of the world after his father's death and first saw Belleterre, for a brief moment he had hated his father for keeping him away from his heritage. Belleterre meant beautiful land, and never was a name more appropriate. The rich fields and woods, the ancient, castlelike stone manor house, were a worthy object for the love he yearned to express. It became his life's work to see that Belleterre was cared for as tenderly as a child.

Ten years had passed since he had come to Belleterre, and he had had the satisfaction of seeing the land and people prosper under his stewardship. If he was lonely, it was no more than he expected. Books had been invented to salve human loneliness, and they were friends without peer, friends who never sneered or flinched or laughed behind a man's back. Books revealed their treasures to all who took the effort to seek.

Belleterre, books, and his animals—he needed nothing more.

Spring

Sometimes, regrettably, Falconer deemed it necessary to leave Belleterre, and today was such a day. The air was warm and full of the scents and songs of spring. He enjoyed the ten-mile ride, though he was not looking forward to the interview that would take place when he reached his destination.

He frowned when he reined in his horse at the main gate of Gardsley Manor, for the ironwork was rusty and the mortar was crumbling between the bricks of the pillars that bracketed the entrance. When he rang the bell to summon the gatekeeper, five minutes passed before a sullen, badly dressed man appeared.

Crisply he said, "I'm Falconer. Sir Edwin is expecting me."

The gatekeeper stiffened and quickly opened the gate, keeping his gaze away from the cloaked figure that rode past. Falconer was unsurprised by the man's reaction; doubtless the country folk told many stories about the mysterious hooded lord of Belleterre. What kind of stories, Falconer neither knew nor cared.

Before meeting Sir Edwin, Falconer knew that he must ascertain the condition of the property; it was the reason he had chosen to visit Gardsley in person rather than summon the baronet to Belleterre. Once he was out of sight of the gatekeeper, he turned from the main road onto a track that swung west, roughly paralleling the edge of the castle.

On the side of a beech-crowned hill he tethered his mount and pulled a pair of field glasses from his saddlebag, then climbed to the summit. Since there was no one in sight, he pushed his hood back, enjoying the feel of the balmy spring breeze against his face and head.

As he had hoped, the hill gave a clear view of the rolling Kentish countryside. In the distance he could even see steam from a Dover-bound train. But what he saw closer did not please him. The field glasses showed Gardsley in regrettable detail, from crumbling fences to overgrown fields to poor quality stock. The more he saw, the more his mouth tightened, for the property had clearly been neglected for years.

Five years before Sir Edwin Hawthorne had come to Falconer and asked for a loan to help him improve his estate. Though Falconer had not much liked the baronet, he had been impressed and amused by the man's sheer audacity at asking a complete stranger for money. Probably Hawthorne had been inspired by stories of Falconer's generosity to charity and had decided that he had nothing to lose by requesting a loan. Sir Edwin had been very eloquent, speaking emotionally of his wife's expensive illness and recent death, of his only daughter, and how the property that had been in his family for generations desperately needed investment to become prosperous again.

Though Falconer had known he was being foolish, he had given in to impulse and lent the baronet the ten thousand pounds that had been requested. It was a sizable fortune, but Falconer could well afford it, and if Hawthorne really cared that much about his estate, he deserved an opportunity to save it.

But wherever the ten thousand pounds had gone, it hadn't been into Gardsley. The loan had come due a year earlier, and Falconer had granted a twelve-month extension. Now that grace period was over, the money had not been repaid, and Falconer must decide what to do. If there had been any sign that the baronet cared for his land, Falconer would have been willing to extend the loan indefinitely. But this . . . ! Hawthorne deserved to be flogged and turned out on the road as a beggar for his neglect of his responsibilities.

Falconer was about to descend to his horse when he caught a flash of blue on the opposite side of the hill. Thinking it might be a kingfisher, he raised his field glasses again and scanned the lower slope until he found the color he was seeking.

He caught his breath when he saw that it was not a kingfisher but a girl. She sat cross-legged beneath a flowering apple tree and sketched with charcoal on a tablet laid across her lap. As he watched, she made a face and ripped away her current drawing. Then she crumpled the paper and dropped it on a pile of similarly rejected work.

His first impression was that she was a child, for she was small and her silver-gilt tresses spilled loosely over her shoulders rather than being pinned up. But when he adjusted the focus of the field glasses, the increased clarity showed that her figure and face were those of a woman, albeit a young one. She was eighteen, perhaps twenty at the outside, and graceful even when seated on the ground.

In spite of the simplicity of her blue dress, she must be Hawthorne's daughter, for she was no farm girl. But she did not resemble her florid father; instead, she had a quality of bright sweetness that riveted Falconer's attention. His view was from the side and her pure profile reminded him of the image of a goddess on a Greek coin. If his old tutor, Mr. Grice, could have seen this girl under the apple tree, even that old curmudgeon might have wondered if all humans were inherently sinful.

She was so lovely that Falconer's heart hurt. He did not know if his pain was derived from sadness that he would never know her, or joy that such beauty could exist in the world. Both emotions, perhaps. Unconsciously he raised one hand and pulled the dark hood over his head, so that if by chance she looked his way, she would be unable to see him. He would rather die than cause that sweet face to show fear or disgust.

When he had made his plea for money five years earlier, Sir Edwin had mentioned his daughter's name. It was something fanciful that had made Falconer think her mother must have loved Shakespeare. Titania, the fairy queen? No, not that. Ophelia or Desdemona? No, neither of those.

Ariel—her name was Ariel. Now that Falconer saw the girl, he realized that her name was perfect, for she seemed not quite mortal, a creature of air and sunshine. Her mother must have been prescient.

Though he knew it was wrong to spy on her, he could not bring himself to look away. From the way her glance went up and down, she was sketching the old oak tree in front of her. She had the deft quickness of hand of a true artist who races time to capture a private vision of the world. He was sure that she saw more deeply than mere bark and spring leaves; a pity that he couldn't see her work.

A puff of breeze blew across the hillside, lifting strands of her bright hair, driving one of her crumpled drawings across the grass, and loosening blossoms from the tree. Pink, sun-struck petals showered over the girl as if even nature felt compelled to celebrate her beauty. As the scent of apples drifted up the hill, Falconer knew he would never forget the image that she made, gilded by sunshine and haunted by flowers.

He was about to turn away when the girl stood and brushed the petals from her gown. After gathering her discarded drawings, she turned and walked down the opposite side of the hill, away from him. Her strides were as graceful as he had known they would be and her hair was a shimmering, silver-gilt mantle. But she had overlooked the drawing that had blown away.

After the girl was gone from view, Falconer went down and retrieved the crumpled sheet from the tuft of cowparsley where it had lodged. Then he flattened the paper, careful not to smudge the charcoal.

As he had guessed, the girl's drawing of the gnarled oak went far beyond mere illustration. In a handful of strong, spare lines, she had implied harsh winters and fertile, acorn-rich summers; sun and rain and drought; the long history of a tree that had first sprouted generations before the girl was born and should survive for centuries more. That slight, golden child was indeed an artist.

Since she had not wanted the drawing, surely there was no harm in his keeping it. And, knowing himself for a sentimental fool, he also plucked a few strands of the grass that had been crushed beneath her when she worked.

He watched for the girl as he completed his ride to the manor house, but without success. If not for the evidence of the drawing in his saddlebag, he might have wondered if he had imagined her.

Sir Edwin Hawthorne greeted his guest nervously, gushing welcomes and excuses. He had been a handsome man, but lines of dissolution marred his face and now sweat shone on his brow.

As Falconer expected, the baronet was unable to repay the loan. "The last two years have been difficult, my lord," he said, his eyes darting around the room, anything to avoid looking at the cowled figure who sat motionless in his study. "Lazy tenants, disease among the sheep. You know how hard it is to make a profit on farming."

Falconer knew no such thing; his own estate was amazingly profitable, for it flourished under loving hands. Not just the hands of its master, but those of all his tenants and employees, for he would have no one at Belleterre who did not love the land. Quietly he said, "I've already given you a year beyond the term of the original loan. Can you make partial payment?"

"Not today, my lord, but very soon," Sir Edwin said. "Within the next month or two, I should be in a position to repay at least half the sum."

Under his concealing hood, Falconer's mouth twisted. "Are you a gamester, Sir Edwin? The turn of a card or the speed of a horse is unlikely to save you from ruin."

The baronet twitched at his guest's comment, but it was the shock of guilt, not surprise. With quick mendacity he said, "All gentlemen gamble a bit, of course, but I'm no gamester." He ran a damp palm over his hair. "I assure you, if you will give me just a little more time . . ."

Falconer remembered the neglected fields, the shabby laborers' cottages, and almost refused. Then he thought of the girl. What would become of Ariel if her father's property was sold to pay his debts? She should be in London now, fluttering through the Season with the rest of the bright, well-born butterflies. She should have a husband who would cherish her and give her children.

But a London debut was expensive, and likely any money her father managed to beg or borrow went on his own vices. In spite of the isolation of his life, Falconer was not naive about his fellow man. He was surely not Hawthorne's only creditor; the man had probably borrowed money in every direction and had debts that could not be repaid even if Gardsley was sold.

Falconer felt a surge of anger. A man who would neglect his land would also neglect his family, and a girl who should have been garbed in silks and adored by the noblest men in the land was wearing cotton and sitting alone in a field. Not that she had looked unhappy; he guessed that she had the gift of being happy anywhere. But she deserved so much more.

If Falconer insisted on payment now, her father would be ruined, and the girl would probably end up a poor relation in someone else's house. Unable to bear the thought, Falconer found himself saying, "I'll give you three more months. If you can repay half of the principal by then, I'll renegotiate the balance. But if you can't pay . . ." It was unnecessary to complete the sentence.

Babbling with relief, Sir Edwin said, "Splendid, splendid. I assure you I'll have your five thousand pounds three months from now. Likely I'll be able to repay the whole amount then."

Falconer looked at the baronet and despised him. He was a weak, shallow man, unable to see beyond the fact that he had been spared the consequences of his actions for a little longer. Abruptly Falconer rose to his feet. "I'll be back three months from today."

But as he rode home to Belleterre, he was still haunted by one thought. What would happen to the girl?

Ariel returned to the house for lunch, pleased that she had done several sketches worth keeping. Her satisfaction died when she found that her father had taken the train down from London that morning. As soon as the butler told her, Ariel put one hand to her untidy hair, then darted up the back stairs to her room.

As she brushed the snarls from her hair, she wondered how long Sir Edwin would stay at Gardsley this time. Life was always pleasanter when he was away, which was most of the time. But while he was here, she must tread warily and keep out of his sight. Alas, she could not escape her daughterly duty to dine with him every night. He would criticize her unladylike appearance; he always did. He would also be quite specific about the many ways in which she was a disappointment to him.

Once or twice Ariel had considered pointing out that he didn't allow her enough money to be fashionably dressed even if she had been so inclined, but caution always curbed her tongue. Though not a truly vicious man, Sir Edwin was capable of lashing out when he had been drinking, or when he was particularly frustrated with his circumstances.

Still brushing her hair, she wandered to her window and looked out. She loved this particular view. The clouds were quite dramatic this afternoon; perhaps she could go up on the roof and try to capture the sunset in watercolors. But no, that wouldn't be possible tonight, since she would have to dine with her father.

She was regretfully turning away from the window when a strange figure came down the front steps. It was a tall man wearing a swirling black robe with a deep, cowled hood that totally obscured his face. Since Gardsley was said to have a ghost or two, Ariel wondered idly if one of them was making an appearance. But the man who moved so lithely down the steps, then called for his horse, seemed quite real. Certainly the horse and the Gardsley footman who brought it were not phantoms.

Abruptly she realized that the figure could only be the mysterious, reclusive Lord Falconer, sometimes called the Black Beast of Belleterre. He was something of a legend in Kent, and the maids often talked about him in hushed, deliciously scandalized whispers. Ariel had heard him described as both saint and devil, sometimes in the same breath. It was said that he gave much to charity and had endowed a hospital for paupers in nearby Maidstone; it was also said that he held wild, midnight orgies on his estate. Ariel had looked up the word *orgy,* but the definition had been so vague that she hadn't been able to puzzle out what was involved. Still, it had sounded alarming.

Stripped of rumors and titillated guesses, the gossip about him boiled down to three facts: he had grown up in the Midlands, he was so hideously deformed that his own father had been unable to stand the sight of him, and he now concealed himself from the gazes of all but a handful of trusted servants, none of whom would say a word about him. Whether their silence was a product of fear or devotion was a source of much speculation.

As Ariel watched him swing effortlessly onto his horse, she decided that his deformity could not be of the body, for he was tall and broad-shouldered and he moved like an athlete. With compassion she wondered what made him so unwilling to show his face to the world. Even more, she wondered why Lord Falconer was at Gardsley. He must have had business with her father. In fact that would explain why Sir Edwin had unexpectedly returned from London.

Ariel had just reached that conclusion when Lord Falconer glanced up at the facade of the house. His gaze seemed to go right to her, though it was hard to be sure since his face was shadowed. Instinctively she stepped back, not wanting to be caught in the act of staring. Although, she thought with a hint of acerbity, a man who dressed like a medieval monk had to expect to attract attention.

Dropping his gaze, he turned his horse and cantered away. He rode beautifully, so much in tune with his mount that it seemed to move without the use of reins or knees. Stepping forward again, Ariel watched him disappear from sight. The Black Beast of Belleterre. There was a larger-than-life quality about the man that was as romantic as it was tragic. She began considering different ways to portray him. Not watercolor, that wasn't strong enough. It would have to be either the starkness of pen and ink or the voluptuous richness of oils.

She stood by the window for quite some time, lost in contemplation, until her attention was caught by another figure coming down the steps. This time it was her father, followed by his valet. As she watched, the carriage came around from the stables. After the two men had climbed in, she heard her father order the driver to take him to the station. So he was going back to London without even asking to see her.

Silly of her to feel hurt when their meetings were so uncomfortable for both of them. Besides, now she would be free to go up on the roof and paint the sunset. But

Ariel found that unexpectedly thin comfort. A sunset no longer seemed as interesting; not when she had just seen the enigmatic Lord Falconer.

Yes, pen and ink would be best for him.

Summer

Falconer returned to Gardsley exactly three months after his first visit. The day was another fine one, so, despising himself for his weakness, he took the same detour across the estate that he had taken before. The land was in no better shape than it had been, and the hay would be ruined if it wasn't cut immediately, but he did not care for that. His real purpose was a wistful hope that he might catch a glimpse of the girl. But she was not sketching on the hill today. The blossoms were long gone from the tree and now small, hard green apples hung from the branches.

Regretfully he turned his horse and rode to the house. He had had his solicitor make inquiries about Sir Edwin Hawthorne and the results had confirmed all of Falconer's suspicions. The baronet was a gambler and a notorious seducer of other men's wives. He was away from Gardsley for months on end, and had been hovering on the brink of financial disaster for years.

The solicitor's report had gone on to say that Sir Edwin's only daughter, Ariel, was twenty years old. She had had a governess until she was eighteen; since then, she had apparently lived alone at Gardsley with only servants for company. On the rare occasions when she was invited into county society, she was much admired for her beauty and modesty, but her father's reputation and her own lack of dowry must have barred her from receiving any eligible marriage offers.

Falconer had had trouble believing that part of the report. Surely the men of Kent could not be so blind, so greedy, as to overlook such a jewel simply because she had no fortune.

The butler admitted Falconer and left him in a drawing room at the front of the house, saying that Sir Edwin would be with his guest in a moment. Falconer smiled mirthlessly. If the baronet had had the money, he would have been waiting with a bank draft in hand. Now he was probably in his study trying desperately to think of a way to save his profligate hide.

Falconer was pacing the drawing room when he heard the sound of raised voices, the baronet's nervous tenor clashing with the lighter tones of a woman. The drawing room had double doors that led to another reception room behind, so Falconer went through. The voices were much louder now, and he saw that another set of double doors led into Sir Edwin's study, where the quarrel was taking place. The baronet was saying, "You'll marry him because I say so! It's the only way to save us from ruin."

Though Falconer had never heard Ariel's voice, he knew instantly that the sweet, light tones belonged to her. "You mean it will save *you* from ruin, at the cost of ruining me," she replied. "Even I have heard of Gordstone—the man is notorious. I will not marry him."

Falconer felt as if he had been struck in the stomach. Gordstone was indeed notorious—a pox-ridden lecher who had driven three young wives to their graves. Not only did he have an evil reputation, but he must be over forty years older than Ariel. Surely Sir Edwin could not be so vile as to offer his only daughter to such a man. Yet Gordstone was wealthy and Ariel's father needed money.

In a transparent attempt to sound reassuring, Sir Edwin said, "You shouldn't listen to backstairs gossip. Lord Gordstone is a wealthy, distinguished man. As his wife, you'll have a position in London's most amusing society."

"I don't want to be part of London society," his daughter retorted. "All I want is to be left alone here at Gardsley. Is that so much to ask?"

"Yes, dammit, it is!" the baronet barked. "A girl with

your beauty could be a great asset to me. Instead, you hide here and play with pencils and paints. In spite of your lack of cooperation I've managed to arrange a splendid marriage for you, and by God, you'll behave as a proper daughter and obey me.''

Voice quavering but defiant, Ariel said, ''I won't! I'll be twenty-one soon. You can't make me.''

She was stronger than she looked, that delicate golden girl. But even as the admiring thought passed through Falconer's mind, he heard the flat, sharp sound of flesh slapping flesh, and Ariel cried out.

Sir Edwin had struck his daughter. Nearly blinded by rage, Falconer put his hand on the knob to the study. He was about to fling the door open when he heard Ariel speak again. ''You won't change my mind this way, Papa.''

Though he could hear tears in her voice, she did not speak as if she had been seriously injured, so Falconer paused, his hand still on the doorknob. What happened between Sir Edwin and his daughter was none of Falconer's business, and if he intervened, the baronet would surely punish the girl for it later, when her champion was not around.

''Don't worry—I'll find a way that will change your mind,'' Sir Edwin snapped. ''If you don't marry Gordstone, you won't have a roof over your head, for Gardsley will have to be sold. Then what will you do, missy? Go to your room and think about that while I talk with that ugly brute in the drawing room. If I can't persuade him to give me another extension of my loan, I'll be a pauper, and so will you.''

Falconer turned and retreated noiselessly to the drawing room at the front of the house. He was standing there, looking out the window, hands linked behind his back, when the baronet entered the room.

''Good day, my lord,'' Sir Edwin said in a voice of forced amiability. ''You've come just in time to hear good news. My daughter is about to contract an advantageous alliance, and I will be able to repay you out of the settlement money. You need only wait a few weeks longer, for the bridegroom is anxious for an early wedding.''

Falconer turned and stared at his host but didn't reply. As the silence stretched, Sir Edwin became increasingly nervous. Falconer knew that his stillness disturbed people; once, behind his back, someone had said that it was like being watched by the angel of death.

When he could bear the silence no longer, the baronet said, ''Are you unwell, my lord?''

After another ominous pause, Falconer said, ''I've already extended the loan twice. Since Gardsley is your collateral, I can have you evicted from here tomorrow if I choose.''

Sir Edwin paled. ''But you can't ruin me now, not when a solution is so close at hand! I swear that within a month—''

Falconer cut the other off with a sharp motion of his hand. ''I can indeed ruin you, and by God, perhaps I will, for you deserve to be ruined.''

Almost weeping, the baronet said, ''Is there nothing I can do to persuade you to reconsider? Surely it is the duty of a Christian to show mercy.'' He stopped a moment, groping for other arguments. ''And my daughter . . . will you destroy her life as well? This is the only home she has ever known.''

His daughter, whom the villain proposed to sell to Gordstone. Falconer's hands curled into fists when he thought of that golden child defiled by such a loathsome creature. He could not allow the girl to marry Gordstone. *He could not.* But how could he prevent it?

An outrageous idea occurred to him. To even consider it was wrong, blasphemous; yet by committing a wrong, he could prevent a greater wrong. When he was sure his voice would be even, Falconer said, ''There's one thing that would change my mind.''

Eagerly Sir Edwin said, ''What is it? I swear I'll do anything you wish.''

"The girl." Falconer's voice broke. "I'll take the girl."

Half an hour after Ariel was sent to her bedroom, her father came up after her. She steeled herself when he entered, praying that she would be strong enough to resist his threats and blandishments. She was still shaken by what he had revealed earlier. Though Sir Edwin had never spent money on his estate or on her, she had always assumed that he had a decent private income or he could not have afforded to live in London. But today he had informed her that his entire fortune was gone and she must marry the despicable Lord Gordstone.

Yet she couldn't possibly marry Gordstone. A fortnight earlier her father had brought the man to Kent for the weekend. In retrospect it was obvious that the real purpose of the visit had been for the old satyr to look Ariel over. Once he had caught her alone and pounced on her like a dog discovering a meaty bone. His foul breath and pawing hands had been disgusting. After escaping his embrace, she had spent the days in distant fields and had barred her door at night until he left.

Without preamble her father said, "You didn't want to marry Gordstone, and now you don't have to. Another candidate for your hand has appeared. Sight unseen, Lord Falconer wants you."

"Lord Falconer?" Ariel gasped, her mind going to the dark, enigmatic figure she had so briefly seen. "How can he want to marry a female he has never even met?"

"Ask him yourself," Sir Edwin replied. "He's in the drawing room and wants to speak with you right now." Mockingly he stepped back and gestured her to go ahead of him. "It appears that you'll be the salvation of me in spite of yourself. You can't say I haven't done well by you, missy; you have your choice of two wealthy, titled husbands! Most girls would cut off their right arms to be in your position."

Ariel doubted that many girls would sacrifice a limb

for the privilege of being forced to choose between a revolting old lecher and a faceless man known as the Black Beast, but she kept her chin high when she walked past her father. She gave a fleeting thought to her loose hair, but there was no time to tidy herself. In this her father was right; if she behaved like a young lady, sipping tea instead of roaming the fields, she would be prepared for such a momentous interview. Surely if she were dressed properly, she would be less afraid.

She entered the drawing room with her father's heavy hand on her arm. The Black Beast of Belleterre stood in front of the unlit fireplace, tall and dark and so still that the folds of his robe might have been carved from stone. Trying to conceal the trembling of her hands, Ariel linked them together behind her.

"Here's the girl," Sir Edwin boomed. "So excited by the prospect of receiving your addresses that she rushed right down. Ariel, make a curtsy to his lordship."

As she obediently dipped down, the hooded man said, "Leave us, Sir Edwin."

"That wouldn't be proper." Though the baronet's tone was virtuous, his hard glance at his daughter showed that he didn't trust her to say the right thing without him there.

Sharply Falconer repeated, "Leave us! I will speak with Miss Hawthorne privately."

Ariel surreptitiously wiped her damp palms on her skirt as her father reluctantly left the room. In spite of what he had said and done earlier, she watched him go with regret, for he was a known quantity, unlike the frightening man by the fireplace. Even without the hood, he would have been hard to see clearly, for he had chosen to stand in the darkest part of the room.

Falconer turned to her. "Your father told you why I wish to speak with you?"

Not trusting her voice, she nodded.

His voice was the deepest she'd ever heard, but the commanding tone he had used to address her father was gone. In fact he sounded almost shy when he said, "Don't be afraid of me, Ariel. I asked your father to leave so we could speak freely. I know you're in a difficult position and I want to help. Unfortunately the only way I can do so is by marrying you.''

Startled, she said, "You know about Gordstone?''

"Yes, while I was waiting to speak to your father, I overheard the discussion between you.''

Unconsciously Ariel raised one hand to her cheek where a bruise was forming. When she did, the folds of Falconer's robe quivered slightly and the atmosphere changed, as if a thundercloud had entered the room. Her face colored and she dropped her hand, embarrassed that this stranger had heard what had passed between her and her father. It explained a great deal; apparently the Black Beast of Belleterre was enough of a gentleman that he had been upset by her father's bullying. But that didn't answer a more basic question. Thinking of those ill-defined orgies, she asked, "Why are you willing to offer marriage to someone you've never met?''

After a long silence he said, "No young lady should be forced to wed Gordstone. I had not intended ever to marry, so offering you the protection of my name will not deprive me of anything.'' His tone became intense. "And that is exactly what I am offering—a home and the protection of my name. I will not require . . . marital intimacy of you.''

Her blush returned, this time burningly hot. The maids always lowered their voices when they spoke of the marriage bed, or of the nonmarital haystack. Ariel guessed that the subject might be related to orgies, but that still told her nothing worthwhile. Haltingly she said, "Do you mean that it will be a . . . a marriage in name only?''

He grasped at the phrase with relief. "Exactly. You told your father that you wished to be left alone at Gardsley. I can't give you that, for it's just a matter of time until he loses the estate, but if you like the country, you'll be happy at Belleterre. You'll be free to draw or paint, or do anything else you desire. I promise not to interfere with you in any way.''

Her eyes widened. How could he know about her art and how important it was to her? Vainly she tried to see Falconer's face within the shadows of the cowl, but without success. There was something uncanny about the man; no wonder he had such an alarming reputation. ''Your offer is very generous,'' she said, ''but what benefit will you derive from such a marriage?''

''The warm glow that comes from knowledge of a deed well done,'' he said with unmistakable irony. Seeing her expression, he said more quietly, ''It will please me if you are happy.''

She began twisting a lock of hair that fell over her shoulder. He seemed kind, but what did she know of him? She wasn't sure she trusted disinterested generosity. If she became his wife, she would be his property, to do with as he wished.

Guessing her thoughts, he said, ''Are you wondering if you can trust the Black Beast of Belleterre to keep his word?''

So he knew his nickname. This time when she blushed, it was for her fellow man, for inventing such a cruel title. ''I'm confused,'' she said honestly. ''An hour ago, I scarcely knew that you existed; now I'm considering an offer of marriage from you. There's something very medieval about it.''

He gave an unexpected rumble of laughter. ''If we were in the Middle Ages, you would have no choice at all, and the man offering for you wouldn't be wearing a monk's robe.''

So he had a sense of humor. For some reason that surprised her, for he was such a dark, melodramatic figure. She sank down into a chair and linked her hands in her lap while she considered her choices. Marrying Gordstone she dismissed instantly; she'd become a beggar first.

Perhaps she could stay at Gardsley for a while, but

sadly she accepted that her days at the only home she had ever known were numbered. Even if her father received some unexpected financial windfall, he would soon squander it. He cared only for London society and placed no value on his estate beyond the fact that being Hawthorne of Gardsley gave him position.

She could look for work. Wistfully she thought of Anna McCall, who had been her governess and friend for six years. Anna had been discharged on Ariel's eighteenth birthday because Sir Edwin had not wanted to continue paying her modest salary. Anna had gone to a fine position with a family near London; perhaps she could help Ariel find a situation, for the two women still corresponded. But Anna was older and much more clever, while Ariel was young and vague and had no skills except drawing. No one would want her for a governess or teacher.

If she wouldn't marry Gordstone, couldn't stay at Gardsley, and was incapable of supporting herself, she had only one other choice—accepting Falconer's proposal. Of the paths open to her, it was the hardest to evaluate. Yet even if the man was lying and he wanted to use her to slake his mysterious male needs, he couldn't be worse than Gordstone, and if he genuinely wanted no more than to offer her a home, she might be happy at Belleterre.

Lifting her head, Ariel gazed at the dark stranger who waited patiently for her answer. She wished she could see his face; no matter how misshapen his visage was, it would be less alarming than the hood. Nonetheless, she said steadily, ''If you truly wish it, Lord Falconer, I will marry you.''

Humor again lurking in his voice, he said, ''You've decided that I'm the best of a bad lot?''

''Exactly.'' Her lips curved up involuntarily. ''Apparently I inherited some of my father's gambling blood.''

''Very well then, Ariel,'' he said, his deep voice making music of her name. ''We shall marry. I guarantee that your life at Belleterre will be no worse than your life here, and if it is within my power, I shall see that it is better.''

She could hardly ask fairer than that. Nonetheless, that night in her bed, she cried herself to sleep.

They were married three and a half weeks later, after the crying of the banns. Ariel's father had insisted that she must have a fashionable wedding gown, and he had taken her to a London dressmaker. As always, she'd hated the noise and the crowds of people. Even more, she hated the white silk gown, with its bustle and train and elaborate flounces that made her feel like an overdecorated cake. Most of all, she had hated the corset and steel hoops she must wear to make the dress fit properly.

Just before they left the dressmaker's salon, she heard Sir Edwin tell the proprietor to send the bill to Lord Falconer of Belleterre. So her father would not spend his own money even for his daughter's wedding gown. Any sentimental regrets she had about leaving her home vanished then.

She slept badly during the weeks between her betrothal and her marriage, and she went to the church on her wedding day with dark circles under her eyes. She wouldn't have been surprised if the groom had taken one look at her and changed his mind, but he didn't. Still, she suspected that he was as nervous as she, though she wasn't sure how she knew that when he was completely invisible under his cowled robe. For a moment she had the hysterical thought that she might not be marrying Lord Falconer, for anyone could hide under a robe. She reminded herself sharply that his face might be hidden, but his height and smooth, powerful movements were proof of his identity.

It was a very small wedding, with only Ariel and her father, the vicar and his wife, and an elderly man who stood up with Lord Falconer. Based on a faint but unmistakable scent, the elderly man was a groom. Ariel had invited Anna McCall, but her friend had been unable to come, for the interesting reason that she herself was getting married the same day.

Though the ceremony went quickly, there were several surprises—the first when the vicar referred to the bridegroom as "James Philip." Ariel knew that his family name was Markland, but with a small jolt she realized that she hadn't known his given name. He was a stranger, a complete stranger, and she had agreed to marry him without knowing either his name or what he looked like. She glanced up at his face, but the church was old and shadowy, and the cowl effectively prevented her from seeing anything even though she stood right next to him.

The service progressed. The next surprise came when Falconer lifted her icy hand so that he could slide the ring on her finger. He used both hands to hold hers, and she found his warm touch comforting. Then she glanced down. She hadn't seen his hands closely before, for he tended to hold them so that they were not readily visible. Now she saw that his left hand was so heavily scarred that the two smallest fingers must be almost useless. She could not help but stare in surprise. He saw her reaction and dropped his hands as soon as the ring was on her finger. The sleeve of his robe fell over his wrist, and once more the damage was invisible.

She wanted to tell him that her reaction had been simple surprise, not repulsion, but she couldn't do that now, in the middle of the wedding ceremony. She bit her lip as the vicar concluded the ritual, declared them man and wife, and said with strained joviality that it was time to kiss the bride. Ariel had wondered what would happen at this point. Would her new husband abstain, or would he actually kiss her and she might learn something of what he looked like?

Once again, he surprised her by lifting her right hand and kissing it, very gently. His lips were warm and smooth and firm, just the way lips should be. She wanted to weep, and didn't know why. Then they turned and left the church, married. No wedding breakfast had been planned, for Ariel had guessed that Lord Falconer would be uncomfortable at such an event. Nor would there be a honeymoon; they would go directly to Belleterre where her possessions should have already been delivered.

Just before stepping outside, she saw Falconer give an envelope to her father, but she said nothing until she and her new husband were alone in their carriage. Then, as she disposed her billowing skirts, she said quietly, "How much did it cost you to buy me?"

He shifted uneasily on the leather seat, but didn't avoid the question. "I canceled a loan of ten thousand pounds and gave your father twenty thousand pounds beyond that. He's supposed to use it to settle other debts, though I doubt that he will."

She inhaled the spicy sweet scent of her bouquet, which consisted mainly of white rosebuds and pale pink carnations. "That's a very high price to pay for a good deed. You could have endowed another hospital for thirty thousand pounds."

"I suppose so," he said uncomfortably, "but I consider it money well spent."

Ariel was looking straight ahead, her eyes on the velvet lining of the carriage. He took advantage of that to study her profile again, this time from much closer than on the occasion when he'd first seen her. But today she wasn't that carefree girl under the apple tree. Beneath the veil her flaxen hair was drawn up in a complicated style of coils and ringlets, and her gown made her look terrifyingly fashionable.

Her beauty and sophistication alarmed him; where had he ever found the audacity to offer for such a paragon? It was tragic that because of her father's fecklessness, she was now tied to a man wholly unworthy of her. "A pity that you never had a London Season," he said sorrowfully. "There you could have found a husband to your taste instead of being forced to choose between two unpalatable alternatives."

To his surprise she smiled humorlessly. "I did go to London for a Season when I was eighteen."

He frowned. "Then why aren't you married? You must have been a stunning success."

She began plucking the ribbons that trailed from her bouquet. "Oh, yes, I was a success—proclaimed a Beauty, in fact," she said with unexpected irony. "And there were several proposals of marriage. Fortunately they were improperly made to me rather than my father, so I was able to decline without him learning about them."

Bewildered, he said, "Why did you refuse? Were they all men like Gordstone?"

She twined a ribbon around one slender figure. "None were so dreadful as he, but neither did they want to marry *me*. They just wanted to win the latest Beauty. And win is the right word. Courtship was a sport, and I was one of season's best trophies. None of the men who proposed marriage knew anything about me, or cared about the things I cared about." She glanced up at him, her blue eyes stark. "To be a Beauty is to be a thing, not a person. Perhaps you, more than most men, can understand that."

Her words struck him with the impact of a blow; for the first time he realized just how much more she was than the beautiful child he had seen on the hillside. After taking a deep, slow breath, he said, "Yes, I understand what it is to be a thing, not a person. I don't blame you for resenting that. But even so, you would have been better off married to one of those men, someone who would have given you a real marriage and a position in society."

"I'm not sure I would have been better off. I was telling my father the truth when I said that I preferred a quiet life in the country. He can't bear quiet; I suppose that's one reason we've never understood each very well," she said sadly. Then, visibly shaking off her mood, "I don't believe I've properly thanked you for saving me from

Gordstone. I really do appreciate what you've done.''
After a slight hesitation, she added, ''James.''

Startled, he said, ''No one calls me that.''

She glanced up swiftly. ''Would you rather I didn't?''

''No, please, suit yourself,'' he said, his voice constricted. He was deeply moved to hear her use his name; no woman had done so since his mother had died. Thinking of his mother's death, he dropped his left hand from sight behind his thigh. Ariel had viewed the scars with distaste when he had put the ring on her finger; that was to be expected, since she was without flaw herself. But she had the good manners of natural refinement and had done her best not to show her revulsion.

For the rest of the journey to Belleterre neither of them spoke, but the silence was less awkward than he had expected. When the carriage pulled up in front of his home, he helped her out, then said lightly, as if the matter was unimportant, ''After this moment, you need never endure my touch again.''

He started to remove his right hand from hers, but she clung to it. Softly, her great blue eyes staring up at him, she said, ''James, you mustn't think that you repel me. We are almost strangers, but you have been kind to me, and now we are married. Surely we will have some kind of relationship with each other. I hope it will not be a strained one.''

He pulled his hand from her clasp, knowing that if he felt the touch of her slim fingers any longer, he would want to do more than just hold her hand. ''It won't be strained. In fact, you will scarcely see me, except by chance around the estate.''

She frowned. ''It sounds like a very lonely life. Can't we at least be friends, perhaps sometimes keep each other company?''

It would be very hard to be friends with her, but obediently he said, ''If that is your wish. How much company do you want?''

She bit her lower lip, looking enchantingly earnest.

"Perhaps . . . perhaps we might dine together every night. If you don't mind?"

"No, I won't mind." He reminded himself that her request stemmed from the basic need for human interaction rather than any special liking for him, but even so, joy swirled through him at the knowledge that she had actually requested his company on a regular basis.

She took his arm as they began walking up the steps, surprising him again. She was a brave child, and an honorable one, willing to do her duty. Solemnly he promised himself that he would not take advantage of that willingness.

The servants were lined up inside the house to meet the new mistress. Ariel knew that she would never remember all the names until she knew them better, but she was impressed by the general air of well-being. If orgies were held at Belleterre, they didn't seem to distress the servants. Nonetheless, she sensed deep reserve among them, as if they were doubtful about her. She supposed it was only natural for them to be wary about a new mistress. Once they discovered that she didn't intend to make sweeping changes, they would relax.

Introductions over, Falconer turned her over to the housekeeper to be shown to her rooms. Mrs. Wilcox was remote but polite as she took her new mistress upstairs. As she passed through room and halls, Ariel observed that her new home was furnished in excellent, if rather austere, taste. It was also well-kept, with floors and furniture gleaming with wax and not a speck of dust anywhere.

On reaching their destination, the housekeeper opened the door and said, "Your belongings were delivered and the maids have unpacked them, your ladyship. If there is anything that you want, or if you wish to make changes, you have only to ask."

Ariel's first impression was that she had stepped into a garden, for every available surface was covered with vases of welcoming flowers. She drifted through the

scented rooms, awed by the size and luxury of her ac-
commodations. Not only was there a well-furnished bedroom and sitting room, but another large chamber that
was almost empty. It took a moment for her to realize
that the room was a studio, for there was a north light
and an easel in the corner. Her eyes stung. Had he known
what this would mean to her? He must have guessed;
though he was a stranger, he understood her better than
her own father had.

Behind her a soft Kentish voice said, "I'm Fanny, your
ladyship, and I'm to be your personal maid. Do you wish
to take off your gown and rest before dinner?"

Gratefully Ariel accepted the girl's suggestion, for the
stress of the day had left her exhausted. She slept well
and woke refreshed. Fanny appeared again and helped
her dress. In one of the surprises that was starting to
become commonplace, Ariel discovered an armoire full
of new clothing. Apparently the dressmaker in London
had been commissioned to make her a whole wardrobe
as well as the wedding gown.

Her husband had judged her taste well, for most of the
dresses were loosely cut tea gowns. They would be perfect for daytime in the country, particularly for painting
and walking. The colors chosen were clear, delicate pastels that suited her fair hair and complexion. Ariel was
beginning to suspect that the Black Beast had the eye of
an artist.

When she went down to dinner, she found her husband
waiting in the morning room. He greeted her gravely and
inquired if everything was to her taste. She assured him
that her rooms were lovely, especially the studio. Then
they went together into the family dining room. He tensed
when she took his arm, and she wondered if he found
her touch distasteful.

The family dining room was still very large, and one
end of the room was quite dark even though the summer
sun had not yet set. Ariel had thought that when her husband ate he might put his hood back, but he didn't. Since

his chair was in the dark end of the room and she was a dozen feet away, at the far end of the polished table, she saw nothing of his face.

The dinner was a quiet one until the end, when bowls of fruit had been served. After the footman had left the room, Ariel said, "Do you always sit or stand in the shadows?"

He paused in the act of peeling a peach. "Always."

"Is that necessary?"

"To me it is." Slowly he began slicing away a spiral of peach skin, his long fingers deft. In the shadows it was impossible to see the scars on his left hand. "I have said that you can do whatever you wish at Belleterre. In return, Ariel, I ask that you respect my wishes in this matter."

She bit her lip. "Of course, James."

The rest of the meal passed in silence. When they were done, they rose and went into the hall. Ariel had thought that perhaps they would sit together after dinner, but instead her husband said, "Good night, my dear. If you wish to read, the library is through that door on the left. The selection of books is wide, and of course you are welcome to add anything you want to the collection."

She realized that he had been quite serious when he had said they would see little of each other. Well, she had wanted a quiet life, and it appeared that her wish would be granted. She was just saying good night when a scrabble of claws sounded on the polished marble floor.

Ariel looked up to see a dog trotting eagerly down the hall. It was the ugliest dog she'd ever seen, rawboned and splotchy and of very dubious parentage. But its shaggy face glowed with canine bliss as it reached its master, then reared up and balanced on its haunches.

Falconer scratched the dog's head, and a pink tongue lolled out of its panting mouth. "Did you come to meet your new mistress, Cerberus?"

Amused at the name, Ariel said, "Cerberus has no

interest in me; clearly it's you he adores with his whole canine heart.''

Falconer's robe quivered, as if in a slight breeze. ''It doesn't take much to win a dog's heart.''

Ariel was beginning to realize that she could read the movements of the fabric to determine her husband's moods; very useful, since his face was concealed. Though she was new to the skill of robe reading, she guessed that he was uncomfortable with her comment about being adored. Poor man, did he feel unworthy of even a dog's devotion? With sudden ferocity, she wanted to know more about the stranger she had married; she wanted to know what had made him what he was. In time surely she would. After all, they were living under the same roof.

From the corner of her eye, Ariel caught more motion. Turning her head, she saw a black-and-white cat entering the hall. It moved very strangely, and after a moment she realized that it was missing one foreleg. Still, it seemed to have no trouble getting around. Ariel knelt and rubbed her fingers together, hoping the creature would come to her.

''That's Tripod!,'' Falconer said. ''Her leg was accidentally cut off by a scythe.''

After a disdainful look at Cerberus, the cat hopped over to Ariel and rubbed against her outstretched fingers. She smiled. ''Thank you for condescending to meet me, Tripod.''

Jealously the dog trotted over to ask for some attention. As Ariel ruffled the droopy ears, she murmured, ''What a funny looking fellow you are. You remind me of a picture of a musk-ox that I once saw.''

In a low voice her husband said, ''Any ugly creature is assured of a home here.''

Ariel froze for a moment, feeling that she had committed some dreadful faux pas. Then she rose to her feet and said calmly, ''You are a very kind man, James, to take in waifs and strays. After all, I am one of them. Good night.''

Then she went upstairs to the charming rooms where she would spend her wedding night alone.

Though he had seen her with his own eyes, conversed with her over dinner, Falconer had trouble believing that she was under his own roof. In his mind he never used the name Ariel; to him his wife was *she*, as if she were the only woman in the world.

What he had not expected was how tormenting her presence would be. It had been ten years since he had last lain with a woman, and he had become reasonably comfortable with his monkish life. But no more; though he still wore the robes of a monk, he ached with yearning. He wanted to touch his wife's blossom-smooth skin, bury his hands in her silky hair, inhale her sweet female scent. He wanted more than that, though he would not allow himself to put words to his base thoughts.

After she had gone to bed, he went outside and walked from one end of Belleterre to the other as dusk became night. Cerberus trotted obediently behind, ready to defend his master from the lethal attacks of rabbits and pheasants.

As soon as it was dark enough, Falconer pushed back his hood, welcoming the cool night air, for he burned. He despised himself for his body's weakness; it was unthinkable that a monster such as he could lie with the angel he had married. At least, unlike Gordstone, he knew that he was a monster. But in his heart, he was no better than the other man, for he could not stop himself from desiring her.

It was very late when he returned to the house. To his surprise, when he went upstairs a light showed under his wife's bedroom door. Was she also having trouble sleeping? Perhaps he should go and talk with her, reassure her about her new life.

Though he knew he was lying to himself about his

motives, he literally could not prevent himself from going down the hall and tapping on her door. When there was no answer, he turned the knob and eased the door open, then crossed the room to the bed.

She had fallen asleep while reading, and she lay with her head turned to one side, her pale blond hair spilling luxuriantly over the pillow. She wore a delicately tucked and laced nightgown, and she was the most beautiful being he had ever seen.

He picked up the book that she had laid on the coverlet. It was one of his own volumes of William Blake, the mystical poet and artist. A good choice for a girl who was also an artist. He set the volume on the table by a vase of roses, turned out the lamp, and ordered himself to leave the room.

But he allowed himself one last look. The bedroom curtains hadn't been drawn, and in the moonlight she was a figure spun of ivory and silver. He drank in the sight, knowing that he could never permit himself to do this again, for he could not trust himself so close to her.

When he had memorized her image well enough to last a lifetime, he turned to go. He was halfway to the door when his resolve broke and he went back again. Against his will his hand lifted, began reaching out to her.

With a violence that was all the more intense for being subdued, he turned to the vase of roses and gripped the stems with his left hand. Ignoring the thorns stabbing into his fingers, he stripped the blossoms away with his right hand. Then he slowly scattered the fragile scarlet petals over her like a pagan worshiping his goddess. They looked like black velvet as they drifted down the moonbeams.

One petal touched her cheek and slid over the soft curve, coming to rest on her throat, exactly the way he longed to touch her. As the intoxicating scent of roses filled the air around him, more petals spangled her gilt hair and delicate muslin gown, rising and falling with the slow rhythm of her breath.

When his hand was emptied, he took a shuddering breath. Then he turned and left her room forever.

Autumn

Ariel added a little more yellow paint to the mixture, stroked a brushful across her test paper, then critically examined the result. Yes, that should do for the base shade of the leaves, which were at the height of their autumn color. In the next two hours, she made several watercolor sketches of the woods, more interested in creating an impression of the vibrant scene than in drawing an exact copy. As James said, now that photographers were able to reproduce precise images, artists had more freedom to experiment, to be more abstract.

The work absorbed her entire attention, for watercolor was in many ways the most difficult and volatile medium. When she finally had a painting that satisfied her, she began packing her equipment into the special saddlebags that one of the Belleterre grooms had made to carry her supplies around the estate. The glade was deeply peaceful. Above her head tall, tall elm trees rustled in the wind like a sky-borne river.

It had not taken long for her life to fall into an easy routine. As her husband had promised, she had quiet, freedom, and anything else that money could buy. The size of the allowance he gave her was staggering, and it had been exciting to order the finest papers and canvases, the most expensive brushes and pigments, and never have to consider the cost.

It also proved educational to have such wealth at her disposal. She found that after she had bought her art supplies, there was little else to spend the money on. She scarcely even needed to buy books, for the Belleterre library was the finest she had ever seen. Nor did she have to buy clothing, for she had the wardrobe her husband had given her when they married.

He had also given her an exquisite, beautifully mannered gray mare. Foxglove was the prettiest horse on the estate, for the rest of the beasts were an odd-looking lot. Though quite capable of doing their jobs, they tended to have knobby knees, lop-ears, and coats that were rough even after the most thorough grooming. The pairs and teams didn't match at all. She suspected that, like Cerberus and Tripod, the horses had been given a home because they hadn't been appreciated by a world that valued appearance over capability.

Ariel found the mismatched horses endearing and almost resented the fact that her husband had bought Foxglove for her. Did he think she was incapable of appreciating anything that wasn't perfect? Apparently. Yet because his intention had been to please her, she could hardly complain.

Yes, James had given her exactly the life of peace and freedom that he had promised. She could draw and paint to her heart's content, for she no longer had to spend most of her time trying vainly to oversee her father's neglected estate. Her work was improving, and some of the credit for that must go to her husband, for they often discussed art over dinner. His knowledge of painting was remarkable and his insights very helpful, for her abilities were more intuitive than analytical.

Yet instead of mounting to ride back to the house, Ariel put her arms around Foxglove's neck and buried her face against the mare's glossy, horse-scented hide. She was a very lucky young woman. That being the case, why was she so miserable?

"Oh, Foxy," she said in a choked voice. "I'm so lonely—lonelier than I've ever been in my life. Sometimes it seems as if you're my only friend." Though it sounded perilously like self-pity, the statement was true. If she hadn't asked that her husband dine with her, days on end would have passed without her seeing him.

She looked forward all day to those meals, for he was the pleasantest of companions, well-read and amusing, able to discuss any subject. In spite of her youth and frequent ignorance, he was never rude or disdainful of her opinions; in fact, the discussions were making her much more knowledgeable, and she enjoyed them enormously.

Yet no matter how pleasant the meal, as soon as it was over James would bid her a polite good night and withdraw. She would not see him again until the next evening, except perhaps by chance, in the distance, as he rode about the estate.

In addition the Belleterre servants were a surprisingly reserved group. Ariel had been on easy terms with everyone at Gardsley, but Falconer's people were as distant now as they had been the day she arrived, four months earlier. The one exception was Patterson, the old, half-blind groom who had been her husband's best man at the wedding. He at least was always friendly, though not very forthcoming. Patterson, Foxglove, Cerberus, and Tripod were almost the whole of Ariel's social life. Even her friend Anna hadn't written in months, presumably because she was absorbed in her new family.

With a sigh Ariel mounted and turned Foxglove toward home. She had always been able to live quite happily in her own world; in fact, she had never been lonely until she came to Belleterre. Now she reckoned it a good night when Tripod deigned to sleep on her bed.

She had changed, and the blame could be laid at her husband's door. Solitude was no longer enough because she loved being with him—loved hearing his deep, kind voice, loved laughing at his dry sense of humor. She would have been happy to trail around after him like Cerberus. But she couldn't, for she knew James wouldn't like that. She was just a young and not very interesting female; though he was willing to share one meal a day with her, more of her company would probably bore him to tears. She didn't dare jeopardize what she had by asking for more than he was willing to give.

As she reined in Foxglove in front of the stables, Patterson ambled out to help her dismount. When her feet

were safely on the ground, Ariel impulsively asked a
question inspired by her earlier thoughts. "Patterson, why
are all of the servants so reserved with me? Is it something I've done?"

The old man paused in the act of unpacking her painting materials. "No, milady. Everyone considers you very
proper."

"Then why do I feel as if I'm being judged and found
wanting?" Ariel said, then immediately felt foolish.

The groom took her words in good part. " 'Tisn't that,
milady. You're much admired," he said. " 'Tis just that
folks are afraid you might hurt the master."

She stared at him. "Hurt him? Why would I do that?"
A horrible thought occurred to her. "Surely no one thinks
I would poison him so that I could be a wealthy widow!"

"Not that, my lady," he said quickly. " 'Tisn't that
sort of hurt that folks are worried about." He heaved the
saddlebags from the mare. Without looking at Ariel, he
said, "Don't need a knife or gun or poison to break a
man's heart."

"His lordship scarcely knows I'm alive," she said,
unable to believe the implication. "I'm just one more
unfortunate creature that he brought to Belleterre because I needed a home."

"Nay, milady. You're not like any of the others." In
spite of the cloudiness of his eyes, Patterson's gaze
seemed to bore right through her. "I've known that boy
most of his life, and I know that he's never brought home
anyone like you."

Ariel's mind unaccountably went to the morning after
her wedding. There had been blood red rose petals all
over the bed when she woke. She had been surprised and
a little uneasy, until she decided that some of the flowers had fallen apart and been blown by the wind. But they
had fallen very strangely if it was the wind. She had a
mental image of James scattering her with rose petals,
and an odd, deep shiver went through her.

Was it possible that he cared for her, as a man cared

for a woman? She rejected the idea. He didn't want her for a wife; from all appearances, his nature was as monkish as his clothing.

As she hesitated, caught in her thoughts, Patterson said, "I think he's in the aviary, milady. If you like, I can take your pictures up to the house."

As a hint there was nothing subtle about it. "Please do that, Patterson. And thank you." Ariel's steps were slow as she walked through the gardens to the aviary. If she understood the old groom correctly, James did care about her, at least enough that she had the potential to hurt him. Not that she would ever do so, but the opposite side of that potential was that she might be capable of making him happy. She often felt deep sadness radiating from her husband, and the possibility that she might be able to reduce that was tantalizing.

Her steps became even slower when she came within sight of the aviary. It was an enormous enclosure made of elaborately molded, white-painted cast iron. Not only was it large enough to include several small trees and a little pool, but there was a shed where the birds could shelter during bad weather.

The aviary was home to dozens of birds, most of them foreign species that Ariel didn't recognize. She often came by to watch them fly and chatter and play. In particular she enjoyed coaxing the large green parrot into conversation. Several times she had done sketches of the aviary's residents, trying to capture the quick, bright movements.

But today her gaze went immediately to her husband, who was inside the enclosure. Instead of his usual calf-length robe, he was garbed in a dark coat and trousers such as any gentleman might wear for a day's estate management. However, his head and shoulders were swathed in a cowled hood that concealed his face as effectively as the longer robe.

Ariel had occasionally seen him dressed this way, but always in the distance. Close up, he was a fine figure of a man, tall and strong and masculine. His black coat displayed the breadth of his shoulders. His movements fascinated her—the turn of his powerful wrist when he stretched out his hand so that a small brown bird could jump onto it, his gentleness as he stroked the small creature's head with one forefinger, his warm chuckle when the parrot swooped down and landed on his shoulder with a great thrashing of wings.

The birds loved him, not caring what his face was like. The same was true of all the creatures who lived at Belleterre, and all the humans, too, including Ariel. Or perhaps what she felt for her husband wasn't quite love, but it could be, if given a chance. She yearned for his company, for his touch. In her limited life she had never known anyone like him—not just for the obvious reason of how he dressed, but for his kindness and knowledge. It no longer mattered that she didn't know what he looked like; she was so accustoned to his hood that it had in effect become his face.

But how could an ignorant young woman tell a mature, educated man that she yearned to be more to him? Praying that inspiration would come, Ariel unlatched the door and entered the aviary. Cerberus, who had been lying outside, lurched to his feet and tried to enter with her, but she firmly held him back.

As the door clinked shut behind her, James turned. Surprise in his voice, he said, "I thought you were painting, Ariel."

"I was, but the light changed, so I decided to stop after I did a picture that I was somewhat satisfied with."

A smile in his voice, he said, "Is an artist ever wholly satisfied with her own work?"

She smiled ruefully. "I doubt it. I know that I never am."

While she tried to think what to say next, the parrot flew to a branch and crooned, "Ar-r-riel. Ar-r-riel."

Surprised, she said, "When did he learn that?"

James shrugged. "Just now, I imagine. He's a contrary

creature. Once I spent hours unsuccessfully trying to teach him to say 'God save the Queen.' The only thing he learned that day was the phrase 'Deuce take it,' which I said just before I gave up in exasperation.''

The bird obligingly squawked, ''Devil take it! Devil take it!''

Ariel laughed. ''Are you sure that 'deuce take it' is what he learned that day?''

Her husband joined her laughter. ''It appears that my bad language has been exposed. Sorry.''

''James . . .'' Not sure how to say what she wanted, she took several steps toward her husband.

To her dismay he moved away. ''Have you ever seen one of these parakeets close up?'' He laid a hand on a branch and a bird hopped on. ''Lovely little creatures.'' It was neatly done, as if he was not retreating but had merely seen something that caught his attention.

Ariel felt tears stinging in her eyes. Patterson must be wrong; if James cared for her in a special way, he would not flee whenever she approached. She was struggling to maintain her composure when the blue-breasted parakeet suddenly skipped up her husband's arm and disappeared into the folds of the hood where it wrapped around his throat.

For Ariel it was the last straw. Even that silly little bird, which wouldn't make two bites for Tripod, was permitted to get closer to James than she was. Her loneliness and yearning welled up, and with them her tears. Humiliated, she turned to leave the aviary, wanting to get away before her husband noticed.

But he noticed everything. Quickly he said, ''Ariel, what's wrong?''

She shook her head and fumbled with the door, but the latch on this side was stiff. As she struggled with it, her husband came up behind her and hesitantly touched her elbow. ''Has your father tried to reach you, or upset you in some way?''

It was the most natural thing in the world for her to

turn to him, and for him to put his arms around her. She was crying harder than she ever had in her life, even when her mother died. But dear God, how wonderful it felt to be in his embrace! He was so strong, so warm, so safe. So tall as well—the top of her head didn't quite reach his chin, which put his shoulder at a convenient height. Trying to stop her tears, she gulped for breath, pressing her face into the smooth dark wool of his coat.

"Ariel, my dear girl," he said with soft helplessness, rocking her a little. "Is there anything I can do? Or . . . or are you crying because you're married to me?"

"Oh, no, no, that's not the problem." She slipped her arms around his waist, wanting to be as close as she could. "It's just . . . I'm so lonely here. Would it be possible for us to spend more time together? Perhaps in the evenings, after dinner. I won't disturb you if you want to work or read, but I'd like to be with you."

It was as close as she could come to putting her heart in his hands. He didn't answer for a long time, so long that she thought she might suffocate because she couldn't seem to breathe normally. One hand stroked down her back, slowly, as if he were gentling a horse. Finally he said, "Of course we could, if that's what you want."

"But will you mind?" she asked, needing to know if he was willing or simply indulging.

She felt a faint brush against her hair, from his hand or perhaps his lips. "No, I won't mind," he said softly. "It will be my pleasure."

She was so happy that her tears began to flow again. It gave her an excuse to stay just where she was, in his arms. She would never tire of his embrace, for she felt as if she had come home. Besides happiness, she felt also deeper stirrings that she didn't recognize. They frightened her a little, but at the same time she knew that she wanted to explore them further, for they had something to do with James.

She became aware how much tension there was in her husband. Reluctantly she stepped away, for she didn't want to wear out her welcome. "It's getting late." Suddenly aware of the untidiness of her hair and the stains on her painting clothes, she said, "I must go and change for dinner."

"This evening, if you like, we can sit in the library," he said hesitantly. "I've some letters to write, but if you don't think you'll be bored . . ."

"I won't be." She was almost embarrassed at the transparent happiness in her voice. "I'll see you at dinner." This evening would be the first step, and eventually there would be others. She wasn't sure exactly where the path would lead, but she knew that it was one she must follow.

The meal was the most lighthearted they had yet shared. Falconer wondered if his wife was looking forward to spending the evening together as much as he was, then decided that that was impossible. Still, she was happier than he had ever seen her. Though he hadn't realized until now, when the difference was obvious, she had been growing increasingly quiet, her characteristic glow muted. He reminded himself that even self-contained young women who enjoyed solitude needed some companionship, and for Ariel, he was what was available. He would not take her desire to see more of him too personally—but that didn't mean that he couldn't enjoy it.

They went into the library for coffee, still talking, tangible warmth between them. Falconer was careful not to strain that fragile web of feeling, for he wanted it to grow stronger.

She took a chair and gracefully poured coffee from a silver pot. Garbed in a blue silk gown, she looked especially lovely tonight, her delicate coloring as fresh as spring flowers. As she handed him his cup, she said, "Today I got a letter from my former governess, Anna. Have I ever told you about her?"

When he answered in the negative, Ariel continued,

"After leaving Gardsley, she found a position teaching the two daughters of a widower who lives in Hampstead, just north of London."

He stirred milk into his coffee. "Is the man intellectual or artistic, like so many of those who live in Hampstead?"

She laughed. "So he is. Mr. Talbott designs fabrics and furniture for industrial manufacture and is quite successful with it. He also has the good sense to appreciate Anna. In fact, they married on the same day we did. They went to Italy for a honeymoon and have only just gotten back. Anna apologized for not writing but said that she's been so busy and happy that she didn't quite realize how much time had gone by. She has invited us to visit her in Hampstead—the house is very large." Ariel looked shyly over her coffee cup. "Would you be willing to do that sometime? You'll like Anna, and Mr. Talbott sounds like a wonderful man."

Falconer frowned, but he didn't want to spoil the mood of the evening. "Perhaps someday," he said vaguely.

Ariel regarded him thoughtfully, then changed the subject. They talked of other things until the coffee was gone. Then she stood. Falconer feared that she had changed her mind and was going to go upstairs until she said, "I'll read while you do your letter writing." She gave him a bright, slightly nervous smile. "I don't want to distract you from your work."

When she was this close, it was hard to think of letters, but obediently he went to his desk and started writing. He had a large and varied correspondence, for letters were a way to be involved with people without having to meet them face-to-face.

Cerberus was pleasantly befuddled by having them both in the room and wandered back and forth, flopping first by Falconer, then ambling to the chair where Ariel was reading. Tripod was lazier and simply curled up on the desk on top of a pile of notepaper. Falconer could not remember when he had been happier. The library, with its deep, leather-upholstered furniture, had always been his favorite room, and having Ariel's presence made paradise itself seem inferior.

But the evening became even better. Hearing a sound beside him, he absently put his left hand down to ruffle the dog's ears. Instead, he touched silken hair. Glancing down, he saw his wife curled up against his chair. "Ariel?" he said, startled.

She glanced up, both teasing and apologetic. "Cerberus enjoys having his head scratched, so I thought I'd try it." Her smile faded. "I'm sorry, I shouldn't have disturbed you."

"No need to apologize." He turned his head away so that she couldn't see under the cowl. "I'm ready for a break." As if they had a life of their own, his fingers twined through her shining tresses. He had thought his scarred fingers had little sensation, but now he would swear that he could feel each gossamer strand separately.

With a soft, pleased sigh she relaxed against the side of his chair. For perhaps a quarter of an hour they stayed like that while he stroked her head, slender neck, and delicate ears. As he did, joy bubbled through him like a fountain of light, and his mind rang with the words of Elizabeth Barrett Browning's famous sonnet. *How do I love thee? Let me count the ways. . . .*

For he did love this exquisite girl who was his wife. On their wedding day, when she had expressed her dislike of being courted solely for her beauty, he had felt ashamed, for he could not help but be bewitched by her loveliness. Yet even that first moment, when the sight of her had been like an arrow in his heart, he had sensed that her beauty was even more of the spirit than of the body.

The idyll ended when Tripod, deciding that she needed attention, suddenly jumped down into Ariel's lap. Ariel laughed and straightened up. Falconer started to withdraw his hand, but before he could, she caught his fingers. Then she very deliberately laid her cheek against the back of his hand.

Her skin was porcelain smooth against the coarse scars that crippled his two smallest fingers and made the rest of his hand hideous. Yet she did not flinch. He began to tremble as waves of sensation pulsed through him, beginning in his fingers and spreading until every cell of his body vibrated. For the first time he wondered if it might be possible for them to have a real marriage. She did not seem repulsed by the scars on his hand; was there a chance that she might be able to tolerate the rest of him?

The thought was as frightening as it was exhilarating. His emotions too chaotic to control, he got to his feet, then raised her to hers. Hoarsely he said, "It's time for bed. But perhaps in the morning, you might join me for a ride?"

Her smile was breathtaking. "I'd like that."

He turned out the lights, then escorted her upstairs to her room, the animals trailing along behind. At her door she turned to him. "Good night, James," she said in a soft, husky voice. "Sleep well."

In the faint light of the hall, she looked eager and accessible, her lips slightly parted, her hair delectably disheveled from his earlier petting. Instinct told him that she would welcome a kiss, and perhaps more. But she was so beautiful that he couldn't bring himself to touch her.

"Good night, Ariel." He turned and walked away, feeling so brittle that a touch might shatter him. The idea that they might build a real marriage was too new, too frightening, to act on. He might be misinterpreting her willingness. Or, unspeakable thought, she might believe herself willing but change her mind when she saw him. One thing he knew: if she rejected him after he had begun to hope, he would be unable to endure it.

Ariel went to bed in a state of jubilation. He had been happy to have her with him, she knew it. He hadn't even minded when she had foolishly succumbed to her desire to come closer. Best of all, he wanted her to ride with him. Perhaps they might spend all day together. And perhaps even the night . . . ?

The idea filled her with blushing excitement. She was unclear what happened in a marriage bed, but knew that holding and kissing were involved, and she definitely liked those things; she still tingled from the gentle fire of his touch.

If intimacy began with a kiss, in what exciting place might it end?

Her fevered emotions made it impossible for her to sleep. Finally her tossing and turning elicited a growl of protest from Tripod, who needed her twenty hours of sleep every day. Ariel surrendered and got out of bed. As she lit the lamp on her desk, she decided that the best use of her high spirits was to answer Anna's letter, for she was now in the same elevated mood that her friend had been.

Her stationery drawer contained only two sheets of notepaper, which wouldn't be enough. She must get more from the library. Humming softly, she donned her robe, then took the lamp and went downstairs. The shifting shadows made her think of ghosts, but if there were any about, they would surely be benevolent ones. She must ask James about Belleterre's ghosts; any building so old must have at least three or four.

With ghosts on her mind Ariel opened the library door, then blinked with surprise. In the far corner of the room, framed by dark shelves of books, floated an object that looked horribly like a skull. She gave a sharp, shocked cry.

A flurry of sounds and movements occurred, too quick and confusing for Ariel to follow. The object whirled away, accompanied by a soft, anguished exclamation. Almost simultaneously there came a thump, a swish of fabric, then a resounding slam of the door at the far end of the library.

Shaken and alone, Ariel knew with a certainty beyond reason that something catastrophic had just occurred. She raggedly expelled the breath she had been holding, then walked to the far corner of the room. A low lamp burned on a table; that was how she had seen . . . whatever it was that she had seen. A book lay open on the floor, and she knelt to pick it up—Elizabeth Barrett Browning's *Sonnets from the Portugese*.

Dear God, the other occupant of the library must have been James with his hood down. She tried to recall the fleeting image that had met her eyes when she had entered the room, but try as she might, she could remember no details. The floating object had been the right height for his head; the skull-like whiteness must have been his hair, pale blond like hers, or perhaps prematurely white. Covered by his dark robe, the rest of his body had been invisible in the dark, which had made the sight of him so uncanny.

With sick horror she guessed that he had dropped the book and fled because of her shocked exclamation. She leaned dizzily against the bookcase, the volume of poetry clutched to her chest. He must have thought she was reacting to his appearance with disgust. But she hadn't even really seen him! She had simply had ghosts on the mind, then been disconcerted when she saw something ghostly. But to James, who was so profoundly ashamed of his appearance, it must have seemed as if she had found him repulsive. He would not have fled like that, without a word, if he hadn't been deeply wounded.

Anguished, she realized that this was what the servants had feared. She had the power to hurt her husband, and unintentionally she had done so. He must ache all the more because they had been starting to draw closer together; certainly that fact magnified her own pain.

Determined to explain to him that it had all been a ghastly mistake, she turned out the light he had left, then lifted her own lamp and went upstairs to his rooms. She hesitated outside the door, for she had never been inside and to enter uninvited was an invasion of the privacy that he wrapped around himself as securely as his cowl. But she couldn't allow the misunderstanding to go uncorrected. The pain in her heart was well-nigh unbearable, and he must hurt even more.

She turned the knob to his sitting room, and the door swung smoothly inward, but there was no one inside. Swiftly she searched the sitting room and the bedroom next door. Nothing but solid, masculine furniture and richly colored fabrics. She opened the last door and found herself in his dressing room, but he was not there, either. She was about to leave when her eye was caught by a small, framed picture.

She was startled to see that it was one of her own drawings, but not one she had done since coming to Belleterre. Frowning, she examined it more closely. It was a sketch of her favorite oak tree at Gardsley, and it had been done in springtime. The paper had been crumpled, then flattened, and some of the charcoal lines were a bit blurred. Realizing that it was a drawing that she had discarded, she cast her mind back to when she must have sketched this particular subject. It had been the day that she had first seen James, when he had visited her father. He must have found the drawing then.

She touched the elaborate gilded frame, which was far more costly than the sketch deserved. No one would frame such a drawing for its own sake, so it must have been for the sake of the artist. She felt incipient tears behind her eyes. Yes, he must care for her, little though she deserved such regard.

Swallowing hard, she withdrew and quietly searched the public areas of the house, stopping when she discovered that the French doors in the drawing room were unlatched. The housekeeper would never have permitted such laxity, so James must have gone outside this way.

He could be anywhere. She refused to believe that he

would harm himself—the incident in the library couldn't have been that upsetting—so soon he would come home. Determined to wait up for him, she returned to his rooms and curled up on the sofa with a knee rug around her. But in spite of her intention to stay awake, eventually fatigue overcame her.

She was awakened by his return, even though he made no sound. Her head jerked up from the sofa, and she stared at her husband. His hood was firmly in place, and he was so still that she could tell nothing of his mood. Her lamp was guttering, but outside the sky was starting to lighten.

Quietly he said, "You should be in bed, Ariel."

She drew a shaky breath and went straight to the heart of the matter. "James, what happened in the library— *nothing* happened. I didn't see you, just unexpected movement. That's why I was surprised."

She was still fumbling for words when he raised one hand, cutting her off with his gesture. "Of course nothing happened," he agreed in an utterly dispassionate voice. After a pause he continued, "It occurred to me that since you've been lonely, perhaps you should visit your friend Anna for a few weeks."

Ariel rose from the sofa, the knee rug clutched around her. "Don't send me away, James," she begged. "You don't understand."

As if she hadn't spoken, he said, "You'll like Hampstead—close enough to London to be interesting, far enough away to be quiet. Send Mrs. Talbott a note today and see if it's convenient for you to come." He stepped to one side, holding the door open in an unmistakable invitation to leave. "You might as well go. With winter coming there's much to be done around the estate and I won't have much time for you. I don't want you to be bored, so it will be best if you visit your friend."

Chilled by his manner, she repeated desperately, "James, you don't understand!"

His robe quivered faintly. "What is there to understand?" he asked, still in that soft, implacable voice.

Defeated, she walked to the door. She paused a moment when she was closest to him, wondering if she should take his hand, if touch might convince him where words couldn't.

Sharply, as if reading her mind, he said, "Don't."

A moment later she was in the hall outside and his door had been firmly shut behind her. Numbly she pulled the knee rug around her shivering body and walked down the long passage to her own rooms. Perhaps she should do what he suggested. Not only would she benefit from Anna's warm good sense, but if she was gone for a fortnight or so, it would give her husband time to recover from the unintentional hurt she had inflicted. When she returned, he would be more open to her explanation. Then they could begin again. After all, the incident had been so trivial.

She refused to believe that he might not recover from it.

Talbott House, Hampstead
October 20th
Dear James,
   Just a note to tell you that I've arrived safely. It's wonderful to see Anna again, she is positively blooming. Mr. Talbott is a broad, merry elf who is everything hospitable. He makes wonderful toys for the children. I had wondered if his daughters might resent the fact that Anna went from being their governess to their mother, but they adore her. Apparently their own mother died when they were very young.
   I'll finish this now so that it can go out in the next post, but I'll write a longer letter tonight.
                                        Your loving wife,
                                        Ariel

Talbott House, Hampstead
November 10th
Dear James,
   You were certainly right about Hampstead. It's a

*charming place, full of interesting people. Not at all
like the ghastly society sorts that I met during my Season.*

*Remember the letter I wrote where I wondered
who owned Hampstead Heath? I've since been told
that the gentleman who held the manorial rights to
the heath recently sold them to the Metropolitan
Board of Works so that the area will be preserved
for public use forever. I was glad to learn that, for
people need places like the heath. Walking there reminds me a bit of Belleterre, though of course not
so quiet and lovely.*

*Last night we dined with a young literary gentle-
men, a Mr. Glades. He is something of a radical, for
he teased me about being Lady Falconer. He's very
clever—almost as much so as you—but his mind is
less open, I think.*

*I know you must be terribly busy, but if you found
time to scribble a note to tell me how you are, I would
much appreciate it. Of course, soon I'll be home myself, so you needn't go to any special bother.*

> *Your loving wife,*
> *Ariel*

Belleterre
November 20th
My dear Ariel,

*No need to rush back. I'm very busy doing a survey
of improvements needed on the tenant farms. My re-
gards to your amiable host and hostess.*

> *Falconer*

Talbott House, Hampstead
December 1st
Dear James,

*Last week, to amuse the girls, I made some sketches
illustrating the story of Dick Whittington's cat. Without my knowing, Mr. Talbott showed them to a publisher friend of his, a Mr. Howard, and now the fellow
wants me to illustrate a children's book for him! He*

says my drawings are "magical," which sounds very nice, though I don't know quite what he means by it. While I'm flattered by his offer, I don't know whether I should accept. Would you object to having your wife involved in a commercial venture? If you don't like the idea, of course I shan't do it.

Almost time for tea—I'll add to this later tonight.

I miss you very much.

> Your loving wife,
> Ariel

Belleterre
December 3rd
My dear Ariel,

Of course I don't object to you selling your work. Very proper of Mr. Howard to appreciate your talent.

In fact, perhaps you should purchase a house in Hampstead since you've made so many friends there. It will be convenient if you decide to illustrate more children's books. Find a house you really like—cost is no object.

> Falconer

Talbott House, Hampstead
December 4th
Dear James,

While I like Hampstead, I'm not sure we need a second house, and I certainly can't buy one unless you see it. We can discuss the matter when I come home.

Also, I want to ask your opinion of the financial arrangements Mr. Howard has suggested. I don't particularly care about the money, for your generosity gives me far more than I need, but I don't want to be silly about it, either. Later this evening I'll copy out the details of his proposal, then post this letter in the morning. I look forward to your reply.

> Your loving wife,
> Ariel

* * *

Belleterre
December 6th
My dear Ariel,

   Mr. Howard's contract seems fair. However, I can't recommend that you return to Kent just now, for the weather has been very gray and dismal. Far better to stay with your friends, since Hampstead and London will be more amusing than the country. Besides, from what you've said, I gather that all of the Talbotts grieve when you talk about leaving. And what of the literary Mr. Glades? You said he claims you are his muse— surely you don't want to leave the chap inspirationless.

                                                    Falconer

Talbott House, Hampstead
December 7th
Dear James,

   When I mentioned your letter to Anna, she suggested that you might like to come to Hampstead, and we could spend Christmas with the Talbotts. She says there is much jolliness and celebration. Perhaps too much—I'm not sure that it would be the sort of thing you'd like. Also, as much as I love Anna and her family, I would rather my first Christmas with you was a quiet one, just the two of us. And Cerberus and Tripod, of course. Has Tripod forgiven me for going away? Cats being what they are, she has probably expunged me from her memory for my desertion.

   Eagerly awaiting your reply,

                                        Your loving wife,
                                        Ariel

P.S. The only inspiration Mr. Glades cares for or needs is the sound of his own voice.

Falconer finished the letter, then closed his eyes in pain. He could hear her voice in every line, see her vibrant image in his mind. It was torture to read her letters, and she wrote faithfully every day, with only faint, rare reproaches for his almost total lack of response.

Yet what could he write back? *I am dying for love of*

you, beloved, come home, come home. Not the sort of letter one could write to a woman who had been horrified to see his face.

Drearily he got to his feet and stared out the library window. The fitful weather had produced a brief bit of sunshine, but it was winter in his heart. Loyal child that she was, Ariel would come home if he let her, but to what? Her life in Hampstead was full and happy; what would she have at Belleterre but disgust and loneliness? He could not allow her to return.

Mr. Glades, the literary gentleman, figured regularly in her letters. Clearly the man was besotted with her, though she never said as much; perhaps, in her innocence, Ariel did not realize the fact. Falconer had had the man investigated and discovered that the Honorable William Glades was handsome, wealthy, and talented, part of a glittering literary circle. He was also considered an honorable young man. A bit full of himself, like clever young chaps often were, but otherwise he was exactly the sort of man Ariel should have married.

Falconer leaned heavily against the window frame. He'd once read of savages who could will their own deaths. Though he'd been skeptical at the time, now he believed that it was possible to do such a thing. In fact, it would be easy to die. . . .

He wrapped his arms around himself, trying to numb his despairing grief. The heart of his spirit was dead, and it would only be a matter of time until his physical heart also stopped.

The sunshine was gone and the sky had darkened so quickly that he could see his own face faintly reflected in the window glass. He shuddered at the sight, then returned to his desk and lifted his pen.

Belleterre
December 8th
My dear Ariel,
   I never celebrate Christmas; it's a foolish combi-

*nation of sentimentality, exaggerated piety, and pa-
ganism. Still, I don't want to deprive you of the festivities, so I think you should stay with the Talbotts
for the holidays.*

Falconer

After reading her husband's latest letter, Ariel lay down
on her bed and curled up like a hurt child. She did not
cry, for in the previous two months she had shed so many
tears that now she had none left to mourn this ultimate
rejection. Though James was too courteous to say so out-
right, it was obvious that he didn't want her ever to come
back to Belleterre. She still believed that he had once
cared for her, at least a little, but plainly his feelings had
died that night in the library.

She forced herself to face her future. Though she loved
her husband, he would never love her; he couldn't even
bear to have her under his roof. Therefore she might as
well take his suggestion and buy a house in Hampstead.
There was a charming old cottage for sale only ten minutes' walk from the Talbotts. It had a lovely view over
Hampstead Heath and was just the right size for a woman
and a servant. Though James would have to pay for it,
she vowed to work hard at illustration so that eventually
she would no longer need his money to survive.

Supporting herself now seemed possible; it would be
far harder to make the rest of her life worth living.

Christmas

"Did you have a nice walk?" Anna called.

"Splendid." Ariel knelt and helped little Jane Talbott
from her cocoon of coat, bonnet, scarf, and muff. "Even
in winter the heath is full of wonderful, subtle colors. I
never tire of it."

The older girl, Libby, said, "Hurry, Janie, for we can't
help decorate the tree until we've had tea."

Anna, a tall woman with nut brown hair, entered the

front hall. "Thank you for taking the girls for a walk to wear down their high spirits." She smiled indulgently as the children scampered off to the nursery. "They're so excited that I'm afraid they'll vibrate to pieces between now and Christmas. And if they don't, I will!"

"Courage—only two more days to go." Ariel removed her own coat and bonnet. "Did anything come in the post for me?"

"This package arrived from Mr. Howard." Anna lifted it from the hall table and handed it over.

"Nothing from Belleterre?"

"No, dear," Anna said quietly.

Ariel glanced up and made herself smile. "Don't look so sorry for me, Anna. I daresay this is all for the best."

Her friend's eyes were compassionate, but she was too wise to offer sympathy when Ariel's emotions were so fragile. Instead she said, "Certainly everyone in Talbott House will be in raptures if you buy Dove Cottage. You'll never get Jane and Libby out from under your feet."

"I love having them around," Ariel said. "And Libby has real drawing talent. It's a pleasure to teach her." Glancing at the package from the publisher, she continued, "If you'll excuse me, I'll go up to my room. Mr. Howard said he was going to send another story for me to consider."

As Ariel climbed the stairs, she gave thanks for Anna's understanding. In fact, all of the Talbotts had been wonderful; Ariel did not know how she would have survived the last two months without their warmth and liveliness. As a Christmas present to the family, she had done an oil painting of the four of them together. It was one of the best pieces of work she'd ever done; sorrow seemed to be honing her artistic skills.

As she expected, the package contained the project that Mr. Howard wanted her to do next. He had been so pleased with *Puss in Boots* that he was now talking of doing an entire series of classic fairy tales, all to be illustrated by Ariel.

With a stir of interest she saw that he had sent her two different *Beauty and the Beast* books. Oddly enough, though Ariel had a vague knowledge of the story, she had never read one of the many versions of the old folk tale. Lifting the larger of the volumes, she began to read and soon discovered that it was a much more powerful story than *Puss in Boots*. Moreover, the visual possibilities were enticing.

Ariel was halfway through when the back of her neck began to prickle. In an odd way the tale resembled her own life, though reality was sadder and more sordid. At the end it was a relief to learn that Beauty and her Beast lived happily ever after. Ariel supposed that was why people read such fanciful tales: because real life couldn't be trusted to end as well. But as she set the story aside, she was haunted by the image of the Beast, who had almost died of sorrow when Beauty left him.

The rest of the day was taken up with festivities. She helped the Talbotts decorate the tree. After the girls were sent giggling to bed, the adults went to a nearby house where they shared hot mulled wine and conversation with a dozen other neighbors. The small party helped distract Ariel from her misery. As she went to bed, she gave thanks that the next few days would be so busy. By the beginning of the New Year, she might be prepared to face her new life.

But the old life was not done with her, for she fell asleep and dreamed of *Beauty and the Beast*. She herself was Beauty, young and confused, first fearing the Beast who held her captive, then learning to love him. What turned the dream into nightmare was the fact that her captor was not a leonine monster but James. He was a haunted, noble creature who was dying for lack of love, and as life ebbed from him, he called out to her.

She awoke with an agonized cry. How could she have left him? How could she have let him send her away? Even awake, she heard his voice in her mind, the deep, desolate tones echoing across the miles that separated them. She slid out of her bed, determined to leave instantly for Belleterre.

As soon as her feet hit the icy floor, she realized the foolishness of her impulse. It was three in the morning, and she couldn't leave for hours yet; however, she could pack her belongings so that she would be ready first thing. She threw herself into the task with frantic haste and was done in half an hour.

The thought of the hours still to wait made her want to shriek with frustration. Then inspiration struck. She settled down at her desk with drawing paper, pen, and ink. Feeling as if another hand guided her own, she drew a series of pictures with feverish, slashing strokes. She had not bought a Christmas gift for her husband since he had been so firmly opposed to celebrating the holiday. Now she was creating a gift so vivid that it might as well have been drawn with her heart's blood rather than India ink.

As she wept over the last drawing, she prayed that he would accept it in the spirit offered.

The footman opened the front door of Belleterre and blinked in surprise. "Lady Falconer?"

"None other," Ariel said crisply as she swept past him into the front hall. "Is my husband in the house?"

"No, my lady. I believe he intended to be out on the estate all day."

"Very well." She surveyed her surroundings, unsurprised to see that there wasn't a trace of holiday decoration. "Please ask Mrs. Wilcox to join me in the morning room immediately. Then have my things taken to my room. Be particularly careful of the drawing portfolio."

As the footman hastened to obey, Ariel went to the morning room, which was the smallest and friendliest of the public rooms. While she waited for the housekeeper, Tripod came skipping into the room. The cat was halfway to Ariel before she remembered her grievance. With ostentatious disdain, Tripod sat down, her back turned to the mistress of the house who had dared to go away for so long. Only the twitching tip of her tail betrayed her mood.

"We'll have none of that, Tripod." Ariel scooped the cat into her arms and began scratching around the feline ears. Within a minute, the cat began to purr and stretch out her neck so that her chin could be scratched. Ariel hoped wryly that her husband would be as easy to bring around.

Soon Mrs. Wilcox joined her. Always dignified, today the housekeeper was positively arctic. In a voice that was only just within the bounds of politeness, she said, "Since your arrival was unexpected, your ladyship, it will take a few minutes to freshen your rooms."

Ignoring the comment, Ariel said, "How is my husband?" When the housekeeper hesitated, Ariel prompted, "Speak freely."

Mrs. Wilcox needed no more encouragement. "Very poorly, my lady, and it's all your fault!" she burst out. "The master looks as if he's aged a hundred years since you left. How could you go away for so long, after all he's done for you?"

How bad was "very poorly"? Though she ached, Ariel kept her voice even. She was mistress of Belleterre, and she intended to fill the position properly. "I left because he sent me away," she said calmly. "It was very bad of me to obey him. It shan't happen again."

She set down the cat and stripped off her gloves. "I want every servant in the house put to work decorating Belleterre for the holidays. Greens, ribbons, wreaths, candles . . . everything. Send a man to cut a tree for the morning room, and have the cook prepare a Christmas Eve feast. I realize that time is limited, but I'm sure Cook will do a fine job with what is available. Oh, whenever the table is set in the future, always put my place next to my husband's rather than at the far end."

Mrs. Wilcox's jaw dropped. Ariel added, "And when

doing the decorating and cooking, don't stint on the servants' quarters. I want this to be a holiday Belleterre will never forget. Now off with you—there's much to be done."

"Yes, my lady," the housekeeper said, her eyes beginning to shine. She paused just before leaving the room. "You won't leave again, will you? He needs you something fierce."

"Wild horses won't get me away unless he comes, too," Ariel promised. After all, she needed her husband something fierce herself.

Christmas Eve—the thought of going back to the empty house was almost more than Falconer could bear.

He was so weary in spirit that he didn't notice how brightly lit the house was, but when he entered the front hall he was struck by the scent of pine and holly. He stopped, blinking at the sight that met his eyes. The hall was wreathed in garlands of greenery accented by scarlet berries and bows, and a footman stood on a ladder, tucking shiny holly leaves behind a pier glass for the final decorative touch.

Falconer demanded, "By whose order was this done?"

As the nervous footman fumbled for a reply, a clear, light voice said, "Mine, James."

He would recognize her voice anywhere, yet it was so unexpected that he couldn't believe she was really here. Even when he turned and saw his wife walking down the hall toward him, he was sure he must be hallucinating. Exquisite in a scarlet trimmed gown, her flaxen tresses tied back simply with a luxuriant scarlet velvet bow, she had to be an illusion born of his despairing dreams.

But she certainly looked real. Stopping in front of him, Ariel said, "Come and see the tree before you go up to bathe and change for dinner."

Bemused, he followed her into the morning room, which was scented by tangy evergreens and sweet-burning applewood logs. Ariel gestured at the tall fir that had been set up in one corner. "Patterson chose the tree. Lovely, isn't it?"

Hoarsely he said, "Ariel, why did you come back?"

"I am your wife and Belleterre is my home," she said mildly. "Where else would I be at Christmas?"

"I told you to spend the holiday with your friends."

She linked her fingers together in front of her, the knuckles showing white. "When we married, you offered me a home. Are you withdrawing that offer?"

"You don't belong here." Anguish lanced through him, as if a knife was being turned in his heart. He had thought that she understood and accepted that their lives should lie apart, but apparently not. Now he must go through the agony of saying the words out loud; he must send her away again. "You mustn't blight your life through misplaced loyalty, Ariel. Our marriage is one of convenience only. I'm almost twice your age—you're scarcely more than a child."

"I'm old enough to be your wife," she retorted.

He edged toward the shadowed end of the room, trying desperately to keep his defenses from crumbling. "I never wanted a wife."

"But you have one," she said softly. "Why do you run from me, James? I know I'm not clever, but I love you. Is it so unthinkable that we be truly married?"

"Love?" he said, unable to suppress his bitterness. "How could a beautiful girl like you possibly love a man like me?"

His words acted like a spark on tinder. "How dare you!" she said furiously, looking like a spun sugar angel on the verge of explosion. "Because men think me beautiful, do you think I have no heart? Do you think I am so superficial, so blinded by my own reflection in the mirror, that I cannot see your strength and kindness and wit? You insult me, my lord."

Helplessly he said, "I meant no insult, Ariel, but how can you love a man whose face you have never seen?"

Her blues eyes narrowed. "If I were blind and could see nothing, would you think me incapable of love?"

"Of course not, but this is different."

"It's *not* different!" Her voice softened. "I fell in love with you because of your words and deeds, James. Compared to them, appearance is of no great importance."

When the black folds of his robe quivered she knew that he was deeply affected, but not yet convinced. She knelt by the tree and pulled out the portfolio of drawings she had done for him. "If you want to know how I see you, look at these."

Hesitantly he took the portfolio and laid it on a table. Ariel stood next to him as he paged through the loose drawings. If any of her work had magic, it was this, for the drawings came straight from her heart and soul. The images made up a modern *Beauty and the Beast* and showed exactly how she had seen her husband, from her first glimpse of him at Gardsley to the present. Under each picture she had written a few spare words to carry the story.

James was the focus of every picture, forceful, mysterious, larger than life. Though his face was never shown, he was so compelling that the eye could not look elsewhere. He was the enigmatic Black Beast of Belleterre, his dark robes billowing about him like thunderclouds. He was the compassionate, patient Lord Falconer, caring for everyone and everything around him. And he was James, surrounded by adoring birds and beasts, for every creature who knew him could not help but love him.

Then he sent Ariel away. The last drawing showed him lying in the Belleterre woods on the point of death, his powerful body drained of strength and his great heart broken. Ariel wept beside him, her pale hair falling about them like a mourning veil. The legend below read, "I heard your voice on the wind."

He turned to the last sheet and found a blank page. "How does the story end?" he asked, his voice shaking.

''I don't know,'' she whispered. ''The ending hasn't been written yet. The only thing I know is that I love you.''

He spun away, his swift steps taking him into the shadows at the far end of the room. There he stood motionless for an endless interval, his rigid back to Ariel, before he turned to face her. ''I was ugly even as a child. My mother used to say what a pity it was that I took after my maternal grandfather. But that was normal ugliness and would not have mattered greatly. What you will see now is a result of what happened when I was eight.'' She heard his ragged inhalation, saw the tremor in his hands as he raised them to his hood, then slowly pulled the folds of fabric down to his shoulders.

Her eyes widened when she saw that he was entirely bald. Of course; it explained why she had had the fleeting impression of a skull when she'd seen him in the library. Yet the effect, though startling, was not unattractive, for his head was well shaped and he had dark, well-defined brows and lashes. He might have modeled for an Asiatic warlord in a painting by one of the great Romantic artists.

Voice taut, he continued, ''My mother was taking me to Eton for my first term, and we spent the night at Falconer House in London. That night there was a gas explosion in her bedroom. I woke and tried to help her, but she was already dead.''

He raised his damaged left hand so Ariel could see it clearly. ''This happened when I pulled her body from the burning room. The smaller scars on my scalp and neck were made by hot embers that fell on me.'' He touched his bare head. ''Afterward I was struck with brain fever and was delirious for weeks. They thought I would die. Obviously I didn't, but my hair fell out and never grew back. I was never sent to school, either—it was considered 'unsuitable.' Instead my father installed me at a minor estate in the Midlands, so he wouldn't have to think about me.''

James closed his eyes for a moment, then opened them

again, his expression stark. "Can you be as accepting in the particular as you were in the abstract?"

Ariel walked toward him, and for the first time their gazes met. His eyes were a deep, haunted gray-green, capable of seeing things most men never dreamed of. Coming to a stop directly in front of him, she said honestly, "You have the most beautiful eyes I've ever seen."

His mouth twisted. "And the rest of me? My father refused to look at me, my tutor often told me how lucky I was to have my hideousness visible rather than concealing it as most men do."

She smiled and shook her head. "You're a fraud, my love. I'm almost disappointed. I'd expected much worse."

His expression shuttered. "Surely you're not going to lie and call me handsome."

"No, you're not handsome." She raised her hands and skimmed her artist's fingers over the planes of his face, feeling the subtle irregularity of long-healed scars, the masculine prickle of end-of-the day whiskers. "You have strong, craggy bones—too strong for the face of a child. Even without the effects of fire and fever, it would have taken years to grow into these features. Did you ever see a picture of Mr. Lincoln, the American president who was shot a few years ago? He had a similar kind of face. No one would ever call it handsome, but he was greatly loved and deeply mourned."

"As I recall, the gentleman did have a good head of hair," James said wryly.

Ariel shrugged. "A bald child would be startling, almost shocking. Yet now that you are a man, the effect is not unpleasant—rather dramatic and interesting, actually." She stood on her tiptoes and slid her arms around his neck, then pressed her cheek to his. As tension sizzled between them, she murmured, "Now that you have nothing to hide, will you promise not to send me away again? For I love you so much that I don't think I could survive another separation."

His arms came around her with crushing force. She was slim but strong, and so beautiful that he could scarcely bear it. "Unlike the Beast in your story, I can't turn into a handsome prince," he said intensely, "but I loved you from the first moment I saw you, wife of my heart, and I swear I will never stop loving you."

Her laughter rang like silver bells. "To be honest, in both the books Mr. Howard sent me, the handsome prince at the end was quite insipid. Your face has character—it's been molded by suffering and compassion and will never be insipid." She tilted her head back, her shining gilt hair spilling over his wrists. Suddenly shy, she said, "Did you notice what's above your head?"

He glanced up and saw mistletoe affixed to the chandelier, then looked back at her yearning face. Curbing his fierce hunger so that he wouldn't overwhelm her, he bent his head and touched his lips to hers. It was a kiss of sweetness and wonder, a promise of things to come. His heart beat with such force that he wondered if he could survive such happiness. Instinct made him end the kiss, for they risked being consumed by the flames of their own emotions. Far better to go slowly, to savor every moment of the miracle they had been granted.

Understanding without words, Ariel said breathlessly, "It's time we changed for dinner, for it's going to take some time to decorate the tree. I brought some lovely new ornaments from London. I hope you'll like them."

He kissed her hands, then released her. "I'll adore them."

Christmas Eve became a magical courtship. He discarded his robe. Then they dined close enough to touch knees and fingers rather than being separated by a dozen feet of polished mahogany. Laughing and talking, they turned the tree into a shining, candlelit fantasy. And the whole time, they were spinning a web of pure enchantment between them. Every brush of their fingertips, every shy glance, every shared laugh at the antics of Cerberus and Tripod, intensified their mutual desire.

When they went upstairs, he hesitated at her door, still not quite able to believe. Wordlessly she drew him into her room and went into his arms. As they kissed, he discovered an unexpected aptitude for freeing her from her complicated evening gown.

Her slim, curving body was perfect, as he had known it would be. With lips and tongue and hands, he worshiped her, as enraptured by her response as by the feel of her silken skin under his mouth. She was light and sweetness, the essence of woman that all men craved, yet at the same time uniquely Ariel.

She gave herself to him with absolute trust, and the gift healed the dark places inside of him. He could actually feel blackness crumbling until his heart was free of a lifetime of hurt and loneliness. Such vulnerability should have terrified him, but her trust called forth equal trust from him. Already he could scarcely remember the haunted man who had been unable to believe in love.

In return for her trust, he gave her passion, using all of his skill, all of his sensitivity, all of his tenderness. Their bodies came together as if they were two halves of the same whole that had finally been joined, and when she cried out in joyous wonder, it was the sweetest sound he'd ever heard.

After passion had been satisfied for the first time, they lay tranquil in each other's arms. He had never known such rapture, or such humility.

In the distance, church bells began to toll. "Midnight," he murmured. "The parish church rings the changes to celebrate the beginning of Christmas Day."

Ariel stretched luxuriously, then settled against him again. "Christmas—a time of miracles and new beginnings. What could be more appropriate?"

"Indeed." He brushed his fingers through her hair, marveling at the spun-silk texture. "I'm sorry, my love, I didn't get you a present."

She laughed softly. "You gave me yourself, James. What greater gift could I possibly want?"